ISOLATION WARD

By Martine Bailey

SHARP SCRATCH
ISOLATION WARD

ISOLATION WARD

MARTINE BAILEY

Allison & Busby Limited
11 Wardour Mews
London W1F 8AN
allisonandbusby.com

First published in Great Britain by Allison & Busby in 2025.

Copyright © 2025 by MARTINE BAILEY

The moral right of the author is hereby asserted in accordance with
the Copyright, Designs and Patents Act 1988.

A CIP catalogue record for this book is available from
the British Library.

First Edition

HB ISBN 978-0-7490-3099-5

Typeset in 11/16 pt Sabon LT Pro by Allison & Busby Ltd.

By choosing this product, you help take care of the world's forests.
Learn more: www.fsc.org.

Printed and bound in the UK using 100% Renewable Electricity at
CPI Group (UK) Ltd, Croydon, CR0 4YY

EU GPSR Authorised Representative
LOGOS EUROPE, 9 rue Nicolas Poussin, 17000, LA ROCHELLE, France
E-mail: Contact@logoseurope.eu

To my dear sister, Lorraine,
after whom I named my heroine.

CHAPTER ONE

Monday 26th September, 1983

The TV screen was filled with a vast towered and turreted building that might have been a Baroque palace. Yet at second glance, it was stained as black as soot by Yorkshire rain and creeping mould. The camera pulled back to reveal an asylum complex the size of a village: some of its roofs green with creeping moss, and a scattering of its high Gothic windows boarded up with plywood. Above it all soared an Italianate tower bearing a large pale-faced clock crowned with battlements of black-toothed stone.

The documentary's female presenter came into shot, huddled in a crimson coat and scarf, dwarfed by a monstrous arch topped with rampant stone beasts.

'The inquiry into the scandalous events at Windwell Asylum has delivered its findings. The only possible response is to close down this relic of the cruel Victorian past, and indeed the asylum's grim corridors and tunnels are scheduled to be destroyed. A modern top-security unit is in the process of being built close by, and the Secretary of

State with responsibility for health has assured Parliament that the team in charge will keep the most dangerous criminals in the country safe – and also keep us safe from them.'

'Come on, love. Are you asleep?'

Lorraine Quick raised heavy eyelids to find her mum standing over her in her dressing gown, the television's light flickering across her fine-boned face.

'Yes. Sorry.' Glancing towards the TV, she caught the final shot of a dilapidated mental asylum as *World in Action*'s jazzy organ theme music played out.

Blearily, she noticed the scattering of personality tests and overhead projector slides that surrounded her, and shoved them into her satchel. So much for preparing tomorrow's session. Her newly created job as a specialist in Organisational Change was too busy and exciting to cram into a 9-to-5 day. Tomorrow morning she'd just have to busk her presentation. She switched off the TV and spread a sleeping bag and pillow along the settee. She couldn't blame her mum for keeping her own bedroom, which she now shared with Lorraine's eight-year-old daughter, Jasmine. Any day now, the housing association would surely write to her about a house in Salford's redevelopment scheme.

Also waiting on the table were the school test booklets she had been coaching Jasmine to complete over the last few weeks. Jasmine was bright, but she wasn't familiar with the types of questions used to win a junior scholarship to a grammar school. And if personality testing had taught Lorraine one thing, it was that familiarity with the questions' format was a serious advantage in a test. Yawning, Lorraine marked all the practice questions Jasmine had completed on arriving home from school. Tired out but satisfied with her daughter's improving performance, Lorraine settled down for a contented night's sleep.

Tuesday 27th September

The Lancashire Hospital Board met at 9 a.m. and Lorraine was waiting for them, her first slide ready in place on her portable overhead projector. It was a cold autumnal morning and her old Metro had been almost alone on the multi-lane M61 motorway. A grey dawn had been scarcely breaking, a mere glimmer through the rain, when she first arrived. She yawned and wished she could transform herself into a morning person. After all, she only needed to get through this final week's work before taking a whole two weeks' annual leave on the German tour with her band, Electra Complex.

An approaching flurry of footsteps rang out in the corridor. She took a steadying breath and stood to greet her audience of hospital managers and begin her presentation. She gave a series of reasons why the hospital should take part in her project to use personality testing to help select staff. Mostly, they were self-evident: finding better-suited and more motivated employees, avoiding rogue applicants, reducing high turnover. This morning, only the hospital's general manager was resisting common sense, trying to find a reason not to take part. Former wing commander Frank Chichester was exactly the type of man Margaret Thatcher wanted in a top NHS job: an outsider from the RAF, gruff, tough, and to Lorraine's mind, pretty dense. He kept asking

9

her how his busy staff could find the time to waste on all this 'rigmarole'. She stifled her honest thought, that if his staff were too busy to care about the calibre of who they employed, that had to be his fault.

She put up her final slide, which posed the question of cost to the hospital. The answer was that there was no cost, as Lorraine had managed to find a grant to fund the whole project. Even the no-nonsense medical director managed a smile in her direction, followed by a sly sideways glance at the wing commander.

'I'm for it,' said the chief nurse. 'We need to recruit the best nurses at our first attempt.'

The personnel director spoke up next. 'I'm in favour, too. Unsuitable staff cost us a fortune in re-advertising and retraining.'

They all waited for their boss's response.

Suddenly outnumbered, he caved in and flapped an impatient back of his hand towards her. 'Very well. Liaise with Personnel.'

After the room emptied, she packed her satchel, feeling buoyant. The title of her 'Square Peg Project' always gave her a secret frisson of pleasure. Its origin dated back to a conversation she'd had some six months earlier, with Detective Sergeant Diaz of the Greater Manchester Police. Under the immense pressure of a murder inquiry they had shared a fascination with psychological techniques, and one favour she had done for him was to test his own personality. Their profiles had proved to be uncannily similar: both intuitive introverts who loved working alone, both secretly ambitious and determined. But whereas she was open and rebellious, Diaz's ambitions were fuelled by a disturbed childhood and a profound mistrust of sharing his emotions. They had both agreed that they were square pegs in round holes, unsettled in their jobs, though there was more to it than that. From almost their first meeting she had felt an invisible bond between them, that sparked to life whenever they caught each other's eye or tuned into each other's thoughts. There had been that one glorious but disastrous night when they had curled body around body, talking in the candlelit darkness, opening up their raw, open selves. And then, almost before it had started, it had all turned sour. He had failed to tell her he was already committed to a fiancée named Shirley who was bearing his child.

Furious, she'd told him that it was over. And yet she had named her first crucial project after that conversation they'd shared. Square Peg had felt like a positive decision. Suddenly she laughed out loud. She hoped the symbolism wasn't some sort of sexual Freudian slip. Diaz, if he were here, would laugh at that idea of his having a 'square peg' trying to fit in a round hole. They hadn't ever had a chance to find out.

'Miss Quick?' The receptionist arrived with a phone message in hand. Dreading a calamity at Jasmine's school, she unfolded it: 'New appointment with Mr Morgan, North West Regional Director, at 4 p.m.'

No, no. That clashed with her afternoon presentation at the next hospital on her list. She would have to reschedule. Morgan truly was a selfish git. Still, no way could she ignore a summons from the man who had recently appointed her to this scary but impressive job. And she needn't worry – she had plenty of good news to give him.

* * *

11

The Regional Director of Personnel and Legal Services, to give him his full title, was nothing like the wing commander. Morgan was a former employment lawyer, a deeply introverted man of few words but all of significant weight. She was not offered refreshments. When she began to update him on the success of Square Peg, he lifted his palm to silence her.

'That's not why you're here. You saw that exposé of Windwell Asylum last night?'

She nodded, though she had only glimpsed the last few seconds of footage.

'You know that our health secretary is the ultimate overseer of this country's special hospitals? Those institutions have a history of absolute failure in every way. This cannot continue. As you know, the old Windwell Asylum is being demolished and a modern top-security unit has just been built beside it. That's the easy bit. The bricks and mortar – or should I say razor wire and steel.' Morgan smiled, showing pointed little teeth. 'The hard bit is getting human beings to properly direct what goes on inside those places. The new director, Doctor Voss, is having some issues with his team. Those issues need to be resolved. That's where you come in.'

Lorraine struggled to hide her dismay. One thing she loved about working across the whole northern region was that she could move around freely, without feeling trapped inside an institution. And here was Morgan, trying to send her to one of the most oppressive hospitals in the country.

She could barely follow his words as he described the need for an expert to work with Windwell's senior staff and miraculously transform them into a functioning team.

It wasn't a team-building expert they needed, it was a magician.

'As you're already on the payroll, there seemed no point in looking elsewhere. You'll be seconded for a month to work directly for Doctor Voss. We're depending on you to turn Windwell into a good news story.'

Seconded for a month? Jasmine's scholarship exam was booked for a week hence. And the German tour with the band started next week too.

'When is this, exactly?'

'We've arranged for you to report to Doctor Voss, first thing next Tuesday morning.'

'I'm sorry, I have two weeks' leave booked from next Monday.'

'Cancel it.'

'I can't. I have commitments in Germany.'

Morgan leant back in his leather executive chair and narrowed his eyes at her. 'You've been here two months already. All you've produced so far is a mediocre plan to improve selection. We're looking for positive headlines, big breakthroughs. Here's your chance. A national profile that proves that all this pseudoscience of yours actually works. Convince me to continue funding your job. Your contract is still probationary. I can end it tomorrow if I choose.'

Lorraine could produce no satisfactory response.

'Do I make myself clear?'

'Yes.' She was damned if she'd call him 'sir', like his other subordinates.

She turned around, and briskly left the room.

CHAPTER TWO

Wednesday 28th September to Sunday 2nd October

The rest of Lorraine's week was spent painfully extricating herself from the best parts of her life. Lorraine had only heard about a potential scholarship for Jasmine when accidentally eavesdropping on Morgan's secretary as she chatted to a friend on the phone.

'Yes, it's an exam to get straight into the junior school that feeds into the grammar. All fully funded,' the secretary had crowed. 'And only a very few of us are in the know,' she'd added in an undertone that Lorraine barely caught. Lorraine had investigated the opportunity and discovered an exam for entry at nine years of age. She knew it would be difficult for Jas – but not impossible. And it was a seriously appealing chance for Jas to challenge those privileged 'very few of us', and show them what for.

Lorraine had been working through past papers with her daughter and now reluctantly acknowledged that maybe someone else would need to coach Jas for her exam. Her mum had offered, but she was even less familiar with modern maths than Lorraine. Finally, she had found a retired teacher, a Mrs Levitt. Jasmine wasn't keen, and neither was Lorraine's mum, as the weekly sessions involved two buses into Trafford and back, in the cold and dark evenings after school.

Next, she despondently drove to the band's rehearsal room in Didsbury's bedsit-land and explained that she couldn't join them on the German tour.

'What's the problem? Walk out on the tossers,' protested her oldest friend, Lily.

'It's not just a job, it's everything that comes with it.' She found she was fighting back shameful tears as she ran through her reasoning. 'I'm high on the list for a new house and I need a job to pay the rent. And when we get it, Jasmine can go to a really good school. The primary she's at is chaotic. She's bright and keen, but that's all being slowly thumped out of her.'

Lorraine didn't think the rest was worth explaining. The Square Peg Project was the best use of her interests and enthusiasm she'd ever found. It was always hard for people with her personality type to apply logic to their situation, but this time she forced herself to confront the bare facts. At the end of her month away she'd be back playing with the band. But it felt too high a price; she alone would miss the high point of their musical careers so far.

'Thank fuck you're only the bass player,' said Dale gleefully, which was bloody rude, coming from the band's newest member. 'I know someone who could do it. I mean, it's not like you carry the tunes or anything.'

'Who is it?' asked Lily.

Dale had a mate of hers called Gogo, a name that

Lorraine found patently stupid. Apparently, this prodigy could play any instrument and learn a whole set in no time. 'She's rock solid,' Dale kept saying. 'And she's on the dole, so she could do with the money. And she's got loads of time, too.'

Lily offered to give her a try-out, and that was that. Before Lorraine left them to rehearse in earnest, she pulled Lily onto the attic landing, clutching her sleeve.

'For our friendship's sake, don't make this girl permanent. I'll be back in a month and then I'll be a hundred per cent here for you.'

With genuine hurt in her eyes, Lily complained, 'I totally relied on you. Me and you, it's our band. And now you're off.'

'It *is* our band. We're the only ones who've been slogging away at it for years. We've written nearly all the songs. I promise I won't let you down again.' She stared into Lily's hurt eyes, desperate to connect and convince her. 'I promise you, I'll write some new material while I'm away. Then we can take that out on the road.'

Monday 3rd October

The following Monday afternoon, Lorraine reluctantly loaded her car and hugged her mum and Jasmine goodbye. After finding her way onto the M61 she settled into the monotony of motorway driving. Soon blue and white signs proclaimed Preston and the North and the little car was climbing over the rugged tops above Accrington towards the Pennines, which formed the spiky spine of Britain's back of beyond. Entering the bleak wastelands of high country she felt uneasy, sensing her increasing distance from Jasmine.

Still, the practical arrangements had worked out well. On the whole, money for its own sake disgusted her, the merchant bankers in red braces and yuppies with their designer gear and flashy houses. Yet she was learning that money could give you options. It meant that her mum could leave her crummy job at the newsagent's and look after Jasmine. Guiltily, she had realised she would barely miss the £100 a month she could pay her mum to stay at home and care for her daughter. Jasmine's happiness and safety, her mother's chance to enjoy a decent rest – there were plenty of reasons to succeed at this project.

CHAPTER THREE

The setting sun was casting purple shadows over the surrounding moorland when Kevin Crossley shuffled back into his office after yet another exhausting meeting. He was working late again, a martyr to the closure of Windwell Asylum and the transfer of patients to the new state-of-the-art top-security unit. All of the 430 patients classified as too dangerous or violent ever to be returned to the outside world were currently crowded into Phase One of the multi-million-pound building.

The clock on his wall said six-fifteen. Tonight Kevin had planned to be home by six to prepare for one of the most important encounters of his life. For months he had brooded over his decision and at last everything was in place. He was approaching the end of his career and rather fancied himself as Justice, restoring balance to the scales that weigh good and evil. There had been a great wrong done, he could see that now, and tonight he would make a peace offering and set matters right. It was just his bad luck that hare-brained Doctor Voss had conspired to make him late, interrogating him for the last infuriating hour. Kevin's new boss had wanted to know all the ins and outs of his job as hospital administrator. Voss's questions were typical of a psychiatrist, probings that subtly undermined him for no more reason than that Kevin was a traditionalist. It didn't matter to Voss that he had worked at Windwell for nearly forty years, and run a tight ship as administrator for the last seventeen, never mislaying a file. Case notes, court orders, permits and punishments: almost every piece of paper save for the doctor's prescriptions had been date-stamped, dealt with and signed by Mr K. Crossley.

He despaired of the crazy ideas that Voss was threatening to introduce. His latest madcap notion was to let the patients have a say in how things were run. As if a load of psychopaths could be trusted to run a hospital? He'd like to bet a hundred quid that Doctor Voss wouldn't last long in the job. Windwell had a history of proud traditions that no doctor was going to change. He, Kevin Crossley, would do the job as he'd always done it for the next two years, until he got his gold clock and his generous NHS pension paid out as he'd carefully instructed.

Though he had already cleared his desk, to his irritation, he spotted a new piece of paper awaiting his attention. It was a message on Titan Construction letterhead, handwritten in their usual uneducated scrawl:

> **URGENT**
> *Date: Monday 3rd October, 1983*
> *To: Mr Crossley*
> *From: Security Gate Phase 2*
>
> *Come at once to Seclusion Block Cell 17 Phase 2. Otherwise we have to call the police in.*

What could have gone wrong now? Wearily, he pulled on his overcoat, determined to head off home just as soon as he'd dealt with whatever routine procedure had stumped Titan's staff this time.

Night had fully fallen by the time he set off across the deserted site – sorry, *campus*, as Voss liked to call it. Were the lunatics taking over a flaming university? You couldn't credit it. As he hurried along the concrete pathway towards the new Lego-like building, he glanced over to the distant silhouette of the old asylum. He had arrived there at Windwell Asylum for the Criminally Insane as assistant clerk just after the last war, and even as a newly demobbed twenty-one-year-old he'd had a grander office than this new abode, with its mass-produced plastic furniture, and, of all things, one of those new-fangled personal computers. Paper never lets you down, he'd told Voss. Paper doesn't need electricity and tapping on keyboards to access information. The truth was, he didn't have a clue how to operate one of those weird machines. He missed his old hospital administrator's office in the asylum; the oak-panelled walls and heavy carved Victorian furniture. The one item he'd refused to give up was his wide leather-tooled desk. Giving out orders felt so much easier from behind that symbol of his absolute authority.

Phase Two of the new site was running weeks behind schedule. He walked straight through the gap in the fifteen-foot-high perimeter wall that still awaited delivery of its huge double-locking gates. A bright fluorescent light shone out from the security lodge, but when he rapped on the window no guard was at his post. Call yourself a twenty-four-hour security service, he told himself. Anyone could drive up and nick some equipment. In fact, that was probably all that these security nitwits had called him over to complain about. With his master key he let himself through the pedestrian steel gate, hearing it clang loudly behind him. It was only then that he realised that the inner courtyard wasn't illuminated. Didn't Titan realise that bright lighting during the hours of darkness was an essential component of the high-security policy? When he found that absent guard, he'd enjoy putting the fear of God into him for his negligence. He glanced over to the newly operational buildings of Phase One, noticing that the overcrowded wards of all-male patients were much closer to this unlit area than he'd expected. If the security guard had been present, he could have used the lodge's phone to complain to Titan's duty manager. And even better, he could have borrowed a torch.

He was lingering by the gate, not liking the look of the courtyard's impenetrable blackness, when he spotted a faint light in the seclusion block. Of course – it must be the security guard from the lodge waiting for him. He set off slowly across the courtyard area, fearful of stumbling into a random pile of builders' tools or detritus.

Reaching the open door and finding no one waiting, he called out, 'Hello, it's Mr Crossley here.'

The light barely reached him from a low-wattage glow in the far interior. He listened and heard no movement. Cursing these delays, he stepped inside a corridor that smelt of fresh paint. He groped along the wall to find the light switch, but when he clicked it, no illumination appeared.

'Hello there,' he repeated, less certainly. In the gloom, the seclusion cells had their usual troubling appearance.

The corridor was lined with a series of small, bare rooms designed to isolate difficult patients, entirely empty save that each contained a waterproof mattress. The doors he passed were closed, bearing heavy-duty locking systems and the narrow Judas slits the staff used to observe their charges. Only the very furthest cell stood open, casting a dim light from its interior. Now that he was here, the faint bell ringing in his memory grew louder. Of course; he'd had the misfortune to deal with an incident in another Cell 17 back in the old asylum. Taking hesitant steps forward, he fancied that behind these closed doors someone might be hiding, might be silently laughing at him even now.

Approaching the final, softly lit cell, he could just make out the sign 'Cell 17' beside the door. The door was ajar, but when he thrust it open, he let out a cry of terror. What the hell . . .

Crimson graffiti had been daubed on the facing wall. 'RIP Campbell. Your next.' The interior light was nothing more than a battery-powered storm lamp standing on the floor.

Crossley stood on the threshold, struggling to catch his breath. Junior Campbell was the name of a patient who had been found dead in Cell 17 of the old asylum three years back. A tribunal had been held but the police case had been hopeless, for after all, who was Campbell? He was just a bothersome black lunatic who had always got on the nursing staff's nerves. It had been a terrible strain to go to London and speak at that government inquiry. Still, the management board of the day had kept the whole mess quiet.

Crossley wondered if he could somehow cover the

taunting message up before anyone else saw it. Curious, he stepped inside the cell and touched the red paint, feeling sick with apprehension. Now Doctor Voss would find out about his statement to the tribunal and no doubt judge his loyalty to Windwell as a blot on his career.

A draught sprang up and chilled Crossley's neck. He spun around and for an instant, glimpsed a figure in navy-blue serge and a peaked cap.

'Hey!' he cried out. The next moment he was thrown backwards so that he toppled over, landing flat on his back and banging his head against the newly plastered wall. Before he could raise himself to protest, he sensed the person moving above him, and after the briefest of moments, a rush of air as a heavy object swung down, down, onto his brittle skull.

CHAPTER FOUR

Lorraine saw a sprinkle of golden lights that might be Burnley. It was time to pull off the motorway. She moved the car down through the gears and swung onto unfamiliar A-roads. Soon she could sense a vast emptiness beyond the strip of unlit road as the little Metro crossed mile upon mile of moorland. For a long time she saw no lights at all, save for her car headlamps' reflection on drystone walls and the occasional farm gate. There had been no road sign for more than twenty minutes. The little car was climbing now, and she steered it close to a steep bank, fearing an invisible drop beyond the road's edge.

At a sharp turn her lights picked out a sign: 'Windwell Village'. Thank God for that. She was tired and her head was buzzing from the noisy rattle inside the car's cabin. The silver crescent of the moon faintly illuminated a black shape crouching at the top of the hill that seemed to blot out the stars. Windwell Asylum. She reached its high boundary walls and 'Danger No Entry' signs. Yawning, she scanned the road for signs to Windwell village where some sort of hospital accommodation awaited her.

From the edge of her vision, a young woman sprang out in front of the car. Lorraine slammed her feet down on the clutch and brake. The car slewed left, in a juddering emergency stop. Lorraine had missed hitting the idiot by inches. She was a teenage girl, hippyish, with waist-length fair hair. Now she stood her ground, staring at Lorraine and whooping like an animal, with a bravado she guessed was chemically induced. More teenagers emerged, moving unsteadily across the road. Lorraine let them cross in front of her. First, a lean and classically handsome Asian boy flickered past, then a spike-headed punk, broad and muscular, banged on her car's bonnet, pulling a menacing face before chasing after the others. Last in line was another teenage girl, white-faced and fey, in jeans and cowboy boots. Lorraine could hear them, excitedly talking in stupid voices and making ghoulish whooing sounds. She waited for them to leave, in no mood to tangle with a group of local potheads. As her hand groped for the gearstick, a scrap of conversation reached her.

'—that woman in the car? She doesn't belong here.'

Lorraine set off, juddering over slippery cobblestones as the sparse lights of Windwell village came into view. Parking up at number 16 on the high street, she was relieved to see she had been allocated a stone terraced cottage, a small retreat all to herself.

When Ella first saw the car's headlamps she thought it was a UFO rushing towards them. Then Oona had seemed to fly away like a bat released from the underworld. Somehow,

25

her friend had arrived on the other side of the road. Wow –
Ella blinked and grinned. Tonight Tommo's mate Krish had
shared some amazing hash.

'Who's that woman in the car?' Oona asked. Ella could
just make out a fair head of hair and a pale hand on the
steering wheel. 'She doesn't belong here.'

Tommo was nearby. 'I dunno. Some offcumden.
Probably lost.'

'No.' Oona spoke in the mysterious voice she used when
telling people's fortunes. 'She's here for a reason. Bringing
trouble.'

The woman's car drew away, red tail lights heading
towards the village.

'What's up?' Krish had suddenly appeared at her side.
At first Ella had dreaded meeting this Asian lad Tommo
hung out with, but now she'd warmed to his considerate
nature. Tonight she thought he looked nice; in his crisp
white shirt he shone like an angel.

'Nowt worth fretting about,' said Tommo, waving them
on like a commando leader. 'Right-o. The best way through
the fence's just a bit further on. Everyone, keep your traps
shut. The security bloke will've done his rounds but he i'n't
deaf.'

What an oaf Tommo was, Ella thought. God knows why
Oona was going out with him. He had tattoos for one thing,
stupid Nazi eagles on his forearms. God, that was so . . .
National Front. Oona was always talking about how she'd
first met him in the hospital canteen and seen an animalistic
aura glowing around him. Tommo was overpoweringly
large beside Oona, his hair gelled into crimson spikes. His
clothes were faded black, his favourite an 'A for Anarchy'

T-shirt. And he talked too much, lots of gibberish that he thought was clever but was just bits of old books or lines from boring films.

Next to Tommo, Krish was laid-back and smart. The last time they'd met he'd confided how his uncle insisted he worked in his shop to pay his keep. When she asked what he'd rather be doing, he'd told her about a course in electrical engineering that looked right up his street. He was completely uncool about wanting to go to college. Ella liked that.

Oona was way above Tommo's league, too. It was a whole amazing week since she'd saved Ella, on the night she'd boarded a huge shiny bus to anywhere so long as it was far away. She'd been staring out of the window into the night, like it was some kind of ultra-boring TV channel.

Then someone had said, 'Want one?'

Ella had ignored the voice. Despair pressed against her chest. The darkness up there on the hills. The emptiness, just like her insides. Trying not to think about what she'd done.

'Here you are. Have it later.'

An elegant filter ciggie landed in Ella's lap. She looked around. The girl had a whole packet of twenty golden Bensons. She let the girl light her ciggie with a flashy gold lighter and drew on it, tasting the quality. On the farm she sometimes smoked roll-ups; she rarely had any cash. Carefully, she eyed the girl up using her just-down-from-the-hills eyes. Oona was maybe seventeen, waist-length fair hair like a princess, pop star make-up, the sort of Barbie face that lads really go for. Clothes-wise, her cobweb sweater, flowery maxi-skirt and boots were top gear.

She'd asked where Ella was heading and she'd forgotten, so her story was a right muddle. In the end Oona had asked if she wanted to crash at her mum's place at Windwell.

'Isn't that the loony bin?'

Oona hadn't minded her saying that. 'Yeah, but it's cool. Me and my mum work there so she's got a house with the job. You can have a room in the attic till you get yourself together.'

'Why?' she'd asked, suspiciously. 'Why do you want me to stay?'

Oona had laughed. She'd told Ella – well, it was Eileen back then, before Oona gave her a new, more trendy name – that she was a white witch. She did her best to be a kind person – well, most of the time. It was about karma and all that, about the universe giving back to you what you gave to others.

'Go on, come back to mine tonight. Look, we're almost at my stop.' Oona stood up and put her bag over her shoulder, her Indian bangles jangling.

Staying at Windwell had been great – or cosmic, as Oona would call it. Oona said she liked having a live-in friend. Ella was someone she could moan to about Tommo and her mum, and show off her new clothes to, and educate about all that spiritual stuff. Funny though, that Ella still hadn't felt like telling Oona why she'd run away. Maybe she didn't entirely trust anyone but herself.

Now, as they followed the two guys in the darkness, Oona linked arms with her. 'You OK?'

Ella was dragged out of her stoned reverie. 'Can't we go home?'

'Soon,' she soothed. 'This is such a cool place. You don't want to miss it.'

Ella didn't reply. It was easier to let Oona do the talking. They followed the two guys under the gap in the fence and then under a low-hanging shrub. On the other side the old asylum seemed to rear above them like a great carapace of something that had crashed to earth; an alien ship with sinister intent.

Like kids on a treasure hunt they lit the candles Oona had brought along and trailed onwards, each holding a flickering flame. The hash made them stumble around, their shrieks bouncing around the night sky.

Maybe the moon had chosen that moment to slide out from beneath a cloud, but when she next looked up it was as if the house had risen from the ground like a backdrop in a pantomime. It was a big, very beautiful house; the silver moonlight gleamed down on its blind windows and curly roof mouldings.

'What is this place?' Krish asked Tommo.

'The old nurses' home. Been boarded up for years. Wanna take a look round?'

Too frightened to be left behind, Ella followed them to a small side door Oona and Tommo said they'd discovered on an earlier visit. Back then Tommo had shouldered the entrance to force a gap a foot wide, but they'd had to scarper when a security bloke had spotted them.

'It's a bit small but I think we can all get through.' Oona squeezed herself inside the wooden frame. Krish came next, then Ella launched herself through the black gap and waited. Finally, Tommo had a go and only just scraped through thanks to his beer belly. Now they were all inside.

The first room was just some sort of scullery, a repository of Formica kitchen units and cupboards hanging off their hinges. Next door the proper kitchen was vast and as black as pitch behind boarded-up windows. As Ella thrust her candle forward, she saw the old range all crusty with cinders and a chopping block streaked with gashes and stains. She felt sick to think of all the bacteria festering in here since for ever. Her boots crushed something crunchy on the floor.

'Shit, it's not bones is it?' Panic raised Ella's voice a couple of tones.

In the murk everyone moved closer together.

'Rat poison,' said Tommo, deadpan. 'They use it in all the empty parts of hospitals. Hey, this is boring,' he announced. 'Let's see the rest of it.'

The hallway was like every nightmare you'd ever had of a haunted house. A rickety oak-spindled staircase curling upwards into nothingness. A mouldering ceiling hung with a cobwebbed light fitting. The flooring of black and white tiles cracked beneath their feet as they shuffled across the room. Tommo reached another door and slowly opened it, making the hinges screech.

'It's fucking huge,' said Tommo, dashing in and twirling around to take in the baronial fireplace and three branching light fittings that hung low with dust-sprinkled cobwebs.

Krish was the first to say it. 'Man, what a great party space.'

They decided to stay there for a while to plan their party. Krish got his hash out again and Tommo passed round some bottles of beer. Oona and Ella stuck more candles around the room so it looked amazing in the scintillating amber light.

Krish held up a miniature cassette player. 'Seen this? It's the latest gadget from my uncle. A copy of that Sony Walkman thing from Japan that costs two hundred quid. Only this is made in Hong Kong so half the price.'

They all gathered round the tiny red plastic box scarcely larger than the music cassette tape it contained. Krish handed the flimsy, orange, foam-covered headphones to Oona. When it connected she started to nod to the beat with a wide-eyed stare.

'That's mind-blowing. What are the sounds?' she said, shouting too loudly.

Krish was smiling at Oona; all the lads stared at Oona. 'Michael Jackson's *Thriller*. What d'you think?'

'Pretty cool.' She watched him with that Princess Diana upwards gaze through her eyelashes. Then she gave him her mysterious smile.

'You're kidding,' Tommo mocked. 'That little black kid from The Jackson 5?'

'You haven't even heard it,' she said, frowning.

Ella was plugged in next. She had never heard a stereophonic effect like it; the drumbeat was incredible, the ghostly effects, the bass so deep it rattled her eardrums. It was like a ghost train riding around her skull. Then she grasped what the song was about and yanked off the headphones. 'There's a wolf howling in there. And zombies!'

Krish and Oona laughed. Ella gave the headphones to Tommo who rolled his eyes, listening as he sucked on the hot roach of a joint like some old-style tycoon.

'Shit, man, it's disco. Monkey music.' He pulled off the headphones in disgust. 'You can't beat Wharfedale speakers and a good deck. In the old days tribes danced in a circle, not on their fucking own with some tic-tic-tic driving everyone mad. If we're going to have a party we need to share the beats. I mean who wants to dance on their own?'

Krish stood up to Tommo. 'You're wrong, brother. Soon everyone'll want one. You carry your own sounds round in your head, man.'

Tommo asked, 'What else can you get hold of?'

Krish gave him a beautiful white-toothed smile. 'Colour TVs, ghetto-blasters, video recorders.'

'I'll have another of those radio cassette things,' said Oona. 'My mum loves hers and I want one, too. I can wake up every morning to my music if I load a cassette and set the alarm. It's so—'

Tommo interrupted her. 'Man, I always wanted one of them video cameras. I could record some of the shit that goes down in our unit and sell it to the newspapers.'

Suddenly, he leapt up like a jack-in-the-box. 'Listen. I've just had the best idea ever in the world. Let's make a video here before this place gets knocked down. Show how fucking amazing it is.'

'That's not a bad idea,' said Oona.

Ella could imagine it in her stoned brain. The dizzy clock tower, this massive party room, the empty corridors. It sounded like a horror show.

Oona was really getting into it. 'Krish, do you think a video recorder could pick up, you know, spirits?'

Tommo's eyes were round with excitement. 'Yeah, yeah. You could call up the spirits, Oona. You know, Sally's ghost.'

The last blast of hash had left Ella so stoned that she watched Oona speaking what sounded like incredibly profound words. 'Yeah, we could, you know, literally catch Sally on video. Maybe then they couldn't knock this place down? If they demolished her tunnel with her in it, it would be like, you know – murder?'

Ella tugged on her sleeve. 'Who's Sally?'

Tommo tried to explain. 'Sally was one of Oona's family. Oona's a proper psychic. Tell 'em all about it, love.'

All in a tumble Oona told them about her great-grandmother's sister, Sally, who was Oona's great-great-something or other. She'd seen Sally's records in the admin block, and had even nicked a photo of Sally from the files.

'You know what they gave as the reason for her being locked up here? She had a baby out of wedlock. Talk about the patriarchy. She was locked up here for seven years and then one day she disappeared. The story is, she escaped down into the tunnels to hide from the warders. She must have thought she'd broken free, free of those straitjackets and restraints. Anyway, a sympathetic attendant took pity on her and smuggled food and blankets down to her. But when the Spanish flu broke out, the attendant was put in isolation and no one else knew that Sally was down there—'

Tommo broke in, eager to get to the ghastly ending. 'It were only when a nauseating smell began to spread through the asylum that the superintendent even bothered searching for her. Someone had locked the underground boiler room with her in it, starving to death. So she tried to escape by crawling through a narrow pipe. She were found jammed inside a thirty-inch pipe, boiled by a release of hot water.'

'And now,' Oona crooned with sparkling eyes, 'she's

Windwell's most famous ghost. And because she's my ancestor, I think that gives me a say in this place.'

'Too fucking right,' agreed Tommo. 'Loads of people have seen her. A woman in a brown patient's dress with a face like a skull. She lives in the boiler room in the tunnels that run just below where we are now. It's like a catacomb where zombies rise at night . . .'

He popped his eyes wide, and comically lifted his fingers like talons.

Ella squealed, hating him. 'I'm not going down there.' She turned to Oona. 'He won't make me, will he?'

'Not if you don't want to,' she soothed.

Tommo wouldn't shut up. 'Oona, listen for once, will you. You gotta get the key to the tunnels off your mum, OK?'

'I don't know,' she started to say, resentfully. 'Can't you get it? Your dad's on call, too.'

'Yeah, but my dad actually uses his keys all the time. He hasn't just got a doss of an office job.' In the heavy silence Tommo hectored her again. 'Just do it, hey?'

She ignored him and Krish cut in. 'Hold on, man. Have you got a couple of thousand quid to buy this camcorder?'

'Course I haven't. Can't we just borrow one off of you?'

'Maybe you can rent one.'

'Brill.'

'Only that's the Hong Kong version. The battery don't last that long. Have you got electric down there?'

Oona pointed up to the dust-laden light fitting. 'No, all the power's been switched off.'

'Aw, there must be some way,' said Tommo resentfully. 'Can't you bring a generator?'

'My uncle's got an electrics shop, not a power station.'

Tommo wouldn't let it go. 'Well, the security guys have got lights on in their security hut. Can't we just divert a bit of power?'

'What if we get caught?' Oona protested.

Tommo snapped back at her. 'Oona, everyone except you fiddles their meters. There are loads of ways – coins, bits of paper, divert the wiring.'

'I can have a go,' Krish said. 'When I come back I'll bring me tools down and have a good look round. But the video rental will cost. It's a hundred a night but maybe you could manage fifty?'

Ella was watching him, tracing how Krish's facial bones were as fine as a model's. Beside him Tommo was a Neanderthal.

And that was it, how the idea started. It was agreed that Krish would come back and try to sort out the electrics to make a video of Sally's ghost.

As the two lads walked on back to the road together, Tommo was getting loud and manic.

'When we've got Old Sal on video we'll send it to that *Look North* programme on the telly. Or, hey, the *Fortean Times* . . .'

Somehow Krish escaped Tommo's orbit and dropped back to the girls before they reached the fence. He angled himself between them.

'I'll need to check out the wiring.' He was speaking very softly but Ella could hear his words, and even his subtle insinuation. 'If you could get me the key?'

This time Oona wasn't full of awkward excuses. 'Maybe. OK, yeah.'

Ella cast an anxious glance to where Tommo was waiting, uncertain how he'd react to his girlfriend secretly arranging to meet his friend.

'I'll ring you when I know which day I can get away from work early. Leave the key behind the concrete block by the gap in the fence.'

'Even better, I'll see you there,' murmured Oona.

'Get a fucking move on, you lot,' Tommo shouted.

Ella looked away into the darkness, dissecting what she had just heard.

Krish moved ahead of them then, and followed Tommo under the fence. When they'd disappeared Oona clutched her hand, holding her back.

'No need to mention that to Tommo.'

'Mention what?' said Ella. 'I wasn't listening.'

Oona gave her a tooth-gleaming smile. 'Good girl, Ella.' Then as she crouched to go under the fence, Oona ruffled Ella's hair, just like she was a fluffy pet lamb.

CHAPTER FIVE

Tuesday 4th October

The next morning, Lorraine set off on foot for her appointment with Doctor Voss at his address in Windwell village. She could have kicked herself for failing to get a prior insight into the director on *World in Action*. All she had gleaned were a few scraps from the press describing Doctor Voss as bringing 'new blood', 'a fresh pair of eyes' and 'bright new ideas' to the hospital. Well, he sounded far better prepared than she was.

She was searching for the director's residence amongst the huddle of stone houses on the main street when she was greeted by a striking guy in a duffel coat.

'Lorraine? So good to meet you.' The man who grasped her hand with a firm shake looked disarmingly younger than his thirty-two years. Voss was an athletic Dutchman with straight blonde hair falling to his shoulders that gave him an uncanny resemblance to the American rock singer Tom Petty. She took in bright clever eyes, a rainbow striped scarf and an open smile. When he politely enquired about her accommodation, she thanked him for use of the two-up two-down terrace, with a kitchenette and a back view of scrubby moorland. The previous evening she'd found a dish of what looked like chicken stew and rice in her fridge, along with some sort of fritters. When she'd reheated the food it had tasted like fire on her tongue, so rich with spices it was unlike any food she'd ever eaten. Hunger had kept her eating, and by the time she was halfway through, she decided she loved the first curry she'd ever eaten that hadn't come dehydrated from a Vesta packet.

'Ah, one of Parveen's food parcels. She's the hospital's deputy administrator and a very nurturing woman.'

'I must thank her.'

Doctor Voss gave a reassuring nod and silently gestured for her to continue speaking.

Her mind went blank. Was she being invited to lay bare her private emotions? She didn't know how to tell him that she should never have been given this role. She had no experience in building a team and had never even worked in a mental hospital. In fact, if there was one speciality she'd promised herself never to move to, it was psychiatric care. Other parts of the health service gave the public a reasonable return: babies were born, broken bones mended, diseases were at least eased if not cured. But somewhere like Windwell was the ultimate hard place at the back-end of the service. It housed the rejects from prisons, the untreatable offenders, the human beings who needed to be locked up to keep the rest of the population safe.

'Is there somewhere we can go to discuss my role?' she asked abruptly.

'Yes, of course. The easiest way to explain what I'm

trying to do here is to show you around the asylum.'

Lorraine had to mask her disappointment; she'd been hoping to meet in a peaceful environment where she could ask her prepared questions and share the few team-building ideas she'd scraped together over the weekend. Unwillingly, she followed the director down a rough path towards the massive clock tower that loomed over copper-tinted trees. He marched confidently onwards, secure in leather hiking boots, while Lorraine tried not to trip over in her three-inch heeled black court shoes.

All she knew of Windwell was that it had been built as a hospital for the criminally insane back in 1863, and even then had been plagued with reports of cruelty and neglect. In the last century it had at times been an epileptic colony and then an institute for what were described as mental defectives. Only in the 1960s had it been taken under government control as a top-security hospital, though a string of official inquiries all agreed that the asylum was unfit for any of its avowed purposes.

At last, after passing through a security gate where Voss vouched for her to the guard, they entered a great hall that might have been modelled on a palatial Victorian theatre or Persian court. There were the remnants of a proscenium arch and grand stage, while in the room's centre were heaped piles of patterned tiles and lavish plasterwork stripped from the walls.

'This is the much-photographed ballroom,' he said. 'The public image of a happy place while around and beneath the rot set in.'

Lorraine had finally caught her breath. 'Is that what you feel you have inherited? Rot?'

He lifted his bright gaze to hers. 'Lorraine, I expected a mess. These coercive institutions nearly always breed a psychological darkness inside them. But what happened here, the casual violence towards sick inmates, the hardening of conscience, the culture of brutality amongst the nursing staff – that is a tough stain to scrub away from human souls.'

'I understood that many difficult staff had been removed?'

'Some. But I fear that those who stayed on are already tempted to the same path.'

They walked on for what felt like an endless time, up and down corridors imprinted with suffering. He halted in a white-tiled room that now looked grey with dust and black mould.

'The morgue,' he announced. The shadowy chamber was dominated by a flat steel table, presumably used to examine the dead. There were unidentifiable stains on its surface and an array of pipes and drain holes on its underside. Relics of old freezers and lab benches hung from the scarred walls.

The director gestured towards the metal table. 'In recent years three powerless patients died here of unnatural causes. The most recent inquiry revealed that a young patient named Junior Campbell was murdered but the crime was hushed up by staff.'

Lorraine tensed, not wanting to touch a single object or inhale another breath in this place.

'Just one last thing I want to show you.' Doctor Voss strode to a doorway next to the morgue and unlocked it with a key from his belt chain. When he began to climb down a set of dark stairs, she had to force herself to follow him.

'Sorry, it seems Titan Construction have had to disconnect the electricity,' he said, pulling out a chrome torch which sent cross-hatched beams scurrying across the mottled walls of a low tunnel.

'The underground passages are extensive,' he told her when they reached the bottom. She wasn't sure if there really was less oxygen, but what air remained tasted acrid. She knew that most hospitals sat above a labyrinth of tunnels containing storage areas, miles of heating and water pipes, and even occasional miniature railway systems. But Windwell was nothing like most bright and busy general hospitals. She tried to blank out some of what the director showed her, but the worst parts she guessed would permanently lodge in her mind. He stopped outside a series of narrow rooms, which he told her were Victorian confinement cells designed to block out all sight and sound. Inmates had been imprisoned there for at least a week and up to a month. By the time they were released, many had lost their fragile grasp on normality.

'The real scandal is that many traditional psychiatrists still insist on seclusion as a safe place for their patients. The fact is, it's more often used to give an easy life to the staff. Back when this place was built there was a theory that isolation calmed the mind, but the opposite is true: to be stripped of dignity and human contact, to sleep on the floor while strange eyes watch you through a slot in the door, these are often traumatic experiences for patients. Too often it's the start of a vicious spiral of mistrust and violent retaliation.'

41

Lorraine stepped inside the nearest cell and to her alarm, Voss clicked off his torch. Disorientated, she groped for the damp wall of the cell and steadied herself. Darkness is never absolute blackness, she realised. The insides of her eyelids patterned with dazzling blue and white undulations. Her hand grasped the wall tighter, brushing against something dry and brittle.

In the darkness, Doctor Voss began to speak of his former clinic in Holland, a liberal institution created to maximise his patients' control over their own lives. Patients could sit on committees to decide important issues about their care, and facilities such as a swimming pool were shared with the population of the local town.

'In the Dutch clinic we have a very dramatic induction exercise for all our managerial staff. Each senior manager is locked in such a cell as this, with no light, food or drink, in absolute solitary confinement. Yet unlike the inmates here at Windwell, a limit is set of just one hour. In such a way our managers all develop a remarkable empathy for our patients. What do you think, Lorraine?'

'As a team-building method?' She thought about it for a few panicky seconds. It sounded insane. 'Well, that's certainly a dramatic trust exercise. The culture in Holland must be far more liberal than here.'

Unable to see him, she could sense he was waiting for more. Somehow the darkness made it easier to speak her mind.

'Doctor Voss, I don't think we can ignore the political aspect to my being here. What my manager wants are photos of you and your team out in the great outdoors. They want a wholesome success story. I hope to do more than that, but we'd be fools to ignore what your backers will judge as success. I don't think a story about your team being locked up in the darkness down here is going to be helpful.'

When he spoke he sounded peeved. 'You don't think the nursing staff who favour the old custodial ways will appreciate the gesture?'

'To you and me it's an exercise in empathy.' She paused, reviewing what she'd read of Windwell's prison officer culture, the use of brutality to avoid the ever-present threat of attack from patients.

'Forgive me if I'm speaking out of turn, but mightn't the staff think you're taunting them about that infamous Campbell case? The obvious references are to the seclusion cell Campbell was discovered in, here in this building, and that no one was ever apprehended for the crime. I don't know about Holland, but there can be a particular gallows humour around psychiatric settings here in Britain. Worst of all, they might even try to make the team-building process a focus of cruel jokes.'

This time Voss sounded taken aback. 'Thank you for your honesty. Sometimes I do get carried away with my enthusiasm.'

'Have you managed to rid the new building of seclusion cells?'

Voss shook his head. 'I arrived here too late to change that. There are cells but at least they're light and warm, and I've insisted on strict rules on maximum seclusion periods. Shall we go?'

Again, her hand brushed across something rough and dry. 'Just a sec. Can you shine the torch on my hand?'

Voss's wavering beam focused on a peculiar sight and she sprang back. It looked like a ball of frilly paper, or a dried-up lump of coral.

'What is it?'

Her eyes solved the visual puzzle. 'A posy of dried flowers.' It was tied to the metal bars and when she tried to free it, the dried petals fell to pieces. What did hold together, though, was the circle of a lacy parchment frilled out around the dead flowers. 'Very Victorian,' she murmured. 'A *memento mori*, perhaps?'

'You look pale,' Doctor Voss said, suddenly moving the beam up to her face. She shaded her eyes, blinking. It was true, her skin did feel clammy.

On the way back up the stairs he asked over his shoulder, 'You don't believe in ghosts, do you?'

'No.' Then she added a coda. 'Though coming here, I do believe that places where wicked acts were performed can retain an ugly atmosphere.'

At last they reached the outside and stood in a crack-stoned courtyard overgrown with weeds. She took in welcome breaths of drizzly air.

'You are sensitive,' he murmured, and then added, 'I hope not too sensitive. There is a lot of nonsense about supernatural goings-on in the village. A local man, Professor Leadbetter, is partly to blame. He was once employed here and has assembled what he calls his Black Museum of Criminal Curiosities at his home at Wynd Well Hall. He may still be employed by the university, but he's no longer on our payroll.'

They began retracing their steps on the rocky path and Lorraine did her best to trot along beside him. 'That's the tour I give everyone,' he said eventually. 'Even the minister for health who was here a few weeks ago. Do you know why?'

Lorraine didn't say what she was thinking: to terrify us all into submission? Instead, she managed, 'To show how difficult the task is with that legacy.'

'Very good.' He was studying her as if she were the subject of a psychological assessment. 'I never apologise for this harsh introduction. In fact, I was rather pleased to see how anxious you became. Lorraine, I need an ally. Not someone institutionalised by this place who turns a blind eye to ill treatment. I need someone with an outsider's sensitivities.'

'An ally? Against your team?'

'Yes.'

'Any particular people? Or problems?'

'I'm not breaking confidences if I say that our chief nurse is opposed to most of my changes. I believe the other two members of my direct team, the administrator and treasurer, have their own entrenched methods and I have no choice but to give them a chance. But something's going on. Even Kevin, my administrator, has gone AWOL today. Lorraine, if you can help me form the four of us into a team around my new agenda – well, I would be forever grateful.'

He came to a standstill and reached out to touch her arm, his pale eyes searching her face.

'I'm only here for a month,' she said feebly. All this felt way beyond her capabilities.

'You mentioned problems. Yeah, I have those too. I believe there are financial irregularities. Some areas like catering are haemorrhaging cash, yet the department is understaffed and the food is dreadful. And when I asked Enid, the treasurer, for the annual accounts, she couldn't produce them. So I don't even have a grip on the finances.

'Then there's security. It's not been made public, but the last search of Ferris Ward uncovered five bags of cannabis and an entire pharmacy store of contraband uppers and downers. That could only happen with outside assistance, from a visitor or staff.'

He slowed and turned to face her, sighing. 'It was an incredible stroke of luck that a psychologist raised the alarm and we've been able to regulate the patients' medication. So you see, we have enemies in our midst.'

They had reached the edge of the village, but Doctor Voss lingered on the path as if reluctant to return to public scrutiny. 'Whoever it is, they are striking at the heart of my mission here. I haven't come here to run a high-security prison manned by thugs. I am a doctor, a healer. I want to treat these men and offer them a better future. And to do that, I need to maintain a safe and secure environment.'

Lorraine nodded, feeling as troubled as he looked. She reached into her bag and produced a paper.

'Here's my proposal for the team-building sessions.'

He took it but didn't look at it. 'I doubt any fixed plan will work. We're going to have to deal with big questions as they jump out at us. From tomorrow I'd like you to run a session with the team every Wednesday afternoon. I'll show you around Phase One tomorrow. How about two o'clock? Then we can have our first team-building session at three.'

The director hurried away towards a building site just visible behind the trees, from which the distant roar of diggers and workmen shouting orders reached her. Shivering in the drizzle, she set off back to her accommodation feeling like an absolute imposter. She had arrived here with a plan to establish a way forward. Doctor Voss now seemed to think she could make it all up as she went along. Christ, she wasn't a therapist like him, trained to ask questions and let her clients disgorge their traumas. He had given her an impossible task.

Approaching her cottage she made a snap decision. The rest of the day was her own and she needed to clear her head. Thank God she was in a position to escape this place. Pulling out her car keys, she got into the Metro and set off into open green country, feeling the black cloud of Windwell gradually lift as the institution vanished to nothing in her rear-view mirror.

CHAPTER SIX

Ella had made a proper dinner, a shepherd's pie made with a tin of minced beef and a packet of dried mashed potato she'd found in the kitchen cupboard. She'd wanted to do it as a thank you to her new friend Oona and her mum, for letting her stay at their house, but neither of them had eaten much, and now the dish stood congealing on the kitchen table. Her own parents would never have allowed that. At home it was all 'waste not, want not', and plates had to be scraped clean or the same dried-up leftovers would appear at every meal. Still, it confirmed her idea that there was something the matter with Oona and her mum, Enid. Since Friday evening there had been an atmosphere as heavy as woodsmoke in the house, and she'd heard angry voices raised late at night. Once, she'd heard Enid's raw weeping from behind her bedroom door. As she washed the pots, Ella eavesdropped on the conversation in the living room through a gap in the door.

'What if we lose the house? Where will we go?' Enid's

voice was raised in desperation.

'It won't come to that, Mum. You're great at your job. Just keep him happy like you always have.'

'But I'm not great at my job, am I?' Her voice sounded choked with emotion. 'And now he's found out. And he'll let everyone know. Oh God.'

'You can handle him, Mum. It'll be OK.'

'It's not just him,' Enid protested. 'There's this new woman who's started today. Some sort of spy from the government. You know how all the hospitals have got new managers under Thatcher's plan? I reckon she's in cahoots with Voss to get rid of anyone they don't like the look of.'

'That blonde woman who arrived the other night?'

'I haven't seen her yet, but I've heard Voss has been parading her around. She's moved into number 16. It's not just a visit, she's staying up here. He probably nips round after dark.'

Ella crossed the kitchen to put the plates back on the dresser and peered into the living room through the gap in the door. Mother and daughter were sitting side by side on the settee, Oona protectively hugging her mother close. Enid was gulping down tea from a man-sized mug. And didn't her voice have that quivering, sing-song tone again? As a thank you for her bed and board, Ella had taken on whatever daily chores she thought would help them most. She emptied waste bins, cleaned the windows and had started ironing the two women's pile of laundry. There had been two hidden gin bottles so far, one in the wastepaper basket and another amongst the dirty sheets. At night she sometimes heard someone moving around the house, then going out to the outhouse where all sorts of garden tools and potted plants were stored. That must be where Enid kept her secret bottle stash.

She wanted to help the woman: Enid had a responsible job that came with a nice house and salary, a job that she should be proud of. She supposed that most people had things they were addicted to. With Enid, it was gin, with Oona her spells – or was it the attention she got from pretending to do magic? Ella's own mum had her endless evangelical cleaning, while her dad was forever absent, working on the farm. And then there was Jim, touching his cap to her parents but secretly seeking her out, chasing and needling her.

'Look what she sent me,' Enid exclaimed. 'All these questions.' Now Ella glimpsed Oona leaning over to look at a paper booklet. She strained to catch every slurred word.

'Mum, it's only a team questionnaire. Just fill it in.'

Enid's voice was shrill with panic. 'You don't get it, do you? It's like those assessments the psychiatrists use on the patients. It's meant to get under your skin. Pick out your secrets. I'm no good at all this. You know what it's like here. Everything runs smoothly, so long as no one asks too many questions.'

Oona didn't reply, just picked up the questionnaire and leafed through the pages. Her mum watched, twitchy beside her.

'Look.' Enid pounced on the paper and read out an item. '"My teammates say I always admit to my mistakes: a) Usually, b) Sometimes, c) Rarely." You get it? It's all about getting evidence to give me the sack.'

'Come off it, Mum. I'm sure you'll be fine.'

'It's all right for you! I've got to meet this woman along

with Voss, Brian and Kevin for team sessions. What am I supposed to say? I like and respect my teammates? I bloody hate their guts. It's like – I don't know – like being forced to do the patients' therapy. They'll be able to tell I'm lying.'

'I tell you what,' Oona said gently. 'I see this crap in the post all the time. I'll fill it in for you.'

Enid clasped her daughter's hand like a grateful child. 'Will you?'

'I'll aim for the dead centre of normal. But you must try to be more upbeat. Windwell needs a treasurer. He won't sack you.'

An instant later a chair scraped on the floor and Ella sprang back to the sink. She picked up a dishcloth just as Enid came in, swaying slightly as she carried her empty mug, her cheeks very pink.

'Can I fetch you anything, Mrs Finn?'

Enid shook her head. 'You done in here?' Her thin mouth tightened.

'Yes, Mrs Finn.'

Realising Enid was looking to top up her gin, Ella slipped into the living room. Oona met the questions in her eyes with a disbelieving shake of her head, as if to say, *what the fuck next?* As soon as Enid had disappeared upstairs to her bedroom Oona went straight for her cards. She had a gorgeous pack of tarot cards, very large and lavishly decorated, that she kept wrapped in a piece of silk inside a sandalwood box.

'Did you hear all that?' she asked in a low voice. 'I bet your mum isn't half the trouble of mine.'

Ella flinched, then remembered that Oona rarely expected a reply to that sort of comment. One really useful thing she'd picked up, was that she wasn't that interested in hearing anything much about Ella herself.

As usual Oona jumped in to say, 'I'd better do a reading.'

'Can I watch?'

Oona nodded, mischief perking up her face. 'Yeah, course. Switch off the big light and fetch some candles.'

Oona's candles were special; she had yellow beeswax ones for nature work, pure white for white magic, and a box of black wax tapers used for what she called 'dabbling in the dark stuff'. Tonight she chose ordinary white ones and Ella settled down on the settee beside her. Oona did have a fantastic way with all this spiritual stuff; she made the card turning look graceful, like an artist or magician uncovering a beautiful hidden world. Now, once the cards were shuffled and the candles were burning, she selected her first card.

'To represent my mother I choose the Queen of Wands – a businesslike woman, but reversed.' She laid the card upside-down. 'Mum's always been unreliable, pretty hopeless in fact.'

Even craning to look at it upside-down, Ella could see a slight resemblance to Enid in the Queen of Wands. The skinny, rather mannish body sat squarely on the throne and the face was angular within the frame of chin-length brunette hair.

'Just three more cards I'll turn. The past, the present and future. First, the past.' Oona turned the first card. 'Wow, the Five of Cups. Regrets, loss, sadness. Poor Mum, that is so true. She was a model once, you know. A proper dolly bird back in the sixties.'

'The present.' Oona reverently turned the next card and

gave a small gasp. 'The Emperor – reversed.' Again the card was laid upside-down. This one showed an older bearded man seated on a crown before a vast mountain.

'An important man, the boss or father figure – but here he falls down at the job.'

She dropped her head and mumbled a word. Enid had been going on about a man who had accused her of not being up to her job. It had to be this new man Doctor Voss, but Oona had whispered what sounded like, 'Heavy.'

'The future,' Oona said, in her dramatic fortune-telling voice. She turned the card and frowned. 'That is so annoying. The Moon.'

'What's it mean? It looks very mysterious.'

'Well, yeah, it is. But moonlight's uncertain. Could be hidden enemies, danger, deception, anything we can't yet see clearly. But no idea what. Sorry, that was a pretty shitty reading.' Briskly, she gathered up the cards and started shuffling the deck before replacing them in the box.

But Ella had picked up that final card and was studying it. The illustration showed a sky full of stars and in the foreground, a statuesque maiden wearing robes of white and a crown of stars. In her hand stood a staff topped by a glowing orb. Behind her hung a gigantic full moon, across which flew grotesque moths. Ella tried not to stare as her friend put the cards away, for the golden-haired figure on the card had borne a definite similarity to Oona herself.

CHAPTER SEVEN

Lorraine's time spent away from Windwell revived her usual optimism. It was a beautiful autumn day; the air had a sparkle to it, and a low sun flamed on distant woods, turning the trees a warm russet. Slowly, the solitary steadiness of driving restored her. She parked up at a layby on a high ridge and got out to lean on a drystone wall, closing her eyes to enjoy the chilly remnants of the year's sun. If she could get away into fresh air and open spaces like this every few days, she could begin to enjoy her time away. All she had to do was deliver some sort of team-building sessions and give Morgan some photos of the group enjoying an outdoor experience. She had endured far worse. So what was bothering her? There was something lurking in her consciousness. What had she learnt on her personality testing course: that her personality was intuitive and thin-skinned, great for reading people, but like osmosis, it leached stress and anxiety from those around her.

A gigantic crow hopped past her, its wings fluttering in excitement. A moment later it joined its mate on the road and the pair set to pulling a young rabbit apart. As tubes of scarlet appeared amongst the grey fur, she made her way back to the car. Above her, a hawk hovered very still in the air, its black silhouette eerily steady. If she were ever to believe in portents, these were not good ones.

A sign appeared for Haworth and the Brontë Parsonage, but she didn't feel up to all that pent-up passion. Further on came a bigger sign for Hebden Bridge, the valley town known for its cheap stone houses and influx of hippies. Her spirit rose at the prospect of shops and phone boxes and anonymous strangers.

She liked the place at once: cramped stone back-to-back houses ascended like dominoes from the canal all the way up the vertiginous hillside to the looming crags. In the valley bottom she found wholefood shops, second-hand books and hippy goods, from incense sticks to Afghan coats. A bunch of cider drinkers and off-duty morris men had settled in for the afternoon outside the pub in the square. The latter-day hippies wore their differences like a badge of honour: faded rainbow clothing, straggly beards, wooden beads, many circled by feral dogs and even wilder long-haired kids. Venturing into an alternative-style cafe, she ordered nut pâté and wholemeal toast, served on plates ham-fistedly shaped from lumpen clay. She picked up a newsletter and read about the town's efforts to replace capitalist cash with some sort of barter system. There were invitations to join a women's consciousness-raising group, a band of drummers, or help out at a commune. She tried to picture herself and Jasmine living the communal life and decided she'd be bored. It felt earnest and slightly quaint and a very long way from Salford.

At an outdoor clothing shop, she found a pair of lace-up boots that were so stiff she needed to buy a tin of what the assistant called dubbin to ease the leather. Outside her comfort zone, she also shelled out on a waterproof jacket called a cagoule, thick knitted socks, a jumper and an emergency block of Kendal mint cake on display at the till.

Next, her thoughts ran to how the band were getting on. In a newsagent's shop she leafed through copies of *Sounds*, *Melody Maker* and the *New Musical Express*. None of their reporters had followed Gothenburg and her own band, Electra Complex, to Germany yet, thank God.

At four o'clock she tracked down a phone box and Jasmine at once picked up, sounding happy and chatty. She had enjoyed her exam at the grammar school and now her nan was taking her to the pictures to see the new Star Wars film, *Return of the Jedi*. Lorraine ached to think of missing time with her daughter, and promised other treats when she got home. By the time she rang off, the sky was growing overcast so she headed back to the car, brooding over the injustice of being stranded so far away from her daughter.

Wednesday 5th October

On Wednesday morning Lorraine felt ready to face whatever horrors Doctor Voss had to hurl at her. She dressed carefully, pulling on shapeless black trousers and a decidedly modest blouse, and then pulled her hair up into a plain ponytail. Against her better judgement, she recalled how when she'd first applied to work in Personnel she'd also been offered a second job in the Adolescent Secure Unit. It had sounded interesting, though she had been slightly alarmed by the razor-wire fencing around the building and proliferation of alarm buttons on the interior walls. A few weeks later a female worker had been trapped in the office and raped by an adolescent patient. That could have been me, she'd thought at the time. Now her anxiety was crawling back.

At the security gate of Phase One, Doctor Voss appeared, delighted to see her. The building looked impressive; at a distance it could have been a university, save for the stark fifteen-foot-high perimeter wall. All was contemporary light and angles, in contrast to the old asylum's soot-stained curlicues. She followed Voss through a steel reinforced gate, taking in high mesh fences, a reinforced glass airlock, buzzers, alarms and intercom. A large sign listed the items visitors were banned from carrying: drugs, alcohol, Sellotape, Blu Tack, chewing gum, glass, wires, shoelaces . . .

She emerged into a pale lobby that might have been the entrance to a slick city office. The security guard searched her bag. Scowling, he removed a biro pen, a hand mirror and two paperclips.

'Why did he confiscate those?' she asked Voss after he'd checked them both in.

'They could be used to make weapons or escape aids,' he said breezily. 'Here, have a pencil.' He handed her a stub of leaded pencil. 'Just a moment.' Turning to the burly man on reception, he asked, 'Has Mr Crossley checked in today?'

'No, Doctor Voss. Not seen him all day.'

Lorraine thought she saw a glint of smug amusement on the burly male receptionist's face. Already, she was feeling protective of Voss and his radical ideals.

Voss began the tour by proudly showing her the therapy, education and family visiting areas, spaces whose final design he had been able to influence. Next were an impressive set of workshops, the sports areas and the football pitch. They were inspecting the psychologists' seminar room when he mentioned that this was where they would hold the afternoon's team-building session. It was blandly tasteful, painted in a pale flesh pink, and furnished with wooden tables and sofas.

'What's the mirror for?' Lorraine was beginning to notice incongruities amongst the decor.

'One-way observation. There's a small room behind here that's used for clinical assessments. We have the latest hidden recording systems, too.'

It felt ironic that a session centred on trust and openness should take place in an environment designed to secretly record its subjects. She tried to quell her nerves; the team-building session would start in less than forty minutes. Surreptitiously, she wiped her clammy hands against her jacket.

Voss continued his tour down another corridor that still smelt of new paint.

'Now for the ward I was telling you about. Ferris Ward is officially the Personality Disorder Unit. That's the new term for what was always the Psychopath Unit. As you'll see, it's overcrowded.

'Unfortunately, a recent inquiry recommended that

our psychopathic patients should be entirely separated from other mentally ill patients. There were superficially valid arguments: psychopaths will generally seek to dominate and control other patients they see as weaker than themselves. But the result is that we now have the most violent and malevolent inmates all housed together, with little or no contact with the rest of the hospital. As I mentioned yesterday, I'm alarmed by the discovery of contraband drugs and I've no idea how they got there.'

They had stopped stock-still at a double airlock with a complicated mechanism. For the first time it occurred to Lorraine that she would be locked inside. A surge of bitter bile rose in her throat. 'I'm sorry. Are there any ladies' toilets in the building?'

She had to retreat back through the maze of corridors until she found a hatch where she could request a key. Inside the staff toilet every cell in her body ached to be in another place. Suddenly she made a run for a toilet cubicle and was violently sick into the bowl. She wondered if she was ill, but when she stood up and splashed her face she recognised the source of her pallor and panicky breathing. It was fear.

She returned to where Voss waited and after more doors were unlocked, banged shut and relocked, they reached the centre of the building. At the threshold Voss whispered a warning to her.

'Don't tell anyone your personal details. Not your name, phone number, your address, nothing. They'll be curious but just stay close to me.'

Voss led her into a common room that at first glance might have been any working-class social club: there was a pool table, a pall of cigarette smoke, tatty noticeboards and half a dozen bored-looking young men. She was the only female in the room and studiously tried to avoid making eye contact. Voss started chatting to a man in a blue shirt with epaulettes and a dark tie. She risked an upwards glance towards three men who were brazenly staring at her face and body. Guffaws broke out as they discussed her. A small man in a singlet appeared at her side and she smelt his unwashed sweat as his glittering eyes assessed her.

'An' who might you be, then?' he asked in a Yorkshire accent.

Don't give your name, she repeated silently to herself. 'I'm here with Doctor Voss.'

She risked a proper glance at the patient. His stance was cocky, his skin yellowish and pockmarked, his long stringy hair hanging in rat's tails.

'Doctor Voss,' he taunted. 'The great saviour of Windwell. So tell me—' The little man's fingers touched her back and she flinched away, knocking awkwardly against the wall.

'Sorry,' he said, this time grasping her elbow as if she needed his support.

'I'd like to move on.' She spoke loudly, interrupting the flow of Doctor Voss's conversation. The male nurse in the blue shirt swaggered over to her side, heavy and bull-like.

'Come on, Joey. Don't bother the lady.'

'It's Doctor Voss who's bothering her,' Joey announced. 'He's pretending to be the nice guy, but really he just wants to fuck her.'

The huddle of pool players were openly enjoying the

entertainment, a few of them openly guffawing. Voss summoned a deadpan voice.

'That's a good one, Joey. You trying to read my mind again? Well, you're completely wrong. If only you could be so perceptive about your own desires, hey?'

Voss was calm and casual and it worked. Having failed to shock the director, Joey wandered away.

They moved on to view the rest of the unit. Lorraine thought the bedrooms were better furnished than many a student residence, never mind the average bedsit in Manchester. Each had a bed, study desk, TV and storage area. The whole building struck her as possessing a doublethink reminiscent of Orwell's *1984*. It had the serene façade of a relaxing recreational camp, but every glimpse of a nurse's keychain or double-locked door suggested that security was aggressively pursued. Her intuition was that the residents of Ferris Ward were laughing at their keepers, putting on a mildly rebellious performance for the staff while hiding their true intentions.

'Is Rob in?' Voss asked the nurse.

'I think he went to the library. Let's see.' He knocked respectfully at a closed door.

'Rob Kessler's room,' Voss said quietly. She knew the name, of course. He was Windwell's most infamous inmate, convicted of the murder of four women and sentenced by the courts to never leave the place alive.

'He's not back,' said the nurse. They filed inside.

Dominating the room were hundreds of photographs, mostly from magazines and newspapers, stuck to the walls in a gigantic collage. The images were mostly of women, but it was not always possible to say who or what they were.

Mostly they were close-ups of bodies flexed in countless poses. She recognised an advertisement for stockings that ran over a double-page spread, stretching the model's legs from her toes to crotch. Others were of bikini-clad torsos, shots from underwear catalogues, some topless newspaper page-three poses. Others resembled the sorts of posters supplied by medical sales reps, grisly photos of wounds, anatomical slip-ups, amputations and the saws and clamps required to create them. Lorraine felt outrage that the staff allowed such a lurid display. She wondered what Kessler saw when he selected those photographs. A body, a trophy, a target? All the images lacked the identity of a face. From where she hung back near the door she looked at his neatly made bed, his body-building magazines, his copy of *The Sun* open on the football pages. She knew his face from the press – the cheeky, monkey-like features that had charmed those four women to trust him and lose their precious lives.

She was saved from a potential confrontation with Kessler by the high-pitched sound of a pager bleeping from Voss's belt.

'Excuse me.' He studied the message with a look of bemusement. 'Sorry, Lorraine, I need to check this out.' He looked at his watch and beckoned at her to follow him. 'It's OK, we've still got some time before the others arrive.'

Lorraine followed Voss outside the building and passed through the security lodge of Phase Two. This half of the hospital was still a building site, surprisingly empty save for the sound of hammering and drilling from the building's interior.

'It's a rather odd message,' Voss said over his shoulder. 'Hope it's not another of these attempts to undermine me.'

They crossed a courtyard and entered a brand-new flat-roofed building. The director was trying the electric light switch, but the bulbs stayed dark. They were on a gloomy corridor, marked by a series of closed doors with observation slots and heavy-duty locks.

'Cell 17,' Voss muttered to himself, checking off the numbered doorways as Lorraine followed more slowly in his wake.

He reached it first and, finding the door to Cell 17 ajar, swung it open. He let out a sound she couldn't identify. Then he took a few uncertain steps backwards.

'*Mijn God.*' His hand clutched the wall for support.

Lorraine caught up with him and followed the direction of his staring eyes. A man lay slumped on the floor of a seclusion cell, his eyes bulging and glassy, his body twisted on the floor. She wanted to look away, but the physical stasis of shock held her in its grip. One side of the man's scalp was crusted with blackish dried blood. A thin red cord hung from his neck. Her eye traced it back to where it circled the thick flesh. Above him the murderer had left a message daubed in red paint: 'RIP Campbell. Your next.'

Voss sank to his knees beside the man. For a confused instant she thought he was overcome with emotion. Then her vision cleared and she saw he was struggling to cut away the cord with a penknife.

'Ring for an ambulance, Lorraine,' he ordered, without pausing in his work. 'And the police. I'll try to revive him, but I think it's too late.'

In that moment she felt a jolt of relief that Voss was a trained doctor and knew exactly what to do. And relief, too, that she was coping so far – in fact, she was helping.

Even as she ran to find a phone Lorraine had guessed who the dead man was. He was the fourth member of the team, she was sure of it. Lorraine's call from the security lodge summoned an ambulance in less than twenty minutes. But even long before help arrived, she had returned to Cell 17 and knew it was too late to save Kevin Crossley, Windwell's administrator.

CHAPTER EIGHT

Doctor Voss had asked her to wait for the other team members in the psychology seminar room. She carefully chose which seat to take at the table, leaving the most dominant chair at the head for Doctor Voss and taking the one to his right-hand side. Settling down, she began to search her bag for the notes she had carefully prepared. A small sound made her freeze. It was almost nothing, a thud like that of a soft object being dropped in the next room. She looked up into the observation mirror and saw her own reflection, looking pale and scared. Someone had made a noise directly behind that strange glassy rectangle. Someone was watching her.

'Hello? Anyone there?' Her voice sounded slight in the still air. She walked quickly into the corridor, looking both ways but seeing no one. The unobtrusive door into the observation room stood unlocked. Inside the light was off and no one was lurking behind the door. She wondered if she was hearing things. After all, she'd just seen a murder scene. It was little wonder that her imagination was going into overdrive.

The room was crammed with sophisticated recording equipment and stacks of files. Surely the open door must be a security breach? A full ashtray on the desk below the mirror reeked of smoke. Her fingers touched the butts and sure enough, one felt warm and disturbingly damp with saliva. She raised it to the light and saw the letters 'MEL' remaining where the filter had been squashed. She wiped her hands on her trousers. At the very least, the smoker had seen her arrive and rather than make themselves known, had observed her and then slipped away.

A new movement on the other side of the mirror caught her eye. A woman had entered the seminar room next door. Believing herself to be unobserved, the stranger searched her handbag and lifted out a soft-drink bottle. After anxiously glancing about herself, she took a long draught before closing her eyes in appreciation, and then took a second long swig. Dismayed by what she'd witnessed, Lorraine hurried out to meet her.

'Hello. I'm Lorraine Quick. Are you here for the team-building with Doctor Voss?'

The woman standing before her was wiry to the point of emaciation, the deep lines around her thin lips suggesting hard habits or perpetual dissatisfaction. She watched Lorraine with pale, darting eyes.

'I'm Enid Finn. Is it true about Kevin? Is he dead?' The treasurer's hand was shaking as she lowered herself into a chair. As Lorraine had feared, a distinct waft of alcohol reached her nostrils.

'I believe so. Doctor Voss will be here as soon as he can.'

Annoyingly, before they could exchange any further words, the chief nurse, Brian, arrived. He barged past Lorraine, pointedly ignoring her.

'Have you heard the latest, Enid? What the fuck can happen next, eh?'

Enid shook her head, remaining mute.

Brian stood over the table, gripping a chair back with swollen biceps. He had the build and belligerent manner of a professional wrestler gone to seed: well over six feet tall, sporting a ballooning paunch under his white shirt and tie, his round domed head entirely bald.

He glowered at Lorraine. 'And you? What do you know about it?'

'I have a name. I'm Lorraine Quick. You're Brian Ogden, I presume. I doubt I know any more than you at present.'

'Well, I can't be hanging around here all day. Someone's got to sort things out while Voss is fannying around.'

'We should stay here,' Lorraine said firmly.

'Says who?' Brian was smirking unpleasantly. Lorraine guessed she had no actual authority but didn't shift her gaze.

'Lorraine is right,' said a voice from behind her back. Thank God, it was Voss. 'Now we're all finally together, we're going to stay here till I say so.'

Voss insisted that they all sat together around the table and then stoically gave a brief account of how Kevin had been found dead in one of the seclusion cells in Phase Two. Lorraine couldn't help but feel that he sounded remarkably composed for someone who had just discovered a ghastly corpse, but then again, he was a forensic psychiatrist. He appreciated that they were all shaken, but now Windwell's future success depended on how the three of them could work together. Sensing the imminent start of her session, Lorraine tried to inconspicuously search her bag for her notes. It soon became apparent that the carefully nuanced introduction to team-building she had drafted had disappeared. Shit, how had that happened? Verging on panic, she remembered that yes, she had double-checked the papers when she left the cottage. And she had spotted them earlier, when she put Doctor Voss's stub of pencil away. No, they hadn't been confiscated by the security guard. With a plummeting stomach, she remembered how the persistent patient, Jimmy, had knocked against her a couple of times. No doubt part of his disordered personality was a rare talent in stealing from women's handbags.

She looked up at Enid's blank expression and Brian's hostile disengagement. Doctor Voss was clearly coming to the end of his impromptu opening remarks, asking Enid and Brian if they had brought the paperwork on teamwork Lorraine had issued to them. Enid pushed her team profile and a copy of the ground rules across the table. Brian gave no apology for having failed to complete or bring along the documents, complaining of overwork. Now he was making a case for postponing the whole session, making heavy weather of his own vital importance in running the hospital.

If Lorraine had been facing a kinder audience, she might have told them that her notes had been stolen and agreed to postpone. But that would leave Brian as the winner in this psychological battle, and that was unthinkable. If she showed any weakness he might return to the wards and mock her, no doubt finding it hilarious that a woman had been so easily tricked by a patient. No, she couldn't admit that Jimmy had stolen her papers. But then again, she always used her notes as a prop, a prompt to speak lucidly to a group. And now, with Kevin's corpse at the forefront of her mind, she couldn't remember a single word of what she'd prepared.

'And so, it's over to you, Lorraine.' Voss was eyeing her with an encouraging, though rather strained, expression.

The room fell silent. Brian's small eyes fixed on her, in anticipation of sport. She smiled and nodded, wondering if she looked as hideously nervous as she felt. The silence continued as she scoured her brain for an opening line or two. The trouble was, she didn't trust anyone in this room. And trust had been the theme of her opening session. Then she had a sudden off-the-cuff idea.

'Good afternoon. I'd like to make a suggestion about the way we proceed today. The plan for this first session was to talk about trust. It strikes me that the tragic situation we face is in fact a timely opportunity to consider the trust between members of this management team. I propose that while the police begin their preliminary investigation, we use this session to discuss the impact of Kevin's death on the hospital.'

Doctor Voss was staring at her in open surprise. Slowly, his expression softened, and he gave a tiny appreciative nod.

Enid began to speak. 'My head is spinning with the whole thing, the horror of it. Never mind how on earth we can run the hospital without him. What on earth are we going to do without Kevin? It's a disaster – I mean, even beyond the horrible thing that's happened to him.'

Suddenly Brian stood up, rocking with impatience. 'It's all right for you pen-pushers to sit around yakking but I've got Ferris Ward to secure.'

Doctor Voss refused to be baited. 'The police have secured it, Brian. Your staff know you're here with us.'

Brian would not sit down. 'I need to go.'

Doctor Voss leant back. 'No. There should be no reason for the chief nurse to deal with operational issues at this moment. What we need to do is to follow Lorraine's suggestion. As this hospital's management team, we need to plan the future of the unit without Kevin.'

Brian slumped back down into his chair. He made an attempt to stare down the medical director. Lorraine was pleased to see that he failed.

'OK,' Lorraine said. 'I've sent each of you a list of ground rules. I won't insult you by going through them in detail. But if anyone isn't happy, just say so. Brian, if you're not familiar with the list, would you please share Enid's copy.'

She briefly talked through her ground rules: that nothing must be repeated outside the room, respect to each other must be shown and no personal attacks were allowed. She stressed that everyone should have equal speaking time, intending to ensure that introverts and women should not be domineered. Finally, attendance was compulsory and non-negotiable.

'Sounds good to me,' affirmed Voss. To her surprise, neither Brian nor Enid disagreed.

Still thinking on her feet, Lorraine suggested they all took two minutes' silence to consider their personal concerns around Kevin's death. Promptly, the room fell quiet and she studied her watch. The second hand seemed to take for ever to move around her watch face.

'Time's up,' she said quietly. 'I suggest each of you check in for five minutes. We'll go around the table and give our thoughts on the impact this news about Kevin has on each of us.'

Enid was on Lorraine's right-hand side, so she began.

'Kevin was my friend,' she said in a husky voice. 'We'd known each other for more than twenty years. I— I feel terrible. He lived alone, he had no one to confide his worries to. Since his wife died, I think we were the nearest he had to a family. For him to be killed suddenly like this, it couldn't be worse.'

She continued, battling contrary emotions about the man. Lorraine passed her a tissue as wet tears rolled down her crumpled cheeks. She ended with an appeal that must have been running through all their minds.

'But who could have done it? Who could have hated Kevin so much? And then there's the police running all over the hospital. I suppose we'll all have to answer lots of questions.' Between her thin fingers the soggy tissue was dissolving into shreds.

'Thank you, Enid,' Lorraine said softly, and nodded to Doctor Voss. He spoke in a subdued voice.

'It may sound strange, but I can't help feeling responsible in some way for Kevin's death. After all, I'm his manager and he's been missing for at least a day or even two. I feel highly anxious about us running the hospital without him. And I'm not looking forward to the media impact. Politically, it's a blow to us all. Personally, it feels like a waking nightmare. And in confidence, I can tell you that he was murdered in the seclusion cells. In Cell 17. Why would anyone kill Kevin? And why there? Is it some form of retribution over the Junior Campbell case? I, too, feel absolute horror at what I've just witnessed.'

He raised his head wearily, as if still overcome by the recent memory of finding Kevin's corpse, and scanned each of them in turn.

'I'm also aware of the pressure on me, and on all of us, to be leaders at this time. It's not ideal timing, for you don't know me well, but I want to say that I am here for you all and I am ready to represent Windwell, whatever storms lie ahead.'

Lorraine nodded and glanced apprehensively at Brian. His face was set in a grimace and she wondered if he'd try to walk out again. He shook his heavy head. 'I'm angry,' he growled. 'I'm angry that this happened on my patch. Kevin got on my wick, he was a pernickety old bastard. But who the fuck did it? And how?'

He turned on Voss. 'Is it true that he was found in the same way as Campbell was found?'

Voss gave a tiny nod of his head.

'So I'm the biggest suspect. Campbell's death was also on my watch. I can't believe it. I'm angry at the unfairness of it. The whole thing feels like a set-up and the police will be gunning for me.'

A chilly silence fell. 'Thank you.' Lorraine addressed them all. Thank God the details of the seminar she had planned were returning to her, because what she'd just heard eerily echoed the theme of her stolen notes.

'One of the keystones of a team is trust,' she said quietly. 'To trust someone is about being able to reveal our vulnerabilities to them, something you've each done, in your own fashion, just now. It's about truth-telling and not wasting time on posturing or pretending to be someone you aren't. To deal with the task ahead there will be risks to take and mistakes to be made, uncertainties about the future and the need to ask for help. So thank you. This has been a great start.

'Next up, I'd like to try something quite similar again. Two minutes to reflect alone and then share some ideas.' She looked at the three of them and saw fatigue in their slumped shoulders and tired faces. She needed to inject a change of pace. This time she got up and wrote the question on the flipchart: 'How can the team best act together in response to this crisis?'

After the initial period of silent reflection, the group miraculously offered up ideas and Lorraine jotted down their suggestions on the chart. Enid was clearly the most nurturing amongst them and focused on Kevin's funeral. She wanted to express respect for Kevin despite his awful death and suggested some ideas to commemorate the administrator's long years of service.

'And I think that if I was a member of staff – a nursing assistant or even a cleaner, I'd want reassurance of my own safety,' she added. 'And an honest and dignified attitude from the management team.'

'That's really helpful, Enid,' Voss said when it was his turn. He went on to stress the expectation that all staff should help the police, as that was the fastest way to find the killer. He wanted to send a clear message to all staff about what had happened and how they should co-operate. 'It would be useful too, to hear about the mood on the wards.'

Brian exploded. 'You want me to spy on my staff and come back here with tittle-tattle?'

'I'm sorry you misinterpreted my words, Brian. No, I think we all need as much good-quality information as we can get. I, for one, would appreciate the benefit of your own and your staff's experience.'

'Come off it. You want me to do your job for you!'

Voss raised his fingertips to make a steeple gesture, remaining very calm, a habit Lorraine was beginning to admire.

'No, thank you. I like my own job or I wouldn't be here.' He smiled self-deprecatingly. 'I simply want our very different jobs to begin to mesh together like the spokes of a wheel. Only when the spokes are aligned can we continue on our journey as a safe, functioning hospital unit.'

Wanting to end the session on a high point, Lorraine returned to the chart and wrote a new heading, 'Actions', at the top. Inviting ideas, she jotted down a plan. In lieu of close family, Enid would organise the funeral and pay for suitable flowers and a printed tribute to the dead man. Next, she would include a personal message to all staff about Kevin's untimely death with their next payslips.

'I'll brief all ward staff about giving the news to the patients,' added Voss. 'We can assume they will be just as concerned about their safety as the staff. After all, they can't resign or run away,' he added wryly. 'The presence of the police in the building may greatly alarm them, given that their last contact with the law was almost certainly unpleasant.'

Voss did his best to encourage Brian, as day-to-day manager of all nursing staff, to communicate what was happening on the wards and arrange time off for any police interviews.

'Anything else?' asked Voss.

'What about the running of the admin office?' Lorraine asked. 'Could some stop-gap arrangements be made?'

In the last few minutes it was agreed that Kevin's deputy, Parveen, should be offered a temporary upgrade until a new administrator was found.

'There's a problem,' Enid pointed out. 'Kevin took all the personnel and employment contract work under his wing. Parveen isn't trained in writing contracts and so forth. Maybe we need a temporary stand-in from an agency or other hospital.'

Unsure if her enthusiasm was folly, Lorraine heard herself volunteer her own time. 'I'd be happy to help out. I'm a qualified personnel officer with experience in a large acute hospital.'

Voss looked pleased. 'Excellent. I'd rather not have anyone else new on-site at present.'

Enid and Brian both nodded agreement and Lorraine felt unexpected pleasure at giving practical help to this peculiar team. Returning to routine personnel work would feel like an easy win amongst all this friction.

Voss closed the meeting with an agreement to meet at two o'clock the following Wednesday. A few minutes later she was alone, pulling down the flipchart sheets. Her skin felt clammy and her head was buzzing. Thank God she had earned some time to plan the next session.

She was ready to leave when Voss returned, standing at the doorway watching her. 'Good, you're still here. I was wondering if you'd like to meet up off-site some time.

There's a decent restaurant at the hotel in the next valley. How about dinner together?'

She paused and took in his usual laid-back expression. Was this supposed to be some kind of come-on? She felt an enormous temptation to meet as far away from Windwell as possible and find out more about what he wanted from her.

'Great,' she said.

'Excellent. I'm buried under masses of work this weekend, but we'll set a date next week, if that's OK?'

She nodded, decidedly flattered. The boss was taking her out for dinner. It would be a chance to talk openly and get to know the man behind the job.

CHAPTER NINE

Lorraine went in search of the admin office and found a reception area where visitors were greeted by Jenny, a junior typist. When she asked to see Parveen, she was led to an interior open-plan office where the deputy administrator was working at a new personal computer in a clearly competent fashion. She was an approachable, bespectacled woman in her twenties whose eyes welled with tears at the news of Kevin's death. Nonetheless, after a few minutes mopping her eyes with a tissue, she proved able to sensibly discuss the admin office's workload. Over cups of milky tea she gave a clear outline of Kevin's most urgent tasks to date and agreed to liaise with Doctor Voss and Enid where needed. They had just agreed to upgrade her to acting administrator for the next two months when raised voices reached them from reception. Without warning, the door flew open and the teenager Lorraine had almost driven into on her arrival at Windwell marched into the room. Jenny, following in her wake, protested, 'I told her you were having a confidential meeting, Parveen.'

'What do you want, Oona?' Parveen asked sternly.

The girl stopped stock-still and stared at Lorraine in obvious alarm. Lorraine took in Oona's short patchwork skirt, embroidered waistcoat and a blouse unbuttoned to flaunt a provocative view of her cleavage.

'Mr Crossley had some documents my mum needs to deal with urgently.'

'What documents?' Parveen asked.

'Something I typed for him.' Oona momentarily stumbled over her words as if decidedly unsure. 'I— they're for my mum.'

Parveen looked to Lorraine for guidance and she was happy to oblige. 'I'm afraid that until the police have searched Mr Crossley's office, everything must be left undisturbed,' she said smoothly.

Two spots of red flared on the cheeks of Oona's heart-shaped face. 'Please. It's nothing of importance to anyone else.'

Lorraine shrugged and said, 'Go and ask Doctor Voss. Or the police. But I'm afraid you may be wasting your time.'

With a huff of exasperation Oona turned and left. Parveen rolled her eyes to heaven and Lorraine asked, 'Who was that?'

'Oona is a ward clerk on the Psychopath Unit – sorry, it's called Ferris Ward now. She also helps out here part-time. I'm afraid I'll need her help in the office while I'm acting up. And so will you.'

'Fine. Whatever's necessary. But you've got to keep everything of Kevin's – and mine – securely locked away.'

When Parveen didn't respond, she added, 'This is serious. We can't have just anyone removing documents from Kevin's study before the police have checked it.'

'Sorry. I will. And I'll find you a key, too, so you can keep your work in there.'

Lorraine drained her cup of tea and eyed Kevin's office door with interest. Might she get a chance to look at the unit's personnel records? Enid's, Brian's and Kevin's files all struck her as making potentially interesting reading. Oona had obviously been keen to get hold of something in there for her mum.

'So who is her mum?'

Parveen gave her head a little shake. 'Sorry, I didn't say. Oona's from one of the big families round here. Her mum's Enid, the treasurer. And her boyfriend's Tommo Ogden, Brian Ogden's son.'

'Right,' Lorraine said, wishing she'd known that before she'd done her high-handed act and probably made an enemy of the ward clerk.

Back at the cottage, Lorraine sat at her kitchen table with a selection of team-building manuals spread out before her. She had no idea how to prepare for the next session. She had busked her way through the first meeting, but only thanks to the human need to bond over the shock of Kevin's death. How could she follow that?

Maybe she was simply jittery because Voss had rung her to tell her the police had arrived. She was also still feeling stunned from her phone call to Morgan, a matter of courtesy to tell him what had happened. The bastard had almost seemed to blame her.

'I'm trying to manage this story for the health secretary and you let this happen?' he had barked at her. 'Well? Lorraine?'

'Needless to say, it was beyond my control,' she said coldly. 'Doctor Voss is dealing with it very competently. We used the team-building session to get what's left of the team to handle the lack of an experienced administrator. I volunteered to help him out with some essential personnel duties.'

'I don't like any of this. Tell me what exactly happened to this man.'

She told the regional director how she and Voss had found Kevin in the seclusion cell and the copycat nature of his killing, which so closely mimicked the Campbell case.

'Damn. So it is political.'

'The obvious thought is that it's some kind of protest about the Campbell case. I'm wondering if Kevin covered up what happened to Campbell and sheltered whoever was to blame.'

'Stop right there. I don't want you to breathe a word about these speculations. We need positive news stories. Don't speak to anyone at Windwell about this – not the police, and most definitely not the press. You got that?'

'Yes. Absolutely.'

After a chilly farewell, she slammed down the handset and stared defiantly out of the kitchen window towards the empty moors. How did men like Morgan get away with it? The shrill burr of the phone made her jump. Irritably, she snatched it up again, expecting a lecture from Morgan on discretion and political nous. Instead, it was someone at reception informing her she had to attend an urgent staff meeting in the new unit. If she came over straight away, she might arrive before it got started.

Even after rushing over, she found the room packed with about fifty of the unit's key staff. Not enjoying standing alone and on public view, she looked for an empty single place. From the corner of her eye she was aware of two men seated at the front of the room behind a table. One of them was talking about arrangements for interviews in a vaguely familiar accent. To her relief, Doctor Voss stood up at the front of the room and waved at her to join him. When she reached him he indicated his own seat and whispered, 'Take mine. I'll be speaking soon.'

As she squeezed past him, he made that rather mannered gesture of touching the small of her back to guide her gently past. Having settled in his chair, Lorraine looked about, aware that many curious eyes might have observed Voss's gesture. She met Oona's interested stare and looked away, then Jenny from Admin's amused grin – or maybe that was a smirk? The next moment no one was looking at her. The speaker's voice had halted in a coughing fit and was asking for a glass of water. She heard something familiar in his mumbled apology and looked up properly for the first time. Her stare took in a floppy fringe of black hair, broad shoulders and a familiar battered leather jacket. The speaker's features resolved into Detective Sergeant Diaz. She fixed on him, asking herself a hundred questions.

He was deliberately not looking in her direction, then for a split second he shot her a frosty glance. Her arrival had thrown him off course. When he restarted speaking, he stumbled over his words and flicked through his notebook. She ducked her head down. It was a shock for her, too,

81

seeing him like this. His being here prompted an entire re-evaluation of her stay at Windwell. It had been hard enough already, but Diaz being involved brought a whole other dimension of difficulty and distraction. But still, he was here. She didn't know whether to curse him or whoop with joy.

She glanced up again. Now he was staring determinedly above her head. The older man who appeared to be his new boss was making an appeal for witnesses. Finally, the older man invited Doctor Voss to say a few words and he sauntered to the front of the room, blocking her view of the two detectives. Voss addressed them all as his colleagues, translating the jargon-heavy police-speak into plans for co-operation and compassion. There would be new security measures to keep everyone safe: staff were to walk in pairs or groups, especially to late or early shifts. The security lights would remain switched on night and day. For their own sakes patient visits were temporarily cancelled. He trusted them all to understand that they were his priority. He was a natural public speaker, calm and clever and smooth. Lorraine felt a little spark of pride that he had asked her out to dinner. After all, Voss was an impressive and interesting man. With luck he might even cure her of these awkward feelings she couldn't break free of for Diaz.

CHAPTER TEN

Thursday 6th October

Diaz's old chief super had once called him a wolfhound on the chase and he'd loved that. As a reward for his work at the Memorial Hospital, Diaz had been fast-tracked onto the residential CID course at Barnwell police college. The location had turned out to be a vast Jacobean mansion and a source of seemingly limitless luxury. Diaz had worked like a Trojan, his head fizzing with ideas and theories, so he'd been dreading bad news when he was summoned out of his class by the college's commander. Waiting to be called into his inner sanctum, he reckoned that not everything on the course had gone as well he'd hoped. He'd often left the bar early, after only a couple of beers and a grudging game of pool. Free of tedious company, he'd returned to his private study-bedroom to devour precious material on the new science of criminal profiling. As for team sports, they felt juvenile to him now and he'd loathed running around in the mud like a pillock. Lorraine had warned him about the limitations of his personality, and police college had reinforced it all; now he feared that he didn't match what the senior ranks called a sound character. So when the college commander told him that a certain Detective Chief Inspector Thripp needed a bagman on a murder case in Yorkshire, his blood rushed with joy at getting back on an investigation.

But now he was here at Windwell, his equilibrium had been disturbed by the sight of Lorraine. Jesus, he had fucked up the briefing. His concentration had been punctured by flashbacks from the past: Lorraine's smile, the pliable feel of her body, the burst of hope that he might speak to her alone.

'You ready?' The DCI was watching him now as he stared vacantly at his open notebook.

He jerked up his head. 'Yes, boss.' It was Thursday, the first full day of their investigation, and Thripp had asked him to sit in on Doctor Voss's interview and then cross-reference it against the account of the woman who had accompanied Voss at the crime scene. It was only now that he learnt her name was Lorraine Quick.

Thripp was a lean, balding man, with an ugly lantern jaw and watchful eyes beneath his shaggy brows. He had a much faster brain than Diaz's former boss at Salford, an old-timer now retired. And Thripp had bags of what Lorraine had always said he lacked. Empathy. He was also some sort of born-again Christian, which made Diaz uneasy. He didn't get that happy-clappy stuff at all. He touched the silver crucifix at his throat. You knew where you were as a Catholic. He had always been drawn to the dusty silence, the candles, the soothing prayers.

'Something on your mind, lad?' His new boss was good

at deciphering what you were thinking. It was a bloody nuisance.

'Just checking my questions for the Voss interview,' he lied.

'Good lad. There could be something fishy going on here.'

Doctor Voss was waiting for them in his spacious, coolly furnished office. Modern art hung on his walls and the doctor was dressed like a window dummy in one of those daft Benetton shops, wearing a bright green jumper and coloured socks. It brought it all back to him, the dislike of doctors he'd experienced at the Memorial Hospital. They thought they were God's gift to the human race. Mind you, Voss was a good witness, as well as a smooth talker. After a few minutes the detectives had a clear portrait of Kevin Crossley as a workaholic who vehemently opposed changing any aspect of the hospital.

'So he wasn't too happy about you getting the top job?' Thripp asked.

'I don't suppose he was. In fact, last time I saw him, on Monday afternoon, we had a disagreement about the Citizens Advice Bureau. Kevin found the idea of giving legal advice to patients ridiculous. Whereas I view it as humane and empowering.'

Voss fired up when he proclaimed his ideals. His pale blue eyes shone like one of the hell-raising priests Diaz remembered from the children's home. A man who had proved to be a not very Christian priest at all.

'So how did you see that battle working out, sir?' Diaz asked mildly.

'I would have won it.'

'So your problems must have been somewhat eased by his death?'

Voss stiffened. 'No. That's absurd. Kevin was always well-intentioned, just ultra-traditional. Besides, I have an excellent facilitator helping me rebuild the management team. He would have been under powerful pressure to change.'

Diaz realised the man was referring to Lorraine and couldn't resist a little prod. 'We heard you've got some outside help for that.'

Voss turned to Diaz with keen interest. 'Yes, a development expert called Lorraine Quick. She's just what I need to help the unit move on.'

A tide of heat prickled Diaz's skin. 'How long will she be here?' he asked bluntly. It was what he'd been wondering ever since he'd spotted her. He'd noticed Voss's proprietorial circling of her waist when she arrived at the briefing. In fact, that was when he'd completely lost his bloody mental thread.

'She's here till the end of the month. Longer, I hope.'

Thripp asked the next question and Diaz spent a while brooding. A few minutes later he got back into his stride, though reining in his aggression towards Voss.

'Do you have any idea at all what Kevin might have been doing in the seclusion cells that night?'

'No. But I could see he wanted to be somewhere else during our meeting. He was watching the clock closely. He wanted to leave by six. Not wanting to pry, I didn't ask why. He was an excellent administrator and had compiled a report on the total building costs. So after he left, I checked some of his figures on my calculator. It all looked acceptable and I was grateful to him. At around six-twenty Doctor Norris, a research psychologist, came by and we went to the Beckside Hotel to have a drink. He's researching some new therapeutic methods I need to learn about.'

Thripp nodded and Diaz scribbled the facts down. 'And what time did you part company with Doctor Norris?' Thripp asked.

'Nearly eleven o'clock. Doctor Norris and I had dinner and later he dropped me at my house.'

Diaz leant forward, pencil raised. 'As you and Doctor Norris left the unit, did you see Mr Crossley again? Or did anything unusual strike you?'

Voss looked uncomfortable. 'I didn't see him but it did seem rather dark. Maybe I unconsciously picked up that Phase Two's lights were switched off. I should have noticed but I was beginning to relax at the end of the working day.'

Diaz watched him closely. 'How normal would it be for the lights to be off?'

Voss sighed. 'I'm guessing that Titan, our building contractors, could tell you that. But it's not so unexpected. The builders are hard at work and we've had a few stoppages of water and electricity.'

'Another thing,' Diaz asked. 'Why would the door to the seclusion cells not be guarded at night?'

'As I said, you need to ask Titan about that, too. The scheme has not yet been signed over to us.'

Diaz left a long, chilly silence before proceeding in a shirty tone. 'Did you bother checking at all where Kevin Crossley was on Tuesday?'

'Yes I did.' Voss's manner held a hint of petulance. 'I phoned his deputy, Parveen, and she suggested he might have needed a day off from his workload.'

'So he was under considerable strain?'

'Yes. We are all under tremendous pressure.'

Diaz narrowed his eyes, as if not quite convinced. 'And on Wednesday you didn't query Crossley's further absence?'

'I did, I phoned him repeatedly at home but no one answered. I asked around everywhere I went. But I was showing Lorraine around, and dealing with an overcrowded hospital and a rush of urgent assessments to complete for the courts. I thought Kevin might need a few days to calm down after our disagreement. I've already made it quite clear that I'm happy for my staff to manage their own workload.'

Lorraine, again. Diaz bit his tongue and nodded to Thripp, who took over.

'How do you interpret "RIP Campbell. Your next"?'

'Back in 1980 there was an incident here and I guess it's connected to that. A vulnerable patient, Junior Campbell, was found dead in Cell 17, but that was a different place in the old asylum, not this new unit. No one was ever accused of Campbell's murder, but murder it certainly was, for he was not only beaten, but strangled with a red cord.'

Diaz eyed him steadily. 'As a psychiatrist, could you share your thoughts on any connection between the two cases?'

Voss raised his brows and sighed again. 'It's not really my field. But I'd say there's little doubt about its copycat nature. It must be intended to draw attention to the Campbell case.' He rubbed his brow with long, well-tended fingertips. 'Kevin was a witness called to testify at the Campbell inquiry in London. My interpretation is that the perpetrator was violently angry about Kevin's testimony. Yet it's difficult to see how, as administrator, he could have personally been involved in Campbell's death.' He steepled his fingers. 'You have to understand that all this took place three years before I came here.'

'So who else was around then?'

'I read the inquiry report when I was deliberating whether to take this job. It was hardly an enticement to come to Windwell. If I remember correctly, the chief nurse Brian Ogden and his son Tom, known as Tommo Ogden, were both on duty that night. And Kevin would have had overall responsibility for how the incident was reported locally. There was a consultant psychiatrist questioned, who was Campbell's medical officer, but I believe he died some years ago.'

Thripp leant back and assessed Voss coolly. 'Anything else you'd like to add?'

'Yes. According to our contract with Titan, the security guard at Phase Two's lodge should record every visitor who passes through the gate.'

'We're going to check that first thing today, Doctor.'

On the way back through the hospital Thripp turned to Diaz. 'You were a bit tetchy with the doctor, son.'

'He was bloody casual about Crossley vanishing into thin air. I think we should check his alibi with the hotel.'

'Aye, you could say Voss's half-hearted approach to Crossley's disappearance substantially delayed discovery of the body.'

Diaz was buzzing with questions. 'And what about this

hint of some appointment or other Crossley was desperate to dash away to?'

'Follow it up. Find out who he was expecting that night. I want witness statements at every stage.'

'I'm on it, sir.'

'But first things first. That bloke on guard last night, name of Bill Craven. He was sacked by Titan for neglecting his duties this morning and has gone home to Bradford. He's your priority. Get over there now in case he tries a runner.'

'Will do, sir.'

'Something that could be nothing,' Thripp continued. 'Have you heard that this Tommo Ogden is in a relationship with a clerk on his ward? What does that tell you about the way this place is run? Opens the door to fraud and conspiracy, son. If anyone on my patch starts ogling a colleague I transfer them pronto.'

Diaz looked away, mumbling, 'Right you are, sir.'

Back at the hospital's workshop that was now their temporary incident room, youthful Constable Ladlaw, jocularly renamed Laddo, handed Diaz a logbook in an evidence bag.

'From the security lodge, everyone who signed in over the last seven days.'

'I'll take it with us.'

Diaz glanced at the clock on the wall. If Laddo got his foot down now, he'd still be back in time to meet Lorraine at two o'clock.

From the passenger seat, Diaz watched Laddo resentfully, wondering if he'd be able to shake him off. Diaz hadn't recognised the constable at first but Laddo had known him as Shirley's fiancée all right. Ladlaw was the maiden name of Shirley's mother and now he dimly remembered Laddo under his other name, Matt Ladlaw, from the few family gatherings he'd been unable to avoid being dragged to by Shirley. Laddo now seemed to have got the mistaken idea that they were the best of mates and had arranged for the pair of them to share digs on the high street. Worse of all, Laddo's idea of a joke was to rib Diaz about his imminent matrimonial state. On the way to the car they had passed two not especially attractive young women heading into the social club, who had giggled and blurted some rubbish at them. Laddo had nudged him and smirked, 'Better make the most of your freedom, sir, before you get the ball and chain round your ankle.'

Now he tried to ignore the irritating constable while he leafed through the security lodge's visitors' book. Almost all of those who had accessed Phase Two had written 'Titan Construction' beside their names, so he focused on the few exceptions. On Monday morning, Thomas Ogden had signed in at 9.30 a.m., and signed out soon after at 9.53 a.m. At 1.45 p.m. on Monday Doctor Voss had also signed in and then out again after forty-five minutes, seemingly in a hurry, judging from the scrawled signature. Kevin Crossley hadn't signed in at all when he arrived to visit the seclusion block after leaving Doctor Voss's office. Diaz didn't like what he was reading. For Crossley to be last sighted soon after six o'clock on Monday evening and only discovered at 2.55 p.m. on Wednesday was certainly telling him something about this much-revered new leader of the organisation. He leafed through the next few pages

91

and found Doctor Voss's visit just yesterday, on Wednesday afternoon, and noted that Lorraine had been signed in as a visitor. After that, in the confusion of finding the body, neither had signed out. The security guard Bill Craven had also struggled to keep a handle on the crisis, writing a scant account of 'police cars' at five past three and 'ambulans' at seven minutes past, on that chaotic afternoon.

Bill Craven's address was a brick terraced house on a Bradford street where many of his immigrant neighbours had experimented with exuberant red, blue and green doors and windows. An Asian grocer's stood on the street corner with stalls piled high with unfamiliar fruit and vegetables. Diaz was more familiar with a West Indian vibe of thumping reggae systems and the business of ganja being dealt openly in the street. Bradford was different; a woman in a fancy sari topped with a very English rain mac was watching them closely from across the road.

Craven opened the door with stubble on his jowls and what looked like the grey pallor of a hangover. His front room was a filthy pit: piles of crumpled clothes, fag-ends and dirty plates. Both Diaz and the constable refused a cup of tea. Bill's story came out in inarticulate mumbles. He moaned that he been tricked out of his job.

Diaz asked him why he had left his post on Monday night.

'It weren't my fault. This fucking memo arrived from Dugdale, one of Titan's managers. It told me a delivery wagon had a flat tyre near the village sign. Well, all the workmen had knocked off and I had nowt to do. I reckoned I'd only be ten minutes, but I were more than an hour hunting around for it. There were no wagon. It were someone sending me a message and having me on. I get that now.'

'When you left, were the security lights on?' asked Diaz.

'Oh, aye. But when I come back it were as black as sin. I had a torch in the van, so I looked at the fuse box. The switches had tripped, like.'

'Now this is important, Bill. When you left the lodge did you notice anything different, or unusual?'

Bill shook his head. 'Din't see owt different.'

'And when you came back?'

This time he paused a while. 'Yeah, the locker door were open.'

'OK. Your locker?'

'No. Spare one. Mostly got old stuff in it. Rubbish what's been left behind.'

'Can you remember what was in there last time you looked?'

The old fellow's brow corrugated with effort. 'There were an old uniform in there, too small for me. Some magazines. An umbrella. And one of them heavy truncheons, like an old nightstick, in case trouble broke out.'

On the way back to the car Diaz radioed in to the incident room. 'Get some SOCOs down to the security lodge Phase Two. Seems the suspect fiddled with the fuse box. Also check the locker room for prints and the following items: a navy-blue guard's uniform and a nightstick, both believed to have been stolen.'

Back in the incident room Diaz flicked through a bundle of statements and found a new pattern; a number of staff had mentioned a Professor Leadbetter, a man with an apparent grudge against Tommo. The story was that the professor had worked at Windwell but left under a cloud after the Campbell murder. Even more interesting, he had removed some items from the crime site to his home. Why would an academic take souvenirs from the crime scene? Diaz made a note to visit him when he got a chance. To his annoyance, he looked up and saw he was running late for his appointment with Lorraine.

CHAPTER ELEVEN

Lorraine had arrived early for her interview after a weary staff member had been bleeped to escort her inside Phase One. She could see the police incident room through a glass door, bright and busy, with rows of telephones and the buzz of chatter. She lingered in the hallway, nervously watching rain trickle down the glass windows.

Diaz and a younger man appeared in the rain. When his familiar features came into view she couldn't suppress a smile. Instantly, she stifled it. Act like a professional, she told herself. You know he's got someone else and he didn't even have the integrity to tell you about it. Yet still, he also seemed to brighten at the sight of her familiar face.

'Good. Miss Quick, isn't it? We met some time ago, didn't we?' he said, assuming a policeman-like gravity. 'I'm Detective Sergeant Diaz. This is Detective Constable Ladlaw.'

What's all this with the titles, she asked herself. For some reason he didn't want this school-leaver of a constable to spot how well they already knew each other. Her mood sank at the prospect of acting out a charade.

They moved into a small side room and Diaz ran through his spiel. He needed her to give a statement about when she and Doctor Voss had discovered Mr Crossley's body. She started to give her account, trying to keep her gaze fixed on the desktop, but unable to stop from checking his face. After all, wouldn't a witness be curious about how a detective was receiving her words? She had prepared her statement and the words came out on autopilot. She looked up again, and this time she connected with his dark eyes. She slid her eyes down to his mouth. There was the hint of a smile on Diaz's lips.

Suddenly, the fresh-faced constable spoke out loud. 'How long did you leave Doctor Voss alone?'

She looked at him, surprised. 'About ten minutes. I ran to the lodge, made the call and then ran back.'

Diaz leant forward and spoke. 'How was Voss affected by finding his colleague dead?'

'He was surprised. Even shocked. We both were. He was very cool and professional but clearly alarmed.'

'What do you know about Voss and Crossley's argument on Monday night?'

'Nothing. I didn't arrive here until around eight-thirty that night and checked straight into my accommodation. This is the first I've heard of an argument.'

'You spent a fair amount of time with Doctor Voss in your first few days. Can you recall any occasions when he tried to find out where Mr Crossley was?'

She sprang to the director's defence. 'Yes,' she insisted. 'At least twice he asked at reception. And he spoke to

Parveen, Kevin's deputy, frequently.'

Diaz eyed her sceptically. She knew that look and raised her voice in protest. 'It's not Voss. He and Crossley were bound to disagree. They were polar opposites. From what I can tell, Crossley was a details man who had worked here since the year dot. Voss is a visionary, a rare personality with the ability to move this place forward. Crossley no doubt scoffed at Voss's plans.'

'But you don't scoff at him?' Diaz asked. Christ, she had forgotten his capacity to annoy her.

'No, I don't,' she said, feeling stung. 'The frustrating thing is, that if you combined Crossley's grasp of detail with Voss's big picture for the future, they'd have been quite a powerhouse.'

The constable looked back through his notes. 'But surely you never even met Mr Crossley. How can you be so sure of all this?'

Lorraine gave a dismissive shake of her head. If the annoying constable would just bugger off, she could be enjoying a proper conversation with Diaz by now.

'He sent me his team profile,' she said. 'Characteristically, it was by return post and every space conscientiously filled in. And everything I've seen in his results correlates a hundred per cent with what I've heard about him from the staff here.'

'I'd like to see Crossley's profile,' said Diaz.

'I suppose that's possible.'

'And Doctor Voss's.'

Honestly, why was Diaz being such a tosser? She couldn't contain a theatrical sigh. 'I'd have to ask his permission before handing that over. You see, he is still alive and therefore has the right to object.'

'Have you got anyone else's profiles?'

She decided to take a stand. 'The people who completed those questionnaires were given an assurance of absolute confidentiality.'

'Which people?'

She thought of Brian Ogden and knew she couldn't risk enraging the chief nurse. Besides, she hadn't actually received his questionnaire yet. 'Only one other. Enid Finn. The treasurer.'

Diaz gestured towards the constable. 'You got all that?'

The lad's pink face was screwed up in concentration, his head bowed over his notebook. 'Nearly.'

Diaz stood up, gestured towards Lorraine to do the same, then said to the youth, 'I'll be back in a few minutes.'

He ushered her outside and a few moments later they had both slipped around a corner. The grey clouds were heavy but the rain was lessening. She couldn't quite read his expression. He lit a cig and sent a plume of smoke skywards.

'Jesus, Lorraine. I can't believe you're here.' At last he sounded like his old self.

'What's going on? Is it really such a big deal to let that constable know we've already met?'

He grimaced. 'I don't want DCI Thripp to know. I don't think he'd like it. He's not like Brunt back in Salford.'

'Well, that's a relief. If I remember rightly, he was convinced I was after your virtue.' They both gave little snickers of laughter.

'What I mean is, he's one of the God Squad. Evangelical. If he knew we had any history he'd do his best to send you packing.'

'Hold on a sec,' she protested, picking up on his chauvinist assumption. 'I've got a project given to me by a member of the Cabinet. You can go packing if you like.'

She could see his smile glimmering in the gloom. 'I guess we've both got our future careers at stake. So maybe we should collaborate? You're on the inside, Lorraine. You're privy to management chit-chat, the unguarded opinions. Whenever I talk to anyone they clam up. How about it?'

She shook her head in mock regret. How about it, indeed. She would be risking plenty if she was caught breaking confidences, while Diaz would gain plenty in return.

'No,' she said firmly. 'I'm working with the team on something called mutual trust at the moment. Maybe it's an unfamiliar concept?' With satisfaction she noted a wince of pain cross his face as he recalled why she might not trust him. 'Come back and ask me when you've had a chance to think about what trust really means to you.'

CHAPTER TWELVE

Ella was careful to go along with whatever ideas Oona came up with, even the sisterhood ritual. After all, she was getting a perfect private attic space to hole up in, and not a penny to pay. And no one was going to recognise her face in inbred little Windwell, where everyone knew each other from working at the hospital.

They did the ritual in Oona's bedroom one evening while rain battered the windows and Enid was downstairs getting drunk in front of *Family Fortunes*. Oona's room was all polished wood and ethnic throws. Ella threw herself down on a bedroll and breathed in the source of those perfumes and incenses Oona always wafted around. They smoked a joint from a pretty box of pre-rolled spliffs and Oona lit some candles. Then she grasped hold of Ella's forearm.

'Hold your hand out.'

Sleepily, Ella stretched out her arm, then started back at the sight of a massive knife appearing from nowhere.

'What the—'

Oona gripped her hand like a vice and drew the sharp blade across Ella's palm so a line of scarlet appeared. Ella wrenched her arm back.

'What're you thinking? I might need stitches or something.' Honestly, she could have thumped Oona.

'No need to freak out. Haven't you heard, pain's all in the brain?' She flicked back her hair impatiently.

Coolly, Oona stabbed her own palm and squeezed out some fat droplets of blood.

'That's it, let's get started.' Oona reached out and clasped Ella's hand in a mess of sticky blood and held it there. Then Oona began to read from a paper, all slow and trance-like:

Fire, Earth, Air and Blood
We come here as two and leave as one,
Bound eye to eye, heart to heart, soul to soul,
Bound by this pledge, this blade, this blood.
Do you agree to be bound?

She prompted Ella to mumble, 'I do.' Her hand hurt and it didn't feel very hygienic, but later, when she was emptying the bins, Ella noticed that the crumpled-up spell paper was headed 'To Bind Another Soul into Your Power'. That's not very sisterly, she thought, though it was rather funny. Oona, with all her fripperies and witchy chants, clearly thought she was cleverer than Ella and was trying to cast a spell on her. Fat chance of that. Ella kept herself to herself because she was recovering from a bad experience; it didn't mean she was looking to be Oona's zombie follower or something.

Friday 7th October

On Friday Oona took a day off work and slept late. When she came downstairs for breakfast she told Ella they were going to take a walk to see this professor friend of hers who lived at the far end of the village. As they made their way along the high street, Ella stared out through the gaps in the houses at the treeless moors and realised that she was as safe here as anywhere. A few straggly sheep, the occasional tumbledown farm – it truly was the perfect hiding place. If she had to pretend to be Oona's friend, or witch's familiar, that was a small price.

When they reached the open lane on the way to the asylum, Oona took her arm in hers. 'Can you keep a secret?'

Ella nodded. 'Course I can.'

'Well, it's a secret but I've met someone else.'

'Who?' Ella had a horrible notion that she might be talking about Krish.

'I can't say yet. He's very private.'

'Have you known him long?'

'For years, really. But we only got close the last few weeks or so.'

Ella felt a blast of relief. Even Tommo had only known Krish for the last few months.

'You like him?'

'He's wild,' she said with a breathy giggle.

'But what about Tommo?'

Oona lowered her voice. 'I've never told anyone this before, but Tommo – there's so much anger in him. At first I thought it was accidental. You know, holding me too tight, or pinching me too hard. Now it's gone too far. He nearly smothered me last week. I mean, I couldn't breathe. And he meant it.'

Ella woke up from her own thoughts. 'God, Oona, that's awful.'

'And I know Tommo and his dad were involved in that patient Campbell's death. Tommo killed him. I heard them talking about it.'

Ella could believe it. 'You mean the one that died years ago? Isn't that supposed to be connected to Mr Crossley's murder?'

'I know,' Oona said very quietly. 'Do you believe people can get a taste for it?'

Ella thought about that for a few seconds. Little did Oona know that she was speaking to an expert. 'Yes. I do. When people get a taste for wickedness it keeps pulling them back. Just like smoking ciggies – or vodka.'

Oona had stopped in mid-step, frowning. 'Wow, you've really thought about this.'

'I *know* about this,' Ella insisted. 'Listen, you can't keep seeing Tommo.'

'But how can I end it all? What if he gets angry? I mean, he's strong. He could kill me. I don't want to be alone when I do it. You will stay with me, won't you? Help me. Until it's all over?'

'I'll do anything,' Ella said, touching her heart with her fingertips. Maybe she was overplaying her part but she couldn't resist adding, 'I'm your sister, aren't I?'

They passed through a pair of wide gates and stopped to admire the smooth lawns on which Wynd Well Hall was set like a jewel.

'Isn't it fantastic?' Oona gushed. Professor Leadbetter

lived in a rambling mansion like a place in a TV show, with high gables and twisting chimneys.

'So he's your mum's friend?'

Oona looked at her with a gleam in her heavily painted eyes. 'Yeah, from when she was young. She wasn't bad-looking back then.'

Ella nodded. Back at the house she had spotted a photo of Enid from years back, wearing a pink minidress that barely covered her knickers, revealing long skinny legs and a slender body. For the first time, Ella had spotted her resemblance to Oona, that they both shared a prettiness that was also rather hard at the edges with their arched brows and thin lips.

Suddenly, Oona looked rather coy. 'The prof has always had a soft spot for me. He believes I've got special powers. We did some thought experiments ages ago and he thinks I've got genuine ESP.'

'What's that?'

'Gosh, you don't know much, do you? Extrasensory perception. Mind-reading, prophecy, the power I use to cast spells and all that.'

As she followed Oona up to the front door, Ella wondered if her friend was hinting that the professor was her dad. After all, she had seen no evidence of a father figure at Enid's house. The man who opened the door was stooped and dark, rather than the Nordic type she expected. His rheumy brown eyes lay deep in a nest of wrinkles and a neat beard rimmed his jaw with no moustache. He was very well spoken and friendly enough, and ushered them into an imposing living room dominated by a cheery log fire.

'Now girls, a herbal tea or a Yorkshire brew?'

Oona chose something with a strange name and Ella agreed to try it, too. While they waited alone, Oona showed her some of the professor's collections. 'This is the original Wynd Well,' she said, pointing to a framed print of a large cellar with a rectangular pool and all sorts of mystical knick-knacks around it.

'You mean a proper well was here once?'

Oona gave one of her mysterious smiles. 'Yeah, it's still here. A place of miraculous medicinal cures.'

'In the village somewhere?'

She laughed. 'You could say that, yeah.'

Oona treated the place like her own, rifling through drawers and pulling out a cardboard box containing what she called a hand of glory, the mummified hand of a hanged criminal. 'It carries powerful magic,' she crooned over the desiccated, bony thing. 'It's said to give a cloak of invisibility. Thieves once used them to unlock any door.'

Ella watched in amazement as Oona wrapped up the gruesome relic in a large handkerchief and slipped it inside her handbag.

The tea arrived and it was unpleasant with bits of what looked like twigs in it, but the chocolate fingers on a side plate were definitely what people called moreish.

Ella and the professor got talking about that administrator's murder. 'I'm sure the police will need to interview me,' the old man said airily.

'Is it right that Crossley was once out to get you?' Oona asked.

'Crossley was just a glorified paper-shuffler,' he announced as he settled back in his leather chair to light an old-fashioned pipe. 'He objected to my insistence on academic rigour.'

'Aren't you worried about speaking to the police?' Ella asked, suddenly struck by the unwelcome notion they might insist on interviewing everyone living in Windwell. She wondered how she could stay out of their way.

The professor released a cloud of sweet smoke from his mouth. 'I'm not worried. I didn't care for Kevin Crossley but I was hardly going to kill him. And you, Oona, are they going to speak to you?'

'Yeah, tomorrow. There's quite a good-looking sergeant. I hope I get him. I like a strong man.'

The professor laughed. 'Just flutter those eyelashes and he'll believe anything you say. I was wondering actually, have you had any dreams or prognostications about Crossley's killer?'

Oona switched to her actress voice and pouty expression. 'I did cast a little spell to read the future. You know, a basin of water reflecting the full moon. And I dreamt I saw a dark man following Mr Crossley, but I couldn't see his face. I think he's a patient, an old pal of Campbell's.'

The professor leant forward and patted Oona's knee. 'Fascinating. A patient? You must tell the police all about it.' Then he turned to Ella.

'And you, young lady. Where do you hail from?'

Ella nearly choked on her chocolate finger. 'A farm the other side of Bradford. You won't know it.' She had a sudden vision of her parents. And Jim. Had they contacted the police? The last thing she needed were people like the professor knowing where she came from. Then, as usual, she saw he was only being polite.

'Are you possessed of any unusual powers, Ella?'

Ella shook her head. 'I don't know much about it.'

He shook his head and murmured, 'Never mind.'

Oona gave the old man one of her winsome expressions and asked if she could take a look around his library. They moved into another generous room with stained glass and weird engravings stuck on the walls. Ella soon spotted that the shelves were filled with mostly occult stuff like *The Devil Rides Out* and books of spells. Once again, Oona helped herself to an item while the professor was distracted. Soon after, Oona seemed to grow bored and they left.

Back on the drive, Oona pulled a book out of the pocket of her long velvet coat and showed Ella the cover. It was called *Mystic Manifestations: Phantoms or Fraud?* Ella leafed through it and started to smile. There were illustrations of Victorian gentlemen seated around tables, presumably sitting in the dark, having spooky tricks played on them. In one picture, a scary disembodied hand was raised at the table edge. The next image showed how it was done. One of the men had a false hand attached to his boot and was waving it from a dark-clad leg nonchalantly crossed over his knee. Other pictures depicted people dressed as veiled ghosts, crawling on their knees or waving rings of light or tambourines around their baffled guests.

'Listen,' Oona said in her most plaintive voice. 'You know how you promised to help me? When we make the video, let's play a trick on Tommo – see how the big bully likes a taste of his own sick medicine.'

'You want to give him a fright? Make sure a ghost appears?' Ella had already guessed from the pictures what her friend had in mind.

'Yeah, we'll put a little show on for Tommo. We'll have such a freaking time. A video to remember!' As they reached the gates of Wynd Well Hall, Oona was skipping along and called out, 'Let's go and see how Krish is getting on.'

The October daylight was fading fast. They had to walk the same convoluted path from the gap in the fence to the asylum and soon cold spikes of rain needled their faces and hands. Worse, the cut Oona had made in Ella's palm was giving her gyp even though she'd put a big plaster on it. Inside the deserted asylum it felt like an icebox and the wind whistled and moaned in the building's upper storeys. They passed through a nightmare of a room, a sort of operating theatre, before Oona produced a key and unlocked a door that appeared to open on utter darkness. There was something about the steps leading down into the earth that reminded Ella of the slippery cobbles that led to the barn. Jim's hand had gripped her like pincers as he steered her into the blackness. Ella hung back, her limbs suddenly weak. She had told herself she must never go down into the tunnels.

Oona shouted back up at her, 'What's up now? There's a light on. Krish is here already.'

Scared of being left alone, Ella forced herself down the steps towards a bare light bulb, her eyes darting fearfully over the walls. She reckoned the air must have been trapped down here for centuries; it smelt heavy with damp spores. Then Krish came into sight and beamed a white-toothed smile at both of them, and she was unaccountably happy to see him again. He ushered them both on to follow him along the passage, zigzagging the torch beam across cold-sweating brick.

They halted by a big old meter whirring softly on the wall with clamps and gadgets trailing from it. 'Here, I didn't forget your order,' he said to Oona, pointing to a white cube of plastic. 'I was just testing it out.'

It was identical to the cuboid radio cassette Oona had bought for her mum. Now Krish turned a knob on the side in a steady click, click, click. A digital display lit up in shocking pink.

He pressed another button, and the voice of Bob Marley singing 'Get Up, Stand Up' filled the silent tunnel. Oona mouthed along to the funky guitar and pounding bass, jiggling her hips, inching towards Krish. Ella wanted to laugh; reggae really wasn't Oona's thing, she was right off the beat. At home she only played creepy prog rock discs like Black Sabbath or Coven. Now she slung her arm around his neck and spoke into his ear. 'Cool. You're a love. Is it a knock-off?'

Krish laughed nervously, edging backwards to free himself. 'Well, it's a copy. A fiver to you.'

He stuffed it back in its cardboard box covered in foreign writing and took her fiver. Grinning, he pointed the torch at a gorgon's head of cables sprouting from the wall.

'Look, I've got juice coming in off the main line. And the best thing is it's all for free.'

Just then a sound started up around them: a breathy whistling that made Ella erupt in goosebumps. She grabbed Krish's arm. 'What's that?'

'Just the pipes,' he said breezily. 'Air in the pipes.'

The sighing and whispering rose and fell for a few more eerie moments and then died away. She wondered if they had started it up by coming here and making noises. She imagined it was the asylum's creaky lungs, waking from a century's slumbers to find all its patients had vanished away. If only she and Krish had been on their own, she would have talked to Krish about it.

Oona barged her way between Ella and Krish. 'Actually, that's a really interesting sound effect. Do you know how to switch it on and off?'

Krish swivelled the torch beam up to the ceiling, where dozens of mouldering pipes were suspended. 'No. Could be any of those pipes.'

Oona wouldn't let it drop. 'You're doing the sound for our video, aren't you? Could you make a tape of those sound effects? Like a ghostly voice?'

'I could have a go.'

Oona was growing twitchy with excitement. 'You have got the electric fixed up in the boiler room?'

Krish shook his head. 'No, I didn't say that. I thought you could film in this tunnel.'

Her face slumped in disappointment. 'Krish. Sally died in the boiler room. If she's going to manifest, it will be there.'

'It's too far from the connection. I haven't got the gear.'

'Please. Can't you get it? For me?'

He lifted his open palms in a gesture of denial. 'If I can't, I can't.'

Oona pulled a face of abject misery, so he said, 'Honestly, Oona. How are you going to call up a ghost anyway?'

In the gloom Oona's smile looked decidedly mischievous. 'Actually, Ella and me are thinking of playing a prank on Tommo. He's never believed in my powers.'

Krish couldn't help but grin. 'Give him a scare, you

mean?' He started chuckling. 'Sounds like a laugh.'

'It's going to be a scream,' Oona squealed. 'And you've already done great, Krish, I mean you are a genius. So please, how can we make the camcorder work in the boiler room?'

Krish thought for a sec, then relented. 'I suppose I could order a longer cable. But not till a big job my uncle's doing is finished. Not this weekend, maybe the weekend after. And I want something in return.'

'What's that then?'

'It's here at Windwell that an old bloke was murdered, right? The night we were in that haunted house place?' Oona nodded. 'Well, I don't want any questions from the cops.'

'What's your problem?'

'Listen, my uncle'd have me strung up if the fuzz came sniffing round his shop. He don't bother with import duty and all that shit. I already rang Tommo and he's cool with it. What about you two girls, can you forget I came over?'

'Yeah, course I can,' Ella said enthusiastically.

Krish gave her that gorgeous smile again. 'I owe you.'

'All right, if Ella will, we'll forget you were here. But only if you sort the gear out. You can make it the weekend after? We need to get planning and raise the ghost before the whole place is demolished.'

Oona's face lit up as she remembered something else. 'Hey, did Tommo tell you he's got a stash of mushrooms? We can get together for a mushroom party.'

Krish was eyeing Oona shrewdly. 'Magic mushrooms? No need for spells and that with them things. There's going to be ghosts coming out of the walls.'

'Maybe.'

He turned to Ella with a soft expression. 'What about you, Ella? You cool with that?'

'I've never tried them. Are they dangerous?'

'Aw, you'll love them,' Oona said. 'Just do as I say. A friend of mine once freaked and I brought her down. The colours and everything are brill.'

As they climbed back up to ground level, Oona pushed on ahead in that follow-my-leader way of hers. Ella and Krish walked behind her and halfway up he slowed and offered her his hand. 'It's all right,' he whispered. 'It's just a very big old building. There are no ghosts or shit.' She took his hand and though it was her sore hand and his fingers felt calloused, warmth spread through her body.

'I'll look after you,' he said, so quietly that Oona couldn't hear.

Tentatively, she squeezed his hand with her small fingers. But before they reached the dim light of the upper hallway, they reluctantly drew apart so that Oona wouldn't spot them, the two new recruits, defying her and daring to strike out on their own.

CHAPTER THIRTEEN

On Friday evening Diaz had a briefing with DCI Thripp. His superior officer leant forward in his shabby revolving chair and started tapping his pen very fast.

'I had a phone call from the top brass this morning. You only need to know three words. Make an arrest.'

Diaz shook his head in pained disappointment.

Thripp grimaced in sympathy. 'Well, onwards and upwards. How'd you get on with the security guard?'

He passed over a photocopy of the memo sent to Bill Craven to lure him away from his post:

URGENT

To: Bill Craven, Security Gate Phase 2

From: Ron Dugdale, Construction Site Manager

Please assist delivery lorry with flat tyre. Current whereabouts on Blackburn Road approaching Windwell.

'It arrived via the hospital's internal post, delivery time at the security lodge 4.45 p.m.,' Diaz began. 'Whoever forged this knew names, job titles, and that Titan headed paper was kept all over the place, including in a drawer in the security lodge.'

Thripp nodded. 'A definite inside job.'

'It's the same with the pager message that summoned Voss to the scene. It was sent from Crossley's pager which has now disappeared from his office. You know what, sir? I'm wondering if Crossley could have been lured to the seclusion block the same way. Another appeal for help or something.'

'So where's that message?'

'Vanished. The lads are doing a fingertip search of the area but nothing so far. We're also looking for a missing security uniform from the lodge's locker room and a nightstick that's a top contender for the murder weapon. It's possible they've been destroyed or whisked away somewhere.'

Thripp shoved the preliminary reports from the lab across the desk. 'Death was due to blunt force trauma so your nightstick idea fits. The red cord round the neck was more like decoration – he was already dead from the blow to his head when a half-hearted attempt at asphyxiation took place.'

'Presumably to make it a copycat of Campbell's death, as described in the inquiry. Any trace of prints or blood?'

'Nothing back from the labs yet.'

'But they've found something else?' Diaz was trying to read another report lying upside-down on Thripp's desk.

'Two things. First, a short black hair.' Thripp proffered

a photograph of a magnified strand of hair caught on a microscope slide. 'Stuck in the red paint of that message on the wall. All the Titan crew on-site are giving hair samples for elimination.'

Diaz stared at the image, throwing it into the mix of facts and hunches that clustered in his brain.

'And here are the statements from Brian Ogden and his son Tommo. Neither have an entirely convincing alibi. There's a new electronic clocking system, so we can see Brian clocked off at 6.02 p.m. on Monday. Claims he saw nothing unusual. Picked up fish and chips at the Maine Plaice in the village. Bumped into Bill Craven searching for the mystery wagon on the road and they stopped to have a moan about Crossley. Got home at approximately 6.30 p.m., shared the takeaway with Tommo, and then watched the snooker and *Coogan's Bluff* till he went to bed at eleven.'

'What did you make of him?'

'He reminded me of that idea that the warders in a madhouse eventually turn as mad as their patients. Aggressive, suspicious, angry – no, I'd say enraged – at being questioned. Not what you'd call a nurse; he's a brute of a bloke used to throwing his twenty stone about. I'm surprised Voss kept him on.'

'Has he got a record?'

'No. But maybe he's just not been caught yet.'

Diaz had stayed up to study the Junior Campbell inquiry sometime past midnight the night before, and summarised its conclusion.

'Reading between the inquiry's lines, both Brian and his son were suspected of colluding in the Campbell murder back in 1980. It ties in with the message painted on the wall, "RIP Campbell. Your next." And there's that contraction of "you are" to "you're" spelt wrong. We can assume whoever wrote it isn't the best at English grammar. Neither of the Ogdens are known for their brainpower, especially Tommo.'

Thripp nodded. 'You're right, the son is a facsimile of the father but less bright. A shame these mealy-mouthed government inquiries just spout recommendations instead of taking decisive action. But it's hard evidence we're after. Looking at the statements, Tommo Ogden clocked out at 4.55 p.m. on the Monday and says he went straight home for a kip. If you believe his dad, he was eating chips with him around 6.30 p.m. If you don't, he could have been anywhere. At half-seven, he met that ward clerk girlfriend of his and says they hung around the streets.' Thripp looked up with an air of incredulity. 'Windwell on a dark and windy Monday night. She must be easy to please. You're seeing the girlfriend tomorrow.'

Diaz was flicking through his notebook. 'According to the records, Tommo Ogden signed in at the Phase Two lodge at 9.30 on the same Monday morning. He left at 9.53. Again his dad's alibied him, said he sent him over to check they were fitting the right door handles. Still, he had plenty of time to check out the seclusion block, maybe even stow the weapon away on-site.'

Diaz checked off his leads that had led to a blank. 'Voss's trip to Phase Two at 1.45 p.m. was well witnessed, a group site meeting, so he's in the clear for that.'

'How did you get on with the hotel staff? Did they remember Voss and the psychologist?'

'Yeah, they did. Voss has a taste for fine wine and is a generous tipper. He seems in the clear, too. He was well away from Windwell at the hotel till Doctor Norris dropped him off at eleven. The Ogdens are our strongest leads, boss,' Diaz conceded. 'Have either got black hair?'

'No chance. Brian hasn't got any hair. Tommo's is dyed red, punk style.' Thripp despondently sank his long chin into his palm. 'I'm running out of men. We've got resources sunk into the search for the weapon. Titan has more than fifty workers to check out. Security is easy work to get into. Easy for someone with a grudge against Crossley to get a security pass and get close to him.'

Diaz flicked over another page in his notebook. 'Here's something. Crossley's bungalow. He's lived alone since he was widowed a year ago. It was all very neat and tidy as expected, but get this – the table was set for visitors. Three places laid out, teacups and saucers, the lot.'

'Crossley's mysterious meeting. I want you to get the constables to check with the neighbours. Did they see anyone turn up? A car reg would be useful.'

'Will do.' They both lapsed into a thoughtful silence. Then Diaz ventured an idea. 'Boss, I could have a go at creating a profile.'

'What's that when it's at home?'

'What I covered on my course these last few weeks. Instead of just waiting for a lucky break, or for the offender to make a stupid mistake, we use psychology to narrow down the number of suspects. The idea is to draw up a description of the offender based on the crime scene. What does he reveal about himself in the way he commits the crime?'

Thripp's face remained blank, so he rapidly ran through the few successful examples that had impressed him at Barnwell. 'Back in the fifties a psychiatrist called Brussel profiled the "Mad Bomber of New York" and nailed him, even down to his double-breasted suit. And in 1974 a Doctor Tooley made an inspired description of the Great Lines Common murderer in Kent. A young woman staggered into a police station after being attacked and eventually died of her injuries. Tooley came up with a profile describing a young man with a record of indecent assaults, known to be a loner who takes solitary walks in open spaces. The profile led to the conviction of a young male, showing a clear match between the profile and the murderer.

'They were one-offs, but now the FBI's Behavioural Science Unit is identifying what they're calling serial killers in America. They not only teach their agents to read the crime scene for clues, but also do something no one's ever thought of before. They go into jails and ask convicted murderers what went on in their heads. What drove them to murder, how they planned it, how the force could have caught them sooner.'

Thripp was watching him with a sour expression. 'Sounds like you want to be a shrink, lad.'

'No, boss. I just want to find whoever killed Crossley as soon as we can.'

'OK, Diaz. It's payback time for your little holiday at police college. Have a go at this profile description. What do you need?'

'It depends,' he said, not wanting to admit that this would be the first time he'd ever created such a thing. 'I'd like access to personnel files.' He was already thinking he wanted to talk to Lorraine about it.

'OK. But the hard evidence takes priority.'

The boss tapped his pen on the desk again, like Morse code communicating a faster tempo to his thinking. He picked up his phone and got a connection to Doctor Voss. The director was apparently not too thrilled to be summoned to the incident room.

A short while later Voss joined them, and the DCI got straight to the point.

'This is a most unusual location for us, Doctor Voss. We are surrounded by dangerous criminals, a proportion of whom have already committed at least one murder. I need to ask you if an inmate could possibly have killed Mr Crossley?'

Voss's face set in rigid annoyance. 'This hospital's safety record is second to none.'

'But we're talking about Phase Two, Doctor. You aren't overseeing that site yet. We're talking about Titan's protocols, not yours.'

'Yes, but I am responsible for Phase One, which is where all the patients are currently housed. It's simply not possible that one of our patients could temporarily escape from one of the most secure environments in Britain to murder our administrator, and then casually stroll back through locked doors to his own room.'

Thripp waited, tapping his fingers on the desk. Finally, he said, 'This isn't a conversation I want to have, Doctor Voss. Our resources are stretched to their limits. We're taking statements from many of your six hundred staff and over fifty Titan subcontractors. We respect that your patients are your own remit and we're not the appropriate people to interview them. I'd like you to tell me which of your inmates could have done this.'

Voss turned aside, struggling to stay calm. 'Very well, if you insist. I'll conduct a unit-wide assessment of risk, focusing on those with a history of violence.' He considered for a moment. 'I am also seriously lacking the manpower for the job. Tragically, Kevin Crossley would have been just the man to handle that much detail.'

'I don't want to be unhelpful, Doctor. Given the interest at government level, I can possibly draft in some extra police numbers from other forces,' Thripp suggested.

Voss looked horrified. 'Absolutely not. This is a therapeutic environment. Most of our patients associate the police with the most traumatic experiences in their lives. I will oversee my own internal inquiry.' Abruptly, he stood and eyed them with hostility. 'If that's all, I have to go.'

CHAPTER FOURTEEN

Saturday 8th October

On Saturday afternoon Diaz sent Laddo out to fetch Oona Finn, Tommo Ogden's girlfriend. She joined them looking excited and doubtless enjoying all the attention. She was entirely focused on Diaz, presenting a knowing smile and a flirty angle to her head.

'Miss Finn. I have a few simple questions. Could you tell me what you did on Monday afternoon through to the evening?'

'Course I can. I was in work all afternoon and left just before five, went straight home and got there about ten past, went upstairs to get my work clothes off, had a rest, then went out with Tommo.'

'Did anyone see you leave work?'

'Loads of people. Tommo, other people on the ward.'

'And when you got home?'

'Well, my friend Ella was around. She's crashing with us for a while.'

Laddo broke in, pen in hand. 'Ella what? Do you have a surname?'

'Actually, I'm not sure. Just call at our place. She's always there.'

Diaz nodded at her to continue.

'Mum wasn't home yet, she was at a meeting. So me and Ella just had some cheese on toast for tea. Then I met Tommo at half seven. We walked the streets – we both live at home. You can imagine we need some time alone.' She looked upwards suggestively through her lashes. With a flick of her wrist she caressed her golden hair.

Diaz paused to observe her, fixing on the pink lipstick and unbuttoned blouse showing a few inches of eye-catching cleavage. As an attractive teenager she must be well aware that she was fuelling raunchy fantasies amongst men whose punishments included enforced celibacy. He compared her to Lorraine, who had toned down her work clothes to darker and plainer gear, a precaution he considered very wise.

He attempted to tune into her mood and grinned back. 'Come off it, Oona. It was dark and freezing cold. What did you really get up to?'

This time when she smiled, he saw a smear of pink lipstick staining her white incisors. 'Do I have to spell it out?'

'For the record, you do.'

'All right. We drove to the woods and, er, made sweet love.' She lifted her pencilled brows, as if imparting a delicious secret.

'Anyone see you?'

'No. Course not.'

'And what time were you home?'

'About eleven.'

'Anyone see you?'

She seemed to be calculating. 'Mum was in bed. Ella was probably around. Is that OK?'

She picked up a fringed leather handbag from the floor and stood up.

'Hold on. I've not finished.' Oona's composure slightly cracked as she sat down again.

He leant back, noting how she'd been expecting to run her own show. 'How well did you know Mr Crossley?'

'Mr Crossley?' She pulled a face. 'He'd been here since the year dot. I help out in Admin. I did some of his typing.'

'Did you like him?'

'He was all right. Bit of an old fusspot. Like a headmaster.'

'What did your mum think of him?'

She shook her head. 'They'd worked together since for ever. They were cool.'

'Do you ever go over to Phase Two?'

She frowned at him, as if he were asking something outrageous. 'I have been. I take messages over.'

'I see you signed in at the security lodge a couple of weeks ago. Why was that?'

For a moment she stared at him vacantly. 'Oh, yeah. There's been a lot of toing and froing over the plans. My nursing officer sent me with some papers. It was about door handles, basically.'

'So you knew Bill, the security guard.'

'Vaguely.'

'Remind me, what is your job on Ferris Ward?'

'Part-time ward clerk.'

'What does that involve?'

'Not much. Patients' post, staff letters, petty cash, filing.'

'So you work with Tommo Ogden?'

'Yeah, he's a staff nurse on the unit.'

'So how's that working out? You going to the woods to have sex with a male nurse from your ward?'

Oona's chin jerked up aggressively; she didn't like that one bit. Then she softened and shook her head slowly. 'That's not how Windwell people see it. We're cool. No one minds. This is actually quite an easy-going place.'

'Surely a top-security hospital should be the opposite of easy-going?' His jokey smile was turning rigid.

Oona shrugged. 'I wouldn't know.'

He asked, 'Tell me about the patients on Ferris Ward.'

'They're the really hard men. But I always keep them sweet. Sure, they blow up every so often. Rob Kessler's on the unit, you know. There's a journalist who visits him to write his life story.'

It struck him as sadly immature that she would consider that monstrous sadist to be some sort of star patient. Diaz lifted his brows and nodded at her to continue.

'It's a shame, really. Patients so young and clever locked up for life. Some of them are complete shits, though. Totally messed up.'

'I understand Doctor Voss wants to offer them extra therapy.'

'He's crazy. You know what they say on the wards? He won't last six months.'

'Who's saying that on the wards?'

'Oh, you know. The old mob who signed up to the POA.' When Diaz frowned, she translated, 'The hospital used to be run by the Prison Officers' Association. Some say it still is, though the nurses are supposed to join a nursing association.'

'So who do you think killed Mr Crossley?'

She shook her head in bafflement. 'How do I know? It could be anyone.'

'Were you working here when Campbell was murdered?'

'Me? How old do you think I am?' Again she preened her own hair. 'I was still at school.'

'But you were living here with your mum. So what are people saying about Campbell's death?'

'Campbell? I don't know. Maybe it was that psychiatrist who already died who did it.'

Diaz had hoped to find a chatty gossip in Oona, but beneath the winsome exterior he was finding her to be a waste of time. Glancing up at the clock, he was satisfied that he'd get nothing useful from her and told her she could go.

CHAPTER FIFTEEN

Saturday 8th to Sunday 9th October

Lorraine's first weekend at Windwell was feeling empty without Jas and the band to engage her mind. On Saturday morning she decided it would be ridiculous to hang around in Windwell in case Diaz deigned to call on her. Instead, she browsed around Hebden Bridge's shops. The purple blouse she found on a trendy market stall on the cobbled square was £2.99 but she felt she'd deserved it. True, Voss hadn't referred to their prospective dinner date again, but it was always best to be prepared. From a phone box she got through to her mum and Jasmine and listened to their chatter, trying not to let them hear just how much she missed them both.

After picking up an *NME*, she settled down in an earthy café with a wholemeal homity pie and salad. Unbelievably, she found a review of Gothenburg in Berlin and a mention of the support band, Electra Complex. The reviewer had called her band 'spellbinding'. Abandoning her muesli biscuit she let her mug of tea go cold. She told herself she was massively pleased for Lily, though the effect on herself was less happy.

By nightfall she was feeling low, convinced that she had made entirely the wrong decision to back out of the tour and come to Windwell. Without the reassurance of daylight, her mind wandered to places it shouldn't go. She woke from a bad dream with the sight of Kevin's putty-coloured face imprinted like a freeze-frame on her inner eye. Then she started at a sound, a clunk from outside her back door. She switched on the weak lamp and saw that the curtains were trembling in the draught from the ill-fitting windows. Outside, the wind had risen and was whistling tunelessly around the cottage. It was four o'clock on Sunday morning and – there it was again – something was moving in the small stone yard to the rear of the cottage.

She listened hard and hoped it was a stray dog or cat. Or Diaz stumbling around on his way to call on her. If she was honest, she longed for his tough body to shelter her. She needed a barrier against the world, someone to keep her safe. Christ, that was wrong on so many levels. No, he hadn't been in touch and it stung her. She had to face all of this alone; all this mayhem at Windwell, some bloody murderer moving amongst them, and now the noise in the yard.

Another thud sounded from where the back door stood. Christ, that could be the murderer right now. She got out of bed, slipped her coat on over her oversized Clash T-shirt and pulled on leather boots. Downstairs, she stood motionless, listening hard at the back door but hearing nothing but the rattling gale. Defiantly, she moved to unlock the kitchen door and found she'd forgotten to turn the key. It flew open in the blast. She peered outside and saw only dark night, in which the subtle shapes of trees and racing clouds moved wildly. Stepping into the yard, she inched her way towards the drystone wall, beyond which stretched moorland, her hair slapping her face like a whip. Her eyes adjusted. Was that patch of deeper darkness a person hurrying away across the moors?

'Hey, you!' she cried. The gale tore the sound from her lips. She waited, watching and listening, getting soaked in the rain. Across the open land the storm raged, moaning and sobbing like an invisible Fury. She pictured a presence running, crossing the miles of hummocky wilderness, escaping this small patch of civilisation. God, she was cursed by an imagination that could always supply what wasn't really there. The noise must, she admitted, have simply been some debris thrown about by the storm.

Back in the light and warmth of the cottage, she locked the door and put the kettle on, her wet feet freezing on cold lino. It was only when she picked up her mug that she saw it. A small damp object like a decapitated flower. She picked it up; it was wet and slippery, and she thought she had seen something like it before. Back in the old asylum's Cell 17 there had been a small posy just like this one. It was nothing but a fragment of straggly flowers and foliage, wrapped in wilting parchment knotted together with gardening twine. The question was, how had it arrived on her kitchen table? A shard of ice seemed to pass down her spine and she started to shiver. Someone had stepped into her kitchen and left the posy while she was outside.

She gathered her courage to check all around the house, in corners and under tables, then secured the locks and drew all the curtains. Back in her lonely bed she wished even harder that Diaz might come round. He would be home now, she thought. Warm and sleepy in his bed. She played out a sensual scene in her mind: an explosive kiss, the heat of naked skin. But hadn't he been made to share the cottage with that young constable? She must be mad to even think of surprising him.

While she waited for fitful sleep, she pictured the wet and ragged posy on the kitchen table. It was sure to have a significance, for didn't the giving of flowers signify affection? But no, she was kidding herself. This unwanted gift was more sinister, an invasion of her privacy, a warning and a threat.

CHAPTER SIXTEEN

Monday 10th October

Lorraine had decided to call into the admin office at least once a day to check over any personnel-related post set aside for her by Parveen. On Monday morning she was at her temporary desk, as near to a state of relaxation as she had been since arriving at Windwell. She was puzzling over a recruitment problem in the hospital's ancillary grades, most strikingly in the catering department. It was unusual to have a catering staff shortage, given the more than three million unemployed and the reasonable rates of NHS pay. True, there were possible barriers, such as transport difficulties from the nearest towns, and the grim reputation of Windwell itself, but nevertheless, it was an anomaly. Despite the protests of Mr Dobson, the catering manager, she had decided to run a modest recruitment campaign and had just had a promising phone call with the local Job Centre manager.

The office was subdued; Parveen was copying figures from a ledger onto a sheet. Jenny was typing Lorraine's audio dictation, a plastic headset in her ears as she foot-pedalled the tape along.

At ten o'clock, it was their habit to take an informal tea break and that morning, Parveen disappeared into the admin kitchen, a tiny room that housed a kettle, sink and fridge. While they were alone Lorraine set her notes aside and asked Jenny to find Professor Leadbetter's phone number.

'Have you ever met the professor?' she asked Jenny, after she'd spun the Rolodex file and presented her with the number.

'Yeah, he used to work down the corridor. He seemed all right. Mr Crossley didn't like him very much, mind.'

'Have you seen this Black Museum of his?'

'Me? Not likely, I want to sleep easy at night. He's got the cord that killed that patient Campbell apparently, all on display.'

Parveen returned with a tray of tea things but remained standing and expectant.

'Who's left that cake in the carrier bag? It's been in the cupboard for days. It's starting to smell unpleasant.'

After Jenny and Lorraine confirmed that it wasn't theirs, Lorraine was sufficiently intrigued to take a look. A plastic Greenhalgh's Bakery carrier bag stood in the larder cupboard. With the end of her pen Lorraine poked the bag's edges down and found a cardboard box with a cellophane window, revealing the chocolate, cream and black cherries of a large Black Forest gateau. A whiff of sour cream made her back away. Back in the office, she asked her colleagues if they thought it was possible that Kevin could have left the cake.

'It's not something I've ever seen him buy before,' Parveen said thoughtfully. 'But it's not impossible.' Lorraine decided to call the incident room.

Diaz appeared a few minutes later and after taking a look, told Parveen and Jenny to head to the incident room to provide their fingerprints for elimination purposes.

Now they were alone, Lorraine couldn't ignore the awkwardness of their last encounter. The cheek of him still annoyed her; firstly his asking her to share her inside information, and then suggesting that if anyone were to be dismissed from Windwell for an inappropriate relationship, it should be her.

He was perched on the edge of Parveen's desk looking down on her. She got out a file and ignored him.

'Look, I'm sorry about the other day.'

She raised her head. 'I should think so.'

'Listen, my boss wants me to put a profile together. I'd like a proper look around Kevin's office, a shufti at the personnel files. If I come back at five-thirty could you be here?'

'Why do I need to be here?'

'Come on, Lorraine. Let's do it together.' He laughed at her stubborn face. 'You know you want to.'

With a groan she found herself grudgingly laughing out loud. 'Oh, all right then.'

At five-thirty they unlocked Kevin's office and started to make a search, though the police team had already inspected everything. Lorraine speculated on what they might have missed, while Diaz flicked through the files held on Brian and Tommo Ogden, Enid, Kevin, Parveen,

Professor Leadbetter and Oona. Doctor Voss's file was missing, presumably because the particulars of a man of his status were held at the Ministry of Health. Lorraine had already leafed through them all and knew they made dry reading. Every scrap of interesting information must have been compulsively stripped away by bureaucratic Kevin.

'It takes an imagination to create a readable personnel file,' she observed. 'It looks like Kevin had a different talent, to neutralise every speck of humanity.'

A few minutes later Diaz returned the files to their cabinet. 'The only hint of any dirt is in Professor Leadbetter's file. I'm going to have a chat with him. So now can you let me see the profiles?'

'I can only let you have Kevin's. I don't want to let the team down.'

She leant back, expecting him to object, but he didn't.

'Whatever you've got will be great,' he said, with a shake of his head. 'This inquiry is distinctly short on useful leads.'

She fetched her battered satchel, pulled out the results of the team questionnaire that Kevin had completed and laid out his computer-generated printout on the desk.

'Kevin Crossley likes to organise people and projects. He values efficiency and results over feelings,' he read out loud.

As Diaz rapidly scanned it, Lorraine observed, 'He seems to have been a rather closed and rigid man, pernickety and logic driven.'

Diaz was frowning over the final paragraph, which discussed Kevin's shadow side.

'The shadow? Isn't that the darker side of a person's personality?' he asked.

'The shadow side is the least-developed side, those parts we may normally reject or disown. When exhausted or under stress, different personality types can behave in different out-of-character ways that can surprise or even horrify themselves and other people.'

He looked up. 'Do you think that if he was so rigid, he might have found the emotional upheaval around here too much?'

'I think the hospital under Doctor Voss's leadership could have felt threatening and unsafe to him. His whole career was based on being in charge. That argument with Voss just before his murder was out of character and seems to point to him having trouble controlling his emotions.'

She pointed to a phrase on the profile: 'Triggers for a shadow experience: Regrets of past coldness. If threatened by strong emotions, Kevin may excessively focus on his past actions that hurt others. This may lead to hypersensitivity and fear of losing control.'

She decided to risk putting forward a theory. 'Have you heard the rumour that Kevin conspired with the Ogdens to cover up Campbell's unlawful death? With Voss's arrival, might he have been trying to make up for harm done in the past? And in doing so, he got himself killed.'

Diaz nodded slowly. 'What I struggle with is how this rather stiff, sergeant-major type would ever get involved in a cover-up.'

Lorraine considered. 'It could be his obsessive need for order. On the personality testing course, we talked about very extreme obsessive types. As events in Nazi Germany and the Soviet Union have proved, a bureaucratic leader can develop an obsession with keeping their facts tidy at the expense of common morality. I'm not for a moment suggesting Kevin was anything like those extreme leaders, but he was by all accounts compulsive about neatness and order. The Campbell inquiry was a big risk to Kevin's career and he just about survived it.'

She paused and could tell she hadn't convinced him. 'You think Brian and Tommo killed him, don't you? But isn't it just too obvious?'

'Sometimes you can't ignore the obvious.'

'Wasn't there any evidence in that cell where Kevin was found?'

'There was, but it was all dead ends. The best was a black hair stuck in the painted message above Crossley's body. We've just found out it belonged to the guy who mixed the pot of paint off-site. And before you ask, he was verified as playing with his darts team in Carlisle that evening.' He exhaled loudly. 'What about you, any other thoughts?'

'Yes, actually. This antique desk. Why rescue it from the asylum and have it set up here?'

'He liked it,' he suggested.

'It's a beautiful old desk. But while I've been working here, it's come back to me that I've seen this sort of Victorian furniture in hospitals before. Sometimes these desks have private compartments.' She started running her fingers over the edges of the impressive desk and inspecting the drawers. She had noticed that Diaz had been stealing occasional glances at her and she was flattered. Already the spark of working on the case together again was rekindling their liking for each other, the way they fitted together when they were on the hunt, a combination of her intuition and his bullishness.

The sound of a real-life bolt clicking disturbed the air. 'Yes,' she murmured. She had removed a desk drawer and now groped deeper inside the cavity. 'There's something in here.'

He leant over to try and see. 'What is it?'

She sank to her knees on the carpet and pushed her arm inside the small square void. Her face was concentrating, expectant, her head pressed against the desk's front edge.

'Got it.' She pulled her arm free and held up a rectangular pocket diary embossed with the year 1983.

They retreated to the low settee and sat thigh to thigh while she slowly worked through the diary. After all the drama it was a disappointment. There were a couple of appointments marked but Kevin had used only symbols – an asterisk, and a star, against a few random dates. As a code it was pretty unbreakable. Then, impatiently, Lorraine dived ahead to the Monday of Kevin's death, and found something. There was an appointment at seven-thirty in the evening:

7.30 O O A B X O O O

Diaz looked into her face, stumped. 'Any ideas what that could mean?'

'Not yet. Give me time. My first thought is that it looks like a logic test. You remember those from the personality tests I showed you once before?'

She fetched a booklet from her satchel and showed him an example:

ABSTRACT THINKING – Which of the following should come next at the end of this row of letters: xoooxxooooxxx?

a. ooxx

b. oxxx

c. xooo

'Well?' he asked.

'Unlike the intelligence test, the series of letters in the diary hasn't got enough letters to create a logical sequence. We'd need at least another A and an X. So it's not from a test.'

'Could it be a code for a safe?' he asked.

'When I first came in here I asked Parveen if the building had a safe, and she said no.'

'Mm, I will check. Though seven digits does make it an unlikely code for a safe.'

'Have you been to Crossley's house?' she asked.

'Yeah. It was mega-neat and clean but there was no safe. He was definitely expecting someone that evening. There was china for three people laid out on a freshly ironed tablecloth. All waiting for that big cake, no doubt.'

'Three? So not a romantic assignation. Sounds more like a genteel celebration.'

'The neighbours were questioned and no one turned up at seven-thirty.'

'No,' Lorraine said thoughtfully. 'Which means Crossley's guests were probably involved in his murder. I mean, you get an invitation to tea, but neither of you show up? There has to be a reason.'

Lorraine picked up the diary and stared at the appointment without further revelation.

'This diary,' she said. 'Can you say you found it?'

'OK. Though it doesn't feel right to take the credit from you.'

'I don't want anyone to know I've been rooting around.'

The sound of high-heeled footsteps reached them from the outer room. Instinctively, they sprang apart. Diaz sauntered to the far side of the room, taking the diary with him.

To Lorraine's surprise, it was neither a cleaner nor Parveen who appeared at the open office door. It was Enid. At the sight of Lorraine she froze, then stammered, 'What are you doing in Kevin's office?'

'I work here.'

Enid took a shaky intake of breath. 'I thought the police had shut it off. Who gave you the right to come in here?'

Lorraine looked to Diaz, who stepped into Enid's view. 'I did.'

Enid's head gave a little shake of disbelief. She stared at them both with baleful eyes. Lorraine signalled to Diaz to leave them alone.

As soon as he'd gone, Lorraine said, 'It's good to see you. Have you got a minute to talk while we're here on our own?'

Enid nodded and took a seat on the settee, while Lorraine moved from behind the desk to sit a little closer. As on every previous occasion when she had been close to the treasurer, she detected a sweetly pungent smell on her breath.

'How are you getting on?' Lorraine asked.

'I'm fine.'

'I've not had a chance to thank you for all your work on

Kevin's memorial. It's a shame the coroner has had to delay it for the time being.'

At once, Enid's eyes filled with tears. To give her time to recover, Lorraine chatted inconsequentially before returning to the objective of her conversation. 'Enid, is anything on your mind?'

'What do you mean?'

'Listen, I'm going to have to say this. I'm worried you may be drinking in work time and I'd like to help you.'

Her words were met with a gasp of surprise. Enid sprang to her feet, and pointed a trembling finger at Lorraine. 'How dare you accuse me? Is Doctor Voss getting you to do his dirty work?'

Lorraine was taken aback. 'No, he isn't. But I can tell there's something wrong and I want to help.'

'That's rubbish. I'm sick of people accusing me, sick of this place, and sick of your pathetic team games!'

Lorraine made an effort to stay calm. 'I'm sorry you feel like that. If you'd like to talk things over with an impartial person, I can arrange that.'

'No. I don't need your therapy sessions. I'm not mad.' However, Lorraine thought that Enid did look mad. At that moment her skin was flushed crimson and her limbs shook violently. No, not mad. There was a sing-song quality to her voice and an obvious lack of inhibition. She guessed that the treasurer was drunk.

Gently, she made a suggestion. 'Would you like a lift home? I'm afraid it's not wise for you to drive if you've drunk alcohol.'

The poor woman raised her hand to her brow and opened her eyes, blinking as if waking from a violent nightmare. Lorraine offered her a glass of water which she drank greedily. When her breathing slowed, Enid raised pink-rimmed eyes and said meekly, 'I'm sorry. I'm under terrible strain. Could you ring Oona and ask her to drive me home?'

Later, after Enid and Oona had left, Lorraine sat at Kevin's desk for a long while, pondering whether she had handled Enid's drinking too brutally. When Oona arrived she had glared at Lorraine with hard suspicion, though it was obvious she must be well aware of her mother's problem. In search of distraction, Lorraine pulled out Professor Leadbetter's phone number and called him. It rang out a dozen times and no one picked up. Wearily, she packed up and locked Kevin's office, still unnerved by Enid's outburst, and wondering just how unstable the treasurer might have become.

CHAPTER SEVENTEEN

Wednesday 12th October

Lorraine's nerves were playing up again as the next team-building session approached. She had spent hours sifting through a variety of exercises, from the wacky types that were supposed to be fun but would only suit five-year-olds, to heart-searching analyses of where they had gone wrong that might leave them all with clinical depression. In the end she settled on the most obvious choice, a short talk on team roles followed by personal feedback on each of their team role results. Brian had somewhat surprisingly returned his completed questionnaire to her, and so had Enid and also Parveen, who had been invited to join the meetings by Doctor Voss. Now that Lorraine had scored them all, she was dismayed by how clashingly different each of their personalities were. True, the best teams were a miraculous coming together of different skills and talents, but that sort of utopia required them all to appreciate each other's value. At the moment her four subjects were discordantly different in every way.

Parveen was the first to turn up for the session, tapping apologetically on the psychology seminar room door.

'I don't feel I belong here with people like Brian and Doctor Voss,' she told Lorraine. 'I'm only doing the job for a few months. Do you think I could be excused?'

This was familiar territory to Lorraine: helping build confidence in those who showed promise. She reassured her that they were all as new to the process as she was.

'We've only had one session so far and used that to respond to Mr Crossley's loss. Even if you do go back to your old job, it will be an invaluable experience to work with the team. They need you here.'

'I never thought of it like—'

The door banged open and Brian shambled in. Lorraine nodded to him but the big man slumped down and sank his huge head in his hands. Parveen stared at him, clearly intimidated.

Lorraine moved to sit down beside him in the small circle of chairs.

'Brian?' she asked softly. 'You look distressed. But I'll leave you alone if you prefer.'

A throaty sigh emerged from Brian's bronchial lungs but he didn't raise his head. 'I'm all right. Just fucking furious.'

The clock showed ten past three. Where was Voss? To her relief Enid arrived, but didn't acknowledge Lorraine's greeting. She looked worn out and miserable and chose a seat as far from the others as possible. The airless room felt thick with resentment. Lorraine looked through the team questionnaires. Was today really the right day to feed back to Enid that she could be prone to catastrophise small matters? Or that Brian's aggressive persona threatened the

142

future of the team? No, it would be crass and insensitive. Once again, her mind turned hideously blank.

At last Doctor Voss burst in, apologising for his lateness. He had been called in by the detective chief inspector, he complained. There was obviously something wrong with Voss too, judging from his stiff movements and hard expression. Decisively, she put the team profiles away. What these people needed was catharsis, not confrontation. She pulled another quite different exercise from her folder. Then she nervously introduced the session.

'Thank you all for attending today, given that the pressures and problems here have only increased since we last met. First of all, rather than put Parveen on the spot, I'd like to confirm that she is acting administrator and that it's right that she should be here. Welcome, Parveen.'

The others at least had the grace to nod and welcome their colleague.

'Before we start, I suggest we each check in for a minute or so, to briefly tell us how things are going.'

She nodded at Enid, who expanded on the funeral arrangements and tributes to Kevin. 'Nevertheless, it's been a very difficult few days.' Lorraine detected a resentful glance in her own direction. 'Though I must say that Parveen has been a big help to me.'

They continued around the room, Doctor Voss admitting how tough he was finding his job since the police investigation began. Brian nodded, and described the nightmare of covering the wards with trained nurses while the police insisted that they be released to make statements.

Lorraine summed up the situation: despite their difficulties, there had been positive progress as a team. As well as showing respect to Kevin by planning a memorial service to mark his loss, the hospital's staff and patients had all been updated and reassured about the police investigation and security measures. It was a team achievement, a first important step.

Trying to hide her nerves, Lorraine went on to introduce the exercise she'd chosen. They were to form pairs, Doctor Voss with Parveen, and Enid with Brian.

'May I first make a brief point?' Voss suggested. Lorraine nodded. 'In this situation I seem to be the only person addressed by my title. When we meet here in this confidential setting will everyone please call me J-a-n, pronounced "Yan"?'

For some reason they all, including Lorraine, repeated 'Yan', and a scattering of laughter broke out as they earnestly chorused his name. Lorraine inwardly congratulated him on lowering the tension.

'Let's say that Jan,' she paused for effect, 'is Player A and Parveen Player B. And in the second pair Brian is A and Enid is B. Player A, I'd like you to have a two-minute rant about whatever it is that's really bothering you. Player B, I want you to listen carefully while looking out for the points on this handout. Don't hold back, ranters. And of course everything you say is bound by absolute confidentiality.'

Before anyone could protest, Lorraine had separated the two pairs and directed them to different corners of the seminar room. Then with a signal she started a countdown on her watch. At once Voss began speaking fast and energetically, while Parveen listened and nodded.

She could hear just a smattering of words: 'A problematic patient . . . draws attention and gets under people's skin . . .

144

the sentence of the court like a death sentence . . . young, charming . . . murdered at least four innocent women . . . a tragedy . . .'

She was drawn to step a little closer and covertly eavesdrop. 'Everything he's told me has been false, a performance. He even tries to flatter me . . . a superstar expert on hand, like a movie star boasting of hiring the best therapist . . .'

Her concentration was broken by Brian, his voice raised in protest, unburdening himself to Enid. She listened hard to get a taste of his rant. 'Dogsbodies, whipping boys . . . no one cares about our injuries . . . seven accident forms this week, two nurses on long-term sick . . . kicked and punched by those toerags . . . coppers all over us, no chance of safety standards . . . my boys are at breaking point . . .'

The prescribed two minutes ended. Lorraine asked each of the listeners to translate the rant to their partner according to a handout that listed a series of questions:

Listen to your partner:

What do they care about?

What do they value?

What is important to them?

*When **translating** the rant do not include the facts, only the feelings.*

Lorraine studied the two couples. Parveen was tentatively relaying the messages in Voss's rant and he was, thank goodness, nodding intently. Brian and Enid also seemed to have settled into an amicable conversation.

'Thank you. Would you kindly swap places now.' Again Lorraine timed the pair; this time Enid was speaking intensely to Brian: 'I don't know what to say . . . what's happened . . . used to love my work, balancing books is my pride and duty . . . Kevin wasn't happy . . . said he'd had enough . . . so cruel . . . need a break.'

For all her earlier reticence Parveen was breathily confiding in Voss. Lorraine would have liked to have heard more, as her rant uncovered a series of difficulties: 'the paperwork's backed up without Kevin . . . patients' records aren't ready, bills aren't paid . . . say it's all Admin's fault . . . called me a "useless woman" . . . said I'd been to school in the colonies. I'm English born and bred . . .'

Finally they gathered back in their circle of chairs, where Lorraine had set up a flipchart.

The group's mood was hard to read, so Lorraine simply asked, 'Any thoughts? Parveen?'

'It's going to sound strange,' Parveen said slowly. 'But I haven't ever thought about the therapy the doctors work on with the patients. Or that they truly care. Jan's values came through strong and clear to me. Compassion. A belief in redemption. He cares about this man.' She looked over to Voss with shining eyes. 'I feel rather guilty, actually. I thought psychiatrists just handed out drugs. I learnt a lot about you and the hospital.'

'I know what you mean,' Enid added. 'We don't work with patients, so the day-to-day life of the patients and nurses is a bit of a mystery. I also learnt from Brian's description of how he feels. I don't mean to be rude, Brian,' she said, giving him a quick smile, 'but I didn't expect to uncover such strong commitment and loyalty to the hospital. Yet that's what you're passionate about. Your traditions mean so much to you, and you're desperate to keep up nursing standards. You want respect for your boys on the wards, and fear for them when patients attack them.'

Brian didn't meet the others' eyes but he nodded, his mouth pressed tight in resolve. Was it possible, Lorraine wondered, that he might be trying to hide his tears?

Doctor Voss jumped into the ensuing silence. 'I found the surface of Parveen's rant very disturbing. I'm unhappy that you've been spoken to with such disrespect and want to do my best to remedy it. The values you revealed, Parveen, are of the highest order. I heard your commitment to fairness and to this hospital. You care about what happens to us all, the staff and the patients. You are a courageous woman, angered by mistreatment. I hope we don't lose you.'

Parveen flinched, shocked by his praise. 'Thank you, Doctor— Jan.'

Again, Voss's first name released nervous bubbles of laughter.

When it died away Brian had recovered sufficiently to address Enid. 'Like Doctor Jan, as we'll call him from now on – I am also troubled by what Enid told me. You are also a brave woman, Enid. I heard a great deal about your struggles and worries in trying to do your duty. I respect you in your troubles, Enid.'

Then to Lorraine's surprise, Brian pointed at the values Lorraine had jotted down on the flipchart and said, 'Well, this afternoon has been a right turnaround. I've never thought about it before. When something we care about is threatened it's only right to feel angry. Because the heart of a hospital is its values, and it's sharing those values that makes us all better people.'

He pointed a stubby finger up to the flipchart list and read out loud, 'Compassion. Loyalty. Tradition. Justice. Morality. Respect. Courage. Fairness. Duty. Things that some of us thought we'd forgotten about years ago. But there they were all the time, lurking behind our anger, prodding us not to settle for less.'

Doctor Voss waited for Lorraine as she gathered up her notes and folded up her flipchart sheets.

'That was a most surprising session. Well done.'

'I'm amazed. And relieved,' she said.

'I noticed you're putting in some hours in Admin, too. How is that going?'

She decided to get the bad news over with and told him about the staff shortages in catering. 'When jobs aren't filled, the number of patients volunteering in the kitchens rises above safe levels.'

'I don't like the sound of that.'

'I know, it's not good. And meanwhile, virtually no one leaves their professional roles, because they'd lose the extra payments they view as danger money, and their subsidised housing. The nepotism is obvious from the many familiar surnames from the town's main families. If you're looking at barriers to changing things around here, those are two of your biggest.'

'Yes,' he said, 'I might not enjoy it, but this is what I need to hear.'

Lorraine smiled and made ready to leave but he stood

uncertainly in the doorway. 'Actually, I wonder if you're free for dinner this Saturday?'

Lorraine's weekend had been dreary and she didn't fancy repeating the experience. True, there would be gossip if they were seen together. Well, that was tough.

'Yes, I'd like that.'

'I'll book a table for seven-thirty at the Beckside Hotel.'

'Great. I wonder if I can ask a favour?'

He nodded amiably.

'I hear you have a piano in your house. I'm hardly a concert pianist but I do miss playing in my free hours. I wouldn't want to bother you.'

Voss grinned. 'I can't play myself, so feel free to come over and practise when I'm at work. I keep a spare key in the turquoise pot by the back door.'

CHAPTER EIGHTEEN

Thursday 13th October

The professor's home was what Diaz thought of as a mansion, all tall chimneys and poky little windows glittering amidst ancient stonework. The man who answered the door was a stoop-shouldered old bloke, the picture of an academic with his pipe and beard. He led Diaz into an impressive hallway with ceiling beams and dark indecipherable paintings.

When the professor asked how he could help him, Diaz got straight to the point. 'I've heard you have a collection of crime memorabilia. A Black Museum.'

'Yes, yes. I've always had a fancy it might prove useful in a live investigation.'

The Black Museum was a low, windowless room lit by an elaborate array of spotlights set into the ceiling and inside glass display cases. In the first case stood memorabilia from the original Victorian asylum, black and white photographs of lunatics alongside various ugly restraints and medical equipment. Diaz was repelled by a straitjacket made of brown canvas, with mitten-like sleeves and an arrangement of leather straps and buckles intended to enclose the patient's head. Large typewritten cards described the cruel treatments endured by unfortunate inmates. They told of children as young as eleven or twelve imprisoned and allowed no further association with family or parents. New inmates had been stripped of their own clothes, and even necessities such as spectacles or hearing aids.

The second cabinet focused on the tragic death of Sally Finn. Her photograph revealed a young woman with tightly pinned black hair and open features, save for a squint, which made her dark eyes appear to gaze in different directions. Her posture suggested absolute defeat and misery.

'She was imprisoned at Windwell because she was discovered by the rector's wife digging a hole in the woods,' the professor commented cheerily. 'She was trying to bury a dead newborn. It was a common enough occurrence amongst unmarried females who lacked a man willing to marry them. It is quite possible the baby may have died of natural causes. Sally was actually lucky not to be hanged for the crime of infanticide.'

'Can't really call her lucky, can you?' Diaz said, stung at the notion of an abandoned woman delivering a dead baby.

The professor nodded sagely. 'Sally still has something of a local following. There's a belief that she haunts the tunnels running under the old asylum. There have been many sightings of a black-clad woman. Sometimes she appears as little more than a retreating shadow and an echo of footsteps. In other sightings she's seen lingering in the far distance, her clothing ragged and torn. One unfortunate engineer opened a boiler room furnace and was confronted by Sally's badly burnt hands reaching out to grasp him. It's not unusual, of course. These closed institutions are rich in their own mythology.'

'Yes, plenty of tall tales,' Diaz said brusquely. At the Catholic children's home there had been that blue-eyed priest who had carried a whiff of the torturer's fiery brand about him. He had taught the children from his *Book of Saints*, lingering over descriptions of grotesque martyrdoms utilising fire, blades, spikes and inventive machines to break bones and snap sinews. And yet, what were those saints he'd prayed to for intervention, but some kind of ghosts themselves?

'Campbell's murder. I understand you retrieved some evidence from the murder scene.'

The professor chuckled uncomfortably. 'I think you'll find that's also a myth.'

He indicated the next display case, which gave a brief account of the Junior Campbell inquiry and centred on a framed photo of Campbell himself. The victim looked very young and rather scared. The youth had a great vulnerability to his demeanour, despite his shoulders and arms being pumped up with muscles. Yellowing newspaper cuttings shouted the headlines that had made the case notorious: *Patient Death Remains a Mystery, Tribunal Slams Brutal Hospital Regime* and *Patients Terrorised by Staff at Horror Hospital.*

Diaz inspected the length of red cord hanging on a hook beside a label that described it as, 'Hospital-issue cord of the type found upon the body of Junior Campbell.'

The professor sidled up beside him. 'So you see, I didn't

take actual evidence. At the time there was a furniture repair workshop in Occupational Therapy. That's where both this cord and the cord that strangled Campbell came from.'

'I see. But why go to all this trouble?'

The old man sniffed thoughtfully. 'The honest truth is, because I wanted to gather evidence against Tom Ogden and his father. At the tribunal it was my word against theirs. The pair of them got me sacked.'

'Professor Leadbetter, you're clearly an intelligent man. How did matters escalate to the point where you lost your job?'

'Take a seat, Sergeant. I'll tell you everything I know.' They sat down amicably in a couple of deep brocade armchairs. Leadbetter relit his pipe with a match, while Diaz watched him closely.

'Tommo was a freshly qualified nurse when I first met him. He was always kept tucked well under Brian's wing. Everyone knew that Brian wrote the course essays for his son and gave him the easiest shifts. The night of Campbell's death, he gave him a simple enough job. A suicide watch over Campbell. All Tommo had to do was sit there and stop Campbell from hurting himself. It was down in Cell 17. A horrible place beneath the old asylum.'

'Is that the original sign?' Diaz pointed to a metal plaque in the glass case, emblazoned with 'Cell 17'.

'Yes. It should have been an easy night shift, save that Junior Campbell was a very sick young man. He was a broken creature, riding a mental rollercoaster of depression and mania. Did you know that seclusion is the most dangerous place to find yourself in a psychiatric unit?

If the nursing heavy mob have it in for you, no one will ever hear your cries for help. Everyone knew that Tommo had a low tolerance for patient outbursts. No one ever doubted that Tommo beat Campbell up in Cell 17. The investigation found clear wounds on both Campbell and Tommo: bruising, scratches, and Tommo's knuckles were badly grazed and bleeding.'

'So where did the red cord come into it?'

'Good question, Sergeant. Despite the horrendous beating, Campbell's cause of death was asphyxiation. Consider this. Campbell was only twenty, a strong boy, very fit and healthy from his hours in the gymnasium. It will have taken great strength and considerable effort at close physical quarters to kill him. Under normal circumstances, Tommo would have simply been arrested and convicted. But that's forgetting that Brian was the chief nurse and constructed a somewhat ludicrous alibi. Not wanting to rock the boat, the tribunal chose to believe them. I was the only witness to speak out about Campbell's tragic death.' The old man shook his head wearily. 'Can you believe it? A chief nurse committing perjury to save his killer son? We'd all sworn on the Bible.

'Still, I felt I'd done my duty to Campbell. But as soon as it all died down, Brian made sure I lost my job. I had been doing useful work as a research fellow at Windwell, looking into behaviour on the Personality Disorder Unit, the place they renamed Ferris Ward. You must understand that the way management views the wards is incredibly limited. It only asks whether policies are adhered to, and how docile the inmates appear. But beneath and behind that is the true life of the ward: the hierarchy formed amongst the psychopathic patients. There is always a man at the top of the pyramid, a man who terrorises his prey, who dishes out rewards and punishments. There's no doubt that the top man on Ferris Ward had absolute control. He was running the whole show, including the staff, controlling them with offers of easy shifts, favours, drugs, money. Brian Ogden and Kevin Crossley were violently opposed to my research. It undermined them both, uncovering that secret side of the organisation. I proved how fragile their sense of control truly was.'

Diaz nodded. He was not surprised by the professor's information; it was only what he'd learnt about the way some high-security prisons organised themselves.

'Brian Ogden has an army of loyal nurses he controls in a similar fashion. They are dependent on him for decent shifts and perks on the job. One of them made a false complaint about me and my contract wasn't renewed. But I've never forgotten the injustice of it.'

'Isn't Tommo's girlfriend Oona Finn?'

'Yes. Goodness knows what a lovely girl like that is doing with an ape like him.'

Diaz tried not to look too surprised on hearing the genuine affection in the old man's voice, a gentleness very different to his bitterness over Tommo.

'Are you going to create a display cabinet of Kevin Crossley's murder?'

The professor grinned playfully. 'It's a free country.'

'Who do you think was responsible?'

'I'm sure a bright fellow like you has heard of Occam's razor. It's a sensible rule, suggesting that when one is faced with a number of options, it's best to pick the most obvious, least complicated explanation.' The professor was clearly comfortable in lecture mode.

'Given the copycat nature of the crime: the red cord, and the reference to Cell 17, I'd venture an informed guess. Kevin Crossley and Brian Ogden fell out with each other, as co-conspirators will do. I imagine that Kevin was sorely tempted to spill their story to Doctor Voss. As an idealist, Voss would doubtless be happy to blow all these old cobwebs away in the name of progress. Brian and Tommo murdered Kevin as an act of cowardly self-protection.'

Suddenly Diaz felt the need to get outside and breathe the cold, damp air. Yet what had Lorraine said? It was all so obvious that maybe it was true.

As he strode back to Windwell high street he decided to call at Lorraine's cottage. He had been meaning to ever since she'd found Crossley's pocket diary, but Thripp was proving to be a hard taskmaster. When ideas were colliding in his head like this, he often thought about her. In fact, he felt lucky she was here, just when he needed her. He had been working like a Trojan on the offender profile and would have at least a basic outline to discuss with her, though how it had got to Thursday already, he couldn't say. He decided they should meet outside Windwell. There had been a pub he'd passed up on the high tops, one of those stone coaching inns that seemed to be formed from centuries of gritstone. He pictured an open fire and decent ale, and with luck, some hot food. By the time he reached Lorraine's cottage he felt the happiest he'd been in months. She was going to love working on the profile; it was totally her thing.

He rang the doorbell but no sound echoed within. It was

four o'clock already. Peering through the open curtains, he saw that all was dark inside. Annoyed, he had to admit she wasn't home yet. Maybe she was still at the hospital, a fact he hadn't considered. Maybe she was with Doctor Voss.

Pulling out his notebook, he wrote a brief message, asking if she would come to the Black Dog pub with him on Saturday night to discuss his offender profile. He reread it and it sounded like a summons rather than a – a what? Two friends getting together. It had stuck with him, how useless Lorraine had said he was at this emotional stuff when she'd tested his personality. She had called him cold and devoid of empathy. That wasn't how he felt today. Anxiously, he wondered if it would be unwise to let more of how he truly felt show on the outside.

Shit, he couldn't stand here like a gormless idiot all night. He tore out the page, folded it in half and stuck it through the letterbox.

CHAPTER NINETEEN

Lorraine's cottage was thankfully private but hardly palatial. Its interior had been painted with a pale green emulsion presumably left over from a hospital ward. The furniture was saggy and worn, and the bedroom contained such a narrow bed that it recalled a particularly devout breed of nun.

In contrast Doctor Voss's accommodation was decidedly grand, a three-storeyed Victorian stone villa, with its own high-walled gardens and ornate turret room. If her own accommodation had originally been built for a middling hospital worker, Doctor Voss's villa was very much the former asylum superintendent's residence. The turquoise pot was easy to find and Lorraine used the key to open the back door. The elaborately carved upright piano stood in a splendid sitting room at the rear of the villa with wide views of the distant fells. The stained-glass windows cast fragments of a rainbow into the room. She touched the piano's ivory keys and the notes were both a true pitch and pleasantly mellow. Yet still she couldn't shake off a feeling of agitation.

A sense of opportunity struck her, that this might be her one chance to explore the remarkable asylum superintendent's house undisturbed. The air was very still as she crossed the high hallway crowned by an elaborate brass chandelier. Her boots clumped on stone flags in a scullery, and door latches rattled as she explored a refurbished kitchen and outhouses. She wondered who had first lived here in such opulent style while overseeing the lunatics. What type of man chose a role in life that was part prison governor and part custodian of unfortunates and paupers? And which man, she wondered, had overseen the asylum's final decline into scandal, as the shadows grew darker in neglected wards every year? At the top of a wide staircase lay a further suite of grand rooms, thickly carpeted and arranged with ponderous oak furniture.

She found Doctor Voss's study, a workplace befitting both an eminent psychiatrist and a medical director. White concertina blinds covered the windows and bleached Scandinavian furniture held neat rows of medical books. She studied the abstract expressionist artwork on the walls, the flurry of '*Gefeliciteerd!*' Dutch good-luck cards on the mantelpiece. No personal photos yet, but maybe they would appear soon. So far it was the perfect backdrop for a man of intellect and vision.

As the house unfolded, she mulled over her forthcoming dinner date with Voss. Possibilities presented themselves; images of a new life flickered unsteadily in her mind. They liked each other well enough. And didn't she deserve a lucky break after the failures of the last few years? As for

Diaz, she had fancied herself in love with him once, but in the flesh he was just as slippery as ever. What were his plans with his pregnant girlfriend, Shirley? He had hardly rushed around to her cottage to explain what was going on. She told herself that knowing her luck, he probably already had a date fixed to marry her.

Having satisfied her curiosity, she made to return downstairs to the piano, only pausing to use a small bathroom just off the landing. It was a masculine space, very neat and clean with a strong scent of lemon cleaner. She carefully relieved herself, and having washed her hands, dried them on a towel, glancing unthinkingly down into a bamboo waste bin.

The object inside it looked like a small translucent sea creature. Then she understood. It was a used condom. She caught sight of her own startled face in the cabinet mirror. What business was it of hers to spy on Voss's sex life? Yet she couldn't help but wonder – who in this remote backwater was Voss taking to his bed?

Flushing the loo and checking that she'd left no evidence of her intrusion, Lorraine retraced her steps downstairs and settled at the piano. She had promised Lily she would come up with some new material; her being a part of the band was on the line. As soon as she'd set her fingers to the keys, it was hard to pull herself away from what she loved: the chance to explore new melodies, work at her lyrics and escape into sounds more pleasing than the slamming of doors and grinding sound of keys in locks.

On her return to her own cottage, she picked up the note Diaz had pushed through her letterbox hours earlier. She read it, frustrated at not being able to meet him, now she had committed to having dinner with Voss. She hurried around to where Diaz was billeted, but no one answered the door. It felt like a bad omen. Clearly, whatever she felt for Diaz, it wasn't meant to be.

CHAPTER TWENTY

Friday 14th October

News had come from Krish that he'd booked the video gear out for Saturday night. When Friday night came, Oona and Ella met Tommo by the gap in the fence. They followed him in a crocodile file, the beams of their torches zigzagging across broken masonry all the way to the decaying nurses' home.

Inside what Ella thought of as the Haunted Mansion, Krish was waiting for them, wearing another crisp shirt and a musky aftershave. Ella couldn't help comparing him to that tanned male model in that Kouros advert, diving into the deep blue sea. Now she hung back, suddenly feeling too awkward to speak to him. Oona was all over him again, whispering in his ear while Tommo sampled the mushroom tea. Ella saw her friend shove a piece of paper into Krish's hand and him stuffing it inside his work bag. Then Oona started talking loudly about the police.

'Me and Tommo were both interviewed. It was pretty lame. They're not getting anywhere.'

'Just don't send them my way, guys,' said Krish.

Tommo nodded, rejoining them. 'We'll keep you out of it, man.'

The girls lit candles and set them around the room till it looked like a vampire's chapel. Then they poured the tea into paper cups. Earlier on, Tommo had dropped off a huge haul of mushrooms for the night's party, four jam jars oozing with natural psilocybin. Together, Oona and Ella had concocted the murky brown mushroom tea.

Now Ella sipped the cold, earthy liquid, humming along as Debbie Harry's warbling 'Heart of Glass' boomed through Krish's ghetto blaster. In no time her own heart began shivering as the mushrooms kicked in. Soon the chemicals were hitting her brain as waves of excitement tingled down her arms to her fingertips.

When Krish came to sit beside her with his long slim thigh pressing against her leg she felt safe, like a pilgrim who has arrived at a foreign shrine. She also loved Oona. Oh, and tonight even Tommo was all right too, though probably completely doolally. She eyed Krish shyly. He was so beautiful. A minute later she found herself still staring at him, entranced by the white gleam of his eyes in the candlelight.

Someone started talking about what the drugs made them see. Oona said she could feel the cosmos expanding. 'I can see the spirits alive in everything.'

'I can see flowers but sort of pressed flowers, like wallpaper,' Ella said, with some effort.

Krish shook his head. 'I don't see these flowers and shit, man. I see electronic circuits – big ones, small ones, all different colours.'

'Only a guy would say that,' hiccupped Oona, and Ella laughed and laughed.

Hours later, after Ella had wandered ecstatically in the musical labyrinths set off by Krish's playlist, the night seemed to turn sour.

Tommo was giving a long, complicated description of a patient on the unit.

'There's this little guy, right, hardly talks at all. And he says "Then, eh, then, eh, can a typewriter ride an aeroplane?"' Tommo could do the voices and everything. The way he told it, this Lenny had a squeaky voice like Kermit the Frog.

'Aw, that's loony,' Ella said, doubling over with painful laughter.

'You know what, Ella,' he replied. 'It really is. Lenny really is a loony!'

Next Tommo started wringing his hands like a manic Fagin. 'So Lenny's fingers are all burnt black from years of smoking and never knowing how to put them out. So I says, "What happened to your fingers, Lenny?" And you know what he said?'

Ella tried to think but nothing made sense.

'He said – "I rode a typewriter." Get it? He's got black fingers from the ribbon.'

'That's not real.'

'But Ella, it is real,' said Tommo, still mimicking Lenny's crazy walk and hand wringing.

'You're frightening me,' Ella bleated. 'There is no such person. No one rode a typewriter, did they, Oona?'

'Only in their broken heads.'

Krish had been listening. 'How do you do a job like that, man?'

'I get good money and I'll get me own house one day. It's a fucking laugh a minute, that's what it is.'

Ella decided she hated Tommo. She remembered how even Oona was scared of him now. She wondered if that crazy man Lenny was living inside Tommo, like a ventriloquist's dummy that sometimes showed its mad face. It made her own head hurt just to think about it.

'Oona, I don't feel good.'

'Hey, Tommo, get us all some tabs will you?' Oona called irritably. 'You're turning it bad for her with your horrible stories. We could all do with some sleep anyway.'

'Get them yourself.'

'You're a real charmer.'

Oona appeared with a brown glass bottle and mug of water.

'Here love, take these and you can get off to the land of nod,' she urged, helping Ella swallow them.

Krish took his share. Then he appeared beside Ella with a sleeping bag and offered her a space to lie down. It was wonderful to feel the warmth creeping around her body, to press her face into the musty nylon and at last, tumble down, down, into pharmaceutical oblivion.

Ella woke with a pain nagging in her stomach. It took a long time to work out that she needed the loo. After what felt like a lifetime of tossing from side to side on the hard floor, she got up. Krish lay in a deep, beautiful sleep beside her, his long lashes like black feathers, his tousled hair a crow's nest. She stood over him, watching him breathing. No one had mentioned him having a girlfriend; she hoped he didn't have to go through all that arranged marriage shenanigans.

Leaving the candlelit room she felt her way through darkness, heading to where she thought the bathroom might be. Faint fluorescent after-images still glowed on her retinas. The damp-stained walls pulsed with paisley patterns. If she hadn't been bursting to empty her bladder she might have wandered in the gloom for hours, entranced by her own inner light show. It was the sound of slow-motion water dripping that drew her up a set of creaking stairs. Behind a heavy door she at last found the bathroom. The windows were only half boarded up, so she could make out mouldering dark wood and crazily stained porcelain. Though the gigantic toilet smelt bad, she emptied herself and then groped towards the sink.

A metallic groan met her attempts to turn the taps, so she wiped her hands on her jeans. Above the sink was a mirror smeared with muck. She was startled to see her reflection. Suddenly all her universe-ranging perceptions were snapped back into that one neat human figure.

'Weird,' she murmured to herself. For a long time she stared into the mirror, fascinated. In a drug-induced epiphany, she wondered why she had never before noticed this mirror-world that lurked inside the looking glass. When she was straight her mind was so . . . limited.

Then she saw another movement in the mirror. A man. It took a giddy moment to realise that the figure in the mirror was a real man in the real room – behind her.

'No,' she cried. Then the mirror figure reached out to her in the real world and trapped her in his arms.

For a plummeting moment she was lost between reflection and reality, completely confounded. Yet hang on, was it Krish?

'Nowt to be scared of.' It was Tommo's ugly voice.

Listening to the uncanny drip, drip, drip from the pipes, she felt a ghastly explosion of fear.

'Just checking you're all right. Don't fret. I'll look after you.'

She was frightened. Too frightened to move. In the mirror her face was narrow and doll-like. In the mirror two heavy arms slithered around her like steel pythons.

'You don't want to listen to that bitch, Oona,' he murmured. 'Just relax.' Stubby fingers worked their way inside her T-shirt, like splayed icicles on her midriff. Her heart beat so loudly, so much faster than the metronomic dripping. How had she got here? In a lucid moment she understood the reason for this imprisonment. Tommo was holding her so tight that she could feel it – that bulge in his trousers that was digging into her backside.

'No need to say owt,' he whispered. 'I'll look after you.' Muscular fingers found her bra. She couldn't fight him so she turned dead, fossilising into stone. Her terror had triggered the echo of past terrors, but she mustn't think of that. Deep in the pit of her mind were the memories – squashed down and sickening, like the stuff in the farm's sump after slaughter day.

Tommo was still mumbling to himself, urging himself on. She stopped breathing. Maybe she could disappear. Maybe she could die. After all, she deserved to die. Because the memory that was threatening to break its chains was this: she had stabbed a man and no one must ever find out.

A click rang out. The buckle of a belt being unclasped. An involuntary sob escaped her mouth. Then everything changed.

'You fucking creep.' The voice was a she-wolf's growl. Distantly, Ella heard Oona and Tommo argue like a pair of snapping dogs. She didn't move, still standing like calcified stone, until long after Tommo had unhanded her. She stared at herself inside the mirror, a moon-carved statue with eyes as blind as opal beads.

'You OK?' She woke from stony visions to see a boyish face creased with concern.

'Are you real?'

'Ella, it's me, Krish. For real.'

'Thank God.' She turned to him and gripped his arm and felt herself trembling. It was a struggle to make up sensible words.

'Don't look in the mirror any more.' How wise he was. How amazingly wise.

Suddenly Ella started to laugh. 'Jesus Christ,' she choked. 'Those mushrooms were strong.'

Krish grinned back. He had purple-bronze lips and white teeth like a toothpaste advert.

'You're telling me, love.'

They laughed again, and it was like a dentist's sweet gas rising from a high-pressure canister.

'Come on. Let me show you round.' He reached out his hand to pull her away with him. Once they were walking she didn't let go; he was a planet guiding a fiercely loyal satellite. He wanted to show her his secret place.

'Don't tell the others,' he said, and quickly kissed her hand. That made her feel more special than if her path had been scattered with petals and pearls.

* * *

Outside the sky was grey and pink and a church bell distantly chimed. In a rustling tree a blackbird began to sing his fluting song. The drug had nearly worn off, but still Ella felt a trace of magic as she followed Krish between a gap in a tumbledown wall. There was a path, almost obscured by shrubbery, but Krish confidently pushed through the spiky branches. Then they came to a circular open space.

'What do you think? I found it the other day when I was fixing the electric.'

He was so proud of his discovery, just like the way he had been bursting to show how he'd connected the wires. Whereas that had been a descent to hell, this was the opposite.

Krish pointed to a tiny building made of rocks that sheltered a hollow basin. Inside, a trickle of water fell into a pool. She joined him to admire the rough-hewn shrine decorated with white pebbles. It reminded her of something she'd recently seen. 'Oona showed me a picture of a healing well that's the original Wynd Well. But that's underground somewhere.'

He was interested. 'Then this might be a run-off from the original place. It were blocked with all this rubbish but I've cleared it out.'

'It could be one of those ancient healing wells. Wow.'

Together, they dipped her fingers in water that was like newly melted snow. Then she cradled her two hands to make a cup and drank. It numbed the inside of her mouth like frost, travelling in iceburn down her gullet.

She decided that her reinvention could begin today, drawing a thick black line under the last few months' awful events. She had been given a golden chance to try again.

She felt so lucky to be here – it was beautiful in the way that very old, time-ravaged places evoke a kind of paradise.

She reached inside the little prayer house and saw that Krish had set out tiny objects: a figure of a god playing a flute, a sprinkling of flowers and two charred joss sticks.

'Last week I came here to like, you know – try and meditate before I started work.' He looked bashful but secretly pleased with himself, hopping a little from foot to foot.

'It's beautiful.'

He set two new joss sticks in the arms of the figurine. When he lit them with his plastic lighter, they flared and slowly released twists of perfumed smoke. Then he sprinkled some biscuit crumbs from his pocket in front of the figure. Finally, he spoke rhythmically and quietly under his breath. Ella caught the recitation of indecipherable phrases but the only word she recognised was 'Krishna'. She didn't feel excluded, only privileged to listen to him, though he turned and grinned sheepishly at her a couple of times. She studied the sharp triangles of his shoulder blades beneath the thin white shirt and the long flexing of his legs inside his blue jeans.

With a bow of his head, he finished and turned to her, seating himself beside her with a serene hint of a smile.

'Where are you from?' she asked. If he had said Alpha Centauri she might have believed him.

'Bradford,' he grinned. 'But my family are from Bengal.'

She couldn't move her eyes from his face. His eyes were so dark, with a slightly lazy cast, and his hair fell like raven's wings down to his shoulders.

As if on cue a sparrow fluttered down from the sky with

its bouncing, up and down flight. Cautiously it landed, swivelling its face from side to side. Slowly, it hopped down to the figurine's open hand, and finally, with a last dart of its beady black eye, it pounced on a beakful of the biscuit.

'They take my offerings to the gods.'

There was no need to talk. Just holding hands, sitting in silence was enough. Sometimes they turned to each other and smiled deep, penetrating, love-igniting smiles. Those smiles were better than any kiss, she thought. That could come later.

'Krish,' she asked, a lump swelling in her throat. 'Can you help me get away from here?'

He nodded. 'I'll do anything.' Then with puzzlement in his eyes he asked, 'What's the matter?'

She tried to summon the words. 'It's not just Tommo,' she began, and saw in Krish's face that he understood.

He touched her cheek. 'Do you want to be with me?'

Her throat burnt so painfully that she only sniffed and mumbled, 'Yeah.'

He kissed her forehead and it felt like a blessing.

'I'll take next week off work. It's time I moved on from my uncle's place.' He hesitated, and then said, 'Tommo's paying me good money for the filming stuff tomorrow. Do you mind if we go ahead? We'll need cash wherever we're going.'

'Just one more night? And then we'll get away from here?'

He nodded and she clasped his hands as if she were drowning, and he was her one hope of ever rising back to the surface again.

CHAPTER TWENTY-ONE

Saturday 15th October

On Saturday evening Ella and Krish met in his uncle's van, parked on Windwell's high street. They had arranged a time half an hour before Oona was due to arrive and now they clung to each other.

'I wish I didn't have to meet Tommo again. He scares me,' she whispered.

'It's the last time,' he said softly. 'I'll look after you. If he touches you again, he's dead. We've just got to get this flaming video over with and get our cash off of him.'

She pushed her face into his chest and closed her eyes. 'OK.'

He kissed her on the lips, at first very gently, but then with a pressure that she guessed was passion. It was the first true lover's kiss of her life and it made her feel a bit dizzy, partly from holding her breath, but also from a funny feeling she had never experienced before.

'How long will this filming take?' he asked, when they both took a breather.

'Oona'll be along any minute. She'll know.'

'Remember, just keep calm, love. And as soon as we've got the dough—'.

A startling tappety-tap on the van's window made them both spring apart. Oona's face was scowling in at them both as the door creaked open. Ella had been as near to sitting on Krish's lap as the gearstick would allow.

'Don't mind me,' she said, gesturing at Ella to budge up so they could share the passenger seat. She cast a black look at them both and said, 'I'm disappointed in you both keeping secrets. I suppose I'm the last to know.'

Ella wasn't having that. 'What d'you expect after what happened in the bathroom with your boyfriend? Krish rescued me.'

'Tommo's no boyfriend of mine. I saw him mauling you. It's all over between us. He just doesn't know it yet.'

Instantly, Ella felt sorry for this girl who had, despite her weird ways, been her friend in a time of need. She snuggled up close to her. 'OK, well, we're ready to give him the fright of his life.'

Oona confronted Krish. 'So you do get it? All you need to do is bring the gear and stay cool, whatever happens.'

'Yeah, sure. I got the sound tape you asked me for. After what he did to Ella, I hope he'll be as petrified as she was.'

Oona's attention was distracted by a grey Rover parked a few cars along. 'I had a premonition he'd be around. Detective Diaz. He told me I'm one of their top witnesses.'

Krish directed an amused eye-roll towards Ella while Oona studied the detective throwing a cigarette butt out of his car window.

A red Metro drove past them and pulled up outside

Doctor Voss's house. 'There's that woman who's staying at number 16,' said Oona excitedly. 'Look, that detective's watching her.'

Lorraine Quick got out of her car and headed inside the villa's gates. 'Freaking hell. She's going to see Voss.' Oona was straining to watch through the windscreen.

Not long afterwards the pair came out, Doctor Voss all smartened up in a shirt and a suede jacket that must have cost a bomb. The pair set off in the Metro.

'She didn't take long to get her claws into him,' Oona sniped. 'Even my mum thinks she's a government spy. Voss had his hands all over her at the police talk. Is she his girlfriend or what?'

Ella shrugged, but did wonder if Oona was jealous of this woman.

'Look, he's trailing them,' Oona said triumphantly. 'I wonder which one he's chasing, the sainted Doctor Voss or her, the government spy?'

'Right, you two,' broke in Krish. 'Are we ready to teach Tommo a lesson, or what?'

CHAPTER TWENTY-TWO

By the time Lorraine and Voss reached the hotel, she was grateful to the director for providing this break from her own maudlin thoughts. Together they entered an unlikely modern building of glass and brick, with a single-storey frontage and a motel block to the side. The attraction was that it overlooked a vast reservoir, replete with castellated outlet towers and giddy iron walkways. Voss led her to an expensive-looking wine bar area decorated with old casks and French posters, where he ordered her a glass of white wine.

'Windwell is pretty oppressive, isn't it?' she said. 'Do you usually live on-site?'

'Not if I can help it. I prefer to live somewhere livelier, with more varied culture.'

'I bet you do,' she said with feeling. They both laughed.

A few days earlier, on an exploratory walk around Windwell village, she had noticed that the school was sparsely attended and like many of the buildings, had an unfortunate custodial appearance with battlemented walls and heavy gates. There was no public library, cinema or theatre, just the hospital social club, a tatty drinking hole frequented by beer- and darts-loving staff. So now it was especially welcome to take seats on modernist orange chairs and order from heavy leather menus. At first Lorraine quailed at the prices; a steak was £6.95. Then she noticed something called 'Today's Menu', all included, for £10.95, so she chose dishes from that. She hoped she had enough money in her purse when they came to split the bill.

'So, tell me about yourself?' she said, after an awkward silence.

'Hey, that's one of my best lines.' His pale eyes crinkled as he smiled.

'It's a good one,' she laughed. 'Very well tested around here, I'm told.'

'OK, though I admit it's not so comfortable to be on the receiving end.' He took a long sip of wine and said, 'My mum and dad were typical of their generation. They met on the hippy trail in India and I suppose I was their accidental child. So I was dragged from communes to squats and festivals, and didn't get much steady education. But I could read well enough to get into university and get out of that aimless lifestyle.'

'You still see your parents?'

He raised his eyebrows. 'You borrowed from my script again. I'm afraid my parents died in a hostel fire in Sri Lanka five years ago. Hey, you're good at this. Do you fancy taking over my job?'

'I don't think I'm capable of doing what you do.'

'Oh, I'm sure you could. Like most women, you undervalue yourself.'

She reached for her drink. 'I'm sorry, I'm a typical northerner, suspicious of flattery. I mean, I agree that most women do undervalue themselves, but not me. Analyse that, Sigmund.'

Again, they shared wry smiles, then he tapped her arm. 'Actually, I'd like to guess what sort of background you come from. I'd say your family is quite secure and you have good attachment to at least one of your parents.'

She nodded and he continued. 'You had books and music around you. But you're not at all conventional. Where did that come from?'

'My mother is French. My dad is a musician.'

He was studying her so closely that she was getting seriously self-conscious. 'Aha, bohemian. I approve.'

'Not quite as freewheeling as your own upbringing. So you aren't hoping to create a world where everyone is bang on the norm?'

'God, no. Why else would I be here, tending to all these extraordinarily abnormal minds?'

A waitress told them their table was ready, and they followed her into an ultramodern dining room with leatherette chairs and smoked-glass tables.

While waiting for their food, Lorraine chatted about the personnel work she was doing.

'We've not had a single phone call about the administrator vacancy and hardly any applications for the other dozen vacancies at present.'

He pulled a weary face. 'How hard will it be to sort out?'

'I'll have a think and put a plan together.'

He poured out two further generous glasses of wine. 'If it's that easy, wonderful.'

'Actually, if you can find the right administrator and make the place more inviting to outsiders, the situation could improve fairly rapidly. And I do recommend you appoint a personnel manager.'

'You want the job?'

'What, at Windwell?' She hoped she'd sounded sufficiently incredulous.

'Yes. We could say this was your interview and save us both from wasting time.'

'That,' she said, shaking her head, 'is exactly how Windwell got to be in this mess. It's utterly incestuous.'

'But in your case, I'm serious. I'd take you on. Actually, I'm already dreading you leaving.'

She shook her head in bemusement. Crikey, he had to be desperate. To her, the attraction of working permanently at Windwell was pretty well on par with being admitted as a lifer patient. She turned her attention to her 'Orange Surprise' starter, which turned out to be a bowl of fruit topped with orangey water ice and a stalk of mint. So not that surprising. Next came a large steak smothered in a highly alcoholic sauce, and then some sort of cream extravaganza from the dessert trolley. If only she could have been sharing the meal with Jas and her mum. Now that would have been a treat for the three of them.

She was finding Doctor Voss hard to read. When they finished the bottle of wine, he called the waitress over to order two liqueurs. He brushed his hand against hers; clearly keen to touch her, he gazed at her intensely, studying her reaction. She had the odd sense that he was examining her with the same intensity with which he might observe a lab rat in an experiment. Maybe this was how people got together in Holland, but as flirtations went it was feeling distinctly clinical. She forced herself to imagine what Morgan back at Regional HQ would make of it if they got together. No doubt the male double standard would cast her as a trollop, while Voss was simply a bachelor living life to the full. No, she had to focus on what Morgan had actually sent her here to do.

'I mustn't forget,' she announced. 'I need to get some photos of our team in the great outdoors.'

'That's easy.' He pushed a liqueur glass of something green towards her. 'This hotel has an outdoor activity centre. There are brochures at reception.'

'That's great news,' she said with feeling. 'I'll just go and collect them, so I can get it all booked.'

'Don't be long. I'll order coffee in the lounge.'

Lorraine set off for reception with the tipsy feeling that the carpet had turned into spongy waves as she strove to stay upright on her high heels. First, she found the ladies, and discovered that her cheeks were decidedly pink. She drank some cold water and splashed a few drops on her face. With a clearer mind she headed for the reception desk and took her place behind a newly arrived couple who were checking in. As she waited, she glanced through the outdoor activity brochure and found that the range of activities looked perfect – everything from raft-building and archery to orienteering and caving. She felt a surge of confidence that she could deliver the perfect photos to be featured in some ministerial press release.

The couple being checked in were making a seemingly endless number of requests. Lorraine yawned and picked up a promotional leaflet from a rack. 'Special Offer – Two-night Leisure Break, dinner, bed and breakfast – £55 per room.' An idea sprang into her mind. Her mum and Jasmine could come here, for there had to be a coach service from Manchester to Blackburn or Bradford. She could pick them up. In fact, she might even stay with them here. It would be wonderful to treat them, and even better to have them close to her for just a few days.

CHAPTER TWENTY-THREE

From his armchair in the corner of the hotel foyer, Diaz had a perfect view of Lorraine waiting at the reception desk. He'd had another bad day, returning at six o'clock from a series of frustrating interviews, still brooding over the note Lorraine had pushed through the door, regretting that she couldn't meet him that night. He'd sworn and thrown his work on the offender profile aside. Laddo had asked him what was up, and for a paranoid second Diaz had wondered if he'd read the note first. No, Lorraine had had the good sense to stick it in a sealed envelope. Still, he hadn't answered the lad, just slammed the door, needing to get out of the cottage to get his head straight. He couldn't say why he'd got back in the car but driven only as far as Lorraine's house, where he'd chain-smoked and watched her door with grim determination.

He had felt sick to his guts when Lorraine, looking dressier than he'd ever seen her before, emerged from Doctor Voss's fancy house. Robotically, he had switched on the ignition and begun to cautiously follow the Metro as it left Windwell's streets and started to climb the empty twisting road across the moors. When they'd reached the hotel, he had trailed them through the brightly lit entrance door and taken a sidestep into a high-backed chair in the foyer when they disappeared into the wine bar.

Now she had arrived at reception, no more than twenty feet from where he sat with his second pint. She looked rather hot and distracted. He wondered why she was waiting behind a couple checking in, when surely she and Voss were only here for dinner. She was flicking through some leaflets, but he couldn't read the details. The couple finally picked up their luggage and Lorraine moved to the centre of the reception desk. He heard her ask, 'This offer on rooms. Is it available next weekend?'

Diaz stared, uncomprehending, or at least not wanting to comprehend.

'And the bed, is it a double?'

Before he could stop himself, Diaz had crossed the bar area and was standing right behind her. She noticed him, and though she looked surprised, she greeted him with a smile.

'Oh, hi Diaz. I've been trying to get hold of you. I thought you were going to the Black Dog tonight.'

'No. What are you doing here?'

She glanced back towards the dining room, seemingly oblivious to his belligerent tone. 'Doctor Voss suggested we meet off-site to talk about the team-building. Why are you here?'

'It looks like more than a business meeting,' he grumbled. 'You're all dressed up.'

'Thought I should. Who the hell knows what I'm

doing here? I'm at a complete loss, actually.' She looked unfocused – even a bit drunk. Then her eyes met his penetrating look. 'I waited,' she mumbled. 'I waited to hear from you. I thought we were . . .'

Lamely, he said, 'I've been dying to see you again.'

Her expression was hard to read; was it encouragement or disapproval?

'I'm not psychic,' she said. 'But I'm here now. And so are you.'

The way she continued staring at him, urging him on, gave him strength. 'Do you fancy meeting up tomorrow?' When she didn't answer him, he added, 'You've got no other plans?'

'No plans.' She was studying his face. 'You think we can try that pub?'

'Yeah, yeah. I could pick you up at eleven?'

She nodded. 'I'd better get back to the receptionist.'

Diaz paid the barman and left the place, feeling like a new man. It dawned on him how pathetic it had been to spy on them both. Nevertheless, he drove back to Windwell with a glimmer of victory in his heart.

Lorraine found Voss sipping coffee, seemingly lost in the view of the reservoir that gleamed like liquid tar.

'You look very happy.'

'I am,' she said. 'I've got an appointment with the outdoor activity manager on Monday.' She put the brochures down on the table and Voss picked up the leisure break flyer.

'Do you think the team need to stay here for the night?' he asked.

'No. The leisure break's for my mum and daughter. I miss Jasmine terribly and they both deserve a treat.'

Voss's reaction was surprisingly warm. 'You have a daughter? Lorraine, that's delightful.' He asked her all about Jasmine, how old she was, and told her how impressive it was that she was musical and also liked maths. She told him her mum's recent news, that Jasmine had an interview at the grammar school, having gained one of the top three marks in the exam. He congratulated her as if her daughter had won a Nobel Prize. This was not the typical male reaction, Lorraine mused. She wondered if it was a therapy thing, that he considered parenthood to be some elevated state of being. At this rate she'd not only be his personnel manager, he'd have her whisked to the altar and Jasmine officially adopted by the end of the year.

They left soon afterwards, and Lorraine didn't protest when he told her he'd already sorted out the bill, reassuring herself that his salary had to be at least triple her own.

'Motherhood suits you,' he told her on the journey home. 'Your daughter must bring you so much happiness.'

'Well, it's not all party dresses and kittens.' She was carefully manoeuvring the car down the precipitous unlit road. 'It's a logistical nightmare when you have a demanding job.'

'Yes,' he considered. 'Yet to have a small individual you are so powerfully attached to. She must give you great joy.'

'Well, something like that,' she conceded. Then for a while she drove the small car and allowed herself to think of Diaz and what tomorrow might bring.

After she pulled in at Voss's house, he very earnestly asked her if he could take her out again. She would have liked to say no, for apart from finally running into Diaz, the evening had turned out rather heavy and, well – decidedly weird. But what excuse could she give? The only courteous reply was, of course, to say yes. After all, there was no possibility of their seeing each other once the month was up. Without warning, he leant towards her and kissed her briefly on the lips.

'Goodnight and thanks again,' she said, escaping with great relief. Then, accelerating back towards her empty cottage, she treacherously returned to thoughts of Diaz, and looked out for the lit square of curtain behind which she guessed he also waited for tomorrow.

CHAPTER TWENTY-FOUR

Ella could easily believe that the boiler room was a place where ghosts gathered. Krish led her down the dark stairs and along the chilly tunnel. The three of them entered the boiler room together, staring at the mass of crazy ironwork, ancient pipes, dials and gauges. And there stood the furnace against the wall, a metal-studded monster the size of a small garage. Ella heaved the ornate cast-iron door open and baulked to see an interior just like the sort of oven a wicked witch might stuff children inside.

'Aw, it's like a horror film, man,' Krish groaned.

'That's the idea,' Oona shot back with satisfaction, unpacking her embroidered rucksack of magical props. She'd brought the expensive black candles this time, and started setting them up.

Krish started putting the film gear together while relaying his worries to Oona.

'You'll back me up, hey? I've got to get hold of the dough first. Then we teach him a lesson, scare the pants off him, yeah? Then me and Ella are hitting the road.'

'Cool. I do the filming. Tommo reads the script. Then Ella comes out and scares him shitless. You brought that scary soundtrack?'

He passed her a music cassette. 'I used the words you gave me. There's a prog rock group over Barnoldswick way who go for all these way-out sounds. I mixed it with their synthesiser before they came to pick it up.'

Oona slotted it into the radio cassette player and clicked it on. The sound of fizzing waves of static crackled in the air. Then a ghostly little girl's voice whispered, *'Who's there?'*

'Aw, it's like *The Exorcist*. Who is that speaking?' Oona was gaping at the recorder.

'My little niece. She loves playing at ghosts and stuff. I got the idea from the noises in the pipes down here. I mixed two tracks and looped it.'

'Clever boy,' said Oona. 'Tommo's going to lose his freaking marbles when he hears that with the lights out.'

Ella hadn't expected to react to the tape at all, but down here, underground in this room where the real Sally had died, that accusing little voice was the last thing she wanted to hear.

'Who's there? It's me. Risen from the grave . . .'

She shook her head as if she might shake the voice away. It wouldn't go.

'You all right?' Krish asked, picking up Ella's distress.

'Course she is,' Oona snapped. 'Ella, get changed and we can have a quick rehearsal. You never know, Tommo might even get here on time.'

Ella retreated to a dark corner. She was already wearing

most of Sally's costume beneath her clothes, so she simply took off her jeans, pulled on the long brown skirt and tied the knitted shawl over the frilled white blouse Oona had lent her. With Enid's long hippy wig covering her own hair, the black tresses gave her a wild, witchy look. When she'd had a try-out that morning, both girls had agreed she bore an uncanny resemblance to Sally's photo.

Now Ella applied pallid green make-up to her face and hands. Finally, she drew heavy black rings circling her eyes and shadowed the hollows of her cheekbones.

'What do you think?' she asked Oona and Krish tentatively.

They both stared. Oona gave a congratulatory nod. Krish eyed her uncertainly and muttered, 'This is totally mad, in every sense.'

They had a run-through. Ella had to hide in the furnace until Oona gave the signal by intoning: 'Sally is back from the dead.' At that point she was to climb out and appear as if from nowhere to confront Tommo. For the rehearsal, Krish screwed the camcorder onto a tripod and Oona began to film Ella, firstly standing motionless in the flickering candlelight, and then taking tiny steps forward, staring blankly into the lens. Again, she felt the breathy voice on the tape spoke to her alone. '*I'm trapped here all alone. Help me someone, help me . . .*' How had they known to choose those words?

Ella switched the cassette player off. The others didn't even notice; they were bent over the playback screen on the video recorder. Oona beckoned her to see. 'Look. It really is like a Hammer horror film.'

Ella peered at the little screen. 'It doesn't even look like me,' she said. It looked like Sally. Icy goosebumps rose all along her arms.

'I'll rewind the tape back to the beginning,' Oona called. 'Both of you. Back to positions.'

Ella crept back into the furnace, praying that the whole thing would be over soon. What had she been thinking to get dragged into this? She had convinced herself that she was feeling better but maybe that was only because she'd been lying low at Enid's, sleeping the days away, hiding from the past. All she wanted now was to get away from here and start her new life with Krish.

Oona appeared at the cast-iron door and whispered, 'Here's your final prop.' The object was wrapped in a black cloth and when she unwrapped it, she found a large carving knife, with a bone handle and a long, cruel-looking blade.

CHAPTER TWENTY-FIVE

Sunday 16th October

The Black Dog pub was impressive on the outside, a rambling stone warren on the summit of a misty pass, with a primitive painting of a monstrous red-eyed creature on its creaking sign. Inside, it was not much warmer than out, so they headed to the soot-stained inglenook fire and warmed their hands over blistering logs. Lorraine was glad she'd pulled on jeans and her thickest mohair jumper, and Diaz had also dressed down in jeans and a sweater. They both eyed the horse brasses and scattering of rusting farm implements and smirked to each other like a pair of city slickers. He fetched her a cider along with his pint of bitter and they pulled up as close to the flames as they could get without setting fire to themselves.

He nodded towards the bar. 'No proper food, just pies in the warmer or pork scratchings. We could find somewhere better.'

'A pie will do. It's quiet for a Sunday. No one's going to take any notice of us here.'

He put a document case on the table. 'I've had a go at

writing down some thoughts about Crossley's killer. I was dead confident on the profiling course, but it's not like they give you a step-by-step plan how to write one. I started by comparing Campbell's death in 1980 with Crossley's murder.'

She scanned the page of neat boxy writing:

PRELIMINARY PROFILE	
Junior Campbell, 1980	*Kevin Crossley, 1983*
CRIME SITE	
Cell 17, Windwell asylum *Victim in solitary seclusion*	*SC17, Phase 2, Windwell new build. Victim lured to site* *Slogan on wall in red paint: 'RIP Campbell. Your next'*
VICTIM'S ROLE	
Windwell inmate - lifer	*Hospital Administrator*
CAUSE OF DEATH	
Manual asphyxiation, following assault *Note: red cord murder weapon*	*Blow to head with blunt instrument* *Note: red cord crime scene dressing*
CRIME CIRCUMSTANCES	
Knowledge required of security systems *Access to keys, basement layout* *Blood stains and prints: Brian and Tommo Ogden*	*Knowledge required of security systems* *Access to Phase 2 layout, keys, stolen weapon and uniform* *Forensically aware – site cleaned, gloves used*
PERPETRATOR	
Windwell worker or possibly inmate *Possibly working with accomplice* *History of violence likely* *Anger problems, strong and fit*	*Windwell worker or possibly inmate* *Possibly working with accomplice* *History of violence and/or deception* *Organised, manipulative*

DISCUSSION:

The Campbell Inquiry raised serious concerns about the involvement of Brian Ogden and his son Tommo Ogden. Brian Ogden was senior nurse in charge on the night in question. Tommo, then a newly qualified nurse, was on suicide watch outside Campbell's cell. The Tribunal found insufficient evidence to press charges.

The detailed circumstances of Campbell's death were widely circulated in the press and on TV, and printed copies of the inquiry were circulated widely at Windwell.

Was it the same perpetrator or a copycat?

'That's a helpful summary,' Lorraine observed, looking up. 'But as for Tommo or Brian, what's the motive to kill Kevin? Why create such an elaborate set-up? Couldn't the killer just have slipped something nasty into Kevin's teacup, or quietly finished him off at home in a burglary gone wrong? Surely Brian isn't so daft that he'd want all those old allegations dug up again.'

'I agree.'

'So why make it a copycat?'

'The simplest explanation is to put Brian and Tommo in the frame for it.'

'Yes, but doesn't that underestimate you lot?'

'OK, let's say some unknown person is aggrieved that justice still hasn't been done over Campbell's death. And that back then Kevin covered it up as a favour for his mate Brian. The copycat killing gets rid of Kevin and kicks up all the suspicion back to Brian and Tommo again.'

'OK. But why is it happening now, three years after the original crime?'

Diaz nodded. 'Right. So what's changed? Well, the asylum's being demolished. The new unit's being built. Doctor Voss has arrived with his grand plans for a better Windwell. And the new scandal over conditions has just been all over the media.'

'What if someone was putting pressure on Kevin to tell Voss about Campbell's death but he refused. So being killed by the same MO is intended as a taunt at Kevin for his low moral stance.'

'That sounds feasible,' he said.

Lorraine drained her glass and said, 'You know, maybe Tommo's family situation does put him in the picture for Campbell's murder. He was little more than an adolescent when he was left alone to watch over Campbell. It's a risky age for young males, and by all accounts Campbell was seriously deranged and liable to provoke a saint. Tommo's role model is his dad, a tough guy with an aggressive manner. I've been looking into family theory, and that macho, all-male household puts Tommo at risk of difficulties in developing empathy or even normal humanity. What happened to Tommo's mother?'

'She left when the lad was six. Drifted around for a few years and eventually fell off a bridge and drowned last year, with more alcohol than red stuff in her blood.'

Lorraine winced. 'It could also explain why Brian is so protective of his only son. God, the nepotism here.' She shook her head in disbelief. 'And thanks to his dad he got qualified as a nurse.' She picked up her glass and said, 'Want the same again? And a pie?'

'Yeah, anything remotely edible.'

She went to the bar with a mild sense of disbelief that she and Diaz were conversing so easily together. This was new, and she hoped they could keep up this straightforward friendship. Maybe this was the best way they could be as a couple, to share ideas over work and spark each other off. Well, it felt good, and maybe it was enough for her. She was enjoying feeling like a student again, building abstract castles in the air, sharing cheap drinks in a fug of companionship. True, she had been looking at Diaz's hands a lot, at his thick ringless fingers and the strong tendons beneath the skin. His hands were safer to look at than his eyes, those open windows into his fascinating variety of emotions.

'That was rubbish,' Lorraine said, screwing up the serviette her meat and potato pie had arrived in. 'But at least it was hot and filling rubbish.'

'Have you met Tommo's girlfriend, Oona?' Diaz asked.

'The White Witch of Windwell? Yes.'

'Why do you call her that?'

'The story in the admin office is that she's a full-blown Wiccan. Magic spells, tarot cards, the lot.'

'Yeah. Only I get the full-on flirtiness on top.'

'How you must suffer.' She gave him a wry smile.

'Have you met Professor Leadbetter? Rumour has it he's Oona's father.'

She shook her head. 'No.'

'He's definitely on my list. He has a serious grudge against the Ogdens. After he spoke against them at the inquiry he says they made sure he lost his job.'

'An actual motive.'

'Yeah, and he's also created what he calls a Black Museum. He's appropriated items from the Campbell case, including a replica length of red cord.'

'That sounds unusually obsessive. If I remember rightly, Doctor Voss wasn't too impressed by his academic credentials. I'll try to get to meet him.'

'Good. Any other thoughts?' he asked.

'After Kevin died, Oona tried to enter the administrator's office to retrieve something for her mother. She made a fuss but I made sure Parveen now keeps the office locked. Any thoughts on the mysterious cake?'

'Not really. We checked and Kevin pre-ordered it at Greenhalgh's and picked it up that morning.'

'If he was taking it home for this secret appointment of his, it definitely sounds like more pleasure than business,' she mused. 'And maybe he was killed to prevent that meeting going ahead.'

'What are the admin staff saying about it all?'

Lorraine sighed. 'It's mostly random nonsense. That row between Voss and Crossley bothers people. They say that Voss had motive and opportunity.'

Diaz grimaced. 'I'm not his biggest fan.' He leant forward and she had to look away from the directness of his gaze. 'You spent a boozy evening with him. What do you think?'

Lorraine took her time and Diaz lit a cigarette, watching and waiting, taking her seriously.

'To suspect him is ludicrous,' she said at last. 'Why come here to this prestigious job and then sabotage his career by killing his most experienced colleague?'

'I'd say he's a skilled manipulator,' argued Diaz. 'And

I'm guessing there's a "but" to your opinion of him.'

'Well, he is unusual. Unconventional.'

Diaz made an unsuccessful attempt to sound casual. 'How well do you know him?'

'He's effectively my boss but he wants to be – well, more than a friend. It's uncomfortable.'

'Why uncomfortable?'

Oh God, she thought. Diaz was the last person she wanted to ask her why she was uncomfortable. Because I'd rather be with you, you dolt. Instead she plunged into a breathless description. 'Forgive me if this is obvious. He comes from an unconventional hippy background, and still has nonconformist values. He can be self-indulgent and careless of any rules he thinks might block him.'

'Well, we all have our moments,' he said charitably.

'The thing about Voss is that getting what he wants is masked by a very shrewd and discreet persona. On our night out I got the oddest feeling that I was an entertaining research experiment to him. He threw out flattery in spades, which always irks me.'

She told him about an interpersonal skills course she had taught with a wise psychologist. In the breaks between teaching, Lorraine's young assistant had told her and the psychologist that her brother had met the so-called Yorkshire Ripper, Peter Sutcliffe, and ridden in his van on a few occasions.

'And when they went for a drink he was a proper gentleman to the ladies. Held the door open for them and everything,' she confided. The psychologist had nodded and told them that flattery was a common weapon used by psychopaths to create a receptive frame of mind. 'Beware a man showering you in compliments' had stuck with her ever since.

'I'm not saying he's the murderer or—'

'Has he tried it on with you?' Diaz interrupted in an overloud voice.

'No. Nothing more than a light peck on the lips.'

'I see.' He retreated into himself, obviously disgruntled.

'Oh, God. Diaz. Come off it. I'm a free agent. Unlike you,' she added. Unable to resist, she poked at the wound she'd promised herself not to disturb. 'So, are you going to tell me what's going on in your life?'

After a pause, he said, 'Shirley's in hospital. I don't know what's going to happen. I mean, she may lose the baby.'

'Oh, God.' Lorraine looked away, struggling with her feelings. Finally, she asked, 'Are you still going to marry her?'

He bowed his head and pressed his fingers to his brow as if in acute pain. 'I'm not proud of this. I've resisted so far. Her family hate my guts for letting her down. And I may as well tell you this now – Laddo, Constable Ladlaw, is Shirley's cousin, so I feel like I'm constantly under fucking surveillance. Anyway, back to your question. I've decided to wait and see how it goes with the baby.'

'Oh.' She needed time to let all this sink in. More gently, she added, 'Last night you told me that you'd been dying to see me.'

'It's true.'

He raised his eyes to her, a picture of misery. She reached out and grasped his hand. Even just touching him made her nerves hum like wires.

'I'm so sorry,' she whispered. His fingers squeezed hers

in return and the warmth held her very still. His eyes shone and he blinked. What were they going to do?

She scraped her chair backwards, suddenly unable to bear another second of confusion. 'I've really loved today,' she said huskily. 'But I need time to think. Can you give me a lift home now, please.'

CHAPTER TWENTY-SIX

Monday 17th October

Diaz had been yawning at his desk in the incident room all of Monday morning. Then at last he'd been waved through to take his profile in to show Thripp.

Thripp was not looking too happy in the cramped broom cupboard of an office. 'Give me the headlines. Who have you got your eye on for Crossley's killer? What about this Tommo Ogden?'

'Possibly, sir.' Diaz felt cagey about it. 'He's definitely in the picture for the murder of Campbell back in 1980.'

He ran through the details of his sketchy profile and started to argue against the DCI's assumptions. 'Crossley's killer is rather different. Calculating, and organised. Why would Tommo dress up the crime scene to deliberately incriminate himself? I see why you're interested in him, but surely he's only in the picture for Campbell's death?'

'So, who do you fancy for it?'

He started to give a summary of his suspicions about Professor Leadbetter, reminding him the man had no alibi.

Diaz was interrupted mid-sentence by Brian Ogden barging in without knocking.

'Tommo never came home last night, and now he's missed four hours of his shift. I know my lad. Something, or someone, must be stopping him turning in today. I'm begging you to search for him.'

Seeing that Thripp was about to give the usual 'wait and see' response, Diaz stepped in.

'Have you tried his girlfriend's place?'

'She's at home safe and sound. Though I wouldn't trust that one as far as I could throw her. The young 'uns have taken to hanging around the old asylum. It's dangerous, the floors can give way, it's condemned for a reason. Like I said, he's not hisself, he's a big kid. And they go there to take stuff, and that.'

'Drugs?'

'Aye.'

Finally persuaded, Thripp ordered Constable Ladlaw and a couple of specials to make a search.

Diaz returned to his desk and continued checking statements, but achieved little. He felt stuck with the case and frustrated that he'd blown it with Lorraine. It was nearly noon when Thripp approached him, the furrows on his long face looking even deeper. 'Ladlaw just called in a body in those tunnels under the asylum. Sounds like Tommo Ogden, stabbed in the abdomen with a kitchen knife. I've called the scene of crime bods in. We'd better get over there.'

Diaz hadn't yet had time to visit the condemned asylum standing empty just down the road from the new unit. Now its town-sized scale impressed him, its towers and archways seemingly designed in a fever dream. His pulse quickened as he and Thripp descended a stairway into pitch darkness, their electric torches wavering over moth-eaten lagging and sagging service pipes. The boiler room was a claustrophobic cellar dominated by a gigantic furnace. Tommo's body was lying awkwardly just inside its massive door, his body curling around a dark-handled knife. Diaz overheard a medic announcing that the lad was estimated to have been dead for around thirty-six hours.

Diaz stepped away from the others to try to tune into what the FBI called the indelible traces left by the killer. The room itself was distracting; its sooty airless walls had a grotesque sense of style as dramatic as a film set. Like Crossley's murder scene, he deduced that it had been deliberately chosen by the murderer as a statement, though what message it was relaying he couldn't yet decipher.

That description Lorraine had given of Doctor Voss rang in his mind. The hedonist, the hippy rule-breaker who was cloaked in a protective habit of discretion and secrecy. If there was an event that had heralded these murders at Windwell, maybe it was as simple as the arrival of the hospital's director himself. Not for the first time, he felt an urge to warn Lorraine against Voss.

'Sir, we've found this video cassette inside some recording equipment.'

A scene of crime officer, Malcolm, held the black plastic tape casing in gloved fingers.

Diaz inspected it. 'We should get some prints off that. And check the recording equipment for dabs, too.'

'Plenty of cigarette butts on the floor, too,' said Thripp.

'Lots of them are old, though we're bagging them all,'

said Malcolm. 'And we've got a good selection of human hair. Including some long blonde ones, sir.'

'Good work,' said Thripp. 'I bet they're a match to Oona Finn. Ring me as soon as you can about the prints on the knife.'

The small space was now crowded by the arrival of a police photographer and others in protective suits. Thripp scowled and made for the door. 'We'll leave them to it.'

Once they were back in the tunnel, Thripp asked Diaz his usual starter question: 'First thoughts?'

'Only two, sir. Tommo's murder suggests a further link to the Campbell inquiry, as he was the lad's guard that night.'

'Very different MO,' Thripp challenged.

'But why else murder him here? We're just a few yards from where Campbell was killed. We should check out Campbell's murder scene too, while we're here.'

Diaz recalled the room plan in the appendices of the inquiry document and led the way to a row of wet and mouldy cells. He opened the unmarked iron door standing next door to a sign for Cell 16.

'So where's the sign? A souvenir hunter on the prowl?' observed Thripp.

'In a way. Professor Leadbetter's taken the sign to add to his Black Museum of Criminal Curiosities.'

Inside the claustrophobic space, their torches revealed that the wooden board that must have served as Campbell's bed had rotted and been stained with graffiti. There was no window, just a caged electric light fitting, no longer receiving power.

Thripp grimaced. 'It makes Cell 17 in the new place look like the Ritz.'

Diaz picked up a small posy of flowers from an alcove in the wall. The blooms were desiccated and stiff, tied up in a scrap of paper.

'An offering of sorts?' suggested Thripp, when Diaz shone his torch onto it. 'Bag it up and give it to the SOCOs. Then get them to give this cell a going-over as well. Let's go and find out what Tommo's girlfriend has to say about it all, shall we?'

CHAPTER TWENTY-SEVEN

It was Enid Finn, the hospital's treasurer, who opened the door of the large double-fronted house on Windwell's high street.

Thripp had interviewed her after Crossley's death, but this was Diaz's first meeting with Oona's mother. Her skin was rather lined and she was almost emaciated, but she still had the remnants of a girlish charm in her greying blonde hair and blue-green eyes. She invited them both into a scruffy dining room that smelt of stale cigarette smoke and alcohol.

'Cup of tea?' Glumly stoical was how Diaz would describe her. They let her busy herself in the kitchen while they looked around the room. There was a photo on the pine mantelpiece of a younger Enid looking very different in a miniskirt and knee boots. And lots of school portraits of Oona, transforming from cherubic toddler to a teenager with a fierce stare and a penchant for cheesecloth and jingly-jangly jewellery. Diaz ran his eye over the shelves of a bookcase. Lots of accounting textbooks and bound

folders, alongside mild occult stuff: *The Golden Bough,
Wiccan Magic, Fortune-telling Using Tarot Cards*. Enid
returned with a tray and a nervous smile that didn't extend
to the rest of her face.

'Oona's very upset. Brian came round earlier to tell us
the terrible news, poor man. Go easy on her, won't you?'

Diaz to nodded his head without thinking. 'Was Oona
out with him last night?' he asked.

Enid sat down on a hard chair at the small dining table.
'I think so. She comes and goes, she's a grown-up.'

Oona's feet sounded on the stairs and a moment later
she entered the room blinking, like a performer entering
a floodlit arena. Her mum poured her some tea and made
comforting sounds. Diaz thought that without her face
paint Oona looked what she was, a sulky teenager with
spots and an overindulged sense of her own importance.
Even though it was now two in the afternoon she was
playing the invalid, wearing fluffy slippers and a white lacy
nightdress under a dressing gown.

'OK,' she said at last, sighing as if she were a very old
lady. 'What do you want to know?'

Diaz had his notebook out on his lap. Behind the play-
acting he thought he glimpsed the residue of her former
confidence.

'Thank you for agreeing to see us, Miss Finn,' Diaz said.
'We wouldn't bother you at this difficult time if it wasn't
important. Firstly, can you tell us where you were and with
whom last evening?'

'I was with Tommo,' she said flatly. 'We went to the
woods. It's what we usually do.'

'What time was this?'

'I waited at the bus stop for him to come back from the rugby.'

'The bus stop near the old asylum?'

'Yes. He was about ten minutes late. Then we went to our usual spot.'

Diaz glanced over to where Enid was staring blankly into the gas fire. 'For . . . a bit of privacy?'

A faint smile twitched her lips. 'That's right.'

'And what happened then?'

'Not much. I had Mum's car so I drove him back to town and came home.'

'What time was that?'

She shrugged. 'Maybe ten. I was very tired.'

'And where did you drop him in town?'

'He said he might get a pint somewhere. I dropped him near the Spar shop.'

'Miss Finn. Will you answer this question very carefully.' She raised clear blue eyes that showed no signs of excessive crying. 'Do you ever visit the tunnels under the old asylum?'

'Me? I have done. Yes.'

'Did you visit them last night?'

'I have been to them but not last night, no.'

Her convoluted grammatical construction suggested to Diaz that she was lying.

'Did Tommo go there, or say he was going to meet anyone there?'

She shrugged. 'No. But he might have done.'

He continued to gaze at her. There was the faintest blush now on her cheeks and above the neckline of her lacy nightie.

She lifted her head defiantly. 'Tommo probably went to

see his mates at the social club. Why don't you ask them?'

He let the question hang unanswered.

'Your boyfriend told us that he was upset about his name being connected with Mr Crossley's death. What did he tell you about that?'

She swallowed and tried a bright smile that looked badly askew.

'Nothing much. I mean he did go on about it, but it was all a load of . . . you know, a load of rubbish. It got a bit much for me, actually. I kept hearing all these accusations at work and I didn't know who to believe. I told him I was sick of it, I didn't want to hear any more about it.'

'We need to talk to your friend Ella. Can you call her down here?' A definite flicker of alarm crossed the girl's features.

'She's gone back to her parents.' She was clearly defensive now. 'She got a message that her mum was ill or something. Said she'd be back in a few days.'

'Can you give me her address?'

'She didn't leave an address.'

'Is that right?' The look Diaz shot at her was disbelievingly cynical. He tried to gather more facts about this Ella character, but it was like pulling teeth. They had met on the Bradford bus, she said, and Ella lived on a farm somewhere out in the wilds.

'Very strange,' he observed, 'that this friend of yours disappears the night your boyfriend is stabbed to death?'

'Is it? It's not a crime, you know,' she blustered. 'Going home to your parents.'

Suddenly Thripp broke in, in his gentlest manner. 'I don't want to upset you, Oona. But was there anything going on between Tommo and Ella?'

'God, no. Tommo and Ella, that's hilarious!'

Thripp hesitated, took off his glasses and polished the lenses.

'There's no need to get upset. These are just routine enquiries to find out where everyone was last night.'

When she looked up again, she had regrouped and went on the offensive.

'Your insinuations are making me uncomfortable, and I don't even know anything.' Suddenly her features slackened. On cue her face contorted, and she pulled out a tissue from her pocket but only twisted it round her fingers. They gave her a few long moments but no actual liquid leaked from her eyes.

'How long is this going to take?' she demanded. This was followed by a theatrical sigh. 'We'd really like to know when we can have the funeral, you know? Brian and me, we need to mourn.'

Diaz felt increasingly angry. He had hoped Oona would admit to at least knowing something about Tommo's death. And why should she get so upset about this Ella girl?

When Thripp picked up the questioning again, it gave him a chance to really observe Oona.

'How long had you been in a relationship with Tommo?'

'About six months.' She shrugged, which communicated a decided indifference to her boyfriend.

'And how was it going between the two of you?'

'It was fine.' There was a deeper blush now on her cheeks and throat. 'I really don't know what you want me to say,' she said at last. 'To be honest I feel you're hassling me with no reason.' She wiped her nose.

The normally gentle Thripp fired his last question like a bullet. 'Are you telling us the truth about last night? If you're not, you may be in very deep trouble.'

Oona's face formed a mask of hostility. 'Yes, of course I'm telling the truth. Now, have you finished? I want to see Brian. I'd really rather you left now.'

'You'll be pleased to know we've finished with you for today. Do feel free to go.' He stood and addressed the girl's mother. 'Mrs Finn, would you mind if we take a look at where Ella was sleeping? It's very important that we contact all the young people Tommo knew.'

Oona stared at him as if he'd just slapped her. 'Is that really—'

Enid overrode her daughter's objections and ushered them all up the stairs. They reached a landing and then followed her up a further narrow wooden stairway to a low attic room in the eaves. The bed was neatly made and the surfaces were clean. Enid watched them from the doorway with Oona peering over her shoulder.

Diaz checked under the pillow and searched the drawers. Nothing. Then he spotted a duffel bag stuffed under the dressing table. 'Is that Ella's?'

'It's not ours. So it must be,' said Enid.

He laid out the contents across the dressing table and then carefully bagged up a comb and some paper tissues.

'Thank you. You've been most helpful, Mrs Finn.' As if as an afterthought, he addressed Oona. 'Do you have a comb, please?'

'Me?'

'As I said, it's just a routine means of verifying who was where last night.'

209

'Go and get it,' Enid hissed.

Oona appeared a few minutes later with a face like thunder and a comb, which Diaz asked her to drop into an evidence bag.

'It's nothing to worry about.' Thripp was a picture of reassurance.

As Diaz walked back through the hall the DCI lifted a quizzical eyebrow. Diaz shook his head.

'Check the Ella girl out,' the chief inspector directed him when they got back in the car. 'And get statements from anyone on or near the Bradford bus stop last night. Someone somewhere must have seen something.'

CHAPTER TWENTY-EIGHT

Monday 17th to Wednesday 19th October

Parveen phoned Lorraine at the cottage to tell her about Tommo's murder. There was almost no information, only that the police were all over the old asylum and had found the lad's body down in the tunnels. Lorraine's first thought was of Diaz, and his idea that Tommo had killed Kevin. Was it a revenge killing? Then she remembered Brian, poor man, doomed to have his only son die amidst all the publicity and horror of a murder case. She had intended to explore the remainder of the team's profiles at that week's team-building session, but knew it would be impossible to go ahead with it now. Brian couldn't possibly hope to attend. She made an appointment to speak to Voss, who was no longer taking calls while he managed the crisis.

On Wednesday she found Voss looking despondent, uncharacteristically slumped at his desk with a cup of coffee cooling beside him.

'Any news from the police?'

He made an effort to straighten up and look more lively.

'No, I've just sent them my thoughts on the possibility that a patient attacked the lad. I know I confided my worries about security breaches, but no way – I can't believe a patient made his way to the old asylum.' He gestured at her to speak. 'How are things with you?'

'Confusing,' she said.

'And we've got the team-building session in fifteen minutes. I suppose we'd better go. I've had a message that Brian is going to turn up.'

'What?' Lorraine took a deep breath, feeling she had to speak up or burst. 'Jan. I have to tell you, I'm not sure I'm up to this. Team-building with someone who's just experienced a violent death in the family. It's way beyond my experience.'

He was watching her intently, as if his shining eyes could interpret every blink and breath. She wondered what he saw: panic, anxiety, failure. No doubt she would be sent packing back to Morgan with a black mark against her whole career.

To her surprise he said, 'To be honest, I'm extremely grateful for the sessions you've taken so far and your good sense today. I agree that it's best if I simply say a few words. Today is indeed beyond the scope of anything you were sent here to do.'

In the psychology seminar room, only Parveen was waiting for them. She had made a pot of tea and Lorraine was grateful to her. Next, Enid arrived, walking unsteadily and smelling of spirits. When the door sprang open again, everyone looked up in alarm.

'Brian.' Voss spoke in a neutral tone. 'You are very welcome. You wish to join us?'

212

'If you don't mind.' Brian's voice was a painful croak. 'I can't stay at home on me own today.'

Lorraine poured him a cup of tea, and they waited in silence until Voss began to speak in a subdued tone. 'The last fortnight has been an extraordinarily sad and confusing time for all of us. Yet in the midst of this maelstrom, I find it profoundly positive that we are all here, meeting together. Grief at the loss of a loved one is a lonely process. In the workplace we generally feel pressure to keep a frigid silence about our feelings, to lose our authenticity and hide our unruly emotions.

'If these meetings are, as we agree, about trust, we must not ignore Brian's sorrow over this wicked act. We must not pretend Tommo never existed. We should not judge a person's grief as needing a socially acceptable form, beyond which the bereaved should be blamed for not having sufficiently healed. Now, I would like to ask you all to join hands in silence for one minute. For when the shadows blind us, we all need the comfort of the hand in the darkness.'

Lorraine slipped her left hand into Enid's bony grasp and her right hand inside Brian's ape-like fist. She closed her eyes, willing goodness to circulate amongst them. It was a long sixty seconds and behind her closed eyelids Lorraine saw again a spiky-haired youth running across the road, laughter brightening his face, and then the horror of discovering Kevin Crossley, glassy-eyed, with a red cord hanging around his neck. Convulsively, she tightened her grip on both the hands she held. Gently, Brian stroked her knuckles with his thumb, as if it were she who needed solace.

'Time's up,' Voss said softly. When she opened her eyes they burnt with unshed tears. She wasn't alone. Both Enid and Parveen were wiping their eyes. Even Doctor Voss was blinking and looking away. Brian's head dropped low in his hands.

'Thank you,' said Brian in a choking voice. 'You're a good man, Doctor Jan.' He stroked his barrel-like thighs, as if he were wiping something guilty from his hands. 'I'm sorry, I'm going to have to burden you all with a confession. There is something I need to share before I go and tell the police everything I know.'

CHAPTER TWENTY-NINE

'It were the phone call every parent dreads. A copper ringing you to say your kid has had a motorbike accident. Tommo were just eighteen when he hit a tree in the fog and were rushed to intensive care. *Just survive*, that was all I thought at first. And he did survive. He came home and everything seemed all right. It were the little things I started to notice: him throwing a drink at a stranger because he lost a game of pool, too many issues with patients, losing his rag over odd things, mishearing what people said, going mad because someone told him he couldn't smoke. Poor impulse control, like he were regressing back to being a little kid again. I kept it quiet because he'd passed his exams before the accident, though I wouldn't have bet on him ever passing them again. His IQ dropped but I told meself it were just part of a long recovery.'

'Oh, Brian,' Enid murmured.

Brian's long sigh was more of a groan. 'That were nothing compared to what happened. Most of you won't know it, but Campbell were a pain in the arse and everybody on the ward knew it. He moaned all the time, and if he didn't get what he wanted he threatened to top 'imself. He treated us all like skivvies. He needled my boy till he couldn't help himself. It's no excuse, but it's true.

'That night when we started our shift, Campbell had been put on suicide watch. So I set Tommo to keep an eye on him. "Just phone me if he plays up," I said, and went off to check the other wards. I didn't know that Campbell had just heard that all the computer training he were looking forward to had been suspended 'cos of budget cuts. He were in a right dark place. And he took it out on my boy. Campbell was smart, he'd taunt Tommo till he snarled like a bear chained to a post. He knew my boy were damaged. Called him a thicko, and a daddy's boy, stuff like that, until we'd have to restrain Tommo from going on the rampage.

'I take the blame. I've carried it all these years. When I came back to check on them Tommo had disappeared. Campbell were dead, all beaten up and strangled to death. It were the worst shock of my life – to know that my son had turned into a killer. Campbell had been battered to a pulp. There were blood everywhere. And that red cord pulled tight round his neck.'

Brian looked up at them with ghastly red-rimmed eyes. 'I were like a robot. I locked all the doors leading back to the wards. I found Tommo outside in the gardens, shaking like he were having a fit, and rambling on about rubbish. He were in a right bad way. So I dosed him up with sedatives, and then we rehearsed a story. There would be fingerprints, I knew that, so I made sure my fingerprints were mixed up in his blood.'

216

Brian stopped to wipe his nose on the back of his hand.

'The blood, it were still warm and tacky, like glue. It's true what they say. You feel you'll never scrub that guilty blood off your hands. I had a go at CPR on the lad's body. It were right sick-making. And I'd seen Tommo's knuckles were raw and bruised. It didn't look good.

'Still, it were only one in the morning, so I got my lad to wash himself down and change his uniform. Then I punched him in the face and he fell over like a log, his lights went out. He lay on the floor outside of Cell 17 looking like my little lad again. Then I set up the alarm and when the others come running I told them there must've been a break-in. Campbell were dead and Tommo had been attacked. It weren't a great story. I know the tribunal lot didn't really believe it, but it stopped them sending Tommo down. I couldn't let that happen. He's all I've ever had. I were his dear old dad.'

He set his big hands down on his knees and said, 'I'll get off now, to see the chief inspector.'

Voss leant forward and tapped Brian's arm. 'Would you like me to come with you? As your friend?'

Brian stood up, his whole body seeming to droop. 'No, you're all right. But thank you, Jan.'

The four of them sat in silence for a long while. Then Lorraine made another pot of tea and they made murmuring conversation, strangely reluctant to return to the unforgiving world beyond that room.

In the end, Diaz appeared at the door and stood gravely in front of them.

'How's Brian?' Voss asked.

'I'm afraid we've had to take him into custody.'

'Why?' Enid asked plaintively.

'Perverting the course of justice. I'm afraid that covering up a murder is a very serious matter.'

'Oh no. Poor Brian.' Enid looked distraught. 'Hasn't he suffered enough? Tommo's death is already a kind of natural justice.'

'Well, given the tragic circumstances, Mr Ogden may be considered for bail. That's all I can tell you at the moment.'

Voss rose to leave, and the others began to follow. But as Lorraine made for the door, Diaz gestured at her to wait behind. 'I need to check something with you, Miss Quick.'

When they were alone, he poured himself a cup of tea and sank into an empty chair.

'Any idea yet who killed Tommo?' she asked.

He shook his head. 'We have got a couple of leads. Down in the tunnels we found a video cassette that I'd like you to watch. Someone was filming down there and I'd like to know if you recognise one of the people in it. It's frustrating, that it's not Windwell equipment and there are no useful fingerprints on it. I'm afraid the sequence is rather disturbing.'

Together, they pulled out a large TV monitor in a wheeled cabinet, and Diaz loaded the video cassette and rewound it. When it ran, the screen showed mottled darkness, illuminated by what looked like a couple of candle flames.

'It's the boiler room down in the tunnels,' Diaz murmured.

The disembodied voice of a child whispered, 'I'm back.'

In response, Tommo's voice reached them, asking, 'You

trying to creep me out? Put the fucking lights on.' The lens of the camera juddered across dark space and then focused on a vast square door that was slowly opening.

'Fuck. What's going on?' Tommo asked, clearly agitated. Lorraine had spotted what was freaking him out. Someone was pushing the door further open from its other side and with a gasp, she identified a terrifying face. The figure of a ghoulish woman was emerging from the vast door. As if it were Tommo's own terrified eyes, the camera lens swivelled closer to the figure and Lorraine started back, involuntarily gripping the armrests of her chair. The woman's face was a skull in the darkness, her eyes two black sockets and her hair a snake-like mass of unruly strands. The high ghoulish voice whispered, 'You did it, didn't you? I'm here to see justice done . . .'

The mic picked up Tommo's harsh breathing and muttered protests. 'What are you fucking playing at, hey? You are joking, right?'

The lens remained fixed on the ghoulish figure as she slowly advanced towards the camera. The woman was dressed in Victorian style, with a smudge of white at her throat and a shawl round her shoulders. In her greenish hands she raised a long-bladed knife.

'Get away from me. I can't take no more!' Tommo's voice rose to a shriek. Then, with a muffled bang and reverberating crack, the scene blacked out. Lorraine made to speak, but Diaz gestured towards the screen. For a few seconds confused images danced across the screen. The camera recorded a wave of moving blackness, a hazy image of a brown boot, followed by the close-up pallor of Tommo's hand clawing at the floor. Apparently, the camcorder had fallen to the floor and was picking up the scene at ground level. They could hear Tommo crying like a baby.

Next Lorraine registered a slicing sound and an expulsion of air. Sickened, she understood that though she was being spared the sight of Tommo's murder, she must still endure the sounds of his last moments. Another swishing slice and a grunt of anguish. Then another wet blow. On screen, Tommo's hand scrabbled back and forth along the ground. Next, a hoarse struggle for breath. She dropped her head into her hands. The video player clicked as Diaz stopped the tape.

Lorraine had unconsciously pushed herself as far back into her chair as possible.

Now she released her muscles with a tiny moan. 'What was that thing?'

'I think it was meant to be Sally Finn. A patient who died down there years ago and some believe haunted the place. More to the point, I'd like to know who was playing her.'

Lorraine released a gasp of high-pitched laughter. 'Yes, of course.' She was still waiting for her heart rate to slow down. She got up and poured herself a glass of water. She took a long draught and said, 'Poor Tommo. Who would do that? I don't think that creature was Oona.'

'Neither do I. We found nylon strands of a long black wig. Even if she wore that, Oona's face is very different.'

'Why pretend to be a ghost?' Lorraine asked. 'What's with all the horror references?'

'This is who we think she's trying to imitate.' He held out a black and white photo of a female with similar unruly hair and deep, shadowed eye sockets. 'Sally Finn was a vulnerable Windwell patient who died due to neglect. Just like Campbell.' Lorraine took the print and studied it, repelled by its raw depiction of insanity.

'Do you recognise the girl in the video?' he asked.

Lorraine shook her head. Yet there had been something odd in the clip. Something incongruous.

'Can I see that last confused bit again?' He got up and rewound it. This time, Lorraine could spot the artificiality of the wig and murmured, 'She's wearing black and green make-up.'

She watched Tommo's mounting fear and his halting questions.

'Who is he speaking to?' she asked Diaz

'We don't know.' There were crashing sounds as the camcorder fell to the ground. That sweep of undulating blackness must have been the ghost woman's skirt, she decided. And the boot—

'Stop it there.' Diaz fumbled with the buttons and then rewound the frames very slowly.

'Stop.' One brown boot showed for an instant, beneath the swirls of skirt. There was a black heel and on its brown leather surface she could just make out elaborate curls and points.

'Cowboy boots. Can you go back to the girl's face and pause it?'

Lorraine studied the spectral face, trying to ignore the theatrical paint to trace what lay below it.

'We found some hair in that giant furnace that she was hiding in.'

'Let me guess. Shoulder-length and brown.'

'Yeah. Who is she?'

'The night I arrived here, I saw four young people hanging around on the main road near the asylum. Two of them, Oona and Tommo, seemed stoned. Oona ran straight in front of me; I nearly knocked her over. And Tommo banged on my car's bonnet.'

'You mean that Monday Kevin went missing?'

'Yes.'

Diaz scoffed in annoyance. 'Oona spun us a yarn that she was alone with Tommo in the woods. It never held up. Can you describe the other two people?'

'An Asian lad in a white shirt. And another younger girl in jeans and cowboy boots.'

'What time was this?'

'I got to the cottage about eight-thirty. So, eight-twenty, I'd say. The second girl was smaller than Oona and younger, I think.'

'That's really helpful. Oona's friend was apparently called Ella. She stayed at Enid's house for a few weeks. Almost no one else here has ever seen her, save for Oona, Enid and, apparently, Tommo. And now you.'

'Do you think she befriended Oona to get close to Tommo and kill him?'

'We can't find a surname or an address. And now she's vanished from Windwell. For all our digging around, she might as well be a ghost with no name.'

CHAPTER THIRTY

Lorraine sensed a distant echo in the back of her mind. What did a ghost have to do with this? She considered asking Voss for his advice but he was sinking under a mountain of work. Consulting the hospital's internal directory, she found a number for Doctor Julian Norris, Research Psychologist, a colleague Voss had described as an ally. Doctor Norris sounded surprised when she asked if she could see him, but invited her to his office at once.

He was a tall, raw-boned young man with longish brown curls and John Lennon-style round spectacles with lightly tinted grey lenses. On her arrival he looked up from marking a pile of psychometric tests of a type she didn't recognise.

'How can I help you, Miss Quick?'

'Please, call me Lorraine.'

He leant back, slinging his arm along the back of his chair, and nodded.

She said with her warmest smile, 'I know this is a strange

question, but what can you tell me about the role of ghosts in psychology?'

'That is a peculiar question.' He stared over her head in deliberate thought. 'In the past, ghosts were often symbols of restorative justice. If we look at Shakespeare's plays, ghosts generally intervene when an offence has been committed that would not otherwise be discovered. If you think about Macbeth, Banquo's ghost haunts him until he can scarcely bear his guilt.'

'So a ghost can be a symbol of a guilty conscience?' Lorraine asked.

'Yes, the guilty conscience that just won't leave you in peace. Yet of course, much depends on the context.'

'Well, the context here is of an individual making a violent attack while impersonating a ghost.'

Doctor Norris hesitated, then said, 'Is it possible the motive is the same? To haunt an offender in pursuit of justice?'

'Perhaps.'

Doctor Norris got up and started rifling through his filing cabinet. 'Yes, here it is. I read a research paper recently about persons whom we call "haunted", a specific personality type who reports seeing ghosts and experiencing haunted houses. In extreme cases their obsessions become infamous, attracting what the press calls poltergeist events. Whether or not this is related to play-acting as a ghost or not, I can't say. But they all share the occurrence of transliminality, a term for hypersensitivity to imagery and ideas rising from the unconscious. Think of the visions experienced by mystics, or artists who tap into astonishing patterns and images. How old is the subject?'

Lorraine recalled her brief glimpse of Ella: a pallid, skinny teenager. 'Less than twenty. Maybe as young as sixteen.'

'There's a theory that repressed teenage girls undergoing extreme anxiety are more likely to manifest as these so-called haunters. An example that springs to mind is the Stephen King horror story about Carrie, a shy and unpopular teenage girl who wreaks psychokinetic chaos at her senior prom.'

'So far as I know, the suspect was also shy and withdrawn. Almost no one ever saw her. She scarcely left the building where she was staying.'

Doctor Norris murmured in agreement. 'That fits with the personality profile of a haunter: anxious, insecure, yet at times capable of great hostility, dissociation and even violence.'

He hesitated, and she felt he was examining her closely, his expression hidden behind the grey cast of his glasses. Abruptly, he said, 'I have a client waiting.'

Then just as she reached the door, he added a spiteful coda. 'You mentioned that the subject attacked someone. I've just remembered another correlate with transliminal traits – a positive link to psychoticism. You may be out of your depth. I'd stick to office work if I were you. Leave the clinical analysis to the professionals.'

CHAPTER THIRTY-ONE

Thursday 20th October

Diaz was speeding towards Burnley with Laddo beside him at the wheel. He stared thoughtfully through the windscreen, blind to the barren passes scattered with farmsteads and barns, his system wired at the prospect of making an arrest at last. After leaving Lorraine, he had persuaded Thripp to let him bring Oona Finn in to view the video. Though she had turned on the waterworks at first, the tears didn't last long.

At her first sighting of the ghostly figure on screen, her mouth fell open. 'That's my stuff she's wearing.'

'Who is she?' he asked.

'That's Ella. What's she up to?' As the clip ran on, she at least had the dignity to make sympathetic noises as her former boyfriend's ordeal of terror transformed into the scene of his death.

Diaz switched the machine off and confronted her. 'So what's all this about?'

Oona's face was flushed and her eyes avoided his. 'Listen,'

she said in the manner of a wary confession. 'It could be this. One night Tommo made a grab for Ella. She freaked out. When I first met her, I gathered something pretty heavy had happened to her and she ran away from home.'

'What did Tommo do to her?'

She shook her head dismissively. 'Nothing much. Just felt her up. He didn't go all the way. It was me who stopped him.'

'So where did this happen?'

Oona looked up at the ceiling, a giveaway of someone consulting a memory, and judging whether or not to speak of it. 'Look, I know we shouldn't have been there.'

His growing anger was hard to hide. 'If you keep wasting more time I'll have to charge you. Get on with it.'

'OK, OK. We were in the old asylum. It was a cool place for parties.'

'What did Ella say about Tommo molesting her?'

'Not much. She just packed up and left. I did warn her about him. I mean, I'm sorry he died and all that, but he was a total headcase. It was Tommo's idea to film down there. A sort of protest against the asylum being demolished.'

'So what happened?'

'I don't know. I wasn't there. I'd had enough of Tommo's craziness.' Now she was staring hard at him, maybe assessing how he was taking all this.

'You expect me to believe that, Oona? We found black candle wax on the floor. And some strands of your distinctive bleached hair.'

'I never said I hadn't been there. I did. I used to visit the boiler room to honour Sally, my ancestor. In fact, that's what bugs me, that Ella and Krish messed around with the memory of my ancestor, like she was some sort of mad witch.'

Krish. That had to be the Asian lad Lorraine had mentioned.

'Tell me about Krish.'

'He brought the recording gear along. Tommo told me he's part of some criminal gang with his uncle. They import knock-off gear from India. I never trusted him either, he used to bring drugs over, really strong stuff. And when he heard that Tommo had been feeling up his girl—'

'So Ella and Krish were in a relationship?'

'Yeah. Krish went mental about it. Oh God, you don't think they lured Tommo down there to kill him, do you?'

Diaz watched her pink fleshy face for signs of anxiety. If she was a liar, she was a very relaxed one.

'Where can I find this Krish?'

'I don't know. But Tommo has a corkboard on his bedroom wall where he pins stuff like phone numbers. He kept Krish's number there.'

Now they were descending the valley road, where a mishmash of once grand civic buildings and abandoned mills dominated the town of Burnley. Laddo turned the car towards an area where row upon row of terraced houses stood like toy blocks, raised in tiers up the hillside. Diaz pulled out the business card he'd found bearing the name 'Krish Khan' and a phone number, advertising Khan-Elek, Global Traders in Electrical Goods, Unit 9, Pike Industrial Estate, Burnley.

Khan-Elek was not a shop but a flat-roofed trading unit, its windows obscured by metal grilles. The door was solid, securely locked and operated by a buzzer system.

'Hiya,' said Diaz, leaning into the intercom by the doorbell, speaking in his broadest Mancunian accent. 'I need a video camera, good price.'

They were buzzed into a room stacked with boxes. A heavy man with a bushy moustache and black-framed glasses that magnified anxious, bulbous eyes looked up at them in alarm. Laddo blocked the man's exit from the counter area.

'Where's Krish Khan?' demanded Diaz.

'I don't know that name.'

'Come off it. I'm guessing from what the trading standards guys told me that you're his uncle, Japa Khan. You do know that importing and dealing in counterfeit goods is against the law?' Diaz picked up a small box badly printed with the words 'Soni Walkman', then cast it aside dismissively.

'Here's the deal. We can lock you up for ten years and confiscate your entire stock.' The man stared down at the counter, utterly deflated. 'Your lad's in big trouble. We just need to know where he is.'

The man pointed back towards the door through which they had just entered. 'The function room at the social club. Just turn left round the corner.'

Diaz and Laddo entered the club unchallenged and followed a sign to the function room. It was decorated like nowhere he had ever seen in his life. The walls were draped with red, gold and purple gauzy fabrics, the furniture was gilded gold, and massive pillars bearing golden elephants were hung with tentlike curtains. A group of musicians in scarlet costumes were chatting in a corner, surrounded by drums and pipes and other paraphernalia.

'We're looking for Krish Khan,' said Diaz, holding up his warrant card. An older man stared at them in bewilderment and shook his head. Then a younger lad in a red turban said in a strong Indian accent, 'You just miss him. He get drinks from the car park.' He pointed back to the door through which they'd just entered.

Diaz and Laddo sped off at once, back to the car park where Diaz remembered seeing a large white transit van.

As soon as the two coppers had left the room Krish dashed to the fire exit, only pausing to pull off his turban and embroidered shervani and stuff them in a waste bin. Then, dressed only in jeans and a singlet, he sped out into the back alley and started to run at full pelt. Convinced he could evade the cops, he wound his way up narrow cobbled ginnels that intersected rows of shabby terraced houses, and then darted across a busy road until he reached the back of Khan-Elek. For a few moments he hung back and watched the rear entrance, before cautiously darting inside a small wooden door.

'Ella.' He kept his voice low. Ella appeared at the entrance to the storeroom.

'What are you—'

'Shush. The cops came to the club. Get your stuff.'

'But shouldn't we just—'

'This is it, Ella. They're here to arrest me.'

They were stuffing a few bags with clothes when Krish's uncle descended on them.

'You know what trouble you bring here? That policeman say ten year in jail for fake goods. I take you in and you ruin us all.'

'I haven't got time for all this, Uncle. Can you lend me some cash?'

'Me? And where my Betamax gone? You going to get it back?'

'Sorry uncle. It were an emergency. I'll pay you back. One day'

'No, you never come back.' Krish's uncle marched to the door and held it wide for them to leave. They brushed past him, Ella holding back tears. She had been grateful for a bolthole these last few nights and now she would be on the streets, homeless and hunted.

'Where are we headed? The bus station?' Even to herself, her voice sounded desperate.

She risked a glance at Krish; his face was tight with rage. He reached into his pocket and pulled out his uncle's keys.

'When I say it, run for the van,' he hissed. She hesitated for a second, aware of Uncle Japa still standing at the back door, seeing them off his land. They walked a few more paces, then Krish shouted, 'Go!' He legged it to the driver's side and swung the passenger door open. She swung up into the seat. With a turn of the ignition key and foot to the pedal, Krish set the van roaring off as fast as its wheels could spin.

'*Arey*,' Krish murmured, his hands gripping the wheel, searching the mirror for any trace of the cops. In happier moments he had taught Ella that '*arey*' meant 'oh my', but today it sounded more like a wail of despair.

CHAPTER THIRTY-TWO

Lorraine's mum had sent her a confusing message to ring an obscure foreign number. Now she walked to a public phone box near the Spar shop with a couple of fifty-pence pieces and a shiny new pound coin in her pocket. There was no light at Diaz's bedroom window; he was still working, she thought dismally. After a few clicks and burrs, the phone connection was made and like magic, Lily picked up a phone somewhere in Germany.

'Hi, how's the tour going?'

'Bloody exhausting. I need to sleep for a month when I get back.'

'Are you going down well? What are the crowds like?'

'Not bad. Course, everyone's there for Gothenburg. But we're staying on another week, at least.'

'That's fantastic. Great review in Berlin, though. "Spellbinding."'

'Actually, there's been some interest from a record label in France. A single. "Path of Stars". They were asking whose name to credit on the label. I don't think there's much cash upfront but you never know.'

'Bloody hell. Well, it's Dale's guitar melody. OK, I wrote the words. But we can share it equally with you and whoever drums, so far as I care.'

'OK. I'll let them know.'

'What about recording it?' Lorraine asked.

'Well, they'll organise some recording time.'

'Good, but I mean I want to play on it.'

'Course you're playing on it. You can sing it if you want.'

'Lily, what's up?'

'Gogo's a complete disaster. Even if she turns up on time she's usually off her head. She's a fucking nightmare.'

'God, I'm so sorry.'

'Yeah, well. I hope you've got plenty of holidays to get this recording done.'

'Bucketloads.'

Lorraine's mouth slowly formed a secret smile as the beeps sounded the end of their call. Soon she'd be away from Windwell and recording with the band. And soon there'd be a proper vinyl record of 'Path of Stars' in the shops. Starting to walk back she sung it softly under her breath, imagining lights in the sky above Windwell, of cosmic highways that might take her into unknown worlds.

She didn't check on Diaz again. Instead she went to Voss's villa and found the key in the turquoise pot. The house was very still and airless as she lifted the lid on the piano. With new confidence she picked out hesitant notes, trying to find a tune that did justice to a newly arrived idea in her head. When she struck the right chord it was like a pathway opening before her. She was feeling happy as something new, never ever heard before in the world, emerged. This was what she loved: the chance to work at her music, practise her fingerwork, escape into creating something less mundane than hospital procedures.

She didn't hear anyone come into the room. The sudden pressure on her shoulders scared her so badly that she gave a little scream. She twisted around and saw it was Voss.

'Christ, it's you.'

His hands remained on her shoulders with a gentle pressure.

'I do like you being here. The house feels complete.'

A sudden pressure dropped on the crown of her head and then vanished. Had he just kissed her? She turned around, fully anticipating more of the same, meeting his eyes, parting her lips. Voss tensed and stepped back away from her. Lorraine's gaze narrowed. What weird vibe had she just picked up there? Sometimes she just didn't get him at all.

She told herself that he was an important man, almost famous really. He was probably still weighing up the idea of a relationship. Or maybe he was comparing her to his current conquest.

He had retreated to the window. 'Your daughter is visiting this weekend. Do feel free to invite her here. I'd love to meet her.'

Lorraine knew that Jas would feel horribly uncomfortable here in this large, silent house.

'I'm sorry, we're pretty tied up with all the activities at the hotel. Archery, canoeing, all the things she's never had a chance to do before.'

'It must be gratifying to watch your child develop new skills.'

God, now he was making Jasmine sound like another of his lab experiments. Nonetheless, she was curious enough about Voss to accept his invitation to stay for dinner. Or maybe she was simply feeling as lonely as he appeared to be, and convinced that Diaz would be working late again. They sat down to a surprisingly accomplished bowl of Italian pasta with ham and cheese. She asked him how his plan to increase therapy sessions was getting on.

'Not good.'

He poured them each a glass of wine and leant back, appraising her. 'Can we extend our usual vow of confidentiality to this conversation?'

'Naturally.' She sipped the delicious wine and settled back in the chair to listen.

'I have a patient here at Windwell who of course I can't name. The man is a lifer, a callous killer of many women. He told everyone that before coming here he was a great success, an actor, the subject of a biography by a top journalist, universally popular. He even flattered me, boasting that at last the government had sent for a superstar expert from Holland to treat him, like a movie star able to afford the best therapist.

'I do feel sympathy for the man. He takes care of himself, he is young and attractive, even charismatic. He spoke of the years he had hoped to live in freedom that were entirely lost to him, the shock of his imprisonment being tantamount to a doctor's verdict of a terminal illness. Recently, I did a little detective work myself. I sent for his personal records. Our alpha male was no superman, but a school dropout, a bankrupt with convictions for fraud. He was an obsessive womaniser, using small ads and contact listings in porn magazines, drawing women to him by deception.

'I confronted him with the facts regarding some of the women he had killed: a girlfriend who had the effrontery to call him a liar, a teenager he raped and murdered after she refused to have sex with him, and a mother earning food for her three children as a prostitute. My patient stuck to that old deluded story I've heard so many times, that it was the women's fault, that they provoked him to murder.

'Then I succeeded in breaking through his cover story. He revisited his childhood for the first time. He had been adopted as a small boy, by a foster mother who cruelly abused him; not sexually, but using physical pain and humiliation. By adolescence he was an outcast, rejected first by his birth mother, and then his foster mother. He became a liar and fraudster, preying on women, and ultimately, a thief of women's lives. He was credibly diagnosed as psychopathic and after his conviction, was placed on the Psychopath Unit in the asylum and later transferred here to Ferris Ward. But in our last therapy session I at last uncovered his true self: a small, pitiable being stripped of his armour of fakery. He admitted the truth. He did hate women. Together we glimpsed a new future for him of understanding, even absolution. With tears in both our eyes we arranged our next session to continue this joyful work, the recovery of a man's true identity.'

Voss looked up suddenly, his eyes alight with fury.

'Then Kevin was murdered and my therapy work was the first thing to be cancelled. My patient is currently in the infirmary after trying to end his life. I let him down and now he won't speak to me.

'He's such a tragic figure. He was the subject of my rant at the last team session. I am here to heal patients. Yet I am condemned to fail them. What if this man truly experienced redemption? Why must he be locked up for ever if he repents of his crimes?'

Lorraine wasn't sure how to respond to Voss's outpouring. Telling him that she was grateful for his candour, she gave the excuse that it was getting late and she needed to leave. Her overwhelming reaction was that she needed to mull over Voss's account very carefully, for Voss's patient was without doubt Windwell's most infamous one, Rob Kessler.

CHAPTER THIRTY-THREE

Friday 21st October

At the incident room, Diaz learnt that a man and woman had walked into the police house at Barnard Castle and announced that they were the parents of Eileen Longthwaite, whom they had seen on the TV news described as Ella. By ten-thirty the couple arrived in a squad car at Burnley nick accompanied by a couple of local coppers. Diaz and Thripp awaited them in the interview room they had commandeered.

Mr Longthwaite arrived in mud-spattered blue dungarees, and his wife was zipped into a nylon chequered housecoat beneath an ancient mackintosh. They both stared around the bare room as if it were somehow offensive to them.

Thripp attempted a charm offensive, hoping their journey had been satisfactory and thanking them for coming forward. Mr Longthwaite mostly kept his eyes on the desk, occasionally darting a rapid suspicious glance at the chief inspector.

'You said you had a photograph of Eileen.'

Longthwaite pulled a school photo from his pocket and slid it across the desk. It revealed an absolutely ordinary teenage girl with clear pale skin, shoulder-length brown hair and nothing else of note.

'Thank you. Detective Sergeant Diaz needs to borrow it for a moment.' Diaz left them and showed the photo to Enid, who was waiting in a side room. She agreed that this was the girl she knew as Ella. On his return, Diaz nodded at Thripp and the chief inspector announced, 'I can confirm that your daughter Eileen was the young woman living here in Windwell. She has been here for approximately three weeks. When did you last see her?'

Mr Longthwaite's bony face and thinning hair resembled an animated skull. 'Aye. It were about three week past.'

'Could you tell us about the circumstances of her departure?'

The couple looked at each other, as if affronted.

Thripp was losing his patience. 'We need to find your daughter urgently. Anything you can tell us will be helpful.'

Mournfully, Mr Longthwaite cleared his throat and began. 'She ran away. Eileen started turning bad about two year past, when she were fifteen. She were staying behind late at school, mucking about in the streets wi' lads, and nicking money out of her mum's purse.'

Thripp nodded. 'I see. What happened next?'

'I took her in hand. Took her out of school before she could shame us even worse.'

'How did she react to that?'

'She were like a wildcat. It were terrible. Tried to run away but I caught her. I brought her home and showed her what for.'

'How did you show her what for?'

Longthwaite brightened up a little. 'She weren't too big to take a belting.'

Diaz signalled that he had a question. 'By belting, do you mean that you struck her with your belt?'

'Aye, I did that.'

'Go on,' Thripp urged.

'She did settle down a bit. Helped with the animals and that. Helped her mam.'

Suddenly, Mrs Longthwaite spoke up. 'Or so we thought.' Her lined face tightened into a scowl.

Her husband shook his head, dolefully. 'It were then that she attacked our Jim.'

'Who's Jim?' Thripp asked.

'A while back I took on some outside help. Jim were me mate's lad. I were training him up and giving him a few bob.'

'She seemed to like him well enough,' Mrs Longthwaite added. 'Two young people. We had hopes to pass the farm on to Jim if he'd keep her in line. But then one morning, we couldn't find Jim. It weren't like him.'

Her husband raised his grimy palm to stop her. 'That's enough. Let me tell 'em. When I found our Jim he were bleeding like a stuck pig. I thought it were an accident. But she'd gone and stabbed him with a pair of shears. A little girl like that, she must be crack-headed. And he were a good lad, he told the hospital it were an accident with a chainsaw. Two week he were at the hospital and now he won't come back again. I lost a good worker there, thanks to that one.'

Thripp leant forward and asked, 'What did Eileen say about the attack?'

'Nowt. She scarpered. Took twenty-two pound from our savings and never showed her face again.'

'And Jim, what's his story?'

Mrs Longthwaite averted her disapproving face. 'We're not saying.'

'If you want us to find your daughter, you must tell us everything you can,' Thripp reminded them.

The couple withdrew into themselves again.

Thripp glared at them. 'I don't wish to charge you with withholding information from the police. But if you continue to be unco-operative I may have to.'

Mr Longthwaite raised a tight fist. 'Hold your horses, you. Jim said—'

His wife interrupted. 'We don't want this going beyond these four walls.'

'Very well. Go on,' Thripp murmured.

The husband told his tale as if spitting out pins. 'Jim told us how he were keen on our girl. He had had hopes of running the farm for us. But she were too wild. She'd been creeping down to the village at night and hanging round with rough lads. And now he couldn't stick with her because she were . . . She were expecting.'

Mrs Longthwaite stared at the blank table, her face rigid.

'And when he told her what he thought about her goings-on, she grabbed my sheep shears and attacked him.' Mr Longthwaite looked up at the pair of them, his pinkish eyes grown round with the drama of the situation.

'And where were you when this attack was happening?'

'At chapel. We go to Bible class every Thursday suppertime.'

'Were there any other people around who might have seen something?'

'No.'

His wife interrupted. 'So what'll happen to Eileen? Will it be all over the papers?'

'That depends, Mrs Longthwaite. Our priority is to find your daughter. Does the name Kevin Crossley mean anything to either of you?'

Both parents shook their heads in bafflement.

'Have either you, or Eileen, ever been to Windwell before?'

'Us? Not likely. We're not barmy.'

'Very well. I'd like you to give Jim's details to Detective Sergeant Diaz, here. We'll have to call in a team of specialists to examine the place where Jim was attacked. Now you are free to set off home, and be ready to give my team access.'

CHAPTER THIRTY-FOUR

Constable Ladlaw steered the car along narrow Yorkshire roads while Diaz brooded over Mr and Mrs Longthwaite's account of their daughter's behaviour. Soon after they had entered the room he had noticed a distinctive smell, reminiscent of cowpats and rancid sweat. He had a city lad's intense dislike of the countryside. Now they were climbing through a barren country of gloomy valleys topped by black brooding crags. Why would anyone choose to live out here in this back of beyond?

Jim Judson lived in Scarsgill, a hamlet clinging to a windswept ridge. His home was a shabby council house tinted green from what he guessed must be the area's incessant rain. To Diaz it was Hicksville, fifteen winding miles from the nearest town. Jim lived with his mum and when they called, was up and about, seemingly recovered from his injuries. He repeated Longthwaite's account of Eileen's unprovoked attack almost word for word, and even lifted his T-shirt and dressing to show three deep cuts.

The lad seemed none too bright and Diaz found him mildly disgusting, with his big feet showing through the holes of his socks and his food-stained jumper. How any girl would fancy that acne-cratered face and those droopy wet lips, he didn't know. He had a go at provoking Jim with hard questioning about his lack of qualifications and prospects, but the lad appeared too dim to rise to the bait. As Jim had no prior police contact, he was scrabbling for anything else to go on.

Next they headed to Thorn Gill Farm, which turned out to be a tumbledown stone farmhouse up a muddy track. A group of ragged sheep nervously watched them arrive and an unseen dog barked out an alarm. Diaz asked Mrs Longthwaite if he could see Eileen's bedroom, and was shown a box room devoid of all the usual signs of occupation by a teenage girl. There were a few religious posters, some worthy books on the shelf, and starkly puritanical clothes hanging in the wardrobe. When he asked Mrs Longthwaite for copies of Eileen's school reports, she was a long time searching through boxes. He glanced at them and found no sign of the behaviourally difficult teenager her parents had described. Instead, her teachers wrote of a hard worker, quiet and well mannered.

Trudging to the barn where the attack had taken place, Diaz told Laddo to wait outside and keep an eye out for the SOCOs. He wanted to be alone as he entered a space which suggested a low stone prison, set with cage-like wooden stalls. Pulleys and ropes hung above his head, while around the walls stood abandoned tractor parts and rusting equipment. It struck him as a man's environment, a place where Mr Longthwaite and Jim Judson would be at home, but not one where seventeen-year-old Eileen would choose to attack a tall and muscular farmhand. Yet, according to the video footage, she had killed Tommo Ogden. He stood very still, remembering the FBI advice to mentally scan a crime scene for evidence of the criminal's personality. Eileen must have been drawn here to act out her feelings of anger or fear. In the theatre of his mind, Diaz placed Jim: six feet tall and of threatening, careless appearance. In fact, there was more than a slight resemblance between Jim and Tommo Ogden, for both were thuggish and thickset. Ella was little over five feet tall, slender and fragile. Yet, as he had seen on the video, she was capable of bearing down on a man while carrying a large and dangerous knife in her hand.

He headed to a ladder leaning against a hayloft. According to Jim, that was where the attack had taken place. He looked for bloodstains but could spot none amongst the dirty straw and mud-spattered cobbles. Diaz played around with various hypotheses. Fear seemed to be the dominant emotion. Maybe Ella had been frightened of being trapped here with Jim on this farm and struck out at him. Or maybe when she confessed her pregnancy to Jim, his rejection of her had provoked her to attack him. Maybe Ella had fallen pregnant to some other village thug, but an attempt to pass off her pregnancy as Jim's responsibility had backfired.

On the other hand, Jim would not be the first young man to react to his girlfriend's pregnancy with violence. What worse pressure could there be upon a couple than the imminent arrival of a baby? He should know. This case was driving him mad, the way it raised unwanted questions in his own troubled mind.

* * *

Back at Windwell, he ran through what he'd found with Thripp. The chief inspector seemed only to be half listening.

'Well, Eileen is an odd one herself, isn't she? A loner raised by that strange pair must be a strong candidate for mental problems. It's the public's safety we need to prioritise.'

Diaz thought of the beating Longthwaite had given Eileen and the peculiar coldness the couple had both expressed towards their daughter. So far, it sounded like a typical pattern in the early life of a potential criminal. At college he had learnt about the impact of destructive families, and the repetitive patterns of violence as a child entered adolescence. Yet none of those theories were a certainty: many children survived all kinds of horrific treatment without becoming violent criminals. His instinct was to defend her.

'Eileen was dragged out of school where she was doing well and made into a kind of slave on the farm. It's entirely understandable to me if she's having mental problems, sir. Then she got away to Windwell and Tommo Ogden molested her. And she's pregnant. Don't you think that might give her a decent defence and the chance of a reduced sentence?'

'Don't get carried away, lad. I should say we've got enough evidence to charge Eileen with Tommo's murder. There is the video footage, after all. Her pregnancy makes it even more urgent we find her. I've already spoken to the commander about more resources.'

Diaz held his tongue over the obvious retort. None of this had got them any nearer to their original job: catching Kevin Crossley's murderer.

CHAPTER THIRTY-FIVE

Night had fallen fast as Lorraine worked on into the evening at her kitchen table. The outdoor team-building session at the hotel was coming up the following week. And the day after that, the team would meet for a final review and action-planning session. Yet no training manual could tell her how to rebuild a team from which half its original members had disappeared, since Kevin had been murdered and Brian arrested for concealing a crime. Enid might be the next to lose her job if Lorraine initiated counselling and assessment for her alcohol problem. Lorraine found herself staring at the full moon that glowed amber through the uncurtained window. She supposed Oona might cast spells to the moon, love charms and magical talismans. Lorraine was too rational for that, but she did wonder if such spells had a psychological effect, just as curses were said to frighten susceptible victims to an early grave. Her thoughts drifted to Tommo and Brian and the strange performance by the ghostly girl on the video clip. She hadn't ever seen a ghost and certainly wouldn't count Ella's bizarre performance as an apparition.

The click and thud of the cottage's back gate opening and closing reached her. Through the window she saw a tall human silhouette moving inside her back yard. She stood up, dropping the team-building manual to the floor. Was it Voss? Or God forbid, a stranger. The murderer. She spotted a familiarity to his steady stride. His features came into view. Diaz.

She hurried outside, unable to hold back a smile.

'How's it going?'

He released a puff of exasperated air. 'I'm sorry, I've been working flat out. Had a really bad day. Do you fancy a drink?'

In her thin jumper she could feel the temperature had dropped rapidly. The distant horizon had a lemony glow, and beyond the fence the moorland grasses were moving in the wind like a tidal sea. She had a sudden longing to be somewhere bright and busy.

'I've got a better idea. What about driving over to Hebden and catching a band at the Trades Club? Don't know who's on, but it would be so good to get away from here.'

They set off in the Metro and soon left the cluster of streetlights for the unlit road that wound over the high tops. As she concentrated hard at the wheel, he filled her in on Krish's escape and the disappearance of the lad to God knows where.

'I can't believe it. He had the nerve to send us off to the car park to look for him, and when we got back he'd dumped his costume and scarpered. He's not daft, I'll say that. And though we've found out where Ella came from, we're no nearer finding where she's got to.'

The road wound through a claustrophobic valley bottom until at last Hebden's rural bohemia of funky shops, alternative cinema, pubs and bistros came into view.

The Trades Club was the only music venue she'd ever heard of that operated as a socialist co-operative. Inside, it was a happy throwback to more harmonious times. They climbed up the rickety staircase, following the churning of a sound system. Upstairs the crowd moved in the flicker and spirals of a light show. Some were hippies with beards, dreads and ponytails, wearing felty home-knits, Asian tat and eccentric hats. There were straighter folk too, and a few punks with shaved skulls or mohawks. There were men, women, kids and even strap-on babies – dancing, talking, drinking, having a blast. She and Diaz settled at a table far back from the stage and caught only half a set by a band who sat on cushions and improvised pleasantly enough on guitars, handbells and flute. There was just time to manage a couple of drinks before the barman rang the bell for last orders.

Diaz shook his head, like a terrier with a rat. 'Why would a young girl from nowhere come to Windwell and kill the administrator and a male nurse? What do you think?

'Revenge? Is there a link to Campbell?'

'Not that I know of.' Diaz pulled out a photo of an athletic-looking young man. She stared at it, wondering if she had seen that large-eyed, handsome face somewhere before. 'She'd have been a schoolgirl when he was killed.'

'Well, so much for that theory.' Lorraine picked up her

cider. 'OK, let's forget Campbell, then. Surely Oona's onto something about Tommo molesting Ella?'

'Do you think so? Oona said it was nothing really. Wouldn't the girl get over it without having to stab him to death?'

'No, not necessarily,' she said sharply. 'Tommo was twice her size. Whatever the courts are saying these days, no should mean no.'

'Oh, right. I didn't know you were such a feminist.'

'Course I'm a fucking feminist, Diaz. How would you like to be held down and molested by some bloke twice your size?'

He was watching her, his near-black eyes concerned. 'Sorry. This job. Sometimes I forget how to think like a normal person.'

'Right,' she scoffed. Then she softened. 'My nerves are in shreds, too. Thanks for coming round tonight. You saved me from myself.'

She considered confiding about Voss's guilty account of Rob Kessler's suicide attempt, but just then the barman hovered over them to gather their empty glasses. 'C'mon you two. 'Aven't you got a home to go to?'

Diaz swigged back the rest of his pint, while she thought bitterly – right, if only we had.

'Better get back to the madhouse,' she said.

In the car's weak headlamps the drystone walls were disconcertingly taller than a man's height, lending their route home the look of a stone labyrinth. It was worse when they approached a steep descent which lacked safety barriers. She switched the radio on, murmuring that the music might help her concentrate in the poor light. She peered through the screen, scared of losing the road edges and sending the car tumbling down into the dark valley below. John Peel was playing Siouxsie Sioux singing 'Dear Prudence'. Well, Lorraine told herself, she had come out to play but all they'd done was talk about the safe stuff: the case, work, Windwell. She glanced at Diaz, silently smoking beside her. Then she turned back to the pale grey unwinding of the road.

Shock felt like a metal hand twisting her heart. Two pale green eyes glowed in the dark a few feet in front of them. The car was aiming directly at where the eyes waited, staring from a man's height in the blackness. Her feet strained for the clutch and brake and made contact, then rammed the pedals hard into the floor. A grotesque face was for an instant bleached by the headlamps: demonic eyes, curved horns, large pointed ears.

Unable to stop, she spun the wheel to avoid the precipitous edge, and for what felt like an epoch of time the car hurtled through outer space. Then with a jolt and a bang that knocked the breath from her lungs, the tyres hit the road and the car slid onto its nose with a crunch of scraping metal. For a second it lurched forwards, then swung backwards, then stopped. She held her breath, waiting for the car to take off again and slither down the hillside to their deaths.

'Don't move.' Diaz shouldered the passenger door open and disappeared. She sat very still. He reappeared at the same open door. 'We're OK. Just in a deep ditch. Your door is jammed.' He reached in and grasped her hands, helping her wriggle over to the passenger side. Then he hauled her out into the icy air. The engine had stopped but something under the bonnet was hissing. She backed away and clambered up a steep bank. When she found a fence to lean against, her limbs felt oddly detached from her brain.

'A deer,' she muttered. At the very last moment, she had seen the elegant body and antlered head leaping aside.

He came to her side. 'I'd say your car's written off.'

'No, it can't be. I need it to pick up Jasmine and my mum tomorrow.' She was ashamed to hear her voice cracking with emotion.

'I'm sure your boss Morgan will stretch to hiring a car.'

Then he opened his arms and she leant into him, breathing in tobacco and leather, sinking into his warmth, and feeling safe for the first time in long months.

'More bad news,' he said into her hair. 'I left my radio back at the cottage – the batteries needed a charge. But, shit, if I'm honest, I didn't want to be mithered by Thripp.'

'Any ideas?' She looked up into the gleam of his eyes.

'You'd been driving about ten minutes. You were doing less than thirty, so let's say we'd covered at least five miles. If we turn back to Hebden, we'd have to clamber up that steep pass and hope we don't meet a speeding vehicle. It can't be more than about four or five miles to Windwell. Do you feel up to it? It's mostly downhill.'

Lorraine was getting over the shock and returning to her usual self. She pulled back from him, though her fingertips lingered on his body for warmth. 'When I've run training exercises about survival on a desert island or getting lost in a jungle, the answer is usually to stay exactly where you are. Make a list of your resources and . . . I don't know, make an SOS message out of parachutes for planes to spot. Someone's going to see the car, aren't they? Or drive up here with deliveries in the morning?'

He moved away and stood in the middle of the deserted road to get a view. 'You really shot into that ditch. I can't see the car from the road. More likely someone'll see us walking back when we get nearer to Windwell and give us a lift. Good idea about resources, though. Let's take a look.'

To her joy, in the boot she found a hooded rain mac of her mum's which she pulled on over her thin jacket. Annoyingly, she was wearing a pair of high-heeled boots and thought longingly of her walking gear, still hanging unused in the wardrobe, possibly the biggest waste of money of her life.

'OK then. Let's walk.'

He reached to link her arm, acting as a windbreak as they set up a steady pace. The moon had disappeared behind bands of silver vapour, reducing the road to a muzzy grey patch in the darkness. Around them trees and shrubs whispered, and the occasional shriek of predator and prey reached them from the open land. At one point they halted at a drystone wall beside some loud snuffling. An inquisitive white pony clopped over to them, tossing its mane, its nose nudging their palms. It was like a creature from a fairy tale come to life, she thought, its breath hot and damp, its face almost humanly inquisitive.

They carried on walking.

'How's Jasmine?' he asked.

'Not bad.' She described her frustration about Jasmine's school application. 'So the poor thing doesn't realise it, but I'll be grilling her about how her interview went all weekend.'

'You cruel mother,' he teased.

'Cruel to be kind,' she said firmly. 'She should have a chance to try for a better school. I suppose it's all those stereotypes the press and politicians go on about, that without fathers all kids fail at school and turn out to be juvenile delinquents. Actually, what I've seen with my own eyes is that it's poverty and poor schools that drag most kids down. I just want to see Jas have a chance of a better life.'

He seemed to consider this. 'I wish I'd had someone to push me when I was younger. Talk about low expectations keeping you down. God knows what I'd have done without the force.'

After a long pause he asked, 'How did you learn to be a parent?'

She laughed. 'No idea. Treat Jas as I'd have liked to be treated, maybe.'

Then she fully comprehended his question. 'Has anything happened yet? I mean with the baby?'

'Shirley,' he said slowly, 'apparently has rhesus negative blood. I have rhesus positive. Because of the miscarriages, some sort of immune response has started up. The baby isn't growing or moving much. Shirley's in hospital so they can monitor everything. The last I heard, they may have to bring the birth on early.'

'I am so sorry,' she mumbled.

'There are injections, so it might be all right. It's about fifty–fifty at present. Whatever happens, the baby will be very small and go straight into an incubator.'

She reached for his hand and squeezed it, and felt a returning caress. They walked on without speaking.

Soon after, he stopped beside a fingerpost that was nothing more than a paler streak against the sky. He pulled out his lighter, and though he struggled against the wind, they just managed to read 'Scarcross Cavern 1 mile' on the arm that pointed towards a single-track road.

Diaz edged her towards the byroad. 'One of the locals told me about this place. In fact, I was thinking of taking a look at the cave if I ever get any time off. It's only two miles from Windwell. So if we take this path, we know it's just three miles to get home. What do you say?'

She wasn't sure, but her mind was made up by a sudden drop in the temperature, followed by a rising gust of wind. A splat of rain fell on her face, then another on her hand. She pulled her hood up and nodded.

'Come on,' he urged. 'We might even be able to shelter there.'

It was like wading through ink, their only orientation the occasional glimpse of a low escarpment of pale rock to their left. Distant thunder growled. Finally, rain fell in volleys, like a thousand icy pins. Beneath their feet the rough gravel rapidly filled with puddles.

A blast of thunder cracked right above their heads. A hot wire of lightning split the sky. The flash revealed a wind-battered sign ahead and a path leading up to an entrance. They both made a dash for it and almost fell inside the cave mouth entrance. The metal barrier beside the ticket office was thankfully a mere deterrent, and the rusted bolt gave way. It felt even colder inside the first tunnel, but it was dry, and Diaz went off on a reccy while she shook out her soaking mac and rubbed her red and dripping hands together. Peering back out into the night, she saw that rivulets of dark water were already streaming over the threshold.

Diaz returned with a few bits and bobs. 'There's a tiny side-cave that's been carved out to make a chapel. It's too small and damp to sleep in but I found a few candles. And this might keep us warm.' He lifted up a dark mass that she reached to touch. It was a musty piece of fabric, maybe a wall hanging or bench cover. He lit a small candle and grasped her hand. 'It might be warmer further in.'

She couldn't resist saying, 'Dante entering the underworld.'

'You remember that night?' He looked down on her – his fringe curling and wet, his face filled with a new intensity. It was half a year since he had told her that Dante was his true Italian name, and she had quoted back a line of the poet's *Inferno*.

'How could I forget?' As he led her into the cave's interior she had a sudden premonition, like a vibration before an earthquake. Everything between them was about to change.

CHAPTER THIRTY-SIX

By the candle's shifting light they discovered roped-off areas and well-worn paths, pools and arches, stalagmites and stalactites. Deciding it might be warmer away from the water, they searched a few tunnels, but the noise of the whistling wind was eerie and unsettling. The largest chamber, complete with a rock formation like a great organ's pipes, was less draughty. A smoothed hollow alcove seemed as good as anywhere to rest for a few hours. He stuck the candle on a small stone shelf that she guessed had been used for the same purpose for a very long time.

When he spread out the hanging cloth she spotted the embroidered motto 'Queen Elizabeth II, Silver Jubilee 1977'.

He lay down on it and smiled sleepily. 'You look worn out. And somehow I've got to report to duty in . . .' He checked his watch. 'In six hours. Come here. Let me keep you warm.'

In the beginning, they were simply holding each other

close, seeking each other's body heat. Gently, he kissed her goodnight. And she kissed him back, brushing dry lips, in a way that made it hard to stop. It was as if they were at the edge of a crumbling bank, but she tried to tell herself she'd hold back. Then the current rose and they rolled together into the fast-surging river of pleasure. His skin against hers was warm and taut. The pleasure felt surprising, like something she had forgotten or repressed. They wound about each other, pressing harder against bone and muscle and flesh. This sharing of herself with a man was like a drug, she thought, and all these long months she had forgotten her craving for it. Yet it had been with them all the time, like a mistreated little animal kicked beneath the table. She had forgotten that she loved it to death.

Kisses thirsted deeper, tongues moved over lips and teeth and throats. His taste was salty, turning to sweet as she licked through the sweat. They both moved with instinct now, to pleasure and be pleasured.

Suddenly, he pulled back, touching her cheek with his fingertips. 'Is this it, Lorraine? Is this what you want?'

She leant her head back against the wall and slid her own hands under his sweater. Little hairs tickled her fingers. She could hear herself breathing fast, but couldn't answer.

'God,' she whispered. 'Listen to me.'

He raised his face. 'What is it?'

'I want you, too. But Diaz, listen to me.'

He raised dark eyes that were bleary with yearning. 'What?'

'Maybe it's not the right time.'

'It is for me.'

'I mean, we can't.'

'What?'

'I mean . . .' For a moment she recovered her usual half-joking manner. 'We can't go all the way. Not unless you want two pregnant women on your hands.'

'Fuck. I never thought to bring anything.'

'We never knew what would happen, did we? So . . .' What more could she say? Suddenly, she chuckled. 'Remember when I tested your personality? We've both got plenty of imagination.' She shifted up onto her knees and unzipped her jeans. 'Let's use that imagination,' she whispered. 'I'm up for anything you like, just so long as I don't conceive.'

They scarcely slept; it was impossible to lie still together without provoking more arcs of desire. She wanted never to move from that place again. Hours later, with her jumper balled up beneath her head, she finally dozed, though everywhere was wet with their sweat and spit and a few unstoppable tears.

Before she fell asleep, she stared into the darkness, listening to his steady breath, enjoying the pressure of his arm circling her waist. High in the cold air a speckled patch of emerald glowed in the void. She had no idea what it was, only that it was of the earth, a luminous plant or creature or mineral. Like a path of stars, she thought sleepily, remembering Lily's news and wondering if this was a sign of a brighter future with Diaz at her side. Then her eyelids grew too heavy and closed.

When she woke she was alone, feeling like an entirely new person. A fresh candle burnt on the shelf. Her watch said six-forty, so she pulled on her damp clothes and thought about the luxury of sipping a mug of tea while lying in a hot bath back at the cottage. She halted at the low entrance to the chapel. Beyond stood the tiny room he had spoken of, carved out from the rock with a decorated altar set with one burning candlestick, postcards and a collection box. Carved into the rock wall above the altar was a primitive life-sized figure of a woman holding a baby. A wooden sign on the wall announced 'The Chapel of the Rocks, founded AD 1403, Hail Mary, Full of Grace'. The stone floor and walls were tinted verdigris green from mildew; it was like nowhere she had ever seen before.

Only when she stepped into the musty chill of the chapel did she spot Diaz, hunched on a bench, passing a string of beads through his fingers. His eyes were closed as he muttered to himself. Without a sound she withdrew to wait outside the cave, where the sun hadn't yet risen but the air was rich with the wet earth scent that follows a storm.

Christ, she'd known he was a Catholic from the moment she'd first spotted that silver crucifix around his neck. All night it had been there on his bare chest. Was he feeling guilty and asking for forgiveness? Surely, in this modern age, what they'd done was no sin?

A noticeboard stood in the entrance, and spotting a photograph of a livid green growth on the cave's surface, she began to read. 'Dragon's gold,' it said, 'is a luminous emerald-green moss that lives in Stygian conditions amongst deep crags and caves. *Schistostega pennata* only displays at night, instantly vanishing in daylight.'

'Morning.' Diaz came up behind her, drew her into his

arms and kissed her. She pulled back after a while, to study his face. Deep within his eyes she read easy commitment, and likely more.

'You were praying,' she whispered.

'Mmm.' He pulled back. 'We should get going. If I know Thripp he'll be watching the clock, waiting for me.'

They returned to Windwell through a reborn autumn countryside; the sun rose in a ravishing pink burst, the yellowing fields smelt wet and sweet, and high above them flocks of wild birds traversed the sky. They walked hip to hip, arm in arm. As they approached Windwell, the silhouette of the old asylum crouched on the horizon, and beyond that stood the brutal perimeter walls of the new unit. They halted beneath a tree and kissed against its trunk, hard and breathless.

Pulling away, he said, 'I don't know what to do.' He touched her hair and looked at her as if he'd never truly seen her before. 'I need to think before we go any further.'

She nodded, feeling his pain as if it were her own. 'I won't ask anything of you. I'll get the car sorted out and probably won't see you for a few days while I'm staying at the hotel with Mum and Jas.' Then, because that felt far too harsh compared to her true feelings, she added with a weak smile, 'Though it's going to be hell, not seeing you.'

He blinked and shook his head. 'And I'll do my best to work on the case. Though God knows, I . . . yeah, it's going to be hell.'

'Do you want to go down first? If we appear together, the gossips are going to have a field day.'

'No, I'll see you home. We went to Hebden together and the car got written off. I don't give a toss what anyone says.'

That made her happy. But before they passed the Windwell sign, she unthreaded her arm and walked calmly beside him. When they reached the high street they coolly waved each other goodbye.

CHAPTER THIRTY-SEVEN

Saturday 22nd October

A shiny white Cortina had arrived at Lorraine's cottage, to use for as long as she needed it, all courtesy of Morgan. And so far, after fetching her mum and Jasmine to the hotel, the pair were loving their luxurious leisure break. Jasmine had booked a full day of archery, canoeing and swimming, all costing a fraction of their true price, thanks to the big budget that HQ were spending on Windwell's team-building day.

Lorraine took her mum and daughter upstairs to show them their spacious family room with its picture window view of the reservoir. She gave Jas a hug and asked, 'So if you get in, are you looking forward to changing schools?'

Jas wriggled awkwardly in her arms. 'I'm not going. They're all toffee-nosed twits.'

'But Jas, your marks were in the top three results. You deserve to go.'

'Yeah, but I don't want to.'

'Right, young madam. We'll see about that,' Lorraine snapped back.

Jasmine assumed her most defiant icy glare. 'I'm not going. You can't make me.'

Lorraine's mum interjected. 'Lorraine, let's have a chat about this later.' Lorraine's glare back at her own mother was, she later supposed, an unfortunate echo of her own daughter's outraged expression.

Ten minutes later, while Jas was engrossed in an archery lesson, Lorraine and her mum ordered morning coffee at a table on a nearby terrace.

'So, what's going on with Jasmine?' Lorraine demanded of her mum.

'I knew you wouldn't like it. She was happy about passing the exam – or, I should say, happy about not disappointing you. It all seemed to go wrong when the three finalists had a group discussion observed by the headmistress. On the way home, Jas kept asking me about how certain words are pronounced. Apparently, the headmistress criticised her in front of the other two girls for talking about "skewel" rather than school, and "bewk" instead of book. When they were alone, the other two girls laughed at her.'

Lorraine fell uncharacteristically quiet.

'I don't think she'd be happy there,' her mum said. 'She was very upset.'

'That's outrageous. It's the local dialect, for God's sake.' Of course, she had noticed Jasmine's twangy Salford accent since she'd started at St Joseph's junior. 'It's class discrimination,' she burst out, feeling deeply hurt. 'I'm going to put in a complaint.'

Her mum sighed heavily.

'Don't go sighing like that, Mum. You must agree it's just not fair.'

'I know, love. But neither is it fair to Jasmine if you make a big drama out of it. I've been thinking. Why not check out all the other schools and try to get housing in the most promising areas?'

'I don't see why—' They were interrupted by Jasmine running towards them with a huge grin on her face.

'I got three bullseyes!'

Lorraine opened her arms and welcomed her daughter into them; it seemed she was not yet too big to jump up and settle on her lap.

'You big daft baby,' she crooned, stroking her daughter's pale hair.

A rare burst of afternoon sunshine tinted the hotel's indoor swimming pool a soothing sapphire blue. Lorraine and Jasmine were the only guests in the pool that afternoon as Lorraine lay on her back, floating weightless in the water, watching blue reflections tremble on the ceiling.

After drying off, mother and daughter headed to the hotel's orangery, a warm, palm-filled glasshouse, where a waitress was setting out afternoon tea in front of Lorraine's appreciative mother. Beyond the windows stretched the reservoir, its surface rippling as a sudden shower swept across it in long arcs. They had nearly had their fill of triangular sandwiches, cakes and strong tea from a porcelain pot, when a dark figure approached the glass door. Diaz appeared, as from nowhere. What the hell are you doing here, Lorraine thought silently, as he smiled genially at her little family.

'Can I join you?'

Lorraine's mum was taken by surprise, then recognised him from the time he had helped Lorraine and Jasmine after the tragedies at the Memorial Hospital. 'Oh, it's Sergeant Diaz, isn't it? I didn't know you were here.'

'I'm working at Windwell, too.'

Her mum shot Lorraine a questioning frown and receiving nothing back, waved him towards the empty fourth seat.

'So, do you two work together?' her mum asked.

'Sometimes,' Diaz said, at the exact same moment as Lorraine replied, 'Not really.'

Lorraine watched as these two distinct parts of her life collided, desperate to relax and enjoy her family around her, at the same time as longing to talk to Diaz alone. Together, the combination felt horribly wrong.

By contrast, Diaz seemed entirely comfortable as her mum pressed him to tuck into the cakes remaining on the heavily laden stand. Diaz asked Jasmine about the day's adventures and her daughter was uncharacteristically halting as she told him, glancing up at Diaz with worshipful shining eyes. Lorraine struggled to smile. Why was he ruining her day like this? Hadn't Jasmine got enough on her plate without having to deal with Diaz playing the charming father figure? After all, the chances were that eventually he'd let them both down badly.

Diaz was telling Jasmine and her mum the story of a hiker who two of his fellow officers had just rescued. At the word 'cave' Lorraine felt a mortifying heat creep along her chest up to her throat and face. She barely listened as Diaz recounted how the area's cave network was the largest in

Britain, passing under Lancashire and Yorkshire to emerge in Cumberland. The amateur caver was lucky to be rescued after some children found his rucksack and a camping stove by a cave entrance. The lad had tried to explore a new shaft and slipped down deep before he got stuck. Was this supposed to be some sort of metaphor for what she and Diaz had got up to the previous night? She was grateful to see a waitress checking their progress from the doorway.

'Right,' she announced. 'Everyone finished?'

'I can't eat another crumb,' said Jasmine, clutching her tummy.

'We can't let those last scones go to waste.' Her mum, still imbued with post-war frugality, wrapped what was left in paper serviettes and slipped them inside her handbag.

When they all stood up, Diaz said, 'Can I have a quick word, Lorraine?'

With a knowing look backwards towards the pair, Lorraine's mum hurried Jasmine away.

'What is it?'

'I hope you didn't mind me coming over.'

She did, she really did, but she shook her head. 'Have you had any news about the baby?'

'No.' His hands slid onto her shoulders. 'Lorraine. I want you to go home with your mum and Jasmine on Monday morning. It might not be safe at Windwell. You're an outsider. You found Crossley's body. And you saw this mysterious Ella the night Crossley was killed.'

'I'd go tomorrow, but it's the final team-building day on Wednesday. Morgan's coming, I've got to show up. After that, there's only some action-planning on Thursday. Then I'm going straight home.'

'Well, if you have to stay, can't you book a room here at the hotel? And be careful. No lonely walks or unlocked doors.'

His hands slid up to caress the sides of her neck, and she feared he was going to kiss her, here in this public place.

'OK, I'll get it booked.' Reluctantly, she pulled away from him and looked up into his face and asked, 'What about you?'

'First, I've got to find Ella, whoever she is. Thripp's going public today to try and locate her.' He glanced at his watch. 'I need to get back.'

Suddenly she did want to kiss him goodbye but stopped herself. 'OK. But you be careful, too.'

Upstairs in their luxurious family room, Jasmine was stretched out fast asleep on her single bed. Lorraine paused to enjoy the sight of her daughter at peace, wishing she could lift all her child's present and future disappointments onto her own shoulders. Yes, her mum was right to tell her not to pursue a complaint, however irritating that was. And at least Jasmine was now prepared for whatever life might throw at her in the form of long-division sums or multiplication of fractions. Looking up, she noticed her mother wearing a strange smile as she studied her wayward daughter.

'Detective Diaz seems very keen on you.'

Lorraine slumped down on her own bed with her back to her mother. She wished everyone would just leave her alone.

'So would it kill you to be friendly to him? Lorraine, think about your future. And Jasmine's future. It's like an electric current between the two of you. What's wrong with you?'

Lorraine couldn't find any words. Then suddenly her feelings burst out. 'You don't know anything.' To her shame, hot tears trickled down her cheeks. The next moment her mum was beside her and she buried her face in the warmth of her shoulder. Her mum murmured words of comfort over her daughter's sobbing back.

In broken fragments, Lorraine explained about Diaz's fiancée, the rhesus baby and his loyalty to a woman he no longer loved. She even raged about the ridiculous religion that bound him to these primitive ideas.

Reaching for a hanky, Lorraine asked her mum, 'So what do I do?'

Her mother's face was serious and intense as she collected her thoughts. Lorraine wiped her eyes, though her tears still kept flowing.

At last her mum said, 'I believe our lives are subject to the whims of fortune. Sometimes, if you're lucky, you meet the right person, the person you were meant to spend your life with. It's not only a feeling in your mind, it's in your skin and your cells, like the changes your body makes when giving birth. It is a small miracle.

'This other woman. One of you must win and the other lose. I am your mother. I care only about your happiness, Lorraine. Take what you deserve.'

Lorraine stared hard at her mother, astonished by her outburst. Then finally, she nodded in agreement. She had never known anyone as perceptive about human affairs as this observant French woman. Then she got up and washed her face in cold water and started to get changed for their dinner together. By the time Jasmine opened her eyes, Lorraine's make-up was restored and her façade was perfectly intact again, though still she carried a raw wound that she feared might never fully heal.

CHAPTER THIRTY-EIGHT

Ella and Krish had got as far as Manchester, and to try and keep warm had to hang around heated shopping precincts, in clothes shops changing rooms, or at the smelly backs of restaurants where they sometimes found leftover food in the bins. Their cash had run out and the van's petrol tank was pointing to empty. Today she was on her own while Krish tried to sell some of the gear from the back of the van to a market trader in Cheetham Hill.

She had spent the morning upstairs at the Arndale Shopping Centre, watching all the smart people marching past with their families and their friends, with places to go and money to get there. The previous night she had barely slept, what with the metal floor of the van and the cold drilling into her bones. Yawning, she found a space on a bench and tried not to nod off. Before her stretched the massed TV screens of an electrical shop. She dozed, and then started awake as her chin hit her chest. A red banner moved across the TV screens: 'Police Statement on Asylum

Tunnels Murder'. She hurried to press her face against the shop window. On each of the screens, an old man with a big chin was talking outside the old asylum. It was driving her mad that she couldn't hear a word of what he said. Then they showed a daft picture of Tommo, probably taken when he was off his head in a photo booth. Beneath that one was a caption:

'Thomas Ogden – Murder Victim'

What in God's name had happened to him? A moment later two more faces flashed onto the screen side by side. One was a really bad photo of Krish as a crop-haired schoolboy wearing a school tie and blazer. Beside it was a childish photofit of her, with a blankly plain face, brown curtains of hair and mad staring eyes. This twin image was captioned 'Wanted for questioning'.

The news moved on to images of thousands of people waving placards about nuclear disarmament. She returned to the bench in a daze, desperate to know what was going on back at Windwell. She wished she could speak to Oona. And how was Tommo's dad taking it? Her own mum and dad were probably watching it, too, but even they would hardly associate that photofit with their own daughter.

It was impossible to sit still. She walked up and down the rows of shops. She needed to find out more before four o'clock, when she'd arranged to meet Krish back at the van. In a waste bin she spotted a discarded *Manchester Evening News* and scrabbled through it, ignoring all the usual rubbish about strikes and that AIDS sickness that people were calling the wrath of God. Then she found it, a small column beneath the same two images of her and Krish:

Male nurse found murdered in asylum tunnels

The murdered body of Thomas Ogden, 21, a psychiatric nurse at Windwell Top Security Hospital, has been found in the abandoned tunnels of the former Windwell Asylum. Mr Ogden's remains were found after a search was begun following his father's concerns for his whereabouts. The scandal-rocked asylum is currently being cleared for demolition following the completion of a new secure unit for more than 400 dangerous patients on an adjacent site.

Detective Chief Inspector Thripp said, 'The post-mortem has confirmed that this was a case of brutal murder. We are confident that we will catch the culprit but in the meantime are asking the public for assistance. We are looking for the following persons: Krishnan Khan, male, aged 19, of Asian appearance, from Burnley, Lancashire. He was last seen in the company of an unknown white female of approximately 17 years of age, known as Ella or Eileen, about 5 feet 2 inches tall, with blue eyes and brown shoulder-length hair. They were travelling in a white transit van, registration number BUR23V with the words 'Khan-Elek, Global Electrical Traders' painted on the sides.

Detective InspectorThripp would not speculate on whether the killing is linked with the recent murder of Kevin Crossley, the Administrator of Windwell

Hospital. Less than a quarter of a mile away, the new Windwell Secure Unit was severely criticised in a recent investigation by ITV's World in Action.

Members of the public are warned not to approach Khan or his associate but report their whereabouts by telephone to 0422 894524 or 999.

She returned to where the van was concealed in an empty railway arch off Deansgate and waited for Krish, her thoughts racing madly. She and Krish might be sent to prison for the rest of their lives. Or, if they were crafty and careful, no one might ever find them. She walked back and forth, stamping her cold feet and burying her gloveless hands beneath her armpits.

At last, footsteps. She made to run into Krish's arms but skidded on her heels. Two uniformed policemen faced her, both impossibly tall and threatening. It was the guy in a leather jacket waiting behind them who spoke, while he assessed her with dark Mediterranean eyes.

'Listen, Ella. There's no point in trying to run. We picked Krish up earlier today. It's time to come with us.'

CHAPTER THIRTY-NINE

Ella was starving hungry and frightened by the time they arrived at the police station. She had a microsecond's glimpse of Krish, being led along a corridor, slumped between two policemen. He hadn't even noticed her – then he had gone. First, she had to have her photograph taken, and then roll her fingers on an ink pad to press her prints on some paper. The worst shock came when she had to stand at a desk and the policeman gave a little speech and said she was being arrested under suspicion of the murder of Thomas Ogden.

'No,' she wailed. 'That's not true.' No one took any notice, and she was taken to a nasty-smelling cell with a wipe-down plastic mattress and a metal thing for a toilet.

Her stomach was knotted with panic by the time a policewoman brought her a cup of tea and a biscuit.

'Can I have some more food? And some aspirins, please?' She hadn't eaten anything since a half-bag of chips the previous night.

Nothing arrived, so she lay down feeling horrible and fell asleep.

The next morning, she gobbled down the unpleasant breakfast they brought her on a plastic tray. She had just fallen asleep again when the policeman in the leather jacket came and told her his name was Detective Sergeant Diaz, and that he had come to fetch her to an interview.

'They treating you all right?'

She blurted out, 'No. I shouldn't be here. I didn't kill Tommo.'

He didn't reply, only eyed her sorrowfully, as if he already knew she was guilty.

She had thought she might have to stand up in court, but they only went to another room where the big-chinned man from the TV was waiting with some other policemen. Sergeant Diaz got her a plastic cup of water. Then the questions began.

It all started quite well, with easy questions about her name, age and address. Then the man the others called 'sir' started firing questions at her like a series of random bullets.

'So you were fed up at home.'

'Yes.'

'That was because you'd fallen out with your boyfriend.'

'What boyfriend?'

'Now come on. Your mum and dad have told us all about Jim. You attacked him, didn't you?'

This took some thinking about and she didn't know where to start.

'We've seen his stab wounds. You did that, didn't you?'

Again, she failed to come up with an answer.

'And then you attacked Tommo Ogden.'

'What? I didn't.'

'How come your fingerprints are all over the knife?'

'But it's not true.'

The chief inspector picked up a piece of paper with some smudgy marks on it and said, 'Then explain to me how it is that your fingerprints match the prints on the murder weapon.'

She shook her head.

'Come on, love. There's no point in wasting everybody's time. You'll feel a lot better when all this is over.'

'I don't know what you're talking about. I wouldn't kill Tommo.' As she spoke, her voice wobbled. None of them had liked him in the end, but it was still a shock that he was dead.

The chief inspector was getting impatient. 'Don't waste our time, now. You can get it all over and done with by bedtime. Clear your conscience. How about it?'

Sergeant Diaz slipped a note to DCI Thripp. The older man pulled a face but said that the interview was suspended until the next day.

Diaz was uncomfortable about Thripp's initial interview. He knew his boss had an impressive reputation for clearing cases by gaining quick confessions. But bloody hell, it wasn't how he would have set about it. He still had his notes from the CID course on best practice interviewing, and now he jotted down a few of the questions he'd like to return to. Nothing fancy, just the five Ws – who, what, where, when and, most crucially, why.

After checking that Thripp wasn't around, Diaz bought

a bar of chocolate in the canteen and took it down to the cells. Posting a female constable at the cell door, he went inside and found Eileen lying unmoving on the plastic mattress. To him she was still a child, and when she lifted her face, it was red and tear-stained. As he'd reminded Thripp in his note, the poor kid was pregnant. He'd noticed her stomach was still girlishly flat, unlike Shirley's swelling stomach. He reckoned it was guilt again, this over-concern he felt for Eileen and her unborn baby.

'Here,' he said, offering the chocolate. 'It's not a bribe or anything.'

'Thanks.' She spoke in a tiny, timid voice and took it. 'Will I get a hot dinner later?'

'Yeah, I'll sort something out. Eileen, would you like a solicitor to represent you? I think it would be a good idea.'

'Will my mum and dad have to pay? They won't like that.'

'No. I could call a duty solicitor. It's free.'

'All right.'

He wondered if Thripp was right and she was acting the pathetic victim. No, his gut told him she was telling the truth.

'Listen,' he said in a low voice. 'Tonight I want you to think hard about what happened to you. And why. Just tell us the truth.'

She raised a pair of hopeless, bloodshot eyes. 'It's not worth it.'

'I promise you, Eileen. Telling the truth is always worth it.'

CHAPTER FORTY

In the endless hours of the night she lay awake, clutching her hand to her mouth, fighting hysteria. Intermittently, she was roused by clanging doors and angry men effing and jeffing in the corridor. Her thoughts went round and round in jangling circles. She had to talk to someone. A long time ago she had been strong, but since Jim arrived at the farm, her bright confidence had worn away like fairground gilt. Yet some good things had happened. There had been her history teacher's encouragement, the image she had created of a peaceful life at college. And gentle Krish, who sweetly cherished her, and wanted to go to college too, dreaming of escaping from his own crooked family and starting an electrical engineering business. It had taken Krish to make her realise just how off-limits Jim's behaviour had been. There had been the malevolent influence of her mother too, a silent battle over her identity; the need to live a life entirely the opposite of a woman dedicated to obsessive cleaning and Bible studies.

She remembered a school trip to a jail in a heritage town where the inmates' punishment had once been to pick three pounds of oakum each day. Her classmates had joked and giggled as they role-played being prisoners, picking apart great lumps of tarry hemp. After a few minutes, their fingernails began to flake and bleed. That was how she felt now, silently separating the solid accretion of memory into loose strands that she could offer up to the police.

Monday 24th October

The next morning, Eileen had a full hour's meeting with Maureen Crawshaw, a middle-aged solicitor who helped to supply her with neater, plainer words for what had happened, and to tell it all in a way that hadn't occurred to her before. When Sergeant Diaz questioned her, it was far easier to give answers than when the older man tried to pin her to the wall with his scattergun bullets.

'Now, Eileen, I'd like you to tell us about life on the farm. How would you describe it?'

With Maureen nodding beside her, she began to tell them about her mum and dad, that they were well-meaning but very old when they had her, and wanted her to be religious like them.

'When your dad took you out of school, did you miss your friends?'

'A bit. But mostly I missed my teacher, Mrs Fitton. She was helping me get into college and signing off my forms.'

'Your mum and dad told us you were hanging around with lads in the village. Were you?'

Eileen shook her head irritably. 'That was one of Jim's

stories. It was a lie he spread about me. You can ask Mrs Fitton where I was when I stayed late. We were doing my UCCA forms and looking at grants. I realise now that my parents were poisoned against me by Jim.'

'Is it true that your father beat you with his belt?'

'Yes.'

'How often did that happen?'

'Oh, not too often. Maybe every month or two.'

'Did it leave any marks?'

'Just bruises, really. Then I had to pretend I'd forgotten my PE kit so no one else saw them.'

There was an awkward shift of feelings in the room.

'Can you tell us about Jim?'

She took a deep and nervous breath. She told them how at first it had been quite good having another young person on the farm. But then, how it had turned bad. His crafty tricks, her stupidity in letting him flatter her into sharing a few secret kisses, a bit of what he called teenage fun behind her parents' back. She had been an innocent, ignorant of the touchpaper she had lit. Every Thursday night her parents had gone to Bible class and every Thursday night Jim ruthlessly pursued her. He humiliated her, bullied her, threatened her, and lied about her to her parents. She tried to stop him, she hid in the loft of the house or out in the fields, but he always found her.

Thripp cut in. 'So why, if all this was going on, didn't you just tell your parents?'

Maureen patted her hand and urged her to carry on.

'He told me he'd kill my parents. And then after I'd watched that, he'd kill me. Then he'd have the farm to himself. He would have done it. He'd got a new shepherd's knife to threaten me, to bring me to heel, as he called it. And besides,' she added, 'Mum and Dad thought he was quite the second coming, with his smarmy ways. He was the blessed son my dad always wanted. Next to him I was just a useless girl.'

Maureen discreetly whispered in her ear. 'And another reason,' she added. 'By then I was expecting.'

'If you were so ignorant, how did you know that?' Thripp demanded.

'I live on a farm. I knew. I told Jim. I hoped he'd leave me alone. He didn't. Instead he was full of himself, that he'd sired a bairn. He said we'd have to get married and then he'd have the farm. I couldn't stand it. I told him I was getting rid of it.'

Maureen passed Eileen a paper tissue. When she had finished blowing her nose, Diaz prompted her to continue.

'The next Thursday evening when we were alone again, Jim went mad. He said if I tried to get rid of the baby, he'd tell my parents how I'd been throwing myself at the lads in the village and that's how I'd got tupped. Mum and Dad would disown me. To them I'd be a murderer as well as a whore.

'Or, if I came to my senses and did the right thing, he'd tell them we were getting married and we'd get the farm off them. I'd never felt so trapped, miles from school, my teacher, my classmates. I thought I'd rather die than live there with Jim all my life. The only good thing that happened was that one day a letter arrived for me, and like a miracle, it was me who fetched the post from the box that day. It was from my teacher and she wanted to know if I was still interested in college, because she'd met up with an old friend who would help me get an interview in January. I read that letter about a thousand times – it was like strong medicine, reminding me who I could be if I stood up to them all. Secretly, I started to pack a bag to run away.

'My plan was to wait till they were all asleep and then walk the six miles to Barnard Castle and catch the eight o'clock bus to Bradford, the only big place I'd ever been to. I did steal a bit of money from Dad, I'm sorry but I had to, and I had been slaving away for no pay for years, so I didn't fret about it.

'I waited till one o'clock in the morning. It was freezing outside, there was a deep frost coming, and I was thinking it might take three or four hours to walk to the coach station. I got up and dressed and picked up my bag and set off. The back path to town led around by the old cowman's cottage where Jim slept, so I was extra quiet.

'I don't know why, I didn't think about Jim's dog. Samson was a blind sheepdog Jim kept locked in the barn. But as soon as he heard me crossing the cobbles, Samson started barking fit to burst. I started to run but I slipped on the ice. Jim appeared with a torch and grabbed hold of me. I tried screaming for Mum and Dad but they slept through it, slept through the whole thing. Jim dragged me into the barn.'

Ella stopped to take a sip of water. No one spoke.

'He dragged me to where Samson was going berserk in his big wire cage and yelled at the dog. Samson cowered down, his poor blind eyes rolling nervously, not knowing where the blow might fall. Then Jim shoved me against the cage. He was as strong as an iron man, cursing me, calling me every name for a slut under the sun. And all the time Samson was whining with fear. I kept thinking about the bus and how I was going to miss it and probably never get a chance again.

'Jim undid my jeans and pushed them down to my knees. I fought but he held me in a lock and I couldn't break free. His fingers were pressing between my legs. Course, it had happened loads of times before but this time I had a plan, a chance of freedom, a bus waiting for me.

'I screamed at him to get off me. I told him I was going to call the police. His fist swung around from nowhere, smacking me on the side of the head. The front of my face hit the bars of the cage. While tears dribbled out of my eyes, he ripped off my knickers. The stink of the cage was right in front of me. The dog's white milky eyes stared into mine. He was frightened. Trapped. I thought, Jim keeps us both in cages to torment us. I could feel a tooth hanging on a thread in my mouth. I spat out some blood.

'"Listen, you," he whispered at me. "You've got to learn one thing, right?"

'I couldn't even move my head.

'"You got to learn to shut up," he said.

'So I did. All through it I kept quiet. Even when Samson's nose snuffled against my fingers, licking them, all warm and desperate. It was like he was seeking comfort from me, a fellow prisoner. That blind old dog was the only creature in the world who cared for me. I started crying without making a sound. Then at last Jim made the grunting noise and it was over. He looked dazed as he pulled his pants up.'

She was coming to the end and knew that her next words could never be unsaid.

Sergeant Diaz spoke softly. 'Can you tell us what happened next?'

'I knew, if I was going to do it, it had to be while he was ignoring me, while I was just a sort of carcass leaning on the cage. Now I'd pulled back from him, Samson was making an unholy yowling sound, jumping from one end of the cage to the other. It was as if he was distracting Jim for me.

'He shouted at Samson to shut it. He kicked the cage. I had a chance to look around and saw where the tools hung on nails on the wall. I grabbed the nearest, a pair of sheep shears. The dog wailed again and he kicked it again, catching his jaw so he yelped. He was laughing, watching through the bars as Samson slumped into a pile of raggy fur.'

She looked up at them all, as if waking from a drugged sleep. 'Yes, I did attack Jim,' she said in a flat voice. 'Because he was stealing my family's money and farm, because he'd got me pregnant and was going to make me a slave for the rest of my life, and because thanks to Maureen I now know the proper name for what he did that night and a dozen times before that. Because he was an evil, cowardly, disgusting rapist.'

Tuesday 25th October

The next day's session would be the most difficult, Maureen had warned her. Back in the interview room, Sergeant Diaz announced that he would lead the interview while another man took notes on paper and the chief inspector watched from the sidelines.

Before the onslaught began, Maureen addressed the gathering.

285

'My client wants to clarify a misapprehension you may have formed about her. While in Bradford, Eileen used the money she stole from her father to terminate her pregnancy.'

Eileen was watching Sergeant Diaz. Momentarily, he looked surprised, then said, 'Eileen, would you mind stating the bare facts for the record.'

Thanks to adverts in magazines she'd known where to go. The urine test she had taken at the Pregnancy Advisory Service had been positive. The woman who interviewed her had sat her down with a cup of tea to talk about her options. It could all be arranged in a few days, she said.

Not lifting her eyes from her lap, she gave the address of the place. Then it was done. No need to describe the crowded clinic, the shameful undressing, the stained cotton robe and her arm flexing rigid as the doctor injected in her vein. She had woken in agony, feeling the gouged emptiness inside her, the blood soaking into the old-fashioned cotton pad. She couldn't bear the thought that she had murdered a potential baby.

'I just want to say something,' she blurted out. 'If I'd have gone home to my parents, they would have made me marry Jim and keep it and I'd have destroyed any chance of a decent life. I've cried about it every day, I've felt so awful about it. But I can't and I wouldn't undo it. To have gone home would have been like suicide.'

Maureen whispered in her ear in reassurance. She hoped the worst was over, but Diaz began a further round of interrogation: how had she met Oona, and Tommo, and Krish? She replayed her memories as if watching figures at the other end of a telescope: Oona on the Bradford bus was glittery and insubstantial, their nights at the abandoned asylum heavy with hash and a frisson of fear. She confessed that she had never liked Tommo, that he had been crude and unpredictable, and mostly off his head.

Yes, Tommo had molested her, she admitted, but it wasn't much compared to what Jim did, because Oona had saved her from him.

'Tell me more about Oona,' the sergeant said.

'I'll always be grateful to her,' she replied. 'She was a friend to me when I needed one. She gave me somewhere safe to stay.'

'What was she like?'

'Not like me, really. So pretty. And lad mad. And into her tarot and things. But really generous with her time and food and everything.'

'Would you say your friendship was an equal one?'

Eileen found herself smiling. 'Yeah. Though she thought she was in charge. She was in the beginning. I did sort of follow in her wake at first. I was still feeling bad so I just kind of sleepwalked along behind her.'

She told them about the sisterhood spell and how Oona thought she had bound Eileen's soul, or something creepy like that. 'I'd woken up by then. Tommo called it all mind games and he was right.'

'Did she ever tell you what to think or say?'

'Not really. Only when we did that bonding thing. Look. This is how she cut me with her knife.' She held out her palm to show the deep maroon scar.

'Was that the same knife you used to scare Tommo?'

'I think so. Her ritual knife. It had a carved bone handle.'

The funnel of questions began to narrow.

'Whose idea was it to make the video?'

It was Tommo's, she explained, but soon afterwards Oona decided to use it to scare him. It was about revenge, she told them, for the way he'd treated Oona and for them all to get back at him. She had been told to wait for Oona's special words and then climb out of the furnace to give him a fright. It was a prank, like *Candid Camera* or something.

'And when you made the video, was Oona present?'

'Yeah, course she was. She did the filming. Tommo presented it. Krish did the sound. I was the ghost.'

Returning from a toilet break, Eileen found a huge TV and video recorder had been set up. The video was switched on. Eileen could make out nothing at first but a couple of lighted candles on a black screen.

'I'm back,' whispered an eerie child's voice.

'Who's that speaking?' asked Thripp.

'It's supposed to be Sally back from the dead,' said Ella. 'It's a tape Krish made for Oona.'

On the video Tommo's voice called out, 'You trying to creep me out? Put the fucking lights on.' The camera lens panned towards the furnace door.

'Hang on. Where are all the earlier parts?' Eileen protested. 'We started filming, then Tommo and Oona had a big row. That was all before this bit.' Diaz nodded and raised a palm, suggesting questions would be answered later.

The video showed only the very end of what she expected to see: her own hammy performance, while in the background she heard the recorded taunts and Tommo's gibbering.

Barely a minute into the film, the video camera clearly fell to the floor. Unseen, the boom picked up Tommo's shriek of protest, 'Get away from me. I can't take no more!'

'This is when I decided to leave,' Eileen announced. At the image of her swishing skirt, she explained, 'That's my boot. I made a run for it. I couldn't take any more.'

The floor-level angle continued. Then the sounds began. The slashing. The harsh breathing.

'God, no,' Eileen mumbled. 'What's that?' Her breathing grew ragged. 'Is that Tommo? Is that what I think it is? No, please.' She sank her face into her hands so as not to see what happened next.

Diaz spoke gently. 'I'm sorry, Eileen, as a witness you must try to watch it.'

She lifted her face and winced as she watched, her hand clamped over her mouth.

When the film ended Eileen drank a breathless draught of water. 'I don't understand any of this,' she mumbled.

'So who was still present when you left the boiler room?' Diaz resumed.

Eileen wiped her eyes. 'Tommo was frightened but alive. Oona was still there. And Krish. But he ran after me almost straight away; we were both desperate to get away early. He caught up with me at the top of the stairs. We got out of there as fast as we could.'

'Why the rush?' Diaz asked.

'Everything had gone way out of control.' Eileen suddenly halted and shook her head. 'You know what? Now you ask, I think I had no clear idea at all what was going on.'

'Tell me about the row that took place earlier?'

'Tommo arrived in a bad mood. He said the police were after him over that patient's death, Campbell. And he accused Krish of selling knock-off gear. It was just an excuse not to pay Krish, that's what we thought. Tommo owed Krish fifty quid.'

'So Krish was angry?'

'He wasn't happy,' she said, desperate to defend him. 'I hope you don't think Krish would murder someone for fifty quid? That's ridiculous.'

'But he was angry about Tommo touching you up, as you called it?'

She couldn't deny it. 'He was annoyed,' she conceded. 'But it was Oona who was stirring everyone up. She knew how to wind Tommo up. Even though she wasn't interested in him any more.'

'What do you mean?'

'I don't think she ever really liked him. And now she fancied someone else.'

'Who?'

'I don't know. Someone at work, I think.'

'Why do you say that?'

'She started coming home from work all lit up. Excited.'

Diaz looked intently at her. 'Eileen. This is very important. Can you remember anything, however insignificant, that Oona may have said about the person she fancied?'

Eileen's head was throbbing. 'She did say he was a real man. Tommo was just a big kid, everyone knew that.'

'Thanks for that. Let's return to the video.'

The questions pelted her, on and on, all afternoon. 'Why did Krish make the tape using those particular words?'

'Oona wrote it all down for him.'

'How did your fingerprints get on the knife?'

'Because Oona passed it to me in the furnace.'

'Why did you point the knife at Tommo?'

'Because Oona told me to,' she said weakly.

Eileen was struggling not to cry. So much for her earlier notion that she had stood up for herself. Oona had been calling the shots all along. She stretched her shoulders and rubbed her forehead.

'Just a sec. I remember what Tommo and Oona were arguing about. He said he'd seen Enid's Mini round where that man Mr Crossley died.'

'Tommo said he saw her mother's car at Phase Two?'

'Yeah, but it was Oona who usually drove it. Enid was scared of driving in case she crashed it or got caught drunk driving.'

Tired as she was, Eileen felt the atmosphere in the room spark up with a new energy.

'Can you remember exactly what Oona and Tommo said?'

'She told him it wasn't her who'd been to Phase Two, that's all I can remember. Oh, hang on. She told him how I'd back her up. Oh, yeah. It was all about that Monday night when we first went to the haunted mansion – that was what we called the nurses' home. Oona told Tommo it couldn't have been her driving the Mini when that man died because she came straight home from work just after five. And that I heard her get home from work.'

'Did you hear her?'

'Yeah. She went straight upstairs and played her music. I did hear her.'

'What time did you actually see her in person?'

'Later. I'd say nearly seven. I made cheese on toast and we met the lads at seven-thirty.'

291

'Please think carefully,' Diaz interjected. 'Did you hear Oona's footsteps, or her key in the door, or anything like that?'

She took her time, frowning. 'No. But I did think she was sleeping longer than usual.'

'Did she have that white cube clock radio at the time?'

'Yeah, she'd got it from Krish for her mum but borrowed it herself all the time.' Ella looked up sharply. 'Oh, I see what you mean.'

'So could it possibly have been the clock radio you heard?'

'Well, it could. She loved pre-loading it with her cassettes so it switched on in the morning to Black Sabbath or something. So she knew all about how to set it to come on later.'

'And her mum, Enid. Was she in the house?'

'No. She was at a health authority meeting. We were definitely on our own.'

'Was the Mini parked outside when you left?'

She shook her head, which felt like it had a tight rubber band around it. 'I'm sorry. I can't remember anything else. Can I have an aspirin now?'

'Well,' said Thripp, as soon as he and Diaz were alone. 'What do you make of all that?'

Diaz shook his head in bafflement. 'Turned things on their heads, all right. I can't remember ever interviewing such a self-possessed girl of just seventeen. And it does tie in entirely with what Krishnan Khan said in his interview.'

'They've had plenty of time to concoct a plausible story. But if it's true . . .'

'It did ring true to me. But we need to keep her in custody while we check it all out. For starters, we need to issue a warrant for Jim Judson's arrest on suspicion of rape. Shall I get onto West Yorkshire with the file and tell them to keep us in the loop?'

'Right you are. And meanwhile we need to bring Oona in for questioning as soon as.'

'In a fairer world I'd like to see Eileen's father charged with assault.'

He should have known better than to voice as much in front of his boss. 'Come off it, lad,' said Thripp. 'Spare the rod and all that.'

Diaz sighed, aware of another evening approaching away from Lorraine. It would likely be a long night.

CHAPTER FORTY-ONE

Friday 7th to Monday 24th October

Rob Kessler had woken to find Oona Finn hovering over him. He immediately wished he hadn't woken up, that he'd succeeded in killing himself after all. Fuck it, he was still in Windwell's infirmary, still in the only allocated bed on the unit, still with a throat like he'd swallowed a packet of razor blades.

'I brought your letter over. I know you don't like your post opened. It's from London. It could be from that author friend of yours, about the book he's writing about you.' Oona offered him a sealed envelope from that wanker journalist Felix Alexander as if presenting a bar of fucking gold.

'Leave it on the side.' His voice croaked like some old geezer on his last breath.

She pulled up a chair and settled down beside him and started prattling on. He didn't listen, but he did watch her. For the past month or so, he'd half-heartedly flirted with her. The lads had ribbed him about it, that he was in there with that one, so he'd put on a show, patted her bum or wheedled her to let him touch her hair. He hadn't given a fuck about it, apart from the respect it earned him from the guys.

Now, he studied her frosty-pink lips as they moved, and her earlobes hanging with silver piercings, her thick calves and her rounded thighs beneath her skirt. To his surprise, a sticky wave of interest started rising, not from his groin but originating in some other more primitive part of his brain.

'Good of you to come by,' he murmured, looking into baby-blue eyes that were small and watery. 'I always did like you best of all the women here.'

'Oh.' Her thin skin flushed as blood rushed to her capillaries. 'Well, I like you too, Rob.'

He attempted a smile, though it felt a bit creaky. 'If only I'd met a beautiful girl like you when I was outside. I wouldn't have wasted time on those ugly birds who got me in all this trouble.'

'That's sad.' She faltered, then asked, 'Is that what happened? Were you led on by bad women?'

Rob was beginning to find his groove. 'Sometimes. Though I wasn't always the innocent. A man has his instincts.'

'Oh. Yeah.' She did have a pneumatic, doll-like quality. There was another blush. Her nervousness made her transparent to him. A virgin priest could tell what was on her filthy mind.

'Yeah,' he said. 'Always had bad luck with women. Landed up with some right dogs. No loyalty. No womanly care. Looking back, I never really had a chance.'

She stared at him, open-mouthed. Then she stood

up, all in a fluster. The rosy flush below her throat was a dead giveaway. It was a truth he'd been told years ago by another lifer. There was a type of female who, faced with what they saw as a victimised, sex-starved serial killer, could hardly sit still at the prospect of risking all for the thrillingly dangerous fuck of her little life.

He soon forgot about the ward clerk when the night staff came on and dimmed the lights. Sleepless, his heart still pounded with fury towards that mind-fucker, Voss. When the new director first arrived at Windwell, Voss had told him that if he co-operated with his therapy he'd recommend him for an appeal on his sentence. Not in all the eleven years of his whole-life tariff had any doc ever held up a hope of release. The sessions went well enough till Voss appeared with his medical records, his psychological reports, from way back to when he was a kid. Voss had discovered that the only acting he'd ever done was as part of a con trick on old women, that he'd never had a school certificate to his name, and that he'd been up to his neck in debts.

Voss had asked him, 'Are you aware of your anger towards women?'

'Me? I'm angry 'cos I've got no women. I love women.'

'Robert.' Voss had given him the sort of look a prick of a teacher might give a stupid pupil. 'You don't love women. You killed four women.'

'Only because they drove me to it. It's me who's suffering for it.'

There had been a long silence before Voss spoke again. 'When you were arrested for those offences, it must have felt like you lost who you were.'

'Yeah. I was the top dog. I had loads of women after me.'

Voss leant forward and looked into his face with those all-seeing eyes. 'When a person becomes a resident here, it's like they stare into a mirror and don't know who they are. The courts force them to lose face.'

Rob looked away, out of the window, trying not to listen.

'I want to help you see the truth in that mirror. A man who was once a lonely and vulnerable child, who was unjustly hurt and humiliated by adults. A person who obliterated women because he'd been so cruelly hurt that he could never feel love.'

'What the fuck do you know about love?' Rob snarled.

Rob wanted to yell at Voss to shut up, but his voice box had choked up. Connie. A torrent of images rushed at him. Burns on his feet so he couldn't walk, the stinging rash 'cos he was locked in a cupboard and peed himself, the scar from a hot iron thrown at his head. He had wanted to kill Connie every day of his childhood but she was like a giantess, too massive and strong to fight against. All he'd had were fantasies of murder. And now he wanted to kill Voss too, to wipe him from the face of the earth. He leapt up and swung out at Voss but the director was fast, and lifted his chair up like a shield to protect himself. The shrink must have pressed an alarm beneath his desk because the door flew open. It had taken six screws to manhandle Rob back to the ward and sedate him.

Back on Ferris Ward he had lain crumpled on his bed, his head a black chaos. Was it true that those women had been scapegoats for Connie? For the first time in years he got to thinking about his birth mother, the slag who had dumped him because she'd guessed how he'd turn out – a freak, abnormal, unlovable. It wasn't fair. He'd worked so fucking hard to create a new self, copying cool heroes from movies, hiding his weakness behind a hardman face.

For the next few days Rob had felt like a volcano, spitting fury like fiery rocks. Then, on the morning of his next session with Voss, something shifted in the cooling cinders. It was a mad thought, but maybe it was true that he'd seen Connie in all those women. As soon as – well, as soon as he got used to his latest girl, got a taste for her, maybe relaxed a bit, something funny happened. It was like some puppet-master started jerking his strings; he'd suddenly find fault, misunderstand what she said, mentally preparing himself to hear that she was fucking some other guy, or badmouthing him, or in league with the cops. It was like a relief to finally knock her about and make her pay. A couple of times he'd managed to control it, but that was when he'd got the craving to be alone. When he got the chance he'd go out night-hunting, armed like a warrior, his eyes and ears ranging like a dog, his senses sweeping the streets like radar.

The cops still hadn't found them all, those street girls who coaxed him into dark alleys, or the homeless junkies, or those other girls who missed their bus or got pissed and lost their friends. But, the morning of his seeing Voss again, Rob got it, exactly why he felt that rush of crimson ferocity when he went after a woman. Ignoring his mates, he'd headed off to the library to ready himself in lonely silence. He was high on self-knowledge, desperate to tell Voss, and begin the journey back to re-enter the human race. When the appointment time came he felt ready to spill out the whole sump of bad feelings, the curdled rage, the buried self-loathing.

When he arrived at the therapy room, a screw was waiting with the look of a man mulling over a cruel joke. No, Doctor Voss couldn't make it. He had more important work to do.

Rob stumbled back to his room. Voss had stripped him of his make-believe rags and now he was crucifying him. The letter from Felix Alexander had been waiting for him. In search of balm to his ego, he tore it open. His eyes could barely register that the book had been rejected by all the publishers it had been offered to. They talked about legal issues but Rob wasn't interested in all that shit. At a stroke he had lost his path to redemption and his chance of glory. He wanted to die.

It wasn't true, what Voss had said, that Rob couldn't feel love. He had picked up the photo of Junior, his mate from the old days, his poor broken-headed boy, and took in that sweet, hopeful face that had turned to cremator's ash these three years now. He'd never used the word love back then, just like he'd never used the boy like a faggot – he wouldn't have let him down like that. He'd tried to be the sort of older brother he'd always wished for as a kid. He'd looked out for Junior, told him how to find his way, keep the screws in place, bang muscle, be a man.

Studying Junior's photo, he'd said, 'I'm comin' over now, Junior.'

Then he'd scrabbled around for any means to kill himself. He'd remembered the relaxation tape Voss had given him, a poxy reward for going through this hell. Rob pulled out the cassette ribbon, disembowelling the shiny brown tape till it hung in spools of intestinal plastic. All the gubbins that it stored – the words recorded as magnetic fields or electricity or vibrations or whatever – were twisted uselessly like his poor blasted thoughts. He slung a noose of it around his own neck and twisted it as tight as a garrotte until he blacked out.

Enough of all that shit. He'd been in the infirmary long enough, refusing to see that bastard Voss but taking new meds that kept him cool and in the zone. And now there was a new plan to hatch, a distraction from the swamp he'd been sinking into. On Oona's next visit Rob had been better prepared, buffed up and shaved, with his T-shirt stretched tight over his deltoids. He got straight to business.

'Have you ever heard how, when two special people meet, their life can be like extraordinary? Everything, the chemistry, the mental connection?'

She raised her watery eyes and puzzled over what he'd said. 'Yeah, that's weird, I think that too. I can't help it. I keep thinking about you, too.'

'Hope they're sexy thoughts.'

'God, you're a right one,' she giggled. 'People say I'm special too. I've got powers. The university's looking into it. Magic, psychic stuff, fortune-telling.'

He just about managed to keep his face straight. 'I get that. I felt that kind of aura coming off you. You've got a sympathetic soul.'

'I have,' she said coyly.

'You can't imagine how bad it feels to be stuck in here for ever, with no proper life. Meeting you made me realise what I'm missing. Physical love. Connection. Someone at my level. It's too fucking cruel. If only we could be free. Together. I think about it all the time.'

'So do I.'

'And the maddening thing, is it would be so easy. All I need is a few, let's say, theatrical props.'

'Ooh, I love a bit of drama.'

'It could be so simple.' He reached down and stroked her ankle as he told her his plan. Inch by inch he slid his fingers higher, caressing the soft skin behind her knee on his way to her thigh. Her blood was rising in her reckless, slavish body. She was hooked to his will. There was something dependably mechanical about the whole process, like clamping the clips onto a dead car battery. Just feed the juice into the element, stand back and watch the crappy old motor rumble back to life.

To get a work allocation in Windwell's new kitchen was a privilege reserved only for the hardmen who ran each block. Rob had always worked in the kitchen back at the old asylum, and when they all moved to Phase One, he'd threatened Dobson, the catering manager, with Armageddon if the privilege didn't continue. So here Rob was again, back from the infirmary and king of the storeroom. His moment of madness was over, he told himself. Besides, Rob had already spotted something a bit off about Doctor Voss. He was sure he had pinpointed his weak spot – and that, he assured himself, could always be called on if he needed to play a new hand.

CHAPTER FORTY-TWO

Wednesday 26th October

Against all her instincts Lorraine had been persuaded to take an active part in the outdoor team-building day. With Kevin no longer with them, and Brian arrested, the Windwell team had dwindled to only Voss, Enid and Parveen. Clifford, the hotel's outdoor instructor, had insisted on an even number of participants, so at last Lorraine had dubbined her walking boots and torn the labels from her outdoor gear. On Monday morning she had dropped her mum and Jas off at the bus station, promising to see them at home on Thursday afternoon. Her mum had hugged her for a few more seconds than usual, and whispered, 'Remember, Lorraine. You deserve him.' Lorraine had struggled to return a strained smile.

After two more nights at the hotel, she drove to the train station on Wednesday morning to greet Morgan as he descended from his first-class carriage. Before they reached the car a deluge of rain had given him a fine Yorkshire welcome. Lorraine viewed his pin-striped suit and shiny black leather brogues with apprehension.

Once in the car, he peered at the primeval swathes of empty countryside with distaste. She pointed to the rainbow overhead, its spectrum of colours vivid against the grey clouds. 'Maybe a good omen?'

'Or just another optical illusion,' he snapped. 'All this bad news isn't going down well with the health secretary. Is it too much to ask, he enquired of me, to keep Windwell out of the press for a day or two?' When he got no reply from Lorraine, he added, 'We won't have to actually visit the place, will we?'

'No. The hotel is about five miles away from the hospital.'

Morgan pulled out a train timetable and began to consult it. 'We'll get the pictures taken straight after lunch.'

At the hotel car park Morgan climbed out with a sour expression. 'You'll find me in the bar, Lorraine. I've brought my work with me.' He raised a very slim and lightweight briefcase in farewell.

The sight of climbing ropes, life jackets and safety helmets lined up outside the outdoor centre reminded Lorraine of the adolescent misery of endless double games at her secondary school. 'Spare me,' she muttered, at the prospect of being bullied by some fitness freak with a whistle around his neck. Inside, she found Voss deep in conversation with Clifford, their assigned instructor. He was bearded and brawny but was holding his own against Voss in a debate about the groupthink that beset President Kennedy and his advisors when they invaded the Bay of Pigs. Voss was nodding heartily, looking very Dutch in a black and orange tracksuit with matching headband, which she supposed had something to do with football.

'They won't make us do anything too horrible, will they?' asked Parveen, gravitating to Lorraine's side for reassurance. She looked rather awkward in big baggy trousers, plimsolls and a pink anorak.

'I did ask Clifford to remember we're not all athletic types.'

Parveen shuddered theatrically. 'Good. What can they do? Lock us up for not being able to leap across a river?'

Just then Enid arrived and quickly disappeared, insisting she had forgotten something from her car.

'She'll be fine,' Parveen commented cattily, 'legs like pipe cleaners.' It was true, as Enid was showing every inch of them in short shorts and legwarmers.

Clifford started the morning gently, by giving them a briefing on 'What makes a great team?' Lorraine glanced up at the diagrams projected on the screen and experienced an unhelpful wave of cynicism. She was beginning to wonder if the concept of teams was little more than American corporate hokum. She and Voss had tried to create a management team, but really, look at them – Enid was devoured by anxiety as usual, and no doubt counting the minutes to her next secret pull on a gin bottle. And she and Parveen would truly rather be anywhere else than facing a series of humiliating physical challenges.

Her mind drifted to her band, Electra Complex, a group of people with the single common aim of making music. How badly was that going? Their first big break and she'd had to back away and then be unceremoniously replaced. So much for team bonding in the real world.

Now Clifford was talking about trust and communication. What did that remind her of? She'd had no communication from Diaz since he'd turned up at the hotel on Saturday and she'd had to confess how unsatisfactory it all was to her mother. Four long days had passed since they'd been stranded at Scarcross Cavern, and the sensual pleasure of their night together was ebbing away. Any day now, he would be summoned back to Manchester, and she would have to consider her mum's advice. She felt cold with dread at the prospect of discovering which of them, Shirley or herself, he truly cared about.

Next, Clifford was touching on negative power, the power used by group members to disrupt, delay and destroy whatever progress the organisation was trying to make. Successive inquiries had decreed that Windwell was a failing organisation. She now believed in a Manichean power struggle between light and darkness, between the staff who supposedly ran the place and the inmates they imprisoned and restrained. One day in the library she'd come across an academic paper about the secret side to wards such as Ferris, designed to be isolated from the rest of the hospital. The symptoms occasionally erupted in violence and deceit: in Campbell's murder and its cover-up by the chief nurse, in whatever had motivated Kevin Crossley's murder, in a history of the inmates stealing meds from under the nursing staff's noses. Then there was Dobson's corruption in the catering department, and the teenagers' misuse of the old asylum to make the gruesome video that culminated in Tommo's murder.

She started to wonder not only how, but why it was that Robert Kessler fascinated Voss so powerfully. Kessler had to be the patient Voss had let down by breaking off his therapy. All Voss's ideals were starting to look decidedly frail up against the negative power of hardmen like Kessler. Kessler versus Voss. Truly, she wondered what hope the director had of winning such a contest.

She pictured Windwell as a rickety wooden structure, unable to withstand the secret infestation that burrowed like woodworm into its structure, eating away at the hospital's strength to heal. After all, what was the secret side but the formation of gangs that ran wards like Ferris, secret teams with corrupted goals, gathering intelligence, stealing resources, and undermining every attempt to modernise and enlighten. She was roused from this disturbing image by the sound of Clifford switching the overhead projector off and inviting them to follow him outside.

To her relief, Lorraine was surprised by how enjoyable the morning's events turned out to be. First off was an archery competition, in which the four of them worked together to reach a perfect score of five hundred. Clifford was well versed in team-building exercises, and created a first easy lesson in the power of collaboration. Next, out on the shallow edge of the reservoir, they all buckled on life jackets and helmets. Warily, they eyed the long canoe that bobbed like a crisp autumn leaf on the water.

'It's bound to sink with me in it,' muttered Parveen, half-joking, but simultaneously clutching at Lorraine's arm. Together they waded out and clambered on board, only just avoiding capsizing the wobbling boat.

Clifford was in the bow, while the four of them each took up one of the benches and picked up a paddle.

Clifford explained that this would be an exercise in clear communication. Voss had taken the front bench, and was given the task of steering them. The twist in the exercise was that the remaining three paddlers were instructed to turn themselves backwards on their benches and rely only on Voss's spoken instructions. In the first ten minutes the four of them laughed more and for longer than they ever had before, as Voss failed to direct the canoe in any direction at all. Then Voss and Parveen swapped places and the group did a little better, having grasped that short, deliberate instructions worked best. By the time Lorraine, and then Enid, had a chance to direct the canoe they had cracked it, by allocating numbers to the paddlers and instigating a calm period of practice before setting off. After an hour they paddled back to the shore in rhythmic synchronisation, with a sense of amused pride at their progress.

Morgan was waiting on the shore beneath an oversized umbrella, his brogues deep in sticky mud and his expression frigid. The sight of him started up Parveen and Lorraine's giggling fit again, as the four team members lined up with damp pink faces and, dare she say it, an inner glow of shared satisfaction. By contrast, Morgan refused to relinquish his gigantic umbrella and was therefore photographed by Clifford standing a good three feet apart from the team, like a solitary misfit, quite alone.

Lorraine leant down and whispered to Parveen, 'Look at him, the overrated buffoon.'

'The what?' Parveen queried. 'Over-inflated balloon?'

Lorraine struggled to keep her laughter clamped inside.

Worse, Morgan squelched over, tight-lipped and scowling venomously.

'I'll get a taxi to the station. Don't want to disrupt your fun. Urgent meeting.'

'Very well, sir.'

Then with an exasperated sigh, he snapped, 'It's nothing to laugh about, Lorraine.'

'I know, that, sir,' she said through gritted teeth, the corners of her lips still twitching.

CHAPTER FORTY-THREE

The team devoured the generous buffet lunch back at the centre, all high on adrenaline and group bonhomie. Voss congratulated Lorraine on the day so far, which cheered her, and she also silently congratulated herself that after just one more night spent in the luxurious surroundings of the hotel, this whole Windwell project would be over. What remained of the management team had somehow bonded, though probably more by luck and Clifford's practical experience than any intervention of hers. After she savoured a last currant-studded Yorkshire Fat Rascal washed down with strong tea, Lorraine was almost eager when Clifford arrived to lead the final activity.

They all filed out into a burst of weak sunshine, relaxed and chatting. The path led up a track to a rocky outcrop where a coil of rope and other gear lay waiting for them.

Parveen clasped a hand over her mouth and moaned. 'Not rock climbing, please. No way can I bear all my weight on my fingertips. I'll just have to let go and hope I die quickly.'

Lorraine edged towards Clifford, who was doing something complicated with buckles and ropes. She glanced down over the edge of a precipitous gully and felt her mouth turn dry.

'Abseiling,' he announced cheerily. 'Perfectly safe. One of our clients' favourite trust exercises.'

By the time Clifford asked for a volunteer, Lorraine had decided a strategy to cope with her nerves. 'I'll go first,' she volunteered.

'Right, Lorraine. Kit on.' She stepped into a clip-on harness and buckled a hard helmet under her chin. Clifford's sidekick, a local lad named Marcus, gave a demonstration that made springing backwards over the edge of a seventy-foot cliff look like a ride on a playground swing. He was down on the gravelly bottom in less than a minute, unhooked and waiting, while Clifford hauled the rope back up to the top. In a few moments the ropes were attached to Lorraine's harness, while two guide ropes were thrust into her hands.

Clifford smiled down on her benevolently as he gestured to the rest of the team to gather and listen. 'Now what I haven't fully explained yet, is how this becomes a lesson in trust. You people,' he said, indicating Voss, Parveen and Enid, 'are all going to help Lorraine by calling down instructions. Remember what you learnt this morning about clarity and directness.' He pulled out a piece of white cloth, the size of a narrow scarf. 'Because, while Lorraine descends to the bottom, she's going to be blindfolded.'

She spoke without thinking and with a sharp edge of

sarcasm. 'What? I don't know about that.'

Clifford fixed his gaze firmly on her. 'All you need to do is focus on letting the rope through your right hand and listening to instructions.'

She backed away from him and pushed her palms up, defensively. 'Sorry. I don't think so. I'm a visual person. Honestly, I don't even think I can tell my right from left in the dark.'

To her extreme annoyance Voss began to argue that there was no such thing as a visual person. Panic was rising in her thumping heart as her breathing accelerated.

'I suggest that we do it right now,' Clifford suggested kindly. 'All you need to do is plant your feet right here at the edge, right there on the lip—'

'We'll all be backing you,' Voss was repeating, as if she gave a shit about what he thought while it would be her alone, dangling in the dark.

She took a moment to consider her options. Of course she could absolutely refuse to do this. Yet how would that look to the others? Or maybe she could just go through with it, and rely on Clifford and the team's instructions. It would be horrible, but despite the terror growing in her gut, logic told her that her fear was irrational. If she simply did as she was told, she would almost certainly live to tell the tale.

Fearfully, she edged to stand directly above the drop into the gully and let Clifford repeat the instructions once more. 'Remember, your right hand is the brake. Your left hand should be relaxed, and just hold yourself upright.'

She noticed that everyone had fallen silent. 'OK. I'm going to put the blindfold on you now. But remember, we are all here, and you simply need to relax and guide yourself down at your own pace.' Deftly, Clifford strapped the blindfold over her eyes. Suddenly she felt utterly alone and disorientated.

'Now. Lean back and put some weight into the harness. Work yourself down. That's it. Now, just let yourself walk down the cliff edge.'

She wanted to say that was easier said than done, but instead, she gently let the rope release herself a short way down. After a dreadful moment swinging in the hellish darkness, her feet found the sheer side of the cliff.

'Great, Lorraine. Now just crouch, as if you're sitting on a chair. That's perfect. Your knees bent, your back straight.'

Cautiously, she inched her way down, one step at a time. After a few steps, she found a rhythm. From above, she could hear the team calling, 'Keep going!' She shouted back, 'How far down am I?' and they told her. At last, she heard, 'You're nearly halfway.' Though her heart seemed to be beating at a thousand miles per hour, she continued walking backwards down the cliff, trying not to think about what might happen if the rope failed, or if she let go.

'You're about ten feet above the ground,' Voss called down.

'What do I do?'

Clifford called down. 'Slow down, take the next steps very slowly and Marcus will make sure you land safely.'

She did as she was told, and a pair of arms guided her to the gravelly earth. Suddenly she found herself standing upright on unsteady legs. Marcus pulled the blindfold from her eyes. From the top of the gulley she could hear cheers and applause. An intense sunshine of euphoria filled her mind and body. She had done it.

Parveen was the next to descend and Lorraine found herself encouraging her with every step, protesting that if she could do it, Parveen certainly could. The administrator gave a little scream of fear as she swung over the cliff edge, and a few times she stopped, getting her breath back and gathering her courage, but soon enough she was standing beside Lorraine, almost crying with relief. They shared a congratulatory hug and shook their heads in disbelief.

Voss, it turned out, was an experienced abseiler and had opted to go last. That put Enid on the ropes next. By now the sunshine had vanished and a chilly drizzle was falling, and it seemed to Lorraine that Clifford speeded through Enid's briefing, though from the bottom they couldn't hear a great deal. What did motivate them was Clifford's promise of hot chocolate and biscuits back at the centre as soon as they were all done.

The back of Enid's head, and then her torso, emerged. With a wail, she protested, 'I can't see!'

Clifford was making adjustments, and re-emphasising his instructions. 'No, use your right hand, Enid. No. Just stop and listen.'

Enid did stop, and then restarted the same route downwards at a rapid pace, bouncing and leaping.

'Slow down!' Clifford shouted. 'Enid. Use your right hand to—'

Lorraine saw Enid kick out clumsily against the rock wall and start spinning like a pendulum on the rope. With sickening inevitability, Enid crashed into a rocky outcrop. Enid shrieked in panic, crying for help.

'No!' Lorraine cried out in disbelief. The poor woman was stuck just below the halfway point, her rope caught on a jutting point of stone some way to the left of the abseiling route. Scarlet blood was flowing on Enid's shock-white face. Now she was clawing at the blindfold, sending her body rotating again, round and round, while she wailed, 'I don't want to be a part of this any more. I can't do it!'

'Marcus, run and get the double harness,' Clifford shouted from the top. Then to Enid he called, 'Just stay very still and breathe deeply. I'm coming down the path but it will take five minutes. All you need to do is to stay very still until I get the double harness and can bring you down safely.'

Lorraine picked up the blindfold from where it had fallen near her feet and then looked up. Enid's petrified eyes met hers. The distance up the rocky wall to where she was swinging didn't actually look that far. As she watched, Enid reached down to her with a claw-like hand. 'Can you help me, Lorraine?'

Afterwards, Lorraine found it difficult to explain her actions. That hand, trembling and beseeching her, might have belonged to a member of her own family. Intent only on finding foot- and handholds on the rock face, Lorraine began to climb. Instinctively keeping her body flat against the rock, she edged her way up to the weeping woman, never looking down. By the time she reached Enid the woman had been sick, retching over her bare legs and hands. Still, Lorraine grabbed her hand that was sticky with vomit and shaking as if with a palsy. The sweetness of alcohol lingered in the air, too.

'It's all right,' Lorraine murmured, trying to soothe those frightened blue eyes. 'We've got you. It'll all be over soon.'

CHAPTER FORTY-FOUR

No one could track down Oona at work, so after a shower and change of clothes Lorraine offered to drive Enid back to Windwell. It hadn't been pleasant to wash Enid's alcohol-laced bile off her skin, but she told herself she'd dealt with worse on nights out with the band. Then the hours had dragged on as Voss dressed Enid's cuts and they endured the rigmarole of dealing with the hotel manager's somewhat guarded apology. Accident forms had to be completed and signed. Clifford was pacing around, silent but clearly shaken by a potentially serious injury on his watch.

When they had a few seconds alone in a corridor, Voss asked, 'She was drunk?'

'Yes, she can hide it quite well but I could smell it.'

'I've told her she needs to take a few weeks off work to recover. I'd appreciate your professional advice before you go.'

'Of course. At this rate, there may only be you and Parveen left running the hospital.'

He gave her a look that seemed ridiculously fond. 'I'm asking you again to stay on too.'

'I'm sorry,' she said as kindly as she could manage, though feeling a twinge of guilt. 'My daughter's waiting for me at home.'

By the time Lorraine and Enid set out, the dying sun was casting purple shadows over the barren hills and they met no other headlamps on the twisting road to Windwell. Lorraine mentioned to Enid that she needed to call in at the admin office to check the personnel-related post.

Enid perked up. 'If you're going into work I can pick my stuff up too.'

'Are you sure that's wise? You should be resting.'

'I'd rather bring the hospital accounts home with me.' She could understand why; Enid had failed in the essential core of her job as treasurer, the production of annual accounts.

Phase One's security lights cast a brutal white illumination over the site. After identity checks at the security barrier, the pair ascended the deserted stairs. It was after six o'clock and Jenny and Oona had clearly left for the day, so Lorraine had to use her set of keys to get onto the empty admin corridor. Seeing Enid safely back to her own office, Lorraine settled down at Kevin's desk to peruse the buff file Jenny had labelled 'Personnel Post'. All the papers were freshly opened and stamped with the day's date, and most were simply waiting to be filed or passed on: application forms, requests for references, and new government circulars from Whitehall. Lorraine picked up a fresh bundle despatched from the NHS Pension Agency. There were the usual pension illustrations for staff about to retire but amongst these the name Kevin Crossley startled her. It seemed that Kevin's death in service benefits were to be paid out to a named beneficiary, and the name printed on the letter was extraordinary: Oona Finn. Also in the bundle was a letter confirming her mother's, Enid Finn's, early retirement with immediate effect as recommended by Kevin Crossley. Lorraine skimmed the contents of both letters, and then slowly read them again. Here were two people in line for Kevin's munificence, two very promising prospects for a celebratory tea party at Kevin's home. Yet neither had turned up at his house on that fatal Monday night.

Visual patterns formed in her brain, triangulations linking disparate people, uncovering previously hidden connections. Kevin, Enid, Oona. In Kevin's diary entry for that tragic Monday he had written:

'7.30 O O A B X O O O'

She pulled out Kevin's, Enid's and Oona's personnel files. There would be nothing but the dry and dusty facts, she told herself, but that was exactly what she was searching for. As recently as September, the Blood Transfusion Service had run mobile donor sessions in one of Windwell's classrooms. It was a common practice in every hospital, and Lorraine had generally volunteered to give blood alongside the majority of hospital workers. It meant no more than an hour away from the workplace to be attached to the machine, followed by a short rest with a cup of tea and a biscuit before heading back to work. In Kevin's scrupulously tidy fashion, a carbon copy of the paper slip generated by the transfusion service had been clipped inside each donor's personnel file. She laid them out in order:

Kevin Crossley	Blood Group O
Enid Finn	Blood Group O
Oona Finn	Blood Group O

She remembered the rumour that Professor Leadbetter was Oona's father. It took a while longer, but eventually she located the professor's personnel file. It seemed that blood transfusion sessions were offered to staff each year, and three years ago, Gerald Leadbetter had attended. She noted down his blood group as AB. It was a long time since Lorraine had studied O-level biology, but she had a fair idea of how children inherited their blood types from their parents. She searched the bookshelves and found a leather-bound encyclopaedia. Under a chart headed 'Blood Type and Paternity' she found the relevant data and copied out the details:

Parents	Possible children	Impossible children
O x O	O	A, B, AB
O x AB	A, B	O, AB

If that was correct, and Professor Leadbetter had been Oona's father, her type would necessarily have been A or B. She recalled Kevin's diary entry:

O O A B X O O O

Kevin's summary of their blood types had led to him writing an X after OOAB to indicate that the first option of Leadbetter being Oona's father was incorrect. The three O-types represented by Kevin, Enid and Oona was the only possible sequence to explain Oona's paternity. Still, she wished there were some other way to corroborate her discovery. Surely there was eye colour, too? Enid's eyes were bluish green, and Oona's a clear blue. She had no idea what colour Kevin's or Gerald Leadbetter's eyes were. Well, there was an even better means to prove the case, and that was to ask someone who knew them both. Enid's office was only a few doors away, but to her frustration, Lorraine found that Enid was absent from her desk, though the door stood unlocked. Lorraine returned to the admin office and started to pack her papers away.

In the corner of her eye she caught a blur of movement passing the open door, and followed Enid into her office. The cuts and grazes to her face were not too deep, but Voss had taped large dressings over the worst of them and she looked wounded and exhausted. Surrounding her were what seemed to be barricades made from stacks of financial printouts. Lorraine lifted a pile and set it on the floor before seating herself to give the treasurer the momentous news.

Enid dropped her face into her hands and stared at the mass of paper covering her desk. 'I feel I've woken up after living in the dark for the last few years. I've been hiding in a deep fog of alcohol.' Her voice started to choke with emotion. 'I'm so ashamed of myself. Maybe what you said – a counsellor or a treatment plan. Then I can find a less responsible job.'

'I think that's a very good idea. If you like, I can refer you to Occupational Health before I leave.'

'Yes, I think it's time. Today I felt so – out of control. When you start out you think alcohol is your friend, but it always undermines you. And I'm worried about Oona.

I've let her run wild. I didn't have much time for her when she was younger.'

She studied Lorraine with her gaunt features. 'I'm sorry I said that about your team-building. It was the last thing I wanted, to be challenged to open up and feel better about myself. Today at the cliff I realised that even Voss is a spirit for good. He needs a better treasurer. It's time I resigned and went on my way.'

Lorraine gestured for Enid to allow her speak. 'Before you go any further, I have some news that might affect your plans.'

She decided to begin with the revelation about Oona's paternity, and passed Enid the first letter from the NHS Pension Agency about Kevin's named beneficiary.

Enid studied the letter with the same surprised reaction as Lorraine had experienced. 'What? Why on earth would Kevin leave his benefits to Oona?'

'Enid, I'm sorry if this seems like prying, but could Oona be Kevin's natural daughter?'

The question seemed to knock the air from Enid's lungs.

'Well, technically, yes,' she said in a very quiet voice. 'I did have a brief affair with Kevin. He was rather unhappily married and I was single,' she added defensively. 'We weren't right for each other, but we stayed friends. He wasn't always the fuddy-duddy he became later on. Then, when he remarried, it seemed like the best thing was to forget it ever happened. And I was also involved with Gerald Leadbetter around the same time. Maybe because Oona visited his house when she was a little girl, she got it into her head that Gerald was her father. And I suppose I decided it must be true. Oona and Gerald were like two peas in a pod compared to Oona and Kevin.'

'Do you mind my asking what colour eyes Kevin and Gerald both had? I'm afraid I haven't met either of them.'

'Kevin's eyes were a sort of pale grey. Gerald's are deep brown.'

'From what I know, if Gerald's eyes were deep brown the colour would have been dominant over your lighter eye colour, and Oona would have been very unlikely to be born with bright blue eyes.'

Lorraine then passed Enid her summary of both her own and Oona's blood type, along with those of the prospective fathers. Enid frowned over the chart, baffled.

'But surely Kevin would have told me if he'd worked that out?'

'I believe he meant to when you were invited to tea at his house. It seems he wanted to discuss that he appeared to be Oona's father. I believe you chose not to go.'

'What? I didn't know about it! We'd had a big row on Friday night. And he'd been rather awful to me. I'd been keeping myself topped up all day and he'd challenged me and said I'd have to go. But if he'd held out an olive branch, like that invitation, and told me he was going to acknowledge Oona, of course I'd have rushed around to make it up with him.'

Lorraine studied Enid's agitated expression. 'I wonder why you didn't receive the invitation? Apparently, Kevin was trying to get away early that evening, and had bought a cake, and even laid the table with his best china.'

Enid shook her head. 'I can't think.'

'What did he say on Friday that upset you?'

'This won't go beyond these four walls?'

'Of course not.'

'Well, I'd completely messed up the annual accounts. I was pretty drunk but still, it was too much to bear to be confronted like that. He told me it couldn't go on. He was going to have to sort it out once and for all.'

'Oh, Enid,' Lorraine said with feeling. 'I think Kevin did sort a solution out.' She handed Enid the second letter from the Pensions Agency offering Enid early retirement. Enid scanned it quickly, then slowly looked up at Lorraine, with round, astonished eyes.

'You think he arranged this for me? I thought he was going to sack me. I raged at Oona that I'd lose my job and we'd be kicked out of our home any day soon.'

'How did Oona take the news?'

'I've never seen her so furious. She told me she hated his guts. In fact, I feared she might never be able to work with him again. I was frightened she might . . . lose her own job too, and confront him in a rage. She called him every name under the sun. Goodness, her own father. She hadn't ever liked Kevin, that was the pity. But still . . .'

Lorraine said carefully, 'So if Oona had been personally invited to Kevin's house, and been told to invite you too, is it possible she decided not to pass the invitation on?'

Enid puzzled over this. 'Oh, you mean she was so furious with him that she didn't even tell me? Maybe. What a miserable weekend we had. At first she did hint that I'd be sacked straight away. Then later, she told me some maniac had killed Kevin and I confess, it did feel like a reprieve. I couldn't believe fate had handed back my job and my home. And now I find out that Kevin wasn't the ogre I'd thought he was. Early retirement. It's like a dream come true.'

Suddenly, her eyes locked on Lorraine, searching for the bad news. 'Will it still be given to me even though Kevin was murdered?'

'Your early retirement? Yes, the application was approved before he died. You just need to serve your notice.'

Visible relief and happiness flooded Enid as she stared at the letter. Lorraine could recall that the figure was the not at all insignificant sum of £9,000 pension payable per annum and a lump sum of £27,000.

'Oh, I can't wait to tell Oona all about it. We can leave Windwell. And I can easily afford to buy our own house with this.'

Lorraine was profoundly happy for Enid's sake. But nevertheless, she felt obliged to warn her about at least one of the consequences. 'You do understand that I must report this to the police. I'm afraid it may have a bearing on their investigation.'

'Of course,' Enid assured her, still dazed by her former lover's generosity. 'And tell the police to hurry up and find Oona, won't you? She won't believe it when I tell her we can leave here at last.'

CHAPTER FORTY-FIVE

Tuesday 25th to Wednesday 26th October

Rob's domain was the fresh food store – a private and peaceful spot where he could eat and smoke for a few hours, and then get some other hobbit to carry out whatever tasks were on his sheet. He kept a plastic tub on the top shelf of his store, with orders to Dobson that no one should touch it on pain of torture and slow death. He kept his private treats in there: a baggie of weed, tobacco and Rizlas, some chocolate, and a couple of skin mags. Now he waited for a new delivery to arrive. On his second day it was there in the plastic tub. It was the day he heard how the cops were grilling a couple of teenage kids for Tommo Ogden's murder. The case interested him, and Rob had plenty of intel sources amongst the weaker screws who were anxious to keep their lives nice and easy. Now he read the message with great satisfaction:

Dobson is loading his car with extras tomorrow at 7.
All you need is in the box.

Beneath the note lay a white plastic trilby hat of the sort the staff had to wear in the kitchen, and a black fake beard, just like the one Dobson sported. Rob considered Dobson to be a bigger crook than any of Windwell's inmates. The tosser had no fucking morals, stealing food out of sick men's mouths. If Rob had to jump the catering manager, it would be a pleasure. He considered his options, like a fat kid ogling a selection in a cake shop. To disable Dobson with his bare hands would be exciting, but the potential noise was a risk. His preference was a good sharp blade, but knives were strictly off-limits. He looked around the storeroom and saw nothing. Blubbery and asthmatic, Dobson would be easy to take down. He picked up the plastic-weave trilby and tore off the ribbon from around the crown. He stretched it tight between his hands and closed his eyes, picturing the moment. It was on the short side, but it would do very nicely indeed.

The following night, Rob was back in the storeroom at seven-thirty, feeling more alive than he had in years. He was stretching his nerves again, extending his faculties like a pair of soaring wings. So far, it had almost been too easy; he had got one of his crew to tell some hobbit to change shifts with him that evening, and here he was, crouched behind a barricade of boxes waiting for Dobson to show up. He played with the hat band, twisting and untwisting it tightly like a silken rope.

When Dobson turned up, Rob watched him as he let himself inside the store, huffing and puffing as he hauled boxes of coffee and chocolate away to the loading bay. Soon the toerag was sweating, and after the third trip Rob had waited long enough. As Dobson picked up his next load Rob silently took up position behind him. Gracefully, he slung the white band over his head like a noose and pulled it into the fat creases of his neck. It was a tight fit, but Rob hadn't wasted all those hours banging muscle in the gym. He twisted the two ends and pulled with what felt like superhuman strength. Dobson couldn't make a sound as his windpipe closed but his arms were a fucking nuisance, clawing back against Rob's sweatpants. Triumphantly, he yanked the ribbon like a vice and waited. Finally, the old geezer's weight drooped against him and he let him topple to the ground. In a leisurely manner, Rob stripped off Dobson's gear and pulled on the baggy brown trousers, shirt and essential white coat. Finally, he stuck the adhesive-backed beard in place and set the white trilby on his own head. The Windwell pass and the car keys were in place, along with a fat wallet containing nearly fifty quid. Dobson lay very still but breathing. It was tempting to finish him off, but it was almost a quarter to eight. A guard might turn up on his rounds any second.

Opening the storeroom door an inch, Rob saw the kitchen was empty. He made his way to the loading bay, where the entrance was still wedged conveniently open. A car stood by the ramp, a disappointingly crappy Allegro, but any wheels would do. He slammed down the hatchback and got inside the car, then checked himself in the mirror. Not a single bead of sweat. He had turned on the ignition and was enjoying reacquainting himself with gears and indicators when he sensed movement behind him on the back seat. He had genuinely forgotten this bit; the irritating price he'd agreed to pay.

'Hi, love. Did it all go to plan?' asked Oona.

'Yeah,' he said mechanically.

'This is so exciting.'

Shit. He couldn't offload her here, in Windwell. Maybe later, in some isolated spot. Or maybe she could be useful? A hostage. Nice.

'Dobson's lights are out,' he said. 'Remember. You do exactly what I say. Act natural, right. I'm giving you a lift.'

The girl nodded. Ahead, the security lodge was well lit. Rob drew the car up beside the lodge's window and lifted his pass to show the guard. Instead of waving him through, the guard came out and knocked on Rob's window. Reluctantly, he wound it down a few inches.

'Got my share, Mr Dobson?'

Rob froze. He turned to the girl and muttered, 'Get rid of him.'

She stepped outside and said, 'What's up? We're in a rush.'

The guard shoved his head inside the rear of the car and shone a torch in Rob's face. 'You're not Dobson!'

Rob leant over the seat and launched a punch that hit the guard's head so hard he toppled backwards onto the tarmac. Jumping out of the car, Rob leapt onto the man's prone body and started kicking him in the guts with a sense of giddy exultation.

The girl started whining at him to stop. 'Come on. Someone'll see us.'

He shoved her back into the car, then raised the security barrier. Leaving the guard unconscious at the roadside, he floored the accelerator of the Allegro and roared away through Windwell into the night. He was free again, back in the outside world, his heart pumped up and his brain on fire.

328

'Which way to get across country?' Rob growled.

'There are no streetlights on the Burnley Road. Keep going.'

For another minute the car careered along narrow roads, passing only a few lonely houses and outbuildings. With a jolt Rob braked hard and skidded over to the roadside. In the far distance the land was stained by the hypnotic pulse of revolving blue lights.

'Fuck it. What's another way out?'

When the girl didn't answer instantly, he hit the steering wheel. 'Come on. There must be a farm track or private road.'

'All right. Turn round. There's an empty house on the edge of the village.'

A tense few minutes later, Rob nudged the Allegro up a private drive and the headlamps illuminated a grand house with darkened windows. Switching off the engine, he asked, 'Is everyone out?'

'Yeah, he's away.'

'Got some new gear for me to change into?'

'I suppose so.'

Stepping outside Rob dragged Oona by the arm up to the house, where she retrieved a key from behind a stone and opened the door. Inside, the hallway was quiet save for the loud ticking of a grandfather clock.

Rob found the light switch. 'Nice digs.' He pushed Oona towards the nearest doorway. 'Get some food sorted. Something hot.'

With a baleful backwards look, Oona disappeared. Rob found some good stuff lying around. There was tobacco, a cabinet with whisky and bourbon, and a recent copy of *The*

Times. When Oona appeared with a plate of beefburgers and chips, he gorged himself.

'Some whisky,' he demanded. 'And some bread and butter.' He was in a state of euphoria, revelling in the sheer comfort of the armchair and the richness of a home decorated with paintings, lamps and soft fabrics, after decades of eyeballing only pale green emulsioned walls and easy-wipe vinyl chairs.

Now that he felt pleasantly stuffed, he began to get bored. He started prowling around the rest of the house, in search of a shooter or some other useful weapon. When he came upon the display cabinets, he called out to Oona and was gratified to see how scared she looked. This was more like it, he thought. The prospect of having a bit of fun with her began to play out in his mind.

CHAPTER FORTY-SIX

'Enid, I just need to make a couple of quick phone calls before I drop you at home.'

The treasurer nodded her agreement, and on her way back to admin, Lorraine tried to identify the growing unease that was troubling her. She wondered how long it would take until Enid worked through the implications of Oona's inheritance. And where the hell was Oona?

Anticipating her own return to the hotel, she had been thinking that her route would pass Professor Leadbetter's home, and warmed to the chance to finally acquaint herself with his infamous Black Museum before she left Windwell for good. She found his phone number and connected to an answerphone, leaving as friendly a message as she could muster.

Uncertainties, like invisible spectres, still taunted her. Time was speeding by, yet she needed to work this investigation through to its final end. And to do that she needed to speak to Diaz.

She rang the direct number Diaz had given her. To her irritation, Laddo picked up the phone.

'I'll have to take a message, Miss Quick.' He sounded rather bored, as if she were endlessly bothering him with nonsense.

'Can't you put me through to him? It's very urgent.'

'He's gone to Manchester.'

Manchester? Through gritted teeth, she asked, 'Is it personal business?'

'So you do know?'

'Yes, he told me all about it.'

'So you'll know he won't want you disturbing him.' Lorraine noted the cruel pleasure in Laddo's tone. She swallowed quickly, not wanting to give him the satisfaction of hearing a catch of emotion in her voice.

'Is Chief Inspector Thripp available?'

'He's not to be disturbed.'

'Then can you write this down, please? My message is that Oona Finn is Kevin Crossley's daughter, and is due to inherit his pension fund. It's possible that she and Tommo were involved in his death. You need to interview her urgently.'

To be fair, the constable did sound rather more impressed this time. 'So where can he find you?'

'I'm just dropping Enid Finn off at her home and then having a word with Professor Leadbetter. I'll be back at the hotel for the evening. You will pass this on, won't you, Constable?'

She waited, and detected the sharpness of sarcasm when he replied, 'Naturally I will, Miss Quick.'

Outside, the coming winter was almost tangible, with the

taste of frost in the air. By the time Lorraine had dropped Enid off outside her house, it was after half past eight.

'My car's here,' Enid said, indicating the mustard-coloured Mini parked on the road. 'Oona must be home.'

'But there are no lights on inside,' Lorraine observed.

Enid's hopes overrode the evidence. 'If I know Oona, she'll be upstairs lounging in her room.'

The treasurer turned to clutch Lorraine's hand and shook it triumphantly. 'Thanks again, Lorraine. Not just for my good news, but for . . . You know, being with me when I was so scared.'

Lorraine pressed her other hand over Enid's and privately made a wish that this woman might soon be living in a kinder future.

It was with a sense of duty rather than pleasure that Lorraine headed towards the impressive gates that she'd been told led to Wynd Well Hall. Across the road the old asylum was starkly floodlit, the magnificent clock tower picked out in pallid detail, the clock still stopped at just before twelve. On the ground a number of heavy lorries were moving as workmen in hard hats hauled fencing and equipment around the site. The demolition men, she realised, must be working late tonight.

Lorraine considered turning round and phoning the professor to explain that she no longer needed to see him. And yet she felt a gathering need to visit him, hoping to glimpse an important link in a pattern she guessed might be waiting in the Black Museum. Her intuition pushed her onwards, up the driveway, until Wynd Well Hall came into sight. It was a beautiful manor house, part medieval, with later Jacobean and what looked like Victorian additions.

For a moment she comprehended why Oona might have fantasised about being the professor's daughter.

'Wynd.' She pondered the origins of the word, for it sounded very ancient. Wasn't it the same word as that used in Scotland for a twisting narrow street, something that wended its way, like a river, or perhaps a wellspring? A few of the leaded windows glowed amber in the dark so she reckoned the professor must be at home. She parked as close to the front door as she could and then hesitated, gathering her thoughts, deciding to merely tell the professor that she was searching for Oona. The question of paternity should remain a closed matter between Enid, Oona and whomever they chose to disclose it to.

CHAPTER FORTY-SEVEN

'What's all this about Junior Campbell?' Rob pointed to the display case where the red cord hung beside a photo of the lad.

'This is Professor Leadbetter's house,' said Oona. 'He's interested in justice for Campbell.'

'What the fuck does he know about it?'

'What everyone knows. That Tommo beat up Campbell and then strangled him. That he only got away with it 'cos his dad covered it all up. So he got what he deserved when he was knifed in the tunnels last week.'

Rob snorted. 'You think you know it all, don't you? Tommo Ogden beat up Junior, but he never killed him.'

A satisfying spasm of shock afflicted the girl. 'What?' she asked weakly.

'It was a set-up. Tommo Ogden was the fall guy.'

She looked like she was having trouble making her lips work. Finally, she managed, 'Who did it?'

He couldn't resist the punchline. 'I did.'

'You never. I always heard he was your best mate.'

'You heard of back-door parole? The only way out of Windwell for Junior was in a coffin. Your scrote of a boyfriend had tormented him enough.'

He reached to open the glass cabinet but it was locked. With a lazy movement he picked up an ashtray and threw it hard against the display case, which shattered into pieces. Though glass still stood in jagged shards inside the frame, he reached inside, pulled out the photo of Campbell and studied it intensely.

'Back then I had my own key made by a nutter who'd trained as a locksmith. I went to check on Junior and found him after your moron boyfriend had battered him. I gave him what he asked for. An escape route from Windwell.'

He looked over to Oona with a knowing smile. 'So you did me a favour killing that thicko boyfriend of yours. Did you enjoy it?'

He watched as a different, cornered look appeared on her face. 'Come on, Oona. It takes one to know one,' he challenged.

Her eyes lifted to his, suddenly bright. 'Yeah. It was fun.'

He grinned and reached in the cabinet for the red cord that hung on the hook, and shoved it in his pocket. Then he took a long look at her, at her thick legs, her breasts, and her hands with the pink painted nails.

'Get me a cup of coffee. Hot milk. Two sugars. And while you're at it, think on what I'm going to get for afters.'

He was rewarded by the sight of her fearfully cringing backwards against the wall. Then a mumbling protest. 'I . . . don't want . . .'

'You're a witch, in't you? What you gonna do, bring

your ugly mug boyfriend back from the grave to defend your honour? Oops, sorry, he won't be too happy when he remembers how you murdered him.'

He laughed then, for the first time in a long time. She made a pathetic dash to escape, into the hallway, aiming for the front door. He grabbed her shoulders and shoved her back towards the kitchen.

'You're going the wrong way, babe.'

He shoved her into the big manorial kitchen, all wooden cupboards and fancy knick-knacks. She banged hard against the table edge and stared at him, bug-eyed with terror. He reached out to lift a strand of her hair. It felt like soft nylon. He slid his fingertips down from her shoulder to her breast and squeezed it, watching the fear blank out all her cockiness.

'Fancied a bit of rough, is that it?'

Her painted lips moved, but the only sound was a wordless protest.

'Get on the table.' He watched her move like an unwieldy puppet and then lower herself to sit on the table edge.

'I don't . . .' she managed to croak.

He didn't want to look at her stupid face any more. 'Turn round and bend over. Lift up your skirt.'

When she clumsily flashed her white thighs he opened his flies, but there was nothing doing. He gave her body some half-hearted squeezes. The stupid cow wasn't even his type. There was still nothing happening down below. It was just his luck that he'd have the whole night here with this bird who was so unfanciable. Getting bored, he turned her back round again and slapped her hard across the face. This was more like it. She cried out, clutching her hand to the trickle of blood running from her nose. He looked down on her in growing excitement.

'So what's your game, Oona?'

She was spitting scarlet blood into her palm.

'I haven't . . . got a game,' she gurgled.

'So why'd you get me out? Who's behind all this?'

Her mascara-stained eyes gaped up at him. 'I was just helping you.'

'You trying to tell me it was a fucking coincidence, you coming along with my personal postal service?' He started laughing at her again, then grasped a hank of her hair and tugged, throwing her down onto the floor.

'You got me out of that place with a plan, a car and these nice comfy digs. What did you want in return, eh?'

She was blubbing on the floor, with her skirt racked up showing flabby thighs. He kicked her in the head and she howled.

'They arrested that girl Ella for Tommo's murder,' she blubbed. 'I wanted out—'

From across the hall, the insistent bell of the phone interrupted her burblings. With a final kick he went out into the hallway to listen to an answerphone clicking its miniature cassette tape on. A woman's voice was filling the still air. When the message ended, he rewound it and listened again from the start.

'Hello, Professor Leadbetter? This is Lorraine Quick. I'm working with Doctor Voss at Windwell and I'm the acting personnel manager for the hospital. Anyway, I wonder if I can call round to see your Black Museum before I leave? And I'd like to talk to you about Oona, too. I don't seem to be able to locate her. Listen, I'll be passing your place later, so if you don't mind, I'll call in and have a word, if that's OK? See you soon, bye now.'

Rob listened as the machine clicked off. Lorraine Quick – wasn't that the name of that bird who hung out with Voss, who Oona had rabbited on about being a government spy? She was searching for Oona and she wanted to talk it over with this professor guy. It was handy then, that this Quick woman was coming straight here. He could find out what was going on and stop her blabbing to anyone else. Smart thinking.

Pleased with himself, Rob went back to the kitchen to see what else the girl might know about Quick. But when he got there, the ward clerk had gone. Rob stood motionless, eyeballing every inch of the room.

'Oona,' he crooned. 'You've got a visitor coming to see you.' He moved silently towards the iron-studded back door and found it was locked tight and double-bolted. The bolts were on the inside so she hadn't left that way. He checked under the table. Nothing. He threw open the larder and the broom cupboard. The fucking girl had scarpered. He moved to the window and that was locked, too. There was no sign of her in the garden outside.

'Are you fucking hiding from me?' he demanded. ''Cos if I have to chase you down, you'll wish you'd given yourself up.'

He inspected the fireplace that was big enough to stand inside, picking up the poker and knocking it against the stonework. There had to be another way out. Slowly he paraded around the kitchen, inspecting every cupboard and cubbyhole. There it was, behind a low curtain that he'd taken to be a pantry. It was a low iron-barred door with a Yale keyhole that was firmly locked. He set off for a root about and found that whoever lived here was a most methodical man. In the study he found a set of labelled spare keys, and amongst them one marked 'Cellar door'. He tried the key and it turned silently. Opening it slowly, he felt a damp chill rise and saw stone steps plunging into darkness beyond. He returned to the kitchen, pulling the door locked behind him, and was looking around for a torch without success when a new sound reached him from the hall. It was the doorbell, a high-pitched drill of a sound. He checked himself in a mirror beside the sink. Coolly, he washed a couple of drops of blood from his face and shirt. Then pulling on a flat tweed cap from a hook on the wall, he headed to the front door.

CHAPTER FORTY-EIGHT

The front door opened. Even in the low light Lorraine grasped that the young man approaching her could not be the sixty-six-year-old academic she was looking for.

'Hello, is Professor Leadbetter at home?'

'He is,' the decidedly rough-looking guy said with a fixed, crooked smile. 'But he's on the phone. I'm here doing some jobs round the house. He said for you to come in and wait.'

The muscular guy in a flat cap gestured for Lorraine to cross the threshold into Wynd Well Hall's gloomy interior.

Lorraine's gaze fixed on his craggy face. Though his cap was pulled low on his close-cropped head, there was something familiar about him, she was sure of it.

'OK. I'll just fetch my papers.'

She turned around to where her white courtesy car stood a few yards away. Get inside, lock the doors and race to Windwell, she told herself. That face – it had been all over the papers for years.

The instant she turned her back, a muscular arm lodged around her throat like a metal clamp. She tried to hit out with a backwards kick but his hold didn't loosen. He dragged her inside the hallway and slammed the front door. The next thing she knew, she was smashed against the wall and while she tried to refill her lungs, something painful tightened around her neck.

'Lorraine Quick,' Robert Kessler murmured. 'That bastard Doctor Voss's friend.'

She couldn't breathe, never mind reply. The pain grew more unbearable as she struggled to claw at her neck. Then shock and pain immobilised her. She felt darkness approaching, the black hood of death descending over her senses. She began to droop, oblivion rushing up to meet her.

He loosened his grip and she found she could gasp, in agony, for air. He was winding a red cord around his fingers. Then with a violent tug she was hauled through the house. On the way their feet crunched on broken glass and she glimpsed the shattered front of a display cabinet. Christ's sake, hadn't Diaz told her the professor kept the red cord on display? Brutal insights crashed into her head: Kessler was immensely stronger than she was. He was using the red cord that killed Campbell. He would use it to kill her now. As if on cue, a low, vibrating noise reached them in that perverse room. The pitch rapidly rose to a whine, then carried on thrumming in the air, like a nerve-jangling wall of sound.

'Get a move on,' Kessler grunted. Lorraine guessed it had to be the escape siren going off at the hospital. A few moments earlier and she would have driven like a mad thing to the safety of the hotel. Still, it meant they would soon be after him.

He unlocked a low door and pushed her through it. Her foot dropped into nothingness, then hit a solid step. With a sharp yank her ankle twisted on stone. She managed to right herself and found she was at the top of a steep flight of stairs. Behind her the door slammed, locking her inside. She hobbled down into a bizarre stone chamber dominated by a rectangular pool filled with deep water. The coping around its edges was scattered with what looked like holy offerings: flowers and fruit, goblets and candles. And at the far end of the room a candle burnt beside Oona Finn sitting slumped on the floor.

Lorraine limped to her side. 'What happened to you?' she rasped, her throat still raw and painful.

Oona raised her head and Lorraine froze. One side of her face was still pretty, the other side swollen like a crimson balloon, with a deep wound running from eye to nostril. Her right eyelid was a sticky slit. Mascara clogged her eyes, lipstick smudged over her chin.

'What the fuck do you think? I'm his hostage.'

'God's sakes, Oona. Here.' She got out a hanky and dipped it in the pool before returning to tend the girl. 'Will this help?'

Oona's injuries were like a Halloween mask, but she did let Lorraine gently dab her wounds.

'You need stitches in that cut.'

'Stupid cow,' Oona hissed. 'I'll need more than stitches to put me back together when he's finished with me. And so will you.'

'How did he catch you?'

'He was beating Dobson up in the kitchen. He forced me into his car.'

'You poor thing.' She glanced up at the steps to the door. 'What's he planning?'

'What do you think?' she shrilled. 'To get away. He's got Dobson's car.'

Lorraine looked around the cellar. 'What is this place?'

'The Wynd Well. The healing waters that started this whole fucking hospital lark. The water's supposed to cure you. But it's bugger all help to us now.'

'Is there any other way out?'

'Oh yeah, you think I'd be sitting here now if there was? Up those stairs and past the psycho, that's the only way out.'

'Where's the professor?'

After a heavy sigh, Oona said flatly, 'Gone to a conference in London while they demolish the asylum. Lots of dust, apparently. So where's your plod friend? Diaz not racing to your rescue?'

'He's been questioning Ella, that friend of yours. I saw that video. I'm sorry, Oona, you've been through hell recently.'

'She'll be arrested, won't she?'

'Suppose so.' A hopeless silence fell. Lorraine couldn't stop herself from trying to comfort the younger woman. 'I did leave a message with the police to say I was coming here.'

Then the memory of Laddo's retort surfaced. *He's gone to Manchester . . . So you'll know he won't want you disturbing him.* Now, sitting here in this dank dungeon of a place, she knew for certain where he'd been going. Shirley's baby must be due any day.

'So you're saying we just need to survive until Diaz arrives?'

Lorraine dropped her head into her hands, too choked up to reply. No, she couldn't rely on Diaz. She might die at the hand of Kessler, might never see Jasmine again, because even if Laddo passed it on, Diaz probably hadn't given her message a second's notice. He had Shirley and the new baby to care for. She was on her own. 'I don't know,' she said.

She slumped down beside Oona and flexed her ankle. It didn't seem broken.

'So, Miss Know-it-all, you got any big ideas?' the girl asked.

The day's team session was still fresh in her mind. 'Well, there are two of us. And one of him. We've got to get a grip of ourselves. Try to outwit him.'

Oona wailed in protest. 'You don't know what he's like. He's too strong.'

Lorraine grasped that she had to rouse Oona to work with her. And yes, she had just the news to do it. 'I've just come from your mum with some good news. Kevin Crossley left you a lot of money.'

Oona did at least raise her one good eye and gape at Lorraine. 'Why?'

Lorraine swallowed. 'He was your father. He worked it out after you gave blood at the donor sessions. He wrote in his diary that you and your mum are both blood group O and so is he. Trust me, it's impossible that Professor Leadbetter was your dad. So was it you and your mum that Kevin invited round for tea on that Monday evening?'

Oona leant her head back against the wall, looking

dazed. 'Yeah. On the previous Friday he found Mum drunk at work and they had a big fight. She was crying all weekend about being sacked.'

'Are you sure he wanted to sack her? It looks more like he invited you and your mum round to make amends to you both. He'd arranged your mum's early retirement, as well as making you the beneficiary of his pension.'

'So how much for me?'

'It's in two parts. A lump sum of just under forty-five thousand pounds. And an annual pension of twelve thousand pounds a year. He'd been paying into the pension scheme since he was twenty-one.'

Oona was in a stupor, taking it all in. Only after an age did Lorraine nudge her arm. 'Listen. Will you work with me to get away from Kessler?'

Oona jerked up her head. 'Have I got this right? This mental case is planning to stop me getting my inheritance? Course I want it. Count me in.'

Lorraine stood up and began to inspect the offerings gathered around the ancient well.

'First, we need to identify what resources we've got that could help us.' She began to rifle through the new-age bric-a-brac: a pottery plate decorated with a pentacle, animal skulls and feathers, faded photographs and wrinkled apples. She couldn't find anything sharp or heavy. But she did recognise a few little posies of dried flowers wrapped in paper frills.

'Are these posies yours?'

'Yeah.'

'So you left one in my kitchen one night?'

She could tell that Oona was thinking about her

inheritance now and didn't care a jot about what Lorraine thought of her. 'We were only having a laugh.'

'So what do these posies mean?'

'Those at the pool are offerings. Yours was thorns and weeds. Just a little hex to stir things up.'

'A curse? Thanks a million.' She'd have liked to say that it hadn't worked – only that, well, to tell the truth, everything had mostly gone to shit since she'd arrived at Windwell.

Oona painfully stood up and joined her, then slipped her hand beneath a woven mat.

'This is what we need. A ritual knife.' She lifted a small but dangerous-looking curved knife with a pointed tip. Lorraine searched further afield, finding some damp blankets and a rug they'd need if they had to spend the night there. In the furthest corner, by an ancient drain cover, a collection of cleaning items were crammed in a plastic bucket: a tin of brass polish and a duster, a bottle of drain unblocker and rubber gloves, washing-up liquid and foam scrubbers.

'What's the plan with the knife?' Lorraine asked.

'Jump him when he doesn't expect it.'

'What about hiding at the bottom of the stairs? The side wall blocks his view as he climbs down. We can make up false beds with cushions so he'll be off his guard.'

Together they hauled blankets and cushions across the floor.

'What do you think?' said Oona, taking up a place where she'd be unseen. 'If I wait here and surprise him.'

'Hang on. I should do it. You're injured.'

Oona pulled out the knife, which gleamed in the

candlelight. She tested the blade against her fingertip. 'Ouch. It's a good one.' Oona was smiling up at the flight of dark steps. 'No, you go and lie down. It'll be a pleasure to stick this inside him.'

Thursday 27th October

Now they had a plan, Lorraine was desperate to see it put into action. To her frustration, Kessler did not return. Exhaustion overcame Oona, who slept on the rug with her arms encircling a shabby embroidered cushion. Lorraine checked her watch: it was one in the morning. These might be the final minutes of her life, she told herself fearfully. She struggled to push away a crowd of regrets: that if only she had gone straight back to the hotel she would now be soundly asleep in her bed, or if only she had chosen to travel with Jas and her mum, they would all be together at home. And now she would never see Jas again, or her mum, or Lily, and never see Diaz again, just when the embers between them had sparked into new life. She felt she was hanging weightless in the dark, and that her life, which she pictured as a precious force like a globe of light, was dwindling into oblivion.

No, allowing those thoughts was the way to madness. Thanks to Oona and her knife, she still had a chance to survive this night. She didn't allow herself to sleep. Shivering inside a damp blanket, she focused on her enemy: Rob Kessler. At three in the morning Oona woke up, frightened and gasping for breath. Lorraine fetched water from the pool after splashing her own face back to wakefulness.

The horror of their situation lay in their uncertainty. Had

Kessler perhaps driven away in the night and abandoned them? Or was he upstairs getting drunk, or raving in a psychosis, or quietly drooling over plans for their artfully gruesome murders? Shut the fuck up, she told the pitifully scared voices jabbering in her head.

'What do you know about Kessler?' she asked Oona.

'He's evil.'

'Go on.'

'He'll say anything to get his way. And he's not after sex. It's pain that turns him on.'

Lorraine couldn't stop herself releasing a fearfully whispered, 'Oh, God.'

A few minutes later, she asked Oona, 'How is he going to react to being stabbed if you don't kill him in one go?'

'He'll kill us.'

The damaged half of Oona's face was closest to her. In the low light the girl seemed to be winking in a grotesque parody – not one of humour, but a subtle undermining of each utterance she made.

Lorraine looked away, staring at the faint sheen of light on the black waters of the well.

'He must have some weaknesses.'

Oona snorted. 'He goes to the gym for about five hours a day. So, no. Not a single fucking weakness.'

'His suicide attempt. Was it genuine?'

Oona at least considered the question. 'Yeah. Windwell does grind patients down. For a lifer, death is their only escape.'

'Doctor Voss told me about a patient who must be Kessler.'

'What did he say?'

'I don't suppose the rules of confidentiality count if that patient is about to kill you.' Lorraine struggled to remember all she had heard of Rob Kessler. 'Voss told me he had a difficult patient. I'm sure it was Kessler because he talked about his youthfulness, his strength and that mesmeric way he had with people. Voss summed him up using words like attractive and charismatic.

'Voss was proud that he'd helped him confront one important fact: that Kessler did not love women. Inside every woman he got involved with, he eventually detected an echo of this abusive woman who fostered him called Connie. Each woman had signed her order of execution the moment she got close to him.' Lorraine paused for a moment, then asked, 'So what made him beat you up?'

Oona was breathing rapidly, clearly anxious. 'I told you. He's not interested in sex. He thought he was but when he couldn't get hard, he hit me.'

'Oh God, Oona.'

'I don't get it. I deal with his post and loads of women write to him.'

'That's a recognised syndrome. Hybristophilia. Sexual arousal in response to violent criminals.'

'But look at how he's handled himself. He's the top man on Ferris. He's had to perform to survive. I get that. It's like when I do spells and stuff. It's like a mind game.'

'But don't you think that's rather sad?' Lorraine asked. 'Kessler was about to accept Voss's help to move on from being a vulnerable little boy trapped in a conflict with his tormentor. And then Kevin Crossley was killed and Voss had to cancel their big therapy session. So Kessler tried to kill himself.'

'So what's the fucking point of all this?' Oona said with a sudden burst of spite. 'I'm not going to feel any better about being sliced up because I'll know it's some cruel old foster mother he really hates.'

At seven-thirty a deep rumbling sound caused the wall they leant against to vibrate. Lorraine pressed her ear to the cold stone and tried to identify it. She heard a deep rumble, then a monotonously regular boom, boom, boom.

'Could that be the asylum demolition starting up?' she asked Oona.

'Yeah. That's why the prof went away. The noise.'

To Lorraine it made the situation even more hopeless. With all that racket there was even less chance of anyone hearing them cry out for help, even if they could get past Kessler. The whole area would be a pandemonium of noise.

The sound of rattling reached them from the door at the top of the stairs. Oona picked up the ritual knife, darted to the bottom of the stairway and stood rigid, out of the sightline of anyone descending. Lorraine slumped down on the blanket bed and was dazzled as a beam of electric light swept through the darkness. As if in a nightmare, she watched Kessler's feet, legs, torso and then head emerge into view. Then the entirety of Rob Kessler appeared, an electric torch in one hand and a claw hammer in the other. Lorraine stiffened rigid, barely able to watch as he descended to where Oona waited motionless, the knife raised in her hand.

He was a mere few steps from the bottom. With a complete absence of stealth, Oona moved into his path and showed herself to him without fear.

'Hi, Rob,' she said calmly. 'You might want to know that this bitch was going to try and kill you. Here, take this.'

Lorraine watched in incomprehension as she passed the knife into Kessler's hand.

'Thanks, Oona.' He took the knife off her and they both turned to seek out Lorraine. Kessler's expression ice-cold but Oona's lopsided wink alert with excitement.

CHAPTER FORTY-NINE

'Go and cook me some breakfast,' Kessler demanded. As docile as a lamb, she disappeared up the steps to the kitchen. Lorraine waited for him to follow her and felt hot bile rise in her throat as he instead walked steadily towards her. The shock of Oona's betrayal made it hard to think clearly. Instinctively, she pressed her back hard against the wall as Kessler loomed in front of her. She held her breath, expecting a blow.

'So, you're Voss's woman.'

'No,' she croaked, and then cleared her sore throat. 'I work with him.'

'From the government.'

She sensed a chink in his armour. Kessler had liked telling people Voss was a superstar shrink from a top clinic.

'I was sent by the Secretary of State,' she said shakily.

God help her, he was inspecting her body, her throat, her hair, the opening of her shirt. Maybe he was planning what he would do to those body parts.

His eyes didn't return to her face when he said, 'I can only take one of you. You're better than Oona. That face of hers.' She glanced up for a second and registered a wolverine sneer. 'I won't get far with that ugly mug.'

Suddenly he reached down and grasped her under the chin so that she gasped. He yanked her head up so that her eyes were forced to connect with his cold drilling stare.

'Tidy yourself up. We're leaving as soon as I've eaten.' From upstairs they both heard the homely whistle of a tea kettle.

He let go of her jaw with a slow, dreamy caress that she knew contained nothing as ordinary as the sexual, but some other sensual promise to do with throats and windpipes.

When he'd gone she found her body was shaking, so she leant back against the wall for support. Think, think, she told herself. Dutifully, she washed her face and hands in the well, raked her fingers through her straggly hair and tried to straighten her clothes. Possibilities flittered in her mind's eye. He would return for her very soon and then she would be under his close and constant surveillance, a captive whose survival depended entirely on his whims. These might be her last moments of comparative freedom.

The demolition started up again, the distant booms and screeches and shrieks of machinery and suddenly – Kessler's voice from upstairs.

'Oona? Oona, where the fuck are you!'

Lorraine moved to the centre of the room and listened hard. Kessler was yelling, not at Oona, but in search of her. Was it possible she was hiding? Lorraine almost laughed out loud, though the danger she was in stifled it in her throat. Was it possible that Oona had outperformed Kessler and escaped? Still she didn't dare to climb the stairs but stood motionless, intently straining her nerves to pick up the tiniest clue about what was happening upstairs. She heard the banging of a heavy object. Why? From behind the wall the sound of the demolition was growing louder; she felt trapped between two mighty forces, terrified they might meet and destroy her.

The sound of the key twisting in the door. Lorraine sprang back to her bedding by the wall, hope miraculously rising that she was being rescued. No, it was Kessler hurrying to the bottom of the stairs. He looked wired and angry.

'Right. You're coming with me. If you so much as wriggle you're dead.'

Her mouth was bone-dry but she said it.

'No.'

'You fucking what? Get over here.'

She swallowed hard and forced out the word. 'No.'

He was bearing down on her, a furious ogre from a dark tale, a monster in a dungeon. In retaliation she raised the open plastic container with hands sheathed in thick rubber gloves.

'It's sodium hydroxide. Drain unblocker. It'll melt your flesh and blind you.'

She lifted the container higher and made a feint, as if about to throw the contents at him. He backed away.

'You bitch. I'll chop you into pieces for this when I get my hands on you.'

A sudden chaos of sounds reached them from upstairs: loud footsteps, shouts, commands. The next moment police in protective gear were thundering down into the well room. Kessler tried to make a run for it, but a stick-baton walloped him down to the ground. She saw the flash of handcuffs around his wrists. Mechanically, she screwed the top back on to the drain unblocker and pulled off the rubber gloves.

'Miss Quick. Let's get you out of here.' A riot-helmeted police officer extended his arm for her to lean on. She shuffled up the stairs into the blinding daylight.

Outside in the garden, the white car stood where she had left it in what seemed another life. The garden, the daylight, the movement, sprang up before her like a technicolour dream. A half-dozen police cars and vans circled the gravel drive. In the back of an ambulance she could see Oona having her wounded face tended to, and Enid watching her daughter from the vehicle's steps below. Across the lawn stood the asylum wall and beyond that, the dust clouds and chaos of the demolition site. Only the taller parts of the structure – the steep roof above the hall, the gable ends and the clock tower – were visible over the wall. A pair of cranes were swinging two wrecking balls across the sky, emitting squeals and shrieks. It felt weirdly symbolic, these two endings coinciding, that of the asylum and the capture of Rob Kessler.

Leaning on the policeman's arm, she spotted Enid approaching. The older woman came over as the policeman let go of her arm.

'Oona's safe. And now you are, too,' Enid said, bright-eyed with excitement, grabbing Lorraine's hand. 'She was running down the road into Windwell when Constable

Ladlaw and I found her. We went out searching for her together. Thank God they've got him.'

Lorraine tried to unpick Enid's words, knowing there was something wrong with them. She searched the dozen or so policemen for sight of Ladlaw but couldn't find him. There was no sign of Diaz, either. But she found Kessler, at the centre of a group of officers who were congratulating themselves triumphantly. 'Lock them up,' she murmured.

'What's that?' Enid asked.

'They need to be locked up,' she muttered.

As if sensing her interest, Kessler's gaze found her and stared back, then slowly raised his handcuffed hands and mimicked them strangling his own throat.

Breaking away from Enid, she moved to the helmeted policeman and hunched down against him to whisper in his ear. 'Don't let him stand there,' she told him. 'Lock them both up. Kessler and Oona.'

'They know what they're doing, miss.'

Another ambulance was trundling towards them from the main road. 'We'll get you checked over by the ambulance crew,' he added kindly. 'Then you'll need to give a statement.'

There was a moment of distraction when the ambulance drew to a halt and the driver leant down for a few words with a CID man. It was enough. In that instant Kessler sprang away, running across the lawn, heading into a stand of shrubbery. The arrest collapsed into near-comical confusion. For too long most of the bystanders were stunned, before setting off in chase. Lorraine clutched her police protector and wouldn't let him go. 'They were too

357

slow,' she muttered into his black overalls. 'Don't leave me.'

Daring to glance up, she saw similarly black-overalled police in helmets searching the garden, pointing and shouting directions.

'He's over the wall,' came the shout. She looked in the direction of the asylum, where the cranes had stilled, and the boom of the wrecking balls had fallen silent. Instinctively, Lorraine, her policeman guard and Enid stepped onto the lawn to gain a better view. From over the wall they heard the high-pitched shriek of a warning whistle. In the ensuing silence everyone fell still, as if turned to stone.

'What's that mean?' Enid whispered. No one replied.

A male voice called in panic. 'He's running for the building!'

The whistle sounded with two more short and violently loud bursts. A hush fell on the watchers. A low, trembling boom began to build until its pitch rose to that of shattering crystal. The ground seemed to shake. No, not the ground, for clearly visible above the asylum wall, the famous clock tower, with its face perpetually fixed at three minutes to midnight, began to shake with a freakish palsy. A dismayed gasp spread through all who witnessed its demise. The closest of the tower's side walls fell away with a slithery sound of shattering bricks, revealing a glimpse of its doll's house innards. Then the whole tower shivered and folded itself neatly downwards like a collapsing concertina. The sound was that of thousands of bricks, glass panes and wooden joists crashing to the ground.

They stood, watching yellow clouds rise and disperse.

The clock tower had vanished. Someone called out, 'He went under it.'

And Lorraine hid her face on on the policeman's arm, aware there was nothing left but a smoking heap of memories, sorrowful and brutal, where Kessler's body lay captive to Windwell for ever.

CHAPTER FIFTY

After a medical check-up and a gruelling two-hour wait, Lorraine had given a lengthy statement to Chief Inspector Thripp in his office at Windwell. Two officers she had never met before were in attendance; there was no sign of Diaz, and she didn't want to give the gossips the satisfaction of hearing her ask after him. Her white courtesy car was still part of a crime scene, but a message from Morgan assured her that a replacement car was on its way to Windwell. No one expected her to be in contact with work for at least another week.

It was noon by the time she was dropped off in a squad car back at her cottage on Windwell high street. Her bags were already packed, so all she had to do was have a quick wash before clambering into bed and surrendering to heavy, deadening sleep.

She woke to the sound of knocking and a panicky disorientation about where exactly she was. Pulling a jacket over her oversized T-shirt, she answered the front door. It was Diaz looking unshaven and uncertain.

'I had to see you. How are you?'

'I don't know. Very cold.'

She went back upstairs and lay down on her narrow bed.

'Can you hold me?' she asked.

He lay down beside her fully clothed and wrapped his arms around her. She concentrated all her mind on being held, the warmth, the comforting pressure. One of his large hands lay across her breastbone and she caught the faint scent of hospital antiseptic.

Twisting round to face him she asked, 'How's the baby?'

'In one of those incubators. She's like a tiny doll. Marie, she's called Marie.'

'And Shirley?'

'Tired. Relieved.'

She closed her eyes again and drifted on an ocean of ease. She remembered the day Jas had been born, in the days when no partners save a husband had been allowed on the maternity ward. She had turned up alone with an overnight case packed with a nightie, slippers and dressing gown. She had possessed no idea of what to expect, having had no time or inclination to attend birthing classes full of married couples. The indignities and harrowing pain, the clutching for gas and air, the frightening aloneness, had been eased by just one kindly midwife who sat beside her and held her hand while Lorraine squeezed it bloodless with every contraction. And yet when Jasmine had arrived she'd been a perfect, healthy, blue-eyed beauty of a girl, and it had felt like a miracle that this tiny new human had arrived on earth.

Now Diaz stroked her collarbone, and it was nothing

like how she'd imagined it would be if he came to her bed. Events had drained them both. He was exhausted, too.

'I'm going to have to go soon,' he whispered. Instinctively, she grasped his arm to hold him close for just a little longer. He relaxed again.

'We've arrested Oona,' he said softly. 'For the murder of Kevin Crossley and Tommo Ogden.'

She murmured, 'Thank God. I thought she'd get away with her innocent hostage act.'

'Well, Thripp's bullying interview style worked a treat. He accused her of killing Crossley for her inheritance – she was also the chief beneficiary of his will. Oona was so righteously indignant about not killing him for money that she admitted killing him to protect her mother from the sack.'

Lorraine sighed in sympathy for the girl. 'Can she blame it on Kessler's influence? She's young and impressionable. Will that help her?'

'Not really. It seems the two of them had been getting close for some time, especially since he was in the infirmary. It is a double murder. And she made that crazy attempt to throw the blame for Tommo's murder on Ella.'

'Last night . . .' She felt a shudder rise at the memory. 'I spurred her on with the promise of Kevin's legacy. I'm guessing it won't pay out.'

'Not if she's found guilty. The law of forfeiture means you can't benefit from a legacy left you by someone you murdered.'

He lifted himself on his elbow and gazed down at her. 'Lorraine. I want to keep seeing you.'

It was what she'd kept telling herself she wanted to hear.

What had her mum advised her? *If you're lucky, you meet the right person, the person you were meant to spend your life with. Take what you deserve.*

Yet if she made him leave this woman – and as her mother had predicted, he would leave her – he might hate himself for ever. And he might come to hate her as well, for making him betray his better self. It was like that law of forfeiture, to put something valuable like love at risk, for the sake of immediate gratification. He needed to stay with Shirley and little Marie now to live up to his better self. Her choice stood clear before her.

For maybe the last time she studied his face, touched his sandpaper unshaved cheeks and then let herself plummet into his night-dark eyes. 'No. You should try and make it work. You're a good person. I think that's what you really want to be.'

Without another word he kissed her briefly and left. At the sound of the door closing she moved into the warm patch on the bed he'd just vacated, but it was empty and growing cold. She started to cry for the loss of her hopes, and of all their shared possibilities. She cried with relief at the ending of the terror that she and Oona had endured, and for Enid and Brian, and the loss of their only children. In time, her tears ran dry and she investigated a hard object digging into her side. She retrieved a loop of wooden beads no larger than a bracelet, with a small crucifix attached. Diaz's rosary. It was still warm to her touch. She slipped it around her fingers, liking the solidity of the beads and their calming mobility. She knew he wouldn't return for it. And she was glad he had left just a fragment of proof that she had been guided, not by God, but by a sense of rightness in the world.

CHAPTER FIFTY-ONE

Lorraine's diary entry for Thursday 27th October, seemingly written in another, earlier existence, listed only one appointment for the day:

*2 p.m. Team-building – Final session, review and
action plan.*

The fact was that now only two of the original team remained in post. Under the circumstances, Voss and Parveen must manage any further action-planning between themselves. After her own ordeal, she felt barely capable of calling into the office to say her farewells.

Arriving at Admin, she found that Parveen was the only person to make it into work so far. She hurried over to Lorraine and hugged her in a tight embrace, studying her face. 'Should you even be up and about? You don't look very well.'

'I need to get home today,' Lorraine explained, still

fondly holding the administrator's shoulders. 'I wanted to say goodbye to you, Parveen. You've been a great friend to me.'

'I've learnt so much,' the administrator said with feeling. 'I won't forget what we've been through. Let's grab a few minutes while it's quiet.'

Parveen closed the admin office's outer door, and Lorraine soon learnt that Brian had formally resigned after his nursing registration was called into question. And Enid was at a Bradford police station in the hope of being told that Oona could return home.

'I doubt it,' said Lorraine. 'And where's Voss? Has he really left you manning the fort alone?'

'He's taken a day's annual leave.' The disbelief in her face said it all. 'Jenny and I had non-stop phone calls all morning, so thank goodness the police took over the switchboard. Jenny's at the incident room, helping them out. I was hoping Doctor Voss might realise it's a crisis and come in later.'

'I think I'll go and call on him. After all, I very much doubt I'll ever meet him again.'

'But we must keep in touch,' Parveen insisted, and they exchanged phone numbers, with promises of friendship.

Setting out for Voss's house, she took her last walk along Windwell high street, recognising that her tears seemed to have done her some good, washing away some unhelpful traps her mind had got caught inside. And after all, whatever Oona's selfish motives may have been, the ward clerk had probably saved her life by running away from Kessler and raising the alarm. And now there was a fresh new future unfolding before her again. She had the song 'Green Light' to show Lily. Or at least she would have, when she retrieved it from the storage space inside Voss's piano stool. She began to hum the few random lyrics that she'd started setting around the main chords:

Green light,
The sky shone with green light,
Clutching at emeralds, burning yearning,
In green light

Dawn light,
Our bodies at first sight,
Mother forgive us, straying, praying,
In sunlight

She felt a rise of energy at the prospect of polishing it up at home. To be honest, she wasn't too keen to see Voss again, for there would be plenty of questions about her ordeal, and maybe more of those ridiculous requests that she move permanently to Windwell. She reached the door to his villa and knocked loudly using the handsome brass knocker. No answer. She tried again and even peered through a couple of the ground-floor windows. She hung about for a while in a quandary. Now that it felt like her last chance to recover it, she felt desperate to get hold of her song notes again.

As she had done before, she found the turquoise pot and plucked out the key. Voss would never even know she'd called in. Inside, the hall and downstairs rooms were as peaceful as on every other visit she'd made. The sitting room door was open, so she stepped quietly inside on the plush carpet. Voss had spent some time at home, she could see that, for an empty wine bottle stood on a low table by the sofa and – yes, her eyes were not deceiving her – two red-stained wine glasses stood beside it. An ashtray too, containing burnt-down filter cigarettes – which was odd, as she had never seen him smoke. Beside it was a crumpled yellow packet bearing a camel standing between a palm tree and a pyramid. Picking up a squashed filter, she read the word 'CAMEL' and recalled the sensation of being observed in the psychology seminar room.

She quickly opened the piano stool lid and found her notes, but was not fast enough. Footsteps sounded on the stairs. There was nowhere to sensibly run or hide. She stepped out into the hall brandishing her rescued papers before her. Voss was descending the wide staircase looking unkempt and pink-cheeked, naked but for a pair of sweatpants.

'Lorraine.' He froze on the spot.

She started to explain her reason for calling, but before she could finish a male voice reached them from the upper landing.

'Jan, there's a packet of johnnies in my briefcase.'

Above their heads a creak on the landing brought Doctor Julian Norris into view, wearing only a pair of striped underpants. Voss was trapped between the two of them, clutching the banister. Unlike Voss's lover, Lorraine grasped the situation in an instant.

Lorraine found her voice. 'I'll say goodbye, then.'

By the time she reached the doorstep, Voss had caught up with her. 'Listen, I hoped you might be liberal enough to . . .' His lips stopped moving, the sentence petered out.

Lorraine turned back to face him. 'Liberal enough to what? Let you play happy families with me and Jasmine as a cover for your genuine tastes? How could you preach about trust and authenticity when you're living a lie?' she shot back at him.

Then she made another connection in the pattern of events here at Windwell. Voss had used some very non-clinical adjectives when he talked about Kessler: attractive, charismatic, tragic.

Before he closed the door on her she called back over her shoulder, 'And by the way, you totally screwed up Kessler's therapy, didn't you?'

As she made her way back to the cottage she passed the Spar shop, the hospital social club, the half-empty school, wondering if Voss's simulation of attraction to her had bruised her ego. No, not at all. In fact she had always found his attentions rather irksome. She recalled the time he had been unable to kiss her at the piano; no doubt he had been conducting some peculiar experiment on his own responses. Now she mused upon the tragicomic strangeness of the world, though already guessing that Voss's future trajectory would veer more to the tragic than the comic.

CHAPTER FIFTY-TWO

Thursday 3rd November

It feels better than anything Lorraine has done in years. Like the past is a country you can check out of, and the future a place you can choose from a pinpoint on a map. Salt spray stings her face while far below, navy-blue water speeds past beneath the ferry's white hull. In an hour Lorraine will be heading to Paris to meet Lily at the recording studio. And then, two blissful weeks with the band, to record 'Path of Stars' and try out 'Green Light' as a B-side. Lily has told her there will be gigs, parties, record company meetings and much flowing wine. Her replacement has disappeared back to England; Lorraine is going to be welcomed back into the band.

She needs this break after enduring a meeting with Morgan at Regional HQ. It reminded her that at heart he is an employment lawyer, and must privately have recognised how negligently the organisation had treated her.

'Yes, I'm still seeing a counsellor about the hostage experience,' she told him, overriding her usual tendency to play matters down. 'And I'm taking a holiday in France.'

'Good, good,' he said. 'No need to take annual leave while you're getting over the . . . experience.'

'I've got the photos you asked for.' She handed him the few photos of herself, Voss, Enid and Parveen, grinning manically in the rain while Morgan stood apart from them, scowling under his giant umbrella.

Morgan grunted at the image. 'We won't be needing those.' With one smooth movement he swept them into his waste bin. 'You do know that Voss was asked to resign?'

'No. Why?'

'Someone at Windwell leaked the notes of Voss's therapy sessions with Kessler. They made damning reading. Voss had guessed what Oona Finn confirmed – that Rob Kessler killed Junior Campbell. Voss made no attempt to report his suspicions to the police, though it clearly had a direct bearing on the recent murders. That alone was deemed to be absolute misconduct, never mind the questions over Kessler's escape and hostage-taking. The latest is that he's resigned and left the country.'

Morgan shook his head indignantly. 'The health secretary is aghast. How the hell did that man get the top job inside a high-security organisation?'

She couldn't resist a dig. 'Maybe they need to pay proper attention to their selection methods. They need the Square Peg Project.'

Morgan narrowed his eyes. 'Maybe.'

He stood up to signal his desire for her to leave his office. 'Take as long as you need to recover,' he said. She promised herself that she would.

* * *

It also feels good to be leaving the ravening British press behind. Kessler's escape from Windwell with an attractive young ward clerk and his subsequent death have dominated newspapers for weeks. Lorraine was unable to resist scanning lurid features about Oona, the 'devil's disciple', or even more wildly speculative, 'Satan's sex slave'. The papers got hold of images of Oona and appeared to be playing merrily with press impartiality. The story held a primitive fascination: a tale of a sadistic killer, a daring escape, unintentional parricide, a fortune gained and lost. Lorraine was deeply thankful that Thripp had succeeded in having her name suppressed by the court, and would be giving her testimony in private.

But for now, she is leaving all those worries behind in their wake, along with the difficulties of finding a new home and a better school for Jasmine. Jasmine and her mum are sitting bundled in scarves and hats, scanning the horizon for a first glimpse of the coast of France. Lorraine's trip has prompted her mum to take an overdue visit to relatives in a Parisian suburb; a chance, too, for Jasmine to see more of the world and her own extended family.

Now Lorraine stares into the glassy depths of the sea. She fancies she sees the dark façade of Windwell Asylum down there, that great palace of the insane, now replaced by the airless airlocks, key chains and concrete perimeters of the multi-million-pound secure hospital. The health secretary has drafted a new management structure, a new plan, new policies, but Lorraine knows that such paper weapons crumple and fail against the wiles of broken, scheming minds. And where does Sally roam now? Perhaps she still flitters in her sealed and hollow tomb, beneath the weight of shattered bricks and timber. Death will swallow them all in time. For a vivid moment she sees all the victims' watery faces: Campbell, Kevin, Tommo, Kessler. Death also stalked her, and almost took her, too. As for Oona, after her trial she is doomed to a half-life in prison for the long remainder of her years.

Looking over to where Jasmine is pointing to the low land mass on the horizon, she thinks of love. She has heard no more from Diaz. At times, her sacrifice feels meaningless. The local paper runs a 'Wedding Announcements' column that she will never glance at, for fear of catching the happy couple's face. That would be too much to bear.

From Parveen she has heard the desultory news of Windwell's demoralised state. And then the administrator's voice brightened; she had news from a cousin of hers who was on his way to college. He told her of a university open day in the midlands and a surprising encounter in the car park. While waiting for a coach he had spotted a teenage girl looking terribly alone, staring into the distance amidst groups of lively sixth-formers and serious-looking families.

Then a leather-jacketed Asian lad had strode up to the girl, and he had recognised Krish Khan from visits to his uncle's electrics store. At the sight of him a glorious smile broke out across her face. He was carrying two plastic bags bearing the university's crest, clearly bursting with admissions material.

They rushed to each other and kissed. The cousin had recognised Ella then, and told Parveen that there was something about the way they moved, as if they couldn't get close enough to each other. Then Krish had slid his arms around the girl's slender shoulders and laughed, lifting her feet off the tarmac and swinging her around. It made Lorraine ridiculously happy to hear that Krish and Ella were still, deeply and sweetly, in love.

For now, the ocean rolls invincible. Lorraine's fingers touch the comforting rosary she wears as a bracelet, spinning the beads like a charm. And as the tides of time turn, the tiny gilt crucifix sparkles in a sudden cloud-break of sunshine.

Afterword

The brooding edifice of a mental asylum is an archetype of many gothic tales and horror stories. Familiar depictions are found in Bram Stoker's Whitby asylum in *Dracula*, where the inmate Renfield feeds on flies, or the island location of delusional nightmares in Dennis Lehane's *Shutter Island*.

Setting my story about an imaginary asylum called Windwell, I attempted a corrective to the more lurid creations in fiction. After all, I had experience of the inside of Ashworth Special Hospital, an institution housing men with dangerous, violent or criminal propensities. At that time the hospital had been subject to a series of inquiries, notably the Fallon Inquiry (1999), that uncovered a loss of control by management so extreme that it could reasonably be said that the Personality Disorder Unit inmates were 'running the asylum'. Pornography, alcohol, and illegal drugs were freely on sale and young children were visiting known paedophiles with the knowledge of staff.

As a very modest response to the inquiry, I was helping to assess staff for senior posts using group and individual assessments. I vividly remember my visits, passing through high perimeter walls to enter sequences of airlocks, subject to repeated searches for any item that might be crafted into a weapon or escape aid. The Personality Disorder Unit at the centre of the scandal contained mostly young, bored males who represented such grave dangers to others that they might never be released. My colleagues' repeated warnings not to confide any personal information to inmates, nor allow them access to any keys, or let an inmate get between me and an exit door, left me feeling fearful even without knowing what crimes those men had committed.

I began work on *Isolation Ward* by reading *Institutions Observed* (1986) by the independent think-tank The Kings Fund. The book was a review of the state of England's three top-security hospitals, Broadmoor, Rampton and Ashworth in the 1980s. All three were geographically and professionally isolated; the nursing staff generally wore prison officer-style uniforms and most belonged to the Prison Officers Association. Prescribed drugs were over-medicated, and therapy was rarely offered. The idea of isolation struck me as the theme for my book, initially because of the hospitals' physical and ideological distance from the rest of the NHS. Later, I focussed on the theme of seclusion of patients in isolation cells, an archaic practice inherited from lunatic asylums.

Whilst writing this book I realised that one voice I had not heard clearly was that of the inmates themselves. I turned to Alan Reeves' memoir, *Notes From a Waiting*

Room: Anatomy of a Political Prisoner (1983). It tells of Reeves being sent to Broadmoor for murder as a fifteen-year old, and his shockingly cruel treatment. He gives a first-hand account of a second murder, a successful escape, life abroad and his extradition back to the UK. Reeve believes that it is the special hospitals system, not its inmates, that are monstrous and deserve to be closed down.

In addition, the following books, papers and websites were especially helpful:

Gwen Adshead and Eileen Horne, *The Devil You Know: Encounters in Forensic Psychiatry* (Faber & Faber, 2022)

Len Bowers, 'Factors underlying and maintaining nurses' positive attitudes to patients with severe personality disorder' (Forensic Mental Health R&D Committee, 2000)

David Canter, *Criminal Shadows: Inside the Mind of a Serial Killer* (Harper Collins, 1994)

Peter Fallon QC et al, 'Report of the Committee of Inquiry into the Personality Disorder Unit, Ashworth Special Hospital Volume 1', January 1999

Martine Hilton, 'Psychic Prisons and New Spaces', MSc dissertation, Manchester Metropolitan University, 1999

Patrick Lencioni, *Overcoming the Five Dysfunctions of a Team* (Wiley, 2005)

Patrick Lencioni, *The Ideal Team Player* (Wiley, 2016)

Gareth Morgan, *Images of Organization* (Sage, 1986)

Joel Richman, 'The Ceremonial and Moral Order of a Ward for Psychopaths', in Tom Mason and Dave Mercer (eds) *Critical Perspectives in Forensic Care: Inside Out* (Macmillan, 1998)

Annalisa Ventola, 'A Transliminal 'Dis-ease' Model of 'Poltergeist Agents' (*Journal of the Society of Psychical Research*, 2019)

Acknowledgements

I would like to thank the following people for their help and inspiration. My dear writer friends, Alison Layland and Elaine Walker, who gave me priceless feedback, friendship, and all round support. Also, two intensive periods of writing on retreat in Pembrokeshire were made possible by Alison's generosity.

Thanks also to my friends in The Prime Writers, a group of writers who have all had their fiction debuts commercially published at the age of 40 or more. Thank you especially to Essie Fox, Louisa Treger, Kerry Hadley-Pryce, and Sarah Sykes, who so kindly found time to read advance copies, alongside crime fiction author Tom Mead.

Sometimes conversational snippets get lodged in one's mind and later resurface as ideas in fiction. I developed a useful spark about young people's magical practices in Lancashire from my old friend Martin Peacock of Haslingden Writers. Similarly, my friend and former bandmate Louise Alderman, depicted as Lily in this book, told me of experiences with Wiccans and covens that fed into Oona's personality.

Thank you to all at Allison & Busby, especially Lesley Crooks, Susie Dunlop, Ffion Hâf, Josie Rushin, Daniel Scott and Christina Griffiths.

For encouragement and support at every stage, many thanks to my agent, Charlotte Seymour, and all the team at Johnson & Alcock Literary Agents.

And finally, I'm grateful as ever to my son Chris and my sisters Marijke and Lorraine for their understanding and positivity. Finally, thanks to my husband Martin, for critiquing my early drafts and sharing his tragicomic tales of work as a nursing auxiliary at a Sheffield mental institution, in an abortive attempt to become an art therapist.

Also by Martine Bailey . . .

SHARP SCRATCH

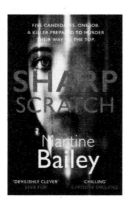

Five candidates. One job. A killer prepared to murder their way to the top.

Salford, 1983. Lorraine Quick is a single mother, a member of a band going nowhere fast, and personnel officer at the grim Memorial Hospital.

A new general manager position is being introduced, and Lorraine's recent training in the cutting-edge science of psychometric testing will be pivotal. As the profiles start to emerge, a chilling light is cast on the candidates. When a lethal dose of anaesthetic is deliberately substituted for a flu vaccine, and a second suspicious death quickly follows, it is clear a killer is at work in the hospital.

Can Lorraine's personality tests lead her to the murderer?

MARTINE BAILEY studied English Literature while playing in bands on the Manchester music scene. She qualified in psychometric testing and over her career, assessed staff for a top security psychiatric hospital and dealt with cases of sexual abuse and violence. Having written historical crime fiction, Bailey's writing has jumped to a modern setting. She lives in Chester.

martinebailey.com
@MartineBailey